THE PROBABLE FUTURE

Alice Hoffman is the bestselling author of many successful novels and screenplays, including *Here On Earth* (Oprah Book Club Choice in 1998), *Illumination Night, Turtle Moon, Practical Magic* (made into a recent major film), *Local Girls, The River King* and *Blue Diary*. She lives in Massachusetts with her husband and two sons.

ALSO BY ALICE HOFFMAN

Blue Diary
The River King
Local Girls
Here on Earth
Practical Magic
Second Nature
Turtle Moon
Seventh Heaven
At Risk
Illumination Night
Fortune's Daughter
White Horses
Angel Landing
The Drowning Season
Property Of

For Children

Green Angel
Indigo
Aquamarine
Horsefly
Fireflies

Alice Hoffman

THE PROBABLE FUTURE

V

VINTAGE

Published by Vintage 2004

2 4 6 8 10 9 7 5 3 1

Copyright © Alice Hoffman 2003

Alice Hoffman has asserted her right under the Copyright,
Designs and Patents Act, 1988 to be identified as the author
of this work

First published in Great Britain in 2003 by
Chatto & Windus

First published in the United States of America in 2003 by
Doubleday

Vintage
Random House, 20 Vauxhall Bridge Road,
London SW1V 2SA

Random House Australia (Pty) Limited
20 Alfred Street, Milsons Point, Sydney
New South Wales 2061, Australia

Random House New Zealand Limited
18 Poland Road, Glenfield,
Auckland 10, New Zealand

Random House (Pty) Limited
Endulini, 5A Jubilee Road, Parktown 2193,
South Africa

The Random House Group Limited Reg. No. 954009
www.randomhouse.co.uk

A CIP catalogue record for this book
is available from the British Library

ISBN 0 09 945386 X

Papers used by Random House are natural, recyclable
products made from wood grown in sustainable forests.
The manufacturing processes conform to the environ-
mental regulations of the country of origin

Printed and bound in Great Britain by
Bookmarque Ltd, Croydon, Surrey

For Tom

ACKNOWLEDGMENTS

Endless gratitude to my editor, Stacy Creamer, and to my publisher, Stephen Rubin, and to my beloved agents, Elaine Markson and Ron Bernstein.

Many thanks to my earliest readers, for friendship, support, and expertise in matters of law, medicine, music, and being human: Elizabeth Hodges, Carol DeKnight, Maggie Stern Terris, Sue Standing, Daniel Kumin, Perri Klass, and Tom Martin.

Thank you to designers Marysarah Quinn and Jean Traina, to Isolde Ohlbaum, and to photographer Debi Milligan. Thanks also to my publishers at Vintage UK and at Chatto & Windus, especially to Alison Samuel.

In memory of
my mother, Sherry Hoffman, who did not believe in limits,
and
my dear friend Maclin Bocock Guerard, a beautiful writer and a beautiful soul.

PART ONE

THE VISION

I.

ANYONE BORN AND BRED IN MASSACHUSETTS learns early on to recognize the end of winter. Babies in their cribs point to the brightening of the sky before they can crawl. Level-headed men weep at the first call of the warblers. Upstanding women strip off their clothes and dive into inlets and ponds before the ice has fully melted, unconcerned if their fingers and toes turn blue. Spring fever affects young and old alike; it spares no one and makes no distinctions, striking when happiness is least expected, when joy is only a memory, when the skies are still cloudy and snow is still piled onto the cold, hard ground.

Who could blame the citizens of Massachusetts for rejoicing when spring is so close at hand? Winter in New England is merciless and cruel, a season that instills a particular melancholy in its residents and a hopelessness that is all but impossible to shake. In the small towns surrounding Boston, the leaden skies and snowy vistas cause a temporary color blindness, a condition that can be cured only by the appearance of the first green shoots of spring. It isn't unusual for whole populations of certain towns to find they have tears in their eyes all through the month of March, and there are those who insist they can see clearly for the very first time.

Still, there are some who are slower to discern the signs of spring. They distrust March and declare it to be the most perilous time of the year. These are the stubborn individuals who continue to wear woolen coats on the finest of days, who insist it is impossible to tell the difference between a carpet of snowdrops and a stretch of ice in this slippery season, even with twenty-twenty vision. Such people cannot be convinced that lions will ever be turned into lambs. In their opinion, anyone born in March is sure to possess curious traits that mirror the fickle season, hot one minute, cold the next. Unreliable is March's middle name, no one could deny that. Its children are said to be just as unpredictable.

In some cases, this is assuredly true. For as long as their history has been known, there have been only girl children born to the Sparrow family and every one of these daughters has kept the family name and celebrated her birthday in March. Even those babies whose due dates were declared to be safely set within the snowy margins of February or the pale reaches of April managed to be born in March. No matter when an infant was due to arrive, as soon as the first snowdrops bloomed in New England, a Sparrow baby would begin to stir. Once leaves began to bud, once the Blue Star crocus unfolded, the womb could no longer contain one of these children, not when spring fever was so very near.

And yet Sparrow babies were as varied as the days of March. Some were calm and wide-eyed, born with open hands, always the sign of a generous nature, while others arrived squalling and agitated, so full of outrage they were quickly bundled into blue blankets, to ward off nervous ailments and apoplexy. There were babies in the Sparrow family who had been born while big, soft snowflakes fell and Boston Harbor froze solid, and those whose births took place on the mildest of days, so that they drew their first breaths while the robins built nests out of straw and twigs and the red maples blushed with a first blooming.

But whether the season had been fair or foul, in all this time there had been only one baby to be born feet first, the mark of a healer, and that child was Stella Sparrow Avery. For thirteen generations, each one of the Sparrow girls had come into this world with inky hair and dark, moody eyes, but Stella was pale, her ashy hair and hazel eyes inherited, the labor nurses supposed, from her handsome father's side of the family. Hers was a difficult birth, life-threatening for both mother and child. Every attempt to turn the baby had failed, and soon enough the doctors had begun to dread the outcome of the day. The mother, Jenny Avery, an independent, matter-of-fact woman, who had run away from home at seventeen and was as unsentimental as she was self-reliant, found herself screaming for her mother. That she should cry for her mother, who had been so distant and cold, whom she hadn't even spoken to in more than a decade, astounded Jenny even more than the rigors of birth. It was a wonder her mother wasn't able to hear her, for although Elinor Sparrow was nearly fifty miles from Boston, Jenny's cries were piercing, desperate enough to reach even the most remote and hard-hearted. Women on the ward who had just begun their labor stuck their fingers in their ears and practiced their breathing techniques, praying for an easier time. Orderlies wished they were home in bed, with the covers drawn up. Patients in the cardiac unit felt their hearts race, and down in the cafeteria the lemon puddings curdled and had to be thrown away.

At last the child arrived, after seventeen hours of brutal labor. The obstetrician in charge snapped one tiny shoulder to ease the birth, for the mother's pulse was rapidly dropping. It was at this very moment, when the baby's head slipped free and Jenny Avery thought she might lose consciousness, that the cloudy sky cleared to reveal the silvery splash of the Milky Way, the heart of the universe.

Jenny blinked in the sudden light which poured in through the window. She saw how beautiful the world was, as though for the very first time. The bowl of stars, the black night, the life of her child, all came together in a single band of light.

Jenny hadn't particularly wanted a baby; she hadn't yearned for one the way some women did, hadn't gazed longingly at rocking horses and cribs. Her stormy relationship with her own mother had made her wary of family ties, and her marriage to Will Avery, surely one of the most irresponsible men in New England, hadn't seemed the proper setting in which to raise a child. And yet it had happened: this baby had arrived on a starry night in March, the month of the Sparrows, season of snow and of spring, of lions and lambs, of endings and beginnings, green month, white month, month of heartache, month of extreme good luck.

The infant's first cries weren't heard until she was tucked into a flannel bunting; then little yelps echoed from her tiny mouth, as though she were a cat caught in a puddle. The baby was easily soothed, just a pat or two on the back from the doctor, but it was too late: her cries had gone right through Jenny, a hook piercing through blood and bones. Jenny Sparrow Avery was no longer aware of her husband, or the nurses with whom he was flirting. She didn't care about the blood on the floor or the trembling in her legs or even the Milky Way above them in the sky. Her eyes were filled with dizzying circles of light, little pinpricks that glimmered inside her eyelids. It wasn't starlight, but something else entirely. Something she couldn't comprehend until the doctor handed her the child, the damaged left shoulder taped up with white adhesive as though it were a broken wing. Jenny gazed into her child's calm face. In that instant she experienced complete devotion. Then and there, on the fifth floor of Brigham and Women's Hospital, she understood what it meant to be blinded by love.

The labor nurses soon crowded around, cooing and praising the baby. Although they had seen hundreds of births, this child was indeed exceptional. It wasn't her pale hair or luminous complexion which distinguished her, but her sweet temperament. Good as gold, the nurses murmured approvingly, quiet as ashes. Even the most jaded had to agree this child was special. Perhaps her character was a result of her birth date, for Jenny's daughter had arrived on the twentieth of March, the equinox, when day and night are of equal length. Indeed, in one tiny, exhausted body, there seemed to exist all of March's traits, the evens and the odds, the dark and the light, a child who would always be as comfortable with lions as she was with lambs.

Jenny named the baby Stella, with Will's approval, of course. For despite the many problems in the marriage, on this one point they agreed: this child was their radiant and wondrous star. There was nothing Jenny would not do for their daughter. She, who had not spoken to her own mother for years, who had not so much as mailed a postcard back home after she'd run off with Will, now felt powerless to resist the mighty forces of her own maternal instinct. She was bewitched by this tiny creature; the rest of the world fell away with a shudder, leaving only their Stella. Jenny's child would not spend a single night apart from her. Even in the hospital she kept Stella by her side rather than let her be brought to the nursery. Jenny Sparrow Avery knew exactly what could happen if you weren't there to watch over your child. She was quite aware of how wrong things could go between mothers and daughters.

Not everyone was doomed to repeat history, however. Family flaws and old sorrows needn't rule their lives, or so Jenny told herself every night as she checked on her sleeping daughter. What was the past, after all, but a leaden shackle one had a duty to try and escape? It was possible to break chains, regardless of how old or how rusted, of that Jenny was certain. It was possible to forge an entirely new life. But chains made out of blood and memory were a thousand times more difficult to sever than those made of steel, and the past could overtake a person if she wasn't careful. A woman had to be vigilant or before she knew it she'd find herself making the same mistakes her own mother had made, with the same resentments set to boil.

Jenny was not about to let herself relax or take the slightest bit of good fortune for granted. There wasn't a day when she wasn't on guard. Let other mothers chat on the phone and hire baby-sitters; let them sit on blankets in the Boston Common on sunny days and on blustery afternoons make angels in the snow. Jenny didn't have time for such nonsense. She had only thirteen years in which to prevail over her family's legacy, and she planned to do exactly that, no matter the cost to herself.

In no time she became the sort of mother who made certain no drafts came in through the windows, who saw to it that there were no late-night bedtimes or playing in the park on rainy days, a sure cause of bronchitis and pleurisy. Cats were not allowed in the house, too much dander; dogs were avoided, due to distemper, not to mention allergies and fleas. It did not matter if Jenny took a job she despised at the bank on Charles Street or if her social life was nonexistent. Friends might fall away, acquintances might come to avoid her, her days of reviewing mortgage applications might bore her silly, but Jenny hardly cared about such distractions. Her only interest was Stella. She spent Saturdays chopping up broccoli and kale for nourishing soups; she sat up nights with Stella's earaches, stomachaches, bouts of chicken pox and flu. She laced boots and went over lessons, and she never once complained. Disappointments, fairweather friends, math homework, illnesses of every variety were dealt with and put in their proper place. And if Stella grew up to be a wary, rather dour girl, well, wasn't that preferable to running wild the way Jenny had? Wasn't it better to be safe than sorry? Selfish pleasures dissolved the way dreams did, Jenny knew that for certain, leaving behind nothing more than an imprint on the pillowcase, a hole in your heart, a list of regrets so long you could wrap them around yourself like a quilt, one formed from a complicated pattern, *Love knot* or *Dove in the window* or *Crow's-foot*.

Soon enough, Jenny's marriage to Will Avery fell apart, unwound by mistrust and dishonesty, one thread and one betrayal at a time. For quite a while there had been nothing holding these two together but a shared history, the mere fact that they'd grown up together and had been childhood sweethearts. If anything, they stayed together longer than they might have merely for the sake of their daughter, their Stella, their star. But children can tell when love has been lost, they know when silence means peace and when it's a sign of despair. Jenny tried not to think what her mother might say if she knew how badly their marriage had ended. How self-righteous Elinor Sparrow would be if she ever found out that Will, for whom Jenny had given up so much, now lived in his own apartment on the far end of Marlborough Street, where at last he was free to do as he pleased, not that he hadn't done so all along.

That Will was unfaithful should have been evident: whenever he lied, white spots appeared on his fingernails, and each time he was with another woman, he developed what Jenny's mother had called "liar's cough," a constant hacking, a reminder that he'd swallowed the truth whole. Every time Will came back to Jenny, he swore he was a changed man, but he had remained the same person he'd been at the age of sixteen, when Jenny had first spied him from her bedroom window, out on the lawn. The boy who had always looked for trouble didn't have to search for it after a while: it found him no matter where he was, day or night. It followed him home and slipped under the door and lay down beside him. All the same, Will Avery had never presented himself as anything other than the unreliable individual that he was. He'd never claimed to have a conscience. Never claimed anything at all. It was Jenny who had insisted she couldn't live without him. Jenny who forgave him, who was desperate for one of his dreams, one that would remind her of the reason she fell in love with him in the first place.

Indeed, if Elinor Sparrow found out they had broken up, she certainly would not have been surprised. She had correctly judged Will Avery to be a liar the moment she met him. She knew him for what he was at first sight. That was her talent, after all. One sentence and she knew. One shrug of the shoulders. One false excuse. She had marched Will Avery right out of the house when she found him lurking in the parlor, and she'd never let him return, not even when Jenny begged her to reconsider. She refused to change her opinion. Elinor was still referring to him as The Liar on the brilliant afternoon when Jenny left home. It was the spring of Jenny's senior year of high school, that feverish season when rash decisions were easily made. By the time Jenny Sparrow's classmates had been to the prom and were getting ready for graduation, Jenny was working in Bailey's Ice Cream Parlor in Cambridge, supporting Will while he managed to ruin his academic career with hardly any effort. Effort, on the other hand, was all Jenny seemed to possess. She washed dishes after a full day of work; she toted laundry to the Wash and Dri on Saturdays. At eighteen, she was a high school dropout and the perfect wife, exhausted, too busy for anything like regret. After a while her life in her hometown of Unity seemed like a dream: the common across from the meetinghouse where the war memorials stood, the linden trees, the smell of the laurel, so spicy just before blooming, the way everything turned green, all at once, as though winter itself were a dream, a fleeting nightmare made up of ice and heartlessness and sorrow.

The month of March had always been particularly unreliable in the village of Unity; the weather could change in a flash, with ninety-degree heat yielding to snowstorms overnight. The town center, only forty minutes north of Boston, halfway between the interstate and the marshes, had a latitude which intersected with the yearly flight of returning cowbirds and blackbirds and sparrows, flocks whose great numbers blocked out the sun for an entire day every year, a winged and breathing eclipse of the pale, untrustworthy sky. People in Unity had always taken an interest in Cake House, the home of the Sparrow family; during the migrations, many came to picnic on the edge of the lane. Most residents couldn't help but feel proprietary, even proud of what had been decreed to be one of the oldest houses in the county. Friends and family visiting from outside the Commonwealth were often taken to a hillock where a fine view of Cake House could be had, if a visitor didn't mind peering through the hedges of laurel or getting down on hands and knees to gaze through the holes in the boxwood chewed by rabbits and raccoons.

The house had begun its life as a washerwoman's shack, a simple edifice with a dirt floor. Mud and weeds had been used as chinking between the logs; the roof had been made of straw. But every generation had added to the building, piling on porches and dormers, bay windows and beehive ovens, as though smoothing icing onto a wedding cake. Here was a crazy quilt built out of mortar and bricks, green glass and whitewash, which had grown up as though it had a life of its own. Local people liked to explain that Cake House was the only building in town, excepting the bakery from which Hull's Tea House now operated, to withstand the fire of 1785, a year when the month of March was so terribly hot that the woods turned to tinder and a single spark from a lantern was enough to set all of Main Street on fire.

History buffs always pointed out the three tilted chimneys of Cake House, each built in a different century, one red brick, one gray brick, one made out of stones. These same experts also made certain not to venture too near the Sparrows' house, even when picnicking, despite the structure's architectural appeal. It wasn't just the NO TRESPASSING signs that persuaded them to keep their distance, nor was it the brambles in the woods. At Cake House, what looked inviting was often poisonous. Take a step, and you might live to regret it. Kick over a stone, and you could easily stumble over a garden snake or a wasps' nest. Out-of-town guests were carefully instructed not to pick the flowers; the roses had thorns that were as sharp as glass and the hedges of laurel, with their pretty pink buds, were so toxic that honey from the blooms could poison a man in a matter of hours.

As for the calm, green waters of Hourglass Lake, where yellow Egyptian water lilies floated, several witnesses had reported that the catfish which swam in the shallows were so fierce they actually crawled onto the grass, chasing after rabbits that had wandered too close to shore. Even the most historically minded residents of Unity—the members of the memorial society, the board of the town council, the librarians who were in charge of the town's artifacts and records—refused to venture very far down the dirt driveway, for there were snapping turtles dozing in the muddy ruts; there were yellow jackets that would sting for no reason. The wildest boys in town, the ones who would jump off the pier at the marsh or challenge each other to run through patches of stinging nettle, would not dare to charge through the reeds on a hot summer day nor dive into the lake where Rebecca Sparrow was drowned so many years ago, with a hundred black stones sewn into the seams of her clothes.

ON THE MORNING of her own thirteenth birthday, Jenny Sparrow had awoken to a chorus of peepers calling from the shallows of the lake. She was hardly responsible back then. Frankly, she was waiting for her life to begin. Right away, in the first hours of her birthday morning, she knew something irrevocable had happened, and that was perfectly fine. Jenny had no qualms about leaving childhood behind, for hers had been miserably lonely. She had spent many hours in her room, with her watercolors and her books, watching the clock, wasting time. She'd been anticipating this morning all her life, counting minutes as she fell asleep, Xing off days on her calendar. The other children in town envied her living in Cake House; they swore that Jenny Sparrow's bedroom was larger than any of the classrooms at school. She was the only one among them who had her own boat and spent idle summer hours drifting across Hourglass Lake, in waters where the turtles would have surely bitten off anyone else's fingers and toes. Her father called her Pearl, the children said, because she had been his treasure. Her mother, it was whispered, let her do as she pleased, especially after the father's death, a sudden accident that was said to have left Elinor Sparrow reeling.

No one was keeping track of Jenny's whereabouts, that much was certain; often, she was the last customer at the soda fountain in the old pharmacy on Main Street. From their bedroom windows, children in town often spied her walking home in the dark, past the old oak tree on the corner of Lockhart Avenue. There she was, untended and unafraid, at an hour when the other children were held back by pajamas and bedtimes and overprotective parents who wouldn't have dreamed of letting them wander about on their own.

Those boys and girls who gazed at Jenny with envy had no idea that during the winter months, the bedrooms in Cake House were so cold Jenny could see her breath in the air, floating out of her mouth in icy crystals. The plumbing in the walls rattled, and sometimes gave up altogether, so that flushing was achieved only by pouring buckets of lake water into the commode. There were bees in the porch columns, birds' nests in the chimneys, carpenter ants at work on the foundation and beams. The house had been cross-stitched together and was always unraveling, a quilt whose fabric was worn and frayed. Things broke, and kept breaking, and nothing was exactly what it seemed. Jenny, that free spirit the children in town spied running past their windows, was seriously afraid of the dark. She was prone to asthma attacks, nail-biting, stomachaches, migraines. She was regularly plagued by nightmares and, unlike the other children, when she cried out in the middle of the night, no one responded. No one ran down the hallway, with a cup of tea or a hand to hold until she could again fall asleep. No one even heard her call.

Jenny's father had died the year she turned ten, and after that her mother had pulled further and further away, retreating behind her closed bedroom door, her garden gate, her armor of distance and discontent. Elinor Sparrow's sorrow over the loss of her husband—a bad loss, a nasty loss, with unexpected surprises—turned from distraction to detachment. Soon enough she was estranged from anything that connected her to this world, Jenny included, Jenny especially, Jenny who would be best served if she learned to stand on her own two feet and take care of herself and not be bogged down with emotions, surely the safer way to navigate this world.

In truth, Cake House was a cold place in which to live, cold in spirit, cold in each and every room. A chill filtered through the windows and under the doors, a rush of unfriendly air that made a person want to stay in bed in the mornings rather than face the day, with quilts piled high, removed from the rest of society, dreaming when life got too difficult, which, frankly, was every day. But this was not the case on the morning of Jenny's thirteenth birthday. On this day, the weather was sunny, with temperatures rising into the sixties. On this day, Jenny sat bolt upright in bed, ready for her life to begin.

She had long black hair, knotted from a restless sleep, and olive skin, just like her mother and grandmother and all of the Sparrow women who had come before her. Like them, she awoke on the morning of her thirteenth birthday with a unique ability that was hers alone. This had been the case ever since Rebecca Sparrow rose from sleep on the first morning of her thirteenth year to discover that she could no longer feel pain, not if she strayed through thorn bushes, not if she held her hand directly over a flame, not if she walked barefoot over broken glass.

Ever since, the gifts had varied with every generation. Just as Jenny's mother could discern a falsehood, her grandmother, Amelia, could ease the pain of childbirth with the touch of her hand. Jenny's great-grandmother, Elisabeth, was said to possess the ability to turn anything into a meal: rocks and stones, potatoes and ashes, all became soup in Elisabeth's competent hands. Elisabeth's mother, Coral, was known to predict the weather. Hannah, Coral's mother, could find anything that had been lost, whether it was a misplaced ring, a wandering fiancée, or an overdue library book. Sophie Sparrow was said to be able to see through the dark. Constance Sparrow could stay underwater indefinitely, holding her breath long past the time when anyone else would have turned blue. Leonie Sparrow was said to have walked through fire, and her mother, Rosemary, could outrun any man in the Commonwealth. Rebecca Sparrow's own daughter, Sarah, needed no sleep except for the tiniest of catnaps; a few moments' peace was said to provide her with the energy of ten strong men and the heart of the fiercest March lion.

As for Jenny, she awoke on the morning of her birthday having dreamed of an angel with dark hair, of a woman who wasn't afraid of water, and of a man who could hold a bee in the palm of his hand and never once feel its sting. It was a dream so odd and so agreeable it made her want to cry and laugh out loud at the very same time. But as soon as Jenny opened her eyes, she knew it wasn't her dream. Someone else had conjured these things; the woman and the bee, the still water and the angel. All of it belonged to someone else. It was that someone, whoever he might be, who interested Jenny.

She understood that this was the gift she'd been given, the ability to dream other people's dreams. Nothing useful, like predicting the weather or perceiving lies. Nothing worthwhile, such as the ability to withstand pain or a talent for seeing through the dark or running as fast as a deer. What good was a dream, after all, especially one that belonged to someone else? Rain and snow, babies and liars, all of it interesected with the sturdy universe of the waking world. But to come to consciousness with a stranger's dream in one's head was not unlike walking into a cloud. One step, and she might sink right through. Before she could stop herself, she'd be yearning for things that didn't belong to her; dreams that made no sense would begin to make up the signposts of her everyday desires.

On that morning, right in the center of the most unreliable month of the year, Jenny was surprised to hear voices rise up from the driveway. Local residents avoided the dirt road, dubbed Dead Horse Lane by the children in town. They might picnic in the lane on the occasion of the spring migrations, but on all other days they circled round the woods, dodging the laurel and snapping turtles, making a wide berth around the wedding-cake house, no matter if it meant a route that doubled back to Lockhart Avenue, the long way into town. The NO TRESPASSING signs were nailed to the trees, and all of the closest neighbors, the Stewarts and the Elliots and the Fosters, knew not to cross the property lines if they wanted to avoid one of Elinor's calls to the police and a nuisance complaint registered down at the courthouse.

Yet there were voices in the driveway, it was true, and one of them belonged to Jenny's dreamer, the dream that had awoken her to the start of her new life, the dreamer she wanted for her very own. Jenny went to the window, groggy, sleepy-eyed, curious to see whose dream she had shared. It was a mild day and the air smelled like mint. Everything was sweet and green, and Jenny's head spun from the pollen. The bees had already set to work, buzzing away in the buds first forming in the laurel, but Jenny ignored their droning. For there he was, standing at the edge of the driveway, a local boy named Will Avery, sixteen years old and already looking for trouble at this early hour. His younger brother, Matt, as thoughtful an individual as Will was undisciplined, trailed after him. Both boys had spent the night on the far side of the lake, having dared each other to do so; the winner could not bolt for twelve hours straight, not even if the dead horse of legend rose from the still water. As it turned out, they'd both made it through till morning, despite the frogs and the mud and the season's first mosquitoes, and now the boys' laughter rose up through the air.

Jenny stared at Will Avery through the mossy haze of spring. Right away she knew why she felt dizzy. She had always been in awe of Will and too shy to speak to him. He was handsome, with golden coloring and a brash manner, the sort of boy who was far too interested in having a good time to adhere to any rules or consider anyone other than himself. If anything dangerous was about to ensue, any reckless mischief at all, Will Avery would be there in no time flat. He did well in school without even trying, all the same he loved a good party; he lived to take chances. If there was something to enjoy, wreck, or burn down, he'd be the first one in line. People who knew Will tended to fear for his safety, but those who knew him best of all feared far more for the safety of those around him.

Now that Jenny had shared his dream, she felt emboldened. It was as though Will Avery belonged to her already, as if their dreaming and waking life had twisted around each other and their lives were now interwoven, one and the same. Jenny shook the knots from her hair and crossed her fingers for luck. She willed herself to be the fearless woman in his dream, the one who would walk through water for the person she loved, the girl with the dark hair who wasn't afraid to go after what she wanted most of all.

Come here, Jenny said softly, the very first words she uttered on the first morning of her thirteenth year.

The sound of the peepers was filling her head. Spring fever was in her blood. Other girls her age knew what they wanted for their birthdays long before the day arrived: silver bracelets, gold rings, white roses, presents tied in silk ribbon. None of these possibilities had interested Jenny Sparrow. She hadn't any idea of what she desired most until she saw Will Avery. Then she knew: she had to have him.

Turn now, she said, and that was when Will looked up at the house.

Jenny quickly pulled on her clothes. She ran downstairs in her bare feet and went outside, into the mild, green air. She felt as though she were flying, as though Cake House were disappearing behind her with its sodden, abandoned rooms turning to ashes. If this was desire—the cold grass under her feet, the scent of mint as she breathed in, the ferocious speed of her pulse—she wanted more of it. She wanted it all the time.

The spring migration had occurred only days earlier, filling the sky with birds. Cowbirds, too lazy to rear their own offspring, were perched beside the nests of sparrows and jays, already tumbling out the azure and dappled eggs that rightfully belonged inside, replacing them with their own larger progeny that were genetically timed to hatch first. The sunlight was surprisingly strong and hot for March; it was the sort of heat that could go through a person's clothes, straight into the bloodstream. Before this morning, Jenny had been quiet and moody, afraid of the dark and of her own shadow. Now, she was someone else entirely: a girl who blinked in the glittery light, someone who could fly if she wanted to, a person so brave that when Will Avery asked if he could see inside Cake House, she didn't hesitate for a moment. She took hold of his hand and led him right up to the door.

They left Will's brother crouched down behind the forsythia, goosebumps rising on the poor boy's arms. Will shouted for his brother to come along with them, but Matt, always so cautious, thoughtful to a fault, refused. He'd heard stories about what had become of trespassers at Cake House. Even at the age of twelve, Matt Avery was law-abiding. Certainly, he wanted to view the Sparrows' house as much as anyone, but he was also a student of history, and he knew what had happened to Rebecca Sparrow more than three hundred years earlier. Her fate made him queasy. It made his throat go completely dry. He was well aware that local boys had been calling the dirt road Dead Horse Lane for centuries, and that most people avoided this place; even the old men in town swore there was a skeleton floating just below the lily pads and the reeds. Matt stayed where he was, glowering with shame, unable to break any rules.

Will Avery, on the other hand, would never let a dead horse or an old superstition deter him from having a good time. He'd even gone swimming in the lake once, back when Henry Elliot had bet him twenty dollars that he wouldn't have the nerve, and the only price he'd had to pay afterward was an ear infection. Now a pretty girl was escorting him across the lawn, and he'd be damned if he backed off, despite the rumors in town. He kept on even when Matt shouted for him to come back, reminding Will that their mother would soon discover they hadn't slept in their beds. Let good old Matt hide in the shrubbery. Let him fear some witch who'd been dead for more than three hundred years. When Monday came around, Will would be the one who would be announcing to his friends that he'd been inside the Sparrows' house and had lived to tell the tale. Before he was through, he might snag a kiss he could brag about, perhaps even filch a souvenir of his exploits to show off to the crowd that would gather admiringly in the school yard, hushed at the very thought of his exploits.

Just thinking about the adulation to come thrilled Will. He liked to be the center of things, even back then. He smiled at Jenny as they sneaked in the front door, and his smile was a gorgeous thing to behold. Jenny blinked, surprised by his attentions, but then she smiled back. This was not an unexpected response. Will had already learned that girls responded when he seemed to be attracted to them, so he tightened his hold on Jenny's hand, just the slightest bit of pressure, enough to assure her of her appeal. Most girls liked anything that passed for charm; they seemed to appreciate his interest, whether or not it was real.

Do you have anything that belonged to Rebecca? Will asked once they were headed down the hall, for that was what everyone wanted to see: something, anything, that had once belonged to the witch from the north.

Jenny nodded, even though she felt as though her heart might burst. If Will had asked her to burn down the house at that moment, she might have agreed. If he'd asked for a kiss, she most definitely would have said yes. *This must be love*, she thought standing there. *It can't be anything else.* She could not believe Will Avery was actually beside her. She, who was all but friendless, more alone than Liza Hull, the plainest girl at school, now had Will all to herself. She wasn't about to say no to him. She brought him into the parlor, even though she'd been instructed never to allow anyone there. Guests were not invited to Cake House, not even on holidays or birthdays. And should some delivery man or door-to-door salesman manage to get inside, he would certainly never be brought into the parlor, with its threadbare rugs and the old velvet couches no one sat upon anymore, so that their pillows spit up dust, whenever they were fluffed. Even the paperboy threw the *Unity Tribune* from the foot of the driveway and was always paid by check, via the mail, so that Elinor didn't have to see him. Occasionally, the plumber, Eddie Baldwin, was allowed into the house, but he was always asked to remove his muddy boots and Elinor made certain to stand over him as he plunged frogs out of the toilet or unclogged water weeds and tea leaves from the kitchen sink.

Most importantly, no outsider was ever to be shown anything that had belonged to Rebecca Sparrow. Those busybodies over at the library, who were always begging for a trinket or a scrap of cloth for their history of Unity displays, were never allowed past the front door. But of course this day was different from all the rest, and this visitor was different as well. Had Jenny been hypnotized by Will Avery's dream? Is that what convinced her to bring him over to the far corner of the parlor where the relics were kept? Was it love that caused her to reveal her family's most treasured possessions, or was it only spring fever, all that filmy green light so thick with pollen, those peepers in the muddy shallows of the lake with their dreamy chorus, calling as if the world were beginning and ending at the very same time.

Along with everyone else in town, Will Avery wanted to see exactly what Jenny herself had always done her best to ignore, what she'd branded the Sparrows' own private and personal museum of pain. What family was foolish enough to keep the things that had hurt them most of all? The Sparrows, that was who, although Elinor and Jenny did their best to ignore that pain. The corner where the display was kept was dusty and neglected. There were oak bookshelves lining the wall, but the leather-bound books had been untended for decades, the seashells that had once been pink had turned gray with age, the hand-carved models of bees and wasps had been attacked by carpenter ants, so that the wood fell to sawdust when touched. Only the glass case had been protected, kept well out of harm's way.

Jenny snatched off the embroidered coverlet, meant to safeguard the family heirlooms from sunlight and ruin. When he saw what was before him, Will gulped down a mouthful of air, for once in his life at a loss for words. What he'd always assumed was nothing more than rumor was indeed quite real. Now he'd have a story to tell. He started to grin right then, right there. Now they'd all be gathering around him on Monday, and if they didn't believe what he told them about Rebecca Sparrow, at least he himself would know it was true.

He leaned forward, affected in some way he didn't understand, almost as if he'd had a heart. There in the glass case before him were the ten arrowheads people talked about, handed down through the generations, preserved under glass, much the way another family might document their history with photographs or newspaper announcements of weddings and births. Against a field of satin, fading from red to pink, but carefully arranged, were three more pieces of the Sparrow archives: a silver compass, a tarnished bell, and what Will thought at first was a coiled snake, but which was, in point of fact, a plait of dark, braided hair.

Still, it was the arrowheads that kept Will's attention; they were handmade, filed out of the local stone. Each one had a line of blood at the tip. Whether these mementos had been kept as proof of human cruelty or human frailty was uncertain. All that was known was what a farmer named Hathaway had written of his own experience in his journal, indexed in the historical records room at the library on Main Street. Hathaway had gone down to the docks to retrieve a mirror, an extremely expensive gift for his wife, in the time when the marshes were still a deep harbor, not yet filled in by mud and silt. But after claiming his treasure, ordered a year earlier and all that time at sea, Hathaway had stumbled over the roots of a twisted swamp ash; before he had time to steady his hold, the mirror had fallen and broken into a hundred bright pieces. Hathaway had stood there for a very long time, wondering how he would explain himself to his wife; he stayed so long, in fact, that he'd been the only witness when Rebecca Sparrow walked over the broken glass, her arms piled high with laundry, barefoot and bleeding, but not uttering a single cry.

As soon as the boys on the farms around Unity discovered that Rebecca Sparrow could not feel pain, they began to shoot at her with arrows, for sport. They tracked her as they would a pheasant or a deer, relentlessly, forsaking the rules of charity. They cheerfully took aim whenever they came upon her at the far end of Hourglass Lake, where she took in laundry from the wives in town who could afford to send dirty homespun and linens out to be washed by someone whose hands were already burned from lye. Several of these boys left behind guilt-ridden letters, now in the Unity library, documenting the fact that their target never once flinched. Rebecca only slapped at herself, as though fending off mosquitoes; she kept to her work, washing the woolen laundry with the strongest soap, made out of ashes and fat, carefully soaking the delicate silks in green tea. She didn't notice when she'd been struck, not until she went home and undressed. Only then did she discover she'd been wounded by one of their arrowheads. She had no idea she'd been hurt until she traced a finger over the trail of blood that had been left behind.

WAS IT ANY WONDER that Jenny was so apprehensive as her daughter's thirteenth birthday drew near? She so dreaded the day she had already bitten her nails down to the quick, a girlhood habit that reappeared in trying times. Perhaps others forgot their own histories, but Jenny remembered hers only too well. She remembered racing across the cool, dewy grass as though it had happened hours ago. She could instantly bring to mind the trill of the peepers and the way her heart had felt, thumping against her chest as she and Will stood in the parlor, examining the memento case. It was this memory that caused Jenny to stay up all night long on the eve of Stella's birthday, perched on a chair beside the bed as her daughter slept. It was the fact that thirteen had been reached yet again that left Jenny's dark hair in knots, her complexion ashen, her nails bitten until her fingertips bled.

Let her wake as she was when she closed her eyes. That was all Jenny asked for. That was all she begged for on this March night that was perfectly equal to the day, unique in all the season. *Let her be the same sweet girl, unburdened by gifts or sorrow.*

There they were, the guarded and the guardian, but it was impossible to ward off time, no matter how vigilant or alert an individual might be. Jenny knew the hour had come when she heard the morning traffic echo on Commonwealth Avenue and Storrow Drive. Blink and the years passed right by you. Turn around twice and you were walking in the land of the future. Daylight was breaking over Marlborough Street, and it would continue to do so even if Jenny kept the curtains drawn and the door bolted shut. Newspapers were being delivered, trash was collected in the alleyways, pigeons were cooing on windowsills and telephone lines. The day had begun, cool and clear and absolutely impossible to avoid.

Stella opened her eyes to see her mother staring at her. Always a sign of trouble, to have your mother huddled over you, watchful as a bulldog with all those knots in her hair. Always a bad start to a day, birthday or not. Stella leaned up on her elbows, her eyes rimmed with sleep dust. She hadn't bothered to unbraid her hair and now a halo of stray bits stuck up from her scalp. All night she had dreamed of dark water, and now she blinked in the sharp morning light.

"What are you doing here?" Stella's voice was still dream-infected. Jenny understood why the words sounded liquid; she had dozed off and caught a bit of her daughter's dream, and it brought her little comfort. Jenny Sparrow knew precisely where the water was darkest, where it never seemed to end, and so she'd drunk coffee and cola and kept alert. "What are you looking at?" Stella asked when her mother didn't respond, annoyance creeping into her voice.

How was Jenny to explain when she herself didn't know? She was searching for a sign of something burning up inside her little star, that was all. An ability that was bound to set her apart, just as surely as if she were a giantess, or a girl who ate fire, or a woman who could walk over glass without feeling the slightest bit of pain.

"I just wanted to know what you wanted for your birthday breakfast. French toast? Waffles? Eggs over easy? I've got raisin bread. The kind with the walnuts."

If it had to happen, let it be something simple and helpful, the ability to mend clothes with a single stitch, perhaps, or a talent for trigonometry. Let it be an aptitude for foreign languages, or an open heart, or a resilient nature. If worse came to worst, perhaps she could see in the dark, always a welcome attribute, or quiet wild dogs with a mere gesture.

"I don't eat breakfast anymore. For your information. And I can't be late. I have a math test first period and Miss Hewitt doesn't care about birthdays. She doesn't care about anything but algebra." Stella had tumbled out of bed and immediately began to search through a rumpled pile of clothes on the floor.

"Would you like me to iron that?" Jenny asked when Stella's disheveled school uniform had at last been unearthed and pulled from the tangle of jeans and underclothes.

Stella eyed her uniform, then shook out the blue skirt and blazer. "There," she said, with the hot edge of defiance that had surfaced at the start of ninth grade. Stella had skipped a year of school, passing directly from fourth to sixth grade. She'd been so quick, such a good reader, naturally they'd been proud of her abilities. But now Jenny wondered if they hadn't made a mistake, if Stella hadn't somehow been rushed into something she wasn't ready for.

"All better," Stella said of her clothes. As she turned, she caught her mother staring at her. Yet again, and this time with a sour expression, as though in studying her daughter, Jenny had happened upon head lice or fleas. "Is there something wrong with me? Is that why you keep looking at me that way?"

"Of course not." At least there was no green light, no calling frogs, no fork in the road that would surely lead to disaster. "Although you might want to brush your hair."

Stella peered at herself in the mirror. Too tall, too thin, with teeth that weren't quite crooked enough for braces and hair that looked like straw left out too long in the rain. She scowled at her own reflection, then turned to face her mother, still defiant. "My hair's fine the way it is, thank you."

Last night, Jenny had counted backward through time until she reached Rebecca Sparrow, the lost girl who was their first recorded blood relation. Stella, she'd realized, was the thirteenth generation in their history. That ominous, unlucky number. Why, some people wouldn't keep thirteen dollars in their pocket, some architects passed directly from the twelfth to the fourteenth floors, insuring that no elevators would stop at that ill-fated destination. And now here Stella was for an entire year, stuck with that number, trapped by her own destiny. Thirteen, no matter how the years were counted. Thirteen, until the next twelve months had passed.

"How about a present?" Jenny brought forth a gift box. She had shopped carefully, trying to pick something Stella might like, but such an endeavor was hopeless. Jenny wasn't surprised at the disappointment that showed on Stella's face as soon as the cashmere sweater she'd chosen had been unwrapped.

"Pink?" Stella said.

Nothing Jenny did seemed right; that was the only thing they could agree upon lately.

"Do you even know me?" Stella carefully folded the sweater back into its box. True enough, everything in Stella's closet was black, navy blue, or white.

Something had begun to go wrong between mother and daughter around the time Will left last summer, or maybe it had begun in those last few months of their marriage, when all Will and Jenny could do was fight. They had sunk so low that Jenny had flung a glass of milk at Will after finding a woman's phone number in his jacket pocket. He'd responded by smashing her favorite platter on the floor. They'd stopped to look at each other then, panting, surrounded by broken crockery and white puddles of milk. Then and there, they knew the marriage was over.

Will had packed up that night. He'd gone off, even though Stella had tried her best to hold him back. She'd begged him to stay, and when he wouldn't, she ran to the window to watch as he waited for a cab.

"He won't go," Stella had whispered hopefully, but hope faded when the taxi pulled up. When it was clear Will was leaving, as it should have been for several years, Stella turned on Jenny. "Call him back." Stella's voice was perilously high. "Don't let him go!"

But Will was already gone, and he had been for ages. Jenny thought about the day when she saw him on the lawn; his dream had been her first taste of desire. But no matter how many nights they had spent together since, she had never again been granted access to his dreams. She was quick to pick up her landlady's dreams, and the dreams of her neighbors; such things came to her unbidden, eclipsing what dreams she might have had on her own. There were the overheated sex dreams of the young man on the first floor, so feverish, Jenny had trouble looking him in the eye when they met by chance at the incinerator. There were the cool, spare dreams of the old woman at the end of the hall, images of Nile-blue landscapes from half a century earlier that always refreshed Jenny, even when she'd been standing on her feet at work all day. Walking through the Boston Common, she'd been privy to bits and pieces of the dreams of homeless men who dozed on the benches, dreams of warm woolen coats and turkey dinners, dreams of everything these men had lost, and everything that had been stolen from them, and all that they'd thrown away.

And, yet, with her own husband, there was only emptiness, the blank space of an individual who could fall into slumber without a single thought, without a care in the world. Dreams as empty as Marlborough Street after he'd gotten into the cab on the evening he left, dark as the brown twilight of Boston that always fell so quickly, like a curtain drawn across window glass.

"I hate you," Stella had said that night. She'd gone into her room and closed the door and it had been that way ever since, much like the closed doors of Jenny's childhood, only in reverse. Her mother then, her daughter now. Even today, on her birthday, Stella didn't want Jenny near.

"Do you mind if I get dressed, or do you have to watch me do that, too?" Stella had her hands on her hips, as though she were speaking to an intrusive maid who couldn't follow instructions, a poor fool she had to put up with until the day when she was finally all grown up and free.

Jenny went into the kitchen, where she fixed herself a cup of coffee, then warmed a corn muffin for Stella. Jenny was of the belief that breakfast was the most important meal of the day, no matter what Stella might say.

"I'm just fixing you a bite," Jenny called when she heard Stella moving about in the hallway. "Just to keep your energy up."

Jenny grabbed the muffin and a tall glass of orange juice; she started for the living room, but when she reached the doorway, she stopped at the threshold. Stella had been rummaging through the hall closet, searching for her black boots, but she'd found something else instead. Now she sat cross-legged on the floor examining the box that had arrived from Unity. A very bad start to an enormously untrustworthy day.

Jenny had thought she'd hidden the gift well, fitting the large packing crate neatly behind the jackets and coats. She had assumed there'd be no reason for Stella to look in the closet before Jenny found the opportunity to get rid of this birthday present, the way she'd gotten rid of all the others for the past thirteen years. Every time Elinor Sparrow had sent a gift, Jenny had destroyed it before Stella could discover the gift and be won over. It made no difference if the box contained a doll or a sweater, a music box or a book; anything with a Unity postmark was sent down to the incinerator. But now the past had reached out to them, drawing them back to everything Jenny had left behind. Why, on this morning she wouldn't have been surprised to find a snapping turtle in her own bathroom sink, or a mud puddle under the hall carpeting, perhaps even a memento from the museum of pain carefully wrapped in tissue paper and twine, fallen into her daughter's hands. There was no way to stop this now: Stella had already pulled off the tape. Packing niblets had spilled onto the carpet.

"Well, well," Stella said, in a tone that included delight and fury at the very same time.

Inside the box was Jenny's toy house, the one her father had made for her, an exact replica of Cake House, with all three chimneys set in place. There was the garden gate, painted a freckled green, and the birds' nests, formed of sticks and string, positioned above the porch. There was the forsythia and the hedge of laurel, with tiny felt leaves glued to each wavering branch and even tinier bees fashioned out of satin and cherry stones, clinging to the pale, gauzy blossoms.

"When were you going to show this to me?" The packing stuff clung to the skirt of Stella's uniform in white puffballs. "Never?"

Jenny's father, Saul, had spent a full year building the house, but after he died, she never played with it again. The miniature house went from a shelf in her bedroom to a corner in the parlor to a storeroom in the cellar, and there it had moldered for years. Now, someone had cleaned the floors with a toothbrush. The rugs had been washed; the kitchen table, whittled out of local pine, was shiny with furniture wax. It was lemon oil, Jenny realized, a scent which reminded her of her father and often caused her to cry.

Stella lifted the model of Cake House onto the trestle table in the hall.

"Did you plan to destroy it, like you have everything else my grandmother's sent me?"

Jenny took a step backward, as though she'd been slapped. There were tears in her eyes, brought on by the lemon oil. She opened her mouth to try to explain herself, but there were no excuses. Just as Stella had suspected. No reason at all, other than selfish pride.

"Don't tell me you thought I didn't know." Red spots had appeared on Stella's cheeks. Had she grown overnight? Had she always looked quite so adult? So extremely self-righteous? "How stupid do you think I am? I've known since my seventh birthday. I followed you down the hall and watched you throw my present into the incinerator chute."

"Of course I don't think you're stupid," Jenny said. "I was only . . ."

"Trying to protect me? Making certain I wouldn't be contaminated. By what? A teddy bear? A dollhouse? Or did you think she might pack my presents in poison? Maybe if I touched one, arsenic would course through my bloodstream. Was that it? Or maybe I would just know that someone cared about me."

"Stella, you don't understand my mother. How manipulative she is, now that she wants something. That something is you. She can rectify her mistakes. But she was never there for me. She only thought about herself."

Stella actually laughed, but the sound was bitter. She'd practiced sneering in front of the mirror, and now she put that practice to use. "You can't be serious." Stella grabbed her boots and was pulling them on. Her mouth was pinched; her skin white as ice. "She was the one who thought only of herself? And of course you're perfect. This is exactly what she said would happen. She told me you'd try to turn me against her. She said you'd blame her for everything."

"What do you mean, she told you?" Everything Jenny had ever wanted for her daughter seemed to be slipping away in this very instant, on this very day. Everything she had tried to do so right seemed to have somehow gone terribly wrong. "Have you been talking to your grandmother?"

"I've been talking to her for years. That's right! We call each other when you're not around. When you can't butt in and ruin things for us the way you ruin everything."

Stella wound a scarf around her neck. Her eyes were cold, flecked with yellow. The same eyes her father had. She had more of his attributes than she had ever imagined. She realized that in the instant when she saw that she'd hurt her mother. She didn't have to be the good girl, minding her manners, doing as she was told. Stella could tell that the balance of power had shifted and it felt good. Somehow, while her mother wasn't paying attention, Stella had gained control.

"Well, I love this present my grandmother sent, and I don't care what you think. If it's not here when I get home from school, I'm leaving. I mean it. I'll move in with my father."

"Oh, Stella, don't be ridiculous." Will was too self-centered to take care of anyone; he hadn't even had Stella sleep over at his place. In order for her to stay at his apartment, he'd have to clean up, he'd have to go to the market, buy milk and bread, set his alarm clock, think about someone other than himself.

All the same, Jenny felt pinpricks of fear along the back of her neck. People lost each other all the time, didn't they? People walked right out of each other's lives.

Keep your mouth shut, Jenny warned herself. *Wait this day out and be smart. Thirteen*, she reminded herself. *That's all it is. It's a number, but it's an illness, and like any virus, it will pass.*

"I mean it," Stella said as she set out for school, already late, but taking her time, flushed with her new sense of power. "I'll leave and I won't come back."

Jenny had said these same words to her mother, and not long after, she'd made good on the threat. She was wise enough now to let Stella go without further argument. After she heard the front door close, she forced herself to look at the little house that had been sent from Unity, even though the mere sight made her feverish. She'd forgotten how like a wedding cake it was, with its circular structure painted white. She'd forgotten how pretty it could seem from a distance, if you didn't know any better, if you hadn't been inside. There was her bedroom at the rear of the house, with the sheer curtains in the windows, the place where she'd spent so many lonely hours as she waited to grow up. There was the front door she'd slammed after that last fight with her mother, when she ran to meet Will and escape from Unity. And there, in the corner of the parlor, behind the sofas sewn from velvet scraps, beside bookcases that had been carefully stained to resemble golden oak, was a copy of the glass memento case. Ten tiny arrows, their tips painted scarlet, had been set in two neat rows.

All around the house, laurels had been set out, planted in plaster, blooming forevermore, made out of felt and wire. The original hedge in Unity was said to be the tallest in the Commonwealth, unflagging and hardy, growing taller each year. Jenny ran her fingers over the tiny bees that were attached to the blooms and felt a thrumming in her fingers. She could smell wild ginger and lake water, a rich, damp scent that got into your clothes and your hair and stayed there, stitched to you with muddy thread.

Seeing it all again, the hedgerows and the frayed rugs, the memento case full of arrowheads and the garden gate, Jenny Sparrow realized that all things really did come back to you. Action brought reaction; salt thrown into the wind flew back into your own eyes. It stung more with each passing year; it could blind a person who wasn't careful. Like it or not, time had passed. What Jenny had feared most of all had already occurred, and there was no way to prevent it or ignore it or deny it had happened.

Stella had turned thirteen.

II.

ON THE WAY TO SCHOOL, Stella hiked up the blue skirt of her uniform and loosened her braids, so that her hair fell down her back, nearly to her waist. Her one and only friend, Juliet Aronson, had informed her that her ashy hair was her best feature. As far as

Stella could tell, it was her only good feature, so she might as well flaunt it. Anyway, braids were worn by the kind of girl her mother wished her to be, the sort who wore pink sweaters and was voted class president, who excelled in after-school activities, from the drama club to the Mathletes. Clearly, that was not the sort of girl Stella happened to be.

As soon as she turned off Marlborough Street, Stella stopped on the corner and took a tube of lipstick from her backpack. The shade was called Cheap, a scarlet tint that made her look sullen and out of sorts. It was perfect. Juliet Aronson had told her she looked ten years older when she wore it, and Juliet was an expert when it came to matters of rebellion, makeup, and fate.

Stella rubbed at her temples as she approached the Rabbit School for girls, a place she had despised since kindergarten. She probably would have hated the school even if she hadn't been a charity case, one of the few scholarship students, an outsider from the time she was five. She forced herself to push through the crowd outside the heavy oak doors, and went to hang her coat in her locker. Standing there, under the fluorescent lights, Stella realized it wasn't exactly a headache she was experiencing, more like something fizzing inside her brain. All through homeroom she felt exhausted, drained, per- haps, from the fight with her mother, who continued to pry into every aspect of her life, allowing her not the slightest bit of privacy, not even in her dreams.

It had always been impossible for Stella to keep a secret from her mother, or to even attempt to have a private life. If Stella dreamed about walking on the ledge of a tall building, the following morn- ing, over a plate of waffles Stella was all but forced to eat, Jenny would turn the conversation around to a study that documented the fact that everyone had a few irrational fears. If she dreamed about one of the boys at the Cabot School after a dance, one of the many who never even noticed her, the very next morning her mother would announce that Stella did not have permission to date until she was sixteen, as if anyone would ever ask her, as if she'd say no if they did.

"Are you sleepwalking?" Juliet Aronson called to her as Stella made her way through the corridor. "Wait up!"

Because Stella had skipped fifth grade, Juliet Aronson, although in the same class, was a year older. She had short brown hair and gunmetal eyes and enough audacity for two people; she had a knack for getting her own way. There are lessons to be learned in a ruined childhood, and Juliet had learned these well. She had, for instance, convinced the headmistress that a physical therapist had insisted she must wear high heels because of a defect in her spine. The dark fuchsia lipstick Juliet had on? Much needed, due to a reaction to the sun, which caused her to break out in blood blisters without the deep shade to shield her delicate mouth. Now Juliet was clip-clopping after Stella in her two-inch heels; she was out of breath by the time she'd reached her friend by the stairs. "I've been calling to you all the way down the hall, birthday girl."

"I wish I was thirty," Stella said. "Then I'd be running my own life."

"You do not wish that. You'd have wrinkles. You'd be all worried about why you weren't married yet, and why you were wasting yourself on some crappy job or some dopey man who was already married and playing you for a fool. Enjoy your youth, kiddo. Trust me, you'll be fourteen before you know it. From experience I can tell you it sucks. Here. This will help." Juliet handed over a shopping bag. "Happy thirteen."

Stella smiled in spite of her pounding head. The Rabbit School was a competitive place, one of the few all-girls private schools left in Boston, and Juliet Aronson was the only other charity case in her grade. Birds of a feather flocked together, that was true enough; Juliet and Stella were lucky to have each other. As a team they made certain to reject everyone else before they themselves were cut to the quick. Neither, after all, could afford to shop on Newbury Street or go to summer camp in Maine. Stella's mother had a steady but small salary, and her father earned very little at the music school where he taught sporadically. The other girls at Rabbit had whispered about Will Avery for days when he'd come to the Harvest Fair Fund-raiser so obviously loaded, turning on the charm for Señorita Smith, who was a fool for any man who remotely resembled her vision of Don Quixote.

Don't let them see if you're hurting, Juliet had advised just last week. Neither one had received an invitation to Hillary Endicott's birthday party at the Museum of Fine Arts—*I don't think you'd fit in,* Hillary had told them after the Harvest Fair, her tone friendly, as if her pronouncement of what they were lacking had been an act of mercy, until Juliet spat on her expensive leather boots. To make up for Hillary's party, they'd gone off to snag some silk scarves at Saks instead. *Act like you don't care,* Juliet had told Stella as they ducked into the Boston Public Library, where they could sit comfortably in the reading room and sift through their loot. *And after a while you won't feel a thing.*

Not caring was Juliet's real expertise. Ten years earlier, in a well-publicized criminal case, Juliet's mother had poisoned her father. After several years of foster care, Juliet now lived with her mother's youngest sister, a graduate student at Emerson College, in an apartment in Charlestown. The aunt was the one who'd finagled the scholarship to the Rabbit School when Juliet was in sixth grade, not that Juliet had cared whether or not they accepted her. She was miles past acceptance, years beyond anything remotely resembling hope.

"Go ahead, open it," Juliet said of the present she'd given to Stella. "You're going to love it."

Inside was a black dress, stolen from the designer department on Saks' second floor, perfect in every way, skimpy and sheer, the sort of thing Stella's mother would never allow her to wear. This beautiful dress belonged to another universe, light-years away from the pink cashmere sweater, which she hoped would spend the rest of its natural life boxed up, relegated to the bottom of a dresser drawer.

Stella threw her arms around her friend. "I absolutely love it!"

"Actually, it's a good thing I got you something to wear."

Stella looked at Juliet blankly. The pounding in her head was simply miserable.

"Earth to Stella. What is wrong with you? Ever hear of the curse? You're leaking."

They rushed into the bathroom, well aware that they'd be late for Miss Hewitt's math class and the exam they both feared.

"Oh, shit." This was the first time Stella had menstruated and she was near tears. "Why today of all days? I have the worst luck in the world."

"Actually, I think that would be me."

Juliet visited her father's grave every other Sunday, and therefore would not have been available for birthday parties even if she'd been asked. She regularly tore up her mother's letters from Framingham State Prison without reading them. She'd heard it all before: the excuses, the reasons why. None of it mattered to Juliet Aronson. She signed her own report cards, made her own lunches, and kept a rope ladder under her bed, in case a fire should break out in her apartment, for her aunt smoked when she studied and often fell asleep in bed, books open, a cigarette still burning in the ashtray. Juliet was used to disaster, and could therefore always be depended upon to be ready for the next catastrophe to come. Now, for instance, she pulled an extra pair of panties out of her backpack. Always be prepared, that was her motto. Always expect the worst.

"You think this is bad? I got my period for the first time when I was on the T going to Cambridge and I just had to sit there on the train and bleed until we got to the station in Harvard Square. I went to the Coop and refused to leave until they gave me a pair of sweatpants."

Juliet sat on the sink and lit up a cigarette from a pack she'd bought at the corner store; she'd recently convinced the shop owner that she was a twenty-three-year-old graduate student, with a bit of help from her aunt's pilfered ID. "I think I'm supposed to slap you or something. Welcome you into the world of women. My aunt slapped me, but maybe that was because it was her white jeans I was wearing, and I had to throw them away."

"Oh, great. A slap. Terrific." No wonder Stella's head had felt fizzy and why her stomach ached. No wonder she was in such a terrible mood. "Welcome to the world of pain."

Stella had changed her clothes, folding the stained skirt and panties into her backpack, slipping the blue blazer over the new black dress. She realized that the fabric was practically see-through. You had to have courage to wear something like this, even when it was half covered up. You had to have faith that you could pull it off and not look like a total fool. Stella smoothed down the skirt and buttoned her blazer, then went to wash her hands. So far, this business of being a woman had been exhausting.

"I hate my mother," Stella said idly as she dried her hands and dashed on more lipstick. In the flickering light of the washroom she looked especially pale without lipstick and extraordinarily trashy with it. "She watches over me like I'm some sort of wilting flower."

"You think your mother's bad? At least she's never killed any-one."

"Only emotionally."

They laughed as they rushed to Miss Hewitt's class.

"If anyone bothers you about not wearing your full uniform," Juliet whispered, "tell them you're bleeding to death. That ought to shut them up."

"Right." Stella was self-conscious in the black dress. She wondered if she had put on too much lipstick.

"And let me deal with the authority figure. You know how sincere I can pretend to be."

Once inside the classroom, Stella scuttled to her desk while Juliet apologized to Miss Hewitt for their lateness. Juliet explained they'd had female problems, the sort of thing her mother had never had time to explain to her since, Juliet reminded Miss Hewitt, Mrs. Aronson was in the state prison at Framingham and was a vile murderess who had left Juliet to fend for herself in the cruel world. How could Miss Hewitt debate that? How could she dock them points for tardiness? Stella was impressed by Juliet yet again. A loyal friend was so comforting, even on a day as horrible as this. Quickly, Stella set to work on her exam. She had actually studied, hoping to raise her faltering grade out of the realm of the C's, and she might have done exactly that if she hadn't happened to look up after writing her name. Her gaze settled on Miss Hewitt and once it did, she couldn't look away. There, plain as day, was a fish bone, right in the middle of the math teacher's throat.

Stella blinked. She'd been dizzy after all; she probably wasn't seeing straight. But when she looked again, the bone remained exactly where it had been, wedged in tightly. It was a delicate object, white and narrow, a trout bone, perhaps. From its form and shape anyone could tell it would be impossible to cough up once it had caught in the trachea.

Stella's pulse was pounding and her mouth had gone completely dry. Right away, she understood that she had somehow managed to see Miss Hewitt's future, the physical manifestation of the math teacher's fate. Sitting at her desk, ignoring the exam for which she had dutifully studied, helpless against the forces of destiny, Stella's complexion turned ashen. Her heart bumped against her ribs and her head spun. When she fainted, the other girls in the classroom gasped and left their desks so they could gather round. Someone pulled down Stella's sheer skirt, for modesty's sake; another student rolled up her blazer, in order to cushion Stella's head on the hard, tile floor.

Naturally everyone understood the situation once Juliet announced that Stella had gotten her period for the first time and that her cramps had indeed been wicked. The school nurse was called in to assist with smelling salts and a cold compress. At last, Stella came to consciousness, sitting up slowly, hands clutching her aching head. For an instant she didn't know where she was, not until she saw Juliet Aronson's worried face.

"Happy birthday," Juliet said.

It was Juliet who convinced the math teacher to allow Stella to leave early. Poor Miss Hewitt, as unaware of her own dire future as she was blind to Juliet Aronson's manipulations, assured Stella that she could make up the test after the weekend. A taxi was called, her coat was retrieved from her locker, and that should have been the end of Stella's troubles. But on the way home, Stella spied a pea-shaped object inside the taxi driver's skull. She nearly fainted again, but she held herself together with sheer will. She would not act like a baby. She would not let this get the best of her, whatever it might be, a curse or an omen or a crossed wire somewhere inside her head. She opened the taxi's window and forced herself to breathe deeply; just in case there was more to see, she kept her eyes closed all the rest of the way down Beacon Street.

Once home, Stella ran upstairs to the third floor and double-locked the door. She fetched a glass of water from the kitchen, then went to the hallway. She pulled a chair over to the model house sent by her grandmother and attempted to block out the day's events. There was something calming about concentrating on the little house, paying attention to the details, the perfect miniature rugs, the brown and white Spode china, the tiny fireplaces—one red brick, one gray brick, one made out of stone—the glass case in the corner of the parlor, covered with a scrap of embroidered cloth.

Stella was soon lost in the rooms of Cake House, a place she'd never been allowed to visit. She tried her best to forget what an awful birthday this had been. Yesterday, when she'd spoken to her grandmother, Elinor Sparrow had advised her to expect the unexpected. Maybe this was what her grandmother had meant. The fizzing in her brain, the visions, the fish bone, the black dress that was far too grown-up, the way she'd fallen onto the floor of the classroom, wobbly and disoriented in the face of the death.

At least her mother was still at work. Stella had a shred of privacy. She went to her room, where she hid the black dress under her bed, then threw on an old pair of jeans and a favorite white blouse. So often, Stella's birthday began with sunshine only to end with snow flurries, or it started with high winds only to shift into fresh, mild air. You never could tell when it came to the equinox. The weather was already changing. When Stella opened the window, there was a damp scent in the air, one reminiscent of lake water, dark and muddy and sweet. Stella thought about hooks and bones, she thought about tumors that resembled garden peas, about birthdays and blood. She considered it all, and then she went back to the hall to phone her father at the music school.

"Daddy," she said, relieved as soon as she heard his voice. Love was like that, it could give you comfort and solace when it was most needed. It could give you hope when you thought there was none. "Come and get me now."

III.

WILL AVERY was forty minutes late, which, for him, was almost like being on time. When he turned onto Marlborough Street and saw his daughter waiting for him, perched on the concrete steps, he felt a rush of joy. Stella still expected something from him, despite the disappointment he'd been to everyone else. Stella, at least, believed in him, and because of this he tried his best to come through for her—when he could, of course, which wasn't as often as he liked. Better than anyone, Will knew he was careless and self-centered, traits that were as much a part of him as his good looks.

He'd never given these failings much thought, not any more than he'd questioned his blood type or his bone structure, but lately something inside him had begun to shift. In recent months he'd found himself overwhelmed by some emotion he couldn't place. He got teary for no reason. He felt the black, uneven edge of regret whenever he was alone, which, frankly, was most of the time. If he wasn't careful, he'd soon become one of those poor souls who start to cry after two strong drinks, willing to confide in any stranger who happened to be close by, bemoaning the mess he'd made of his life.

"Hey, baby," he called when Stella came running to meet him.

Stella's hair was pulled back; she wore an old navy coat over a white shirt and jeans. Not exactly festive. Indeed, her face was drawn with worry and exhaustion.

"Are you all right? Let me get a good look at you." Will stared at his daughter. He knew how to cheer a woman up. It was the one thing he was good at, other than music. "Gorgeous as usual."

"Oh, yeah, right." All the same, Stella smiled, pleased in spite of herself.

"Where's your mother? Wasn't the plan for us all to go out for a birthday dinner?"

Stella grabbed her father's hand. "Actually, I want to go before Mom gets home. I want to celebrate my birthday with you. She wouldn't understand."

"Ah. Ditching Mom." Will was certainly agreeable to a maneuver such as this. It was a course of action he understood quite well. Every time he'd strayed, every time he'd had too much to drink or disappointed Jenny in some way, he'd done the exact same thing. And when it came right down to it, didn't Jenny Sparrow Avery deserve to be disappointed? She was always so damned hurt. She simply refused to learn from experience. Was it Will's fault that Jenny was naive? Was it his responsibility? Maybe he had done her a favor: waking her out of her dream world, letting her know there was a real universe that was filled with liars and cheaters—people like him who had just as much a right to walk this earth as she did.

Will and Stella hightailed it over to Beacon Street before Jenny was the wiser, laughing as they raced several blocks to their favorite restaurant, the Hornets' Nest, famed for its strong drinks and its heavenly Boston cream pie. It was a happy occasion, just cause for celebration, and for once Will had remembered to get a present—reminded, of course, by a message from Jenny on his phone machine. He'd chosen a bracelet with a gold bell that Stella seemed to love. But before long, Will felt a wash of unease. Stella was chattering, which was very unlike her, and her cheerful manner seemed forced. She had always resembled him physically, with the same fine features and golden coloring. Now Will fervently hoped she hadn't inherited anything of his character. Why, he'd been a liar since the day he learned to talk. Dishonesty had come to him as easily as music had; he had a natural talent, it seemed. A good thing, for he'd never worked at anything. He'd never even considered such a possibility. He'd simply opened his hands and fortune had found him, or at least that had been the case until now.

In all this time, there had been only one person who had managed to see through him. Not Jenny. It had taken her thirty years to realize he couldn't be trusted. No, it was Jenny's mother who immediately knew him for what he was. Elinor Sparrow could tell that he was a liar when she first spied him in the parlor of her house. Will had been reckless in those days, he hadn't been spooked by the dusty rooms in Cake House, but of course he hadn't expected Elinor Sparrow to swoop down on them as they evaluated the belongings of Rebecca Sparrow, kept under lock and key.

Don't move, Jenny had whispered that day when she heard her mother in the hallway. But of course he didn't comply. Will being Will, he found it impossible to obey. As soon as Jenny ran out to the hall to try and divert her mother, Will reached for the key hanging from a hook on the wall. Without thinking twice, he opened the glass case for a closer look. Unfortunately, Elinor Sparrow could not be diverted. Not when she heard the creak of the memento case as it was unlocked and opened. Standing in the hall, she had picked up a sweet, cloying odor, the unmistakable scent of a liar and a thief. And there he was: a foolish boy in her parlor, studying the family archives as though he were a rightful guest, searching through that old and bloody case of pain.

Elinor Sparrow was a strong woman and quite large, more than six feet tall; when she grabbed Will by the shoulder he could feel her fingernails pinching his flesh.

What have you taken? She shook him as though she could shake the truth right out of him. She treated him as though he were a mole in the garden, a rat in the cellar, nothing more than a household pest caught in a trap. *What did you steal?*

Nothing. It was the hot response of a liar, syrupy and much too easily spoken. *You've got it all wrong. I'm just visiting.*

Elinor had jeered at that notion. She had taken note of the way he licked his lips, how his eyes darted to the left; she was unmoved by the satiny tone of his voice. He was marked by the distinctive scent of his lies, a leathery, acrid smell. Elinor would have been able to find him even if he'd been hiding in a bale of straw. That's how this boy stank, like old shoes, like dashed hopes, like someone who might steal a person's daughter if she wasn't careful.

Elinor shook Will harder; she could have easily snapped one of the bones in his shoulder if Matt Avery hadn't heard the ruckus and come running. Matt threw open the French doors, shattering several panes of glass, wielding a shovel he'd found beside the porch. Matt was exceedingly shy and rarely opened his mouth until he'd been spoken to, but now he faced off with Elinor Sparrow, shovel in hand, expression set.

Let him go. Do it now!

Elinor laughed at the sheer nerve of this trespasser. He was all of eleven. Twelve at the most.

What are you planning to do about it? she said scornfully. When Matt paused to think over his answer, Elinor laughed again. *I'll tell you what you'll do. Nothing.*

Matt would never have used the shovel as anything more than a shield, but when Elinor laughed at him, when she began to shake Will once more, Matt leaped forward, accepting the challenge. Not knowing any other way to free his brother, he stomped on Elinor Sparrow's foot. She howled and let go of Will.

I want what he stole, Elinor cried.

But Matt had grabbed Will by the shirtsleeve and waved the shovel in the air to keep Elinor at bay. *My brother wouldn't take anything. He wouldn't want anything that belonged to you.*

Although a bruise was surfacing on the mount of Elinor's foot Matt's certainty had caused her to lose her edge. For a moment at least, she seemed to forget she was the wronged party. The brothers hadn't waited for Elinor to regain her wits. They ran off through the French doors so fast they thought their lungs would explode. They fled past the forsythia and the laurel, not stopping until they reached the end of the driveway. By then they could barely breathe. Matt for one was shaking. But Will threw himself down on the grass, laughing so hard, he nearly choked.

What's so funny?

Matt had forgotten to drop the shovel when they took off running and was still holding on to it, his grip so tight blisters were already rising. Matt Avery couldn't quite believe he'd actually confronted Elinor Sparrow. He hoped when he went to bed that night he wouldn't find an onion stabbed through with pins beneath his pillow. He knew, after all, there were those in town who insisted such would surely be the fate of anyone who crossed Elinor: the gift of a small token that was said to be accompanied by seven years' bad luck.

Matt threw down the shovel and sat beside his brother, who was still chuckling, amused and terribly pleased with himself.

Come on. Matt was always the last to know anything. *Tell me. What's so funny?*

Will had opened his hand in front of his brother's face. There in his sweaty palm was one of Rebecca Sparrow's arrowheads. There was the line marked by blood.

Matt had stood up, furious. *You bastard.* Will couldn't remember having ever heard his brother curse before. *You made a liar out of me.*

Matt took off, cutting through a weedy patch of lawn gone to seed, deaf to Will's pleas for him to grow up and stop being such a nitwit. What was wrong with telling a lie if it served your purpose? Will was ready to share the arrowhead, if that was what Matt wanted. He was amenable if Matt wanted to claim to have been beside him when he stole the damned thing, if Matt wanted to share in the glory. But Matt never turned around. He collected his sleeping bag and lantern from the far side of the lake, and he was long gone by the time Jenny came to look for Will.

She was barefoot when she came down from the house, flushed from the fight she'd just had with her mother. Their arguments were stark, brittle things, with the insults hurled falling like bombs. As soon as Will heard Jenny approach, he slipped the arrowhead into his pocket. She might as well go on thinking the best of him. When she sat down beside him, on that green March day, her skin overheated, her hair still tangled, Will saw that she was beautiful in a way he hadn't noticed before.

If my mother hurt you, she'll be sorry, Jenny told him.

She couldn't hurt me if she tried, Will had scoffed, his shoulder aching. All the same, Jenny's concern had moved him; he wanted more of it. She was interesting in a way the other girls in town who chased after him simply were not.

Did you dream about an angel with dark hair last night? And there was a bee and a woman who wasn't afraid of anything. Not even the deepest water.

Will felt mesmerized. He heard the chorus of the wood thrush, the peepers in the mud. Jenny's looks were exotic for Unity, the long black hair that floated down her back like lake water, the dark, bottomless eyes. Even Will Avery wasn't immune to spring fever. He could feel it creeping up on him, clouding his reason. Everything looked iridescent and new in the glittery sunlight.

That was my dream, he said.

I knew it. Jenny was delighted. *I knew it was you.*

Jenny flicked back her black hair. She smelled like verbena and sleep. Will understood that she trusted him, she believed in him, and the very idea infatuated him. Sitting there beside her, Will temporarily forgot who he was and what he was capable of.

And now, all these years later, he had begun to wonder if it wasn't the angel Jenny spoke of that he sometimes saw in the dark, waiting on street corners, standing over his bed. It was a hallucination, surely, but one that seemed to follow him around these days. This vision was apparent to him in the bar of the Hornets' Nest most every night. It was the reason he was drinking too much on the occasion of Stella's birthday, already on his second Johnnie Walker by the time the salads arrived.

This was one of those nights when he was sure to wind up teary-eyed. Time had passed; his little girl a teenager who would surely see him for who he was before long. Stella was busy playing with the bell on her bracelet; she seemed moody, not at all herself, although the fact that she was distracted allowed Will the opportunity to flirt with the waitress, a pretty girl who was clearly too young for him. Probably a graduate student who would expect him to have long conversations about things that mattered to her, her future, for instance, or her opinion. Seduction, Will had found lately, was so much damn work. It was far easier when someone knew you, when you could let down your guard.

"Does your mother ask about me much?" he inquired of Stella.

Stella shook her wrist. The little bell on her new bracelet made a cool, metallic sound. "Not much."

"No?"

Her father seemed wounded, so Stella quickly backtracked. "Well, sometimes. But it's not like we communicate or anything. I can't talk to her the way I can talk to you."

Will smiled, delighted. At least someone still trusted him.

Stella leaned forward on her elbows. "Actually, I have something I need to talk to you about right now. Something she'd never understand."

So that was the reason the girl had been so ill at ease all through dinner. Will hoped this wasn't to be a confession that involved sex or drugs. He was no one's moral compass, how could he hope to weigh in with a parental opinion? Stella was looking at him as though she really needed him, and that in itself was a worry. She had the same gold flecks in her eyes he had; the same habit of lowering her voice when she had something serious to discuss.

"I think I can tell what's going to happen to some people," Stella told her father.

Will laughed out loud. He really couldn't help it, not when he thought about all the crap he'd been into at her age. The terror he put his poor mother through, the nights he hadn't come home, all those rules he felt compelled to break, hashish stored in his closet, bags of marijuana in his desk drawer, the fires he'd started when he'd needed a little excitement, the many times he'd misbehaved and poor Matt had covered for him and taken the blame.

"Sorry," Will said when he saw the hurt look on Stella's face. "I'm not laughing at you. I'm just relieved. I thought you were about to tell me something awful."

"It *is* awful."

"Baby, listen, I can tell what's going to happen to people also." He nodded to a rear table where a couple had been bickering all evening. "See those two? They'll be divorced by the end of the year. Take it from me. Oh, and another thing, I can predict that your mother will be furious that we went to dinner without her. I can definitely foresee that."

"I don't mean things like that." Stella leaned closer still. There was the chime of the bell on her bracelet. "I see how they die."

"Ah." Will lit a cigarette and thought this over. Outside, the brown twilight washed over Beacon Street. There were a dozen pigeons on the sidewalk, their feathers pale and gleaming in the fading light.

"I think you should put out that cigarette," Stella advised.

Her tone was suddenly so sure, so adult, Will found he was spooked. He felt something cold drift across his skin. His future, perhaps? His well-deserved fate? He had been coughing a good deal lately and more often than not he awoke with a sore throat.

"Why? Because it will kill me?"

There was a little smile on Stella's lips. "No. Because we're in the no-smoking section."

Will laughed and stubbed out his cigarette in a half-eaten roll. There was indeed a sign on the wall: NO PIPES, NO CIGARETTES, NO CIGARS. "So I'm not about to die of lung cancer any time soon?"

"I can't see it with you. It's only with some people, and I never know who it will be. I don't control it."

Will finished his drink and called for another. He'd begun to relax. This didn't sound too awful. Premonitions, fears, that sort of thing; surely, it was bound to pass. She had probably fooled around with a Ouija board or a pack of fortune-telling cards. It was nothing when compared to the troubles some people had with their children: schizophrenia, anorexia, kleptomania. What were a few visions compared with all that? The way Will figured the situation, Stella was passing through some developmental stage, a natural fear of death mixed with anxiety caused by her parents' breakup. He'd read a book about children reacting to divorce—actually half a book, since the philosophizing bored him silly. But now he wondered if he should have read all the way to the end. He wondered if Jenny hadn't been right; they probably should have gone into family therapy, but of course Will had refused. It didn't seem worthwhile to pay for an expensive hour of questions and answers when all he would tell were bold-faced lies.

"Can you see it with anyone here?" Will had decided to treat Stella's alleged affliction as though it were a parlor game. *Tell me how many aces I have in my hand, how many one-eyed jacks, how much time I have on earth.* "What about those two in the corner?"

Naturally he would choose them, two young, attractive women in their thirties, clearly enjoying a night out. One of the women had honey-colored hair, pulled back from her pale face; her companion was wearing a black dress, not unlike the one Juliet had given Stella, and a dozen silver bracelets on her arms.

Stella looked over at the corner, then quickly turned back to her father. Her face was drained of all color. One instant was all it took. One look and she knew. She could smell her father's whisky and the faint odor of tobacco that clung to him. Dishes were clattering as the table beside them was cleared.

"The one in black will die in bed when she's an old woman. Her heart will stop."

"Okay. That's good." Will was relieved and more than a little drunk. "That's a fine way to die, Stella, if you really want to know. Hell, I hope I kick off the same way. There's nothing wrong in seeing that."

Will was cheerful again. *Talk to your teenagers*, the book he'd half-read had advised. *Treat them as though their ideas mattered.*

"Anyway, I'll bet this vision thing is like the flu. Twenty-four hours of seeing death. Take two aspirin and get a good night's sleep, Stella, my star, and you'll be fine in the A.M. Completely clear-headed."

Stella certainly hoped so because these visions were nothing she wanted. They were nothing any thirteen-year-old girl could take comfort in. She forced herself to breathe slowly and evenly;

she hadn't yet told her father all of it. She paid no attention when the waitress delivered the check, along with her scribbled phone number for Will to fold into his wallet. She kept her eyes averted from the second woman at the table in the corner, the one with the honey-blond hair whose throat had been slit.

When the waitress had gone, Stella surprised Will by going to sit in his lap, something she hadn't done for ages. "Hey," Will said, pleased. Maybe he did have a chance to be a better father, a better person all around. "That's my little girl."

It took a while before he realized that Stella was crying, her face hidden against him. He could feel her tears through the fabric of his shirt. He could feel his love for her as well, worthless as it might be.

"It's your birthday, Stell. Don't cry."

"Then promise you'll believe me." Stella's voice was surprisingly fierce. "I mean it. Cross your heart."

She moved back into her own chair so that she could watch as Will solemnly crossed his heart, or at least he traced an X in the place where his heart should have been. He listened as his daughter told him about the awful death of the woman in the corner, how she'd be murdered in her bed, how she'd open her eyes and know the darkness was about to close in, how she wouldn't have a chance if she wasn't warned.

"You have to do something," Stella urged. "You just have to."

Her bright confidence burned through Will and, for a moment, it made him a better man. He had no choice but to try to rise to the occasion of being Stella's father.

"Fine. I'll tell her to lock her windows and beware of strangers, but if they drag me off to the loony bin, you'll have to tell them it was all your idea."

Will Avery went over to the women's table to introduce himself. He pointed out his daughter, the charming girl who was staring at them from across the room. Both women laughed when Will sheepishly brought up Stella's premonition. They'd remembered having overactive imaginations when they were thirteen, they'd believed in ghosts and in love at first sight and look at them now—all grown up and dubious about nearly everything, although not so much so that the blonde didn't give him her phone number, which he slipped into his wallet, alongside the waitress's crumpled note.

"I don't think they believed me," he told Stella as they left the restaurant.

"Then we still have to tell someone else. It's our duty, isn't it? It's our responsibility."

Responsibility, that notion was assuredly Jenny's influence. Always looking forward to the next balanced meal, the next homework assignment, the next chore to be completed. And what of Will's influence? What had he taught his daughter? To let your appetites rule your life? To do as you pleased, no matter who might be hurt?

They had turned onto Marlborough Street and were headed toward home. The air was soft and damp, fishy the way March air can be, clinging to clothes, urging the buds of the magnolias to open. Will never went up to the apartment anymore. He merely dropped Stella off and went on his way, but what way was that, really? The way of three drinks in order to get to sleep? The way of not bothering to speak to another human being most days, let alone think about anyone other than himself?

"We have to do more," Stella insisted. "You have to."

"More," Will repeated.

It was as though the thought had never before occurred to him. Standing in front of the apartment building where he'd lived for so many years, Will found himself thinking of someone other than himself. He wondered if this was the way selfless people felt, this lightness inside, a sensation of weightlessness.

"Promise me you'll do something, Daddy."

Stella looked fragile, like a piece of glass, and yet she was also intractable, absolutely sure of what he must do. How lucky he was to have her. How fortunate to be seen through her eyes.

Will Avery held his hand over his heart and vowed to accomplish what he'd never before attempted or promised. He would, indeed, do more. He kissed his daughter good-night and watched her run up the steps, and then he walked through the dark. He felt as though he were floating up Marlborough Street, as though the damp air had turned to water. He was a fish, swimming upstream. He was an arrow, aimed with trust and devotion. The sky was filled with what Jenny always referred to as dreamlight, a sprinkling of those constellations which she felt brought on more dreams for most sleepers. That was one thing he especially missed about his marriage: he used to love to hear Jenny tell him other people's dreams. He himself had never been much of a dreamer. More and more, sleep was of little comfort to him; it had become flat, the country of regret, the empty inner landscape of a man who has lied for so long he can no longer recognize the truth.

Will wished it had been his dream all those years ago, on that morning when Jenny ran after him. He wished he was capable of imagining dark angels, fearless women, bees that would never sting. Still, there was one angel on earth who believed in him, and he'd made her a promise he fully intended to keep. This was a first for him, something he wouldn't have imagined was in his nature. Astounding what love could do to a person. Amazing the changes it could bring. It could alter history, it could stop and start wars; it could even make an honest man out of Will Avery. By the time he reached the police station, Will was whistling, the sign of a man with a clear conscience. It was true he was a liar through and through, but even a liar could have a heart, despite what some people might think. Even a liar could convince himself he was about to do the right thing.

IV.

THE MESSAGE CAME while Jenny was out picking up lunch, round the corner at the market on Charles Street, having telephoned in her order for a Caesar-salad-to-go and a strong, black tea. That Will Avery would list her as his next of kin seemed ridiculous, considering the fact that they'd barely spoken in the past six months, but apparently he had, for there was a message on her desk informing her that he was being held on suspicion of murder. Evidently, whoever had taken the message hadn't kept it to herself, but had spread it far and wide, from Mortgages to Securities, so that all eyes were already on Jenny as she walked to her desk; people knew she would be shocked when she read the note, which had been taped to her weekly calendar.

Jenny tossed her salad in the trash; she'd never get to eat lunch now. Her stomach had dropped into some bottomless pit and she had a tingly feeling in her fingers and toes, the way she always did before disaster struck. Why, on the day of her wedding, right on the steps of City Hall in Cambridge, her toes were so afflicted she could barely put one foot in front of the other. Anyone else would have known herself to be headed for unhappiness; that should have been apparent simply from the way she'd hesitated on the way to see the town clerk as though it were a tar pit that was waiting for her, rather than wedded bliss. Anyone else would have turned and run, whether or not she had to limp all the way. But not Jenny, she had to go forward no matter what; she couldn't admit when she had made a mistake, a flaw her mother had always accused her of having. *You will never back down*, Elinor had said. *Not for love or money. Not if you're the wrongest person on earth.*

Jenny would be lucky to manage a few gulps of hot tea for lunch as she waited for the police switchboard to connect her with a detective. She was soon informed that her husband was being questioned in connection with a murder that had taken place the week following Stella's birthday. Someone had climbed in through an open window or managed to get through the door in Brighton and slit a woman's throat. There had been no witnesses and no apparent motive. Jenny recalled being frightened by the story on the six o'clock news, a teacher, well thought of and respected, a pretty woman of thirty-three, had met this horrendous fate. Jenny had made a mental note to have a locksmith come round to check if their deadbolt needed updating.

But what had this all to do with them? Plenty, it seemed. Her husband, Jenny was now told, had come to the police before the murder with a great deal of information and was now being held for further questioning. The detectives had been particularly interested when they'd found the dead woman's phone number in Will Avery's possession.

"Ex," Jenny was quick to correct.

"Excuse me?"

"My ex-husband. We were legally separated in the summer, and our divorce should come through anytime. No contest."

"Were you afraid for your safety when you split up?"

"No. Of course not." For her sanity, perhaps; her self-respect, certainly.

"How about after the breakup? Did you have a restraining order filed?"

So that was where this line of questioning was headed.

"Will Avery is constitutionally incapable of violence. I know him better than anyone, and I can tell you right now he practically faints at the sight of blood. Especially his own. If he cuts himself shaving, he has to breathe into a brown paper bag."

Which was exactly what he was doing when Jenny got down to the jail on the far side of Charles Street. Will was in a holding cell, huffing and puffing into a bag that had previously held the detectives' coffees and pastries. They had taken pity on him when he couldn't catch his breath, and pity was what Will Avery deserved. He'd been picked up the night before, and the effects of his drinking showed after a single sleepless night. His complexion appeared yellow rather than golden under the glare of the fluorescent lights; he was unshaven, his hands shook. Will, who had always cared so much about his appearance, looked like a common criminal. Had Jenny passed him on the street she might have taken him for one of those sorrowful, lost men who dozed on the benches in the Common, the ones who dreamed of hot showers, and apple pie, and a world in which every man received what he truly deserved.

When Will wandered into the police station the previous week, cheerfully whistling, ready to tell his outrageous story to anyone willing to listen, they had laughed at him. Having smelled the alcohol on his breath, they made certain he wouldn't be driving home. No car, he assured them; he would be walking—stumbling, actually. He'd been huffy about that, insulted they had thought he'd do anything so foolish as drive. To appease him, the sergeant on duty had taken down Will's complaint about the murder that was to be. Everyone at the station house had a hoot afterward, agreeing that they'd truly heard everything now.

But following the killing in Brighton, one of the officers who'd been on duty that night remembered the report, and he had dug up Will's file. There he found a description of the victim and the exact cause of death, six days before it had occurred.

"You idiot," Jenny said when she was let in to see him. She sat facing Will, their knees grazing.

"That's not in dispute." Will looked at his ex and managed a grin. There was a flicker of what there had once been between them. But it was just that, a flicker, nothing more. They had become more like people who'd been through a war together, comrades with little in common but the battle itself.

"I called my brother. He's getting me a lawyer. Remember Henry Elliot who we went to school with? He practices in Boston now. Apparently, he's one of the best."

"You called Matt?"

It was ridiculous for her to feel wounded that he might not have called her first. But Matt? They hadn't seen much of Will's brother over the years. He'd come to visit when they first moved to Cambridge, and of course they'd seen him at Catherine Avery's funeral. But Will and Jenny had an aversion to their hometown, and once Catherine had passed on, the brothers drifted even farther apart. Matt Avery, after all, had stayed put; he had barely taken a step out of Unity. He had cared for his mother in her last years and worked odd jobs, plowing snow, landscaping, working for the Department of Parks. The brothers had so little in common, and then, of course, there'd been that awful fight. It was the year after Stella was born, when Matt had come to stay for New Year's. There had been some altercation at the party Jenny and Will were throwing, and the two men had wound up on the street, going at each other as though their lives depended on the outcome. By the time the fight had been broken up and Jenny had soothed their outraged landlady and the neighbors who were already fed up with Will's antics, Matt had gone. Now, he'd agreed to pay for an expensive criminal lawyer.

"Blood is thicker than water," Will said hopefully. He was dying for a cigarette, but of course they'd taken everything away from him, including the silver lighter Stella had given him last Father's Day. TO THE BEST DAD IN THE WORLD, she'd inscribed. *Poor thing*, Will had thought, even then. *Bound to be disappointed*. "Maybe good old Matt feels guilty that my mother left him the house. Do you think he was the favorite?" There was that grin again, but only for an instant.

"Of course he was. You barely went to visit her. I'm just glad Matt can afford a top lawyer, because I can't."

"Well, evidently he can. He must have plowed a lot of snow."

They both laughed at the notion of Matt driving through their snowbound hometown, then fell silent. Jenny felt their real worry settle down between them. "We can keep this from Stella. There's no reason for her to know."

"Uh uh. That won't work. It will be in the newspapers. Hell, it's probably already in the *Boston Herald* and the *Boston Globe*. There's no hiding it from her, Jen."

"Then you tell me right now. Tell me the truth for once in your life."

Liar, liar, pants on fire. What velvet tale can you tell? What foolish heart can you break? What shameful alibi can you concoct?

"I didn't do it. I swear I didn't."

Jenny studied him carefully because he really was good at deceit. He could tell her it was raining as they stood beneath a blue sky and she would be convinced she would soon be drenched, through and through. After all these years, she hadn't a clue as to whether or not she could trust him.

"I did make the report. That much is true," Will admitted. "But I did it because I promised Stella I would."

"Oh, so now it's Stella's fault."

He told Jenny what had happened that night, how Stella had confided in him on her birthday, how she'd begged him to report the murder she imagined would soon take place. Now Jenny understood, this was the aptitude that had been visited on Stella when she turned thirteen. This was her talent. An eye for death, an ability to read the human timetable; a nightmare of a gift. And she'd turned to Will, that was the thing; she'd confided in her father, not in Jenny. She had trusted him.

Jenny couldn't help but think of Rebecca Sparrow and all her sorrows. She had found a portrait of Rebecca once, a miniature, perhaps a study for the larger painting that hung in the library. The miniature had been wrapped in water-stained silk and forgotten. Jenny would have never seen it if she hadn't happened upon it as she searched through a cluttered cabinet for a gravy boat. She brought the treasure out to the shed, untied the silk, and found a girl with long black hair who looked as though she'd been crying. A girl who resembled Jenny enough to make her start. It was as though some of her own traits had been captured in paint three hundred years before she'd been born.

Rebecca Sparrow had been taken in by the washerwoman who lived by the lake, taught how to cut up frozen potatoes for starch with which to set collars and cuffs, worked hard, until her hands bled. She'd been instructed that a frog in the wash water brought luck, and had quickly learned that a washerwoman's hands looked ten years older than her natural age. Every blister was a token of the life she'd led. Every burn, a document to her courage.

When Rebecca was barely thirteen, the old woman who had taken her in died suddenly. Rebecca herself then became the washerwoman. It was her fate and her duty; it was all she knew. She built a second shed in the woods, for making soap out of ashes and grease was a nasty, smoky business; there needed to be some distance between the laundry house and the place where Rebecca slept. Rebecca's feet would turn green as she took the path where nothing grew these days, but where there once had been wild ginger and bloodroot and masses of wood violets. Jenny had always wondered if the portrait she'd found—which she guessed must have been given in exchange for laundry done—had been painted before or after Rebecca's thirteenth birthday. Rebecca was too beautiful to be bound in silk and left in a drawer, trapped in a frame carved from ash. This was a tree that no longer grew in Unity; it had been cut down so extensively by the first settlers that it disappeared from the county completely. Jenny decided to keep the portrait in the soap shed, where she felt it belonged, where she imagined it must have hung on a nail so many years earlier. Jenny, who'd had something of a talent for painting, then began to create her own miniatures on tiny bits of canvas or wood, using a brush that contained a single horse's hair and a magnifying glass she found in her father's desk drawer.

The soap shed was the meeting spot that Jenny and Will chose when Elinor forbade them to see each other. Before long, their desire had mixed with the scent of harsh soap that still clung to the air. The windows had no glass and never had; Rebecca hadn't even bothered with oil-soaked paper, she'd wanted the fresh air. Still, the shed was easily warmed by the fires Will set in the enormous hearth where Rebecca's pots of boiling laundry had once been attached to the iron bar which swung out from the bricks. It was one of those fires that nearly destroyed the shed back when Will and Jenny were teenagers. They had stayed all night in the laundry shed, and Will had lingered after Jenny had slipped back to Cake House to get dressed. Later that morning, from her classroom at the Unity High School, Jenny had looked out the window of her earth science class and had spied smoke. Right away, she guessed what had happened. Fire stations from three neighboring towns were called in, along with the Unity division, which some people say was founded by Leonie Sparrow, who could take burning-hot bread from the oven bare-handed and walk through fire without being scorched.

The shed was charred and waterlogged by the time the firemen were through—still, it was standing. Jenny had wondered about Will's carelessness, but afterward, as they'd stood there watching the last of the embers, Will had denied having anything to do with the fire. He'd stood there and chomped on an apple as he explained to Jenny how he'd made certain to carefully put out the fire before he'd left that morning. When he was done with the apple, he threw the core into the still-burning embers in the fireplace. People said whenever the pips of an apple popped noisily in a fire it was a sign that true love was nearby. But on this day there was only the sizzling sound of what had been burned and destroyed and the call of crows overhead.

Elinor Sparrow accused Will of arson. Her lips twitched as they always did whenever a liar was near, but the charges were soon dismissed. There was no proof and no witnesses, and the judge was Catherine Avery's first cousin, Maurice. It wasn't until fifteen years later, after Stella had already been born and they lived in the apartment on Marlborough Street, that the fire was mentioned again. Will and Jenny had been watching a newscast about brushfires sweeping through the California canyons; house after house had burned to the ground and Jenny said something about the blaze being impressive.

The shed went up quicker than that, Will had said.

That was when Jenny knew her mother had been right. He'd stood there and watched Rebecca's shed burn, then lied right to Jenny's face. She'd lost that little portrait she loved and he'd never even bothered to tell her the truth. So why should she be certain now, as she sat across from him in a jail cell, that the truth wasn't once again melting in Will's mouth as he proclaimed his innocence, so that every word came out twisted in an odd, untrustworthy shape.

"I regret it, you know," Will said as Jenny was leaving, in a hurry to get to the Rabbit School before the news of Will's arrest began to filter down to Stella.

There were so many possible reasons for Will's apology, Jenny couldn't begin to guess what he was referring to exactly.

"Regret what?"

"Hurting you."

It was a glimmer of truth that blinked like a firefly, then quickly faded. But, frankly, Jenny felt she had no one but herself to blame for what had gone wrong. She'd been a headstrong girl who'd refused to listen to anyone, a fool, intoxicated by spring fever and her own misguided certainty about love.

"What's done is done. Anything else you want to admit to me while we're at it?"

"Not a thing," Will said, so quickly that it was evident, even to

Jenny, he was lying. All the same, she kissed him good-bye. The fact of the matter was, she regretted it, too.

JENNY RAN ALL THE WAY to the Rabbit School, crossing against red lights, nearly getting herself run down in the process. But she needn't have bothered to hurry. By nine that morning several girls in ninth grade were already discussing the article in the *Herald* which had mentioned Will Avery by name. By ten, two detectives had stopped by to question Stella. By the time Jenny arrived, Stella had a migraine and had taken refuge in the headmistress's office. Her blond hair was unbraided and falling down her back, her lips were stained with lipstick, her face was drawn. When Jenny arrived, she found her daughter huddled in an overstuffed chair that stood on wooden claws. Scores of students had sat in this same chair facing parents who'd been called in and informed their daughters weren't working hard enough, or they were sticking their fingers down their throats to rid themselves of calories; they had failed geometry or cut their arms with razor blades. Now it was Stella who sat there, their perfect star. Stella, who didn't look up, but instead continued to play with her bracelet, so there was a hollow, pinging sound in the room.

On this occasion, the headmistress, Marguerite Flann, had little to say. She left them alone so that Jenny could try to explain what had happened.

"Don't bother," Stella interrupted. "I know why you're here. The police came by to question me. I know what they've done to Daddy."

"They had no right to question you without a parent here." Jenny was outraged, but she couldn't help but take a moment to steal a look at her daughter. "Are you wearing red lipstick?"

"It was only an informal questioning. They told me I didn't have to say anything. But I told them the truth. Actually, it's scarlet."

Jenny sunk into the headmistress's leather chair. *Scarlet.*

"So what was the truth?" she asked Stella.

"I told them that I could see how this woman was going to die, and that I only saw it with some people, but I was so sure about her that I made Daddy promise he'd go to the police. They didn't believe me. They thought I was covering for him."

The intense love Stella felt for her father was evident, and why shouldn't it be? Here in the headmistress's office there was the smell of furniture wax, a scent that always reminded Jenny of her own father, a professor of economics and amateur carpenter. Her father, who had spent a year of his free time building Jenny her model house, who had called her his pearl, who had left his classes in Boston one spring evening only to skid off the road. A sudden cold front had left black ice along the asphalt. It was March, that unpredictable season, and he should have known better, he shouldn't have been driving so fast. He had never returned, but he'd left behind the model of Cake House on his workbench, newly finished, the interior woodwork already oiled so that it smelled especially sweet when Jenny peered inside. To this day, Jenny could walk into a stranger's apartment and begin to cry for no apparent reason, only to discover that the oak dining set or the cherrywood desk had been newly waxed, and that the scent of citrus in the air was lemon polish, the sort her father vowed was best.

Statistics, Jenny had learned early on, never mattered when they applied to you, not if you were the one in a thousand who'd been struck by lightning, not if you were the one whose father wasn't coming home, whether he had crashed his car on an icy road or was sitting in a jail cell. Jenny couldn't help but resent the other girls at the Rabbit School who would leave at the end of the day, worried about grades and clothing and their love lives, when her own daughter would be fretting over the many ways it was possible to lose someone in this world.

"It really was me who saw what was going to happen—I saw it with Miss Hewitt, and with the taxi driver, and then with that woman in the restaurant. The police didn't believe me," Stella insisted, "but he had nothing to do with it. I swear it."

The thirteenth among them, born feet first on the day of the equinox. What had Jenny expected? Had she ever really thought Stella would grow up to be an ordinary girl, one who would blend in with the crowd, who would find only happiness and be spared any sorrows?

"I believe you." Jenny was well aware that her daughter belonged to the day in March when the birds took flight, when the earth shifted and the spring constellations appeared in the sky, the lion and the lamb side by side, sharing one heaven, at least temporarily.

They assumed their worries would remain private, but tragedy isn't like that, it rises through the air, it circulates to be twice-told, then told again. Jenny and Stella had no notion of how many people were aware of Will's situation, until they tried to leave the school. Juliet Aronson, an obvious bad influence, in Jenny's opinion, stopped them at the door, out of breath, full of advice.

"You don't want to go out there," Juliet declared.

Juliet had already come up with a plan; she would go outside and announce that she was Stella Sparrow Avery, thereby distracting the band of reporters gathered on the sidewalk. Juliet had dealt with the likes of these carrion creatures for years, ever since her mother's trial. She was only too happy to get back at them now.

"I think Juliet's right. You'd better go around to the back," Marguerite Flann, the headmistress, suggested, for a crew from Channel Four had arrived. Mrs. Flann escorted them around to the rear exit, which led to an alley. "I think Stella had better stay home for the rest of the week. Just until this hoopla dies down."

And then they were let out in the alleyway, empty except for stray cats. They stared at each other. Little sparks of uncertainty were in the air. The stench in the alley was of garbage, but also of fear.

"No school for a week. You should be happy," Jenny said.

"Right." Stella buttoned her blazer, though the day was quite warm. "I'm ecstatic."

They traipsed down the alley, past the overflowing trash cans and Dumpsters. The Rabbit School van was parked here, used for field trips, along with several of the teachers' cars.

"When we get to the street we may have to run," Jenny said.

"Run?" Stella was even paler than usual, and her socks had fallen down around her ankles. She looked younger than she had this morning, even with that scarlet color she had on.

In fact, they bolted when they turned out of the alley. There was a single shout, and they knew the crowd had spied them. They sprinted down Commonwealth, hoping to throw off anyone who might be tracking them. All the same, two reporters continued to chase them, with the brashest following at their heels when they ducked into the pharmacy. It was the same pharmacy where Stella had stolen her lipstick. *Cheap*, Stella thought to herself as she and her mother hid in the hair products aisle. *Cheap as can be.*

The reporter who'd followed them wouldn't back off. He waylaid them in the hair products aisle. "I just want to talk to you."

"No, you don't." Jenny stepped in front of Stella. "You want to harass us."

The pharmacy owner, an elderly gentleman whom Stella recognized from her past thievery at the makeup counter, came to shoo the reporter out of the store.

"Vulture," he said.

And not the only one. When they finally did get home, taking a long, circuitous route through the Public Garden, then up Charles Street, there were more than a dozen messages on the phone machine from various news organizations, including two talk shows based in New York which regularly interviewed people about their personal tragedies.

"The phone is ringing again," Stella said, her tone anxious when they at last sat down to a pitiful dinner of canned soup and burned toast.

It had done so ever since they got home, with one prying individual or another at the end of the line. The last call had come from Marguerite Flann, who, upon considering the magnitude of the situation and reviewing her options, now recommended that Stella not return to the Rabbit School for the rest of the term. For the child's own good, of course, although it was true that Mrs. Flann herself was getting call after call from the newspapers, and such publicity wasn't exactly approved of by the school.

Now, when they couldn't bear the notion of one more nasty call, Jenny got up and unplugged the phone from the wall. "There. It's stopped ringing."

They both laughed, but Stella soon grew somber. "I'm going to fail math now. And if they don't want me at Rabbit, where will I go?"

"We'll think of something," Jenny assured her. But, in fact, she had no idea of what to do next. There was no school in Boston, public school or private, where Stella would be safe from conjecture and gossip. Already, there had been stories on the six o'clock newscasts on every local station. At eleven, Channel Twelve had footage of Jenny and Stella sneaking down the alley behind the Rabbit School, running away, as though they were criminals themselves.

That night, Jenny fell asleep in a chair by the window. She had been thinking of the model of Cake House her father had made for her. She'd been remembering the stories he told, how he'd said that the cherry trees in the woods all around Unity had grown from stray stones dropped by crows, and the peach trees that were naturalized all over town had washed ashore after a shipwreck. Now when Jenny dreamed it was of a tightrope, set between two great trees, one cherry, one peach, both abloom with thousands of white blossoms, set into their branches like stars. She dreamed of falling a very great distance, down in a spiral, unable to stop herself. She woke just before she hit the ground, in a panic, her heart pounding. For once, she had experienced her very own dream, not someone else's. She knew exactly how to interpret it. She knew just where it led.

Outside the street was pitch black, except for the amber pools on the concrete wherever there was a streetlamp. As soon as she plugged the phone in again, it began to ring. Jenny answered and was greeted by the reporter who had followed them into the pharmacy. He was from one of those dreadful newspapers that printed nothing but trash, still he must have thought himself to be extremely persuasive, for he was trying his best to sweet-talk Jenny into an interview, wanting her daughter's reaction to the news that her father had committed a brutal murder. Jenny's reaction was to hang up on him. He called again. This time Jenny picked up, but she didn't speak. Unfortunately, he did.

"I'm going to get that little daughter of yours to talk to me. You can count on that."

Jenny hung up, then reached for the receiver to dial out before he had a chance to call back again. She'd have to have their phone number unlisted. She'd have to put a new lock on their door. But there was no time for that now. Jenny had already decided what she must do first. It was late now, the hour when the moon was in the center of the sky, when the pigeons were finally silent and daylight seemed like a foreign country, hundreds of miles away. The street outside was completely empty when Jenny dialed the number of Cake House, which she still knew by heart. Amazing how after so many years she remembered that this was the week when the forsythia bloomed, each branch filling with radiant bursts of light. How odd that she could recall the timetable of the train to Unity, odder still that she was able to recognize her mother's voice as soon as Elinor picked up the phone, as though it had been only yesterday when they had last spoken, as though they'd been talking to each other all along.

THE ORACLE

I.

W HAT WAS A ROSE BUT THE LIVING PROOF OF
desire, the single best evidence of human
longing and earthly devotion. But desire could be
twisted, after all, and Jealousy was the name of a rose
that did well in arid soils. Red Devil flourished where
no other rose grew, at the edge of the garden, in shadows. In many ways, a rose resembled the human
heart; some were wild, others were in need of constant care. Although many varieties had been transformed and tamed, no two were exactly alike. There
were those that tasted like cherries and those that
smelled like lemons. Some were vigorous, while others faded in a single day. Some grew in swamps, some
needed bushels of fertilizer. Rose fossils dating back
three and a half billion years had been found, but in all
this time there had never been a blue rose, for the rose
family did not possess that pigment. Gardeners have
had to be satisfied with counterfeits: Blue Moon, with
its mauve buds, or Blue Magenta, a wicked rambler

that was actually violet and had to be cut back brutally to stop it from spreading where it wasn't wanted.

None of these false varieties grew in Elinor Sparrow's garden. She wanted a blue that was true, robin's-egg blue, delphinium blue, blue as the reaches of heaven. Clearly, she was a woman who didn't mind taking on an unattainable task. Other gardeners might have backed down from the rules of genetics, but not Elinor. She wasn't scared off by what others proclaimed impossible any more than she was bothered by the clouds of mosquitoes that rose at dusk at this time of year, as soon as the earth began to warm and the last of the snow had melted.

Elinor Sparrow hadn't cared about gardening until her husband's accident. The garden at Cake House, established hundreds of years earlier, had been neglected for decades. A few of the old roses Rebecca Sparrow had planted still managed to bloom among the milkweed and spiny nettles. The stone walls, carefully chinked by Sarah Sparrow, Rebecca's daughter, were still standing, and the wrought-iron gate put up by Elinor's own great-grandmother, Coral, had not rusted completely and was easily cleaned with boric acid and lye.

Elinor should have built her world around Jenny when Saul died in that accident on a road outside Boston, but instead she walked into the garden and she had never come out again. Oh, she'd gone grocery shopping, she'd passed her neighbors on Main Street on her way to the pharmacy, but all she had truly wanted was to be alone. All she could bear was the comfort of earth between her fingers, the repetition of the tasks at hand. Here, at least, she could make something grow. Here what you buried arose once more, given the correct amounts of sunlight and fertilizer and rain.

Elinor Sparrow had brought forth record-breaking blooms in past growing seasons: scented damasks as big as a horse's hoof, rosa rugosas that would flower until January, Peace roses so glorious that upon several occasions thieves had tried to steal cuttings, until the wolfhound, Argus, whose canines were worn down to nubs, managed to scare the intruders away with a few deep woofs. Seeing all the greenery behind the stone walls, even in the month of March, when the buds were only beginning to form, no one would ever imagine how difficult it had been for Elinor to garden in this place. For two years after Saul died, nothing would grow, despite Elinor's best efforts. It may have been the salt on her skin, the bitterness in her heart. Whatever the reason, everything withered, even the roses that Rebecca Sparrow had planted. Elinor hired landscapers, but they failed to enlighten her and merely suggested she use DDT and sulfur. She sent soil samples to the lab at MIT and was told there was nothing amiss that a little bonemeal and tender care couldn't correct.

One day, when Elinor was working in the garden, nearly defeated, thinking it might not be possible for her to go on, Brock Stewart, the town doctor, stopped by. Dr. Stewart still made house calls back then; the reason he was at Cake House was because Jenny, only twelve at the time, had called and asked that he come. Jenny had a long-drawn-out bout with the flu, accompanied by a hacking cough that wouldn't go away and headaches that were so bad she kept the room dark. She was only in sixth grade, but she had already learned to take care of herself.

"Where's your mother?" Dr. Stewart had asked after he'd examined Jenny. Why, the girl was quite feverish, and she didn't have a glass of water on her night table or a cold cloth for her forehead.

"My mother is in the garden." Jenny was a serious individual, even then. "It's the only thing she cares about, so I put a curse on it."

"Did you?" Dr. Stewart was a fine physician and he never overlooked a child's opinion. "What sort of curse?"

Jenny sat up in bed. She had meant to keep the curse secret, but she was so flattered by Dr. Brock's interest she let him in on the intricacies of the hex.

Come here no more, not in day, not in evening, not in rain, not in sunshine.

Jenny smiled at the doctor, pleased by how solemnly he considered the enchantment. "I looked it up in a book in the library corner in our parlor. It's a verse that keeps the bees away. No garden can grow without them."

"I didn't know that."

As the town's only doctor, Brock Stewart was always amazed by the various ways people found to hurt each other, without even trying, it seemed. He was continually astounded by how fragile a human being was, yet how miraculously resilient; how it was possible to carry on through illness and hardship in the most unexpected ways.

"My father was the one who told me that bees dislike bad language," Jenny went on, her tongue loosened. "What they hate most of all is when somebody in a household dies. They often take off when that happens." Jenny's knotted hair looked perfectly black against her overheated skin. She was a very precise girl who hated flowers, dirt, earthworms, and disorder. She had Scotch-taped a row of her tiny paintings to the walls, intricate monkey-puzzle watercolors in which things fit together perfectly: rug and table, house and sky, mother and daughter.

"I see." Dr. Stewart wrote it all down. Children seemed to like when he did that, even the older ones; they could tell he was paying attention when he committed their comments to paper. "And is there a cure for this curse?"

"If someone dies or if the go-away verse is spoken aloud, the bees won't come back until you offer them cake. Anything sweet will do. And you have to invite them to come back. Politely. Like you mean it. Like you care."

Dr. Stewart phoned the pharmacy and asked them to deliver some antibiotics, then he patted Jenny's feverish head and went out to the garden. Elinor Sparrow was on her hands and knees, weeding a bed in which every shrub had turned mottled and leafless. She barely took notice of people anymore. She was too twisted up by her own terrible fate, far too wounded to pay attention to much of anything other than her empty garden.

"I see nothing's growing," Brock Stewart called out.

"Congratulations on stating the obvious." Elinor didn't like most people, but at least she respected Brock, so she didn't chase him off. Not right away. She had never once caught him in a lie, and that couldn't be said for many folks in town. "Do I get a bill for that opinion or is it free?"

"You've been cursed," Dr. Stewart informed his neighbor. "And you probably deserve it."

Every time the doctor saw Elinor he was reminded of the way she had looked at him on that icy evening when he had to tell her about Saul's accident. She had looked inside him then, as though searching for the truth. She was looking inside him now. Dr. Stewart was a tall man, and there were some children in town who were afraid of his height and his stern manner. But the ones who knew him well didn't fear him at all. They asked him for lollipops; they told him about what mattered most to them, curses and bees and forgiveness.

"You're overlooking all the important things, Elly. Just listen."

They stared at each other over the garden gate. Elinor Sparrow could not believe this man had the nerve to call her Elly, but she let that pass. She listened carefully. White clouds moved across the sky and the light was especially clear, with the luminous, milky quality out-of-town visitors always noticed.

"I don't hear anything." Elinor brushed the dirt from her hands and knees, annoyed.

"Precisely. No bees."

"No bees." Elinor felt like an idiot. Why hadn't she noticed before? The silence was so obvious, the problem so apparent. "Who would have put a curse like that on me?"

Dr. Stewart shrugged. After all these years of being the only doctor in a small town, he knew enough not to place blame, especially when it resided so close by.

"Now that you know what's wrong, you can fix it. Here's how: Feed 'em cake." Dr. Stewart made this suggestion matter-of-factly, much as he would recommend aspirin for headaches or ginger ale and licorice syrup for stomachaches. "Then ask them to come back. And be polite when you do it. Their feelings have been hurt. And they're not the only ones, if you really want to know."

Elinor had gone directly to the kitchen once the doctor left. She searched the pantry until she found a week-old sponge cake, which she doused with brandy and cream. But before she could carry the platter outside, the doorbell rang. It was the delivery boy from the pharmacy, who dropped off Jenny's antibiotics, then rushed back to his car, making a hasty U-turn before Elinor could approach and accuse him of trespassing.

As Elinor Sparrow examined the vial of chalky penicillin, she realized something about her house. Cake House was even more silent than the garden was without bees. She had hurt their feelings, and she hadn't even known it. She had been caught in some sort of web that spun days into months, months into years. She understood exactly where the curse had begun. It was the damage she'd done, it was the way she'd turned away, it was the child left to fend for herself.

Jenny was half-asleep when Elinor came upstairs with her medicine.

"Take this and hurry up," Elinor said.

Jenny was so surprised to have her mother ministering to her that she quickly did as she was told.

"Now get out of bed and come with me."

Jenny threw on her bathrobe and followed, barefoot and confused. She thought of a dozen possibilities for her mother's sudden interest: the lake had overflowed, the pipes in the house had burst, the wasps in the attic had broken through the plasterboard. Surely, it must be a true emergency for her mother to think of her.

"I haven't been paying attention to things." They had stopped in the pantry, so that Elinor could fetch the sticky cake. Ants had crawled onto the plate, and the smell of the brandy was overwhelming. "Now I have to give this to the bees. I have to ask for their forgiveness and invite them to come back." She looked right at Jenny, her tangled hair, her wary expression. "I hope it's not too late."

Elinor took the cake outside. Before she had taken two steps, a bee had appeared to hover above her in the air.

"Was Dr. Stewart the one who told you about the bees?" Jenny was feverish, and being on her feet made her dizzy. She stayed on the porch and leaned against the railing. "I told him a secret, and he went and told you."

"Of course he did. Now let's hope it works."

As for Elinor, she felt light-headed as well. Like a fool, she had thrown something away, and now she was trying her best to get it back. The cake she was holding smelled like spring, a heady mix of pollen and honey, lilacs and brandy. Dozens of bees had begun to follow Elinor across the lawn. Perhaps there was a cure for some things: what was ruined, what was lost, what was all but thrown away.

"Please come into my garden."

Elinor pushed open the gate and the bees followed her inside, but Jenny stood where she was, stubborn, unforgiving.

"Come with me," Elinor said to her daughter.

By then, hundreds of bees were flying over Lockhart Avenue, skimming over the thorn bushes on Dead Horse Lane, buzzing through the forsythia and the laurel.

Jenny was hot from her fever and cold from the chill of the day. She realized that her mother hadn't thought to recommend that she put on shoes; Elinor wasn't that sort of mother, no matter what she might pretend. Jenny's toes had a tingling feeling, the sign of sure disaster. But which way was adversity? She could walk forward or could take a step back, or she could stay exactly where she was, unmoving, which is what she did on that day of a hundred bees. She did not make a move.

Despite Elinor's failed attempt to reconnect with her daughter, Elinor then began to turn more often to Brock Stewart for advice. If a decision needed to be made, she telephoned for his opinion, not that she'd necessarily follow his suggestions. Why, she could spend hours arguing with him, debating an issue, worrying a point. It got so Dr. Stewart's family, his wife, Adele, who was one of the Hapgood cousins, and his son, David, knew when the phone rang at odd hours it probably wasn't a patient or the hospital over in Hamilton. It was Elinor Sparrow. Why the doctor wasn't more put out by her nattering away at him no one understood for certain.

The way Elinor saw it, at least there was one place she could turn for a truthful answer. At least there was one honest man in town. All these years later, with Adele gone, and poor David's young wife gone as well, Brock Stewart was still the only company Elinor could tolerate, except for her dog, Argus. Tim Early, the vet in town, was amazed the wolfhound had made it into his twentieth year, unheard-of for the breed. Dr. Early insisted that Argus was simply refusing to die as long as his mistress was alive. He was that loyal, Dr. Early joked, faithful to the end.

If Elinor had been a more forthcoming person, she might have laughed and said, *Well, then, that means the poor boy doesn't have long,* but instead she merely shot back, *I assume you're still charging as much as you always have,* intimidating Tim Early the way she always did, so that he threw in a bottle of Pet Tab vitamins for Argus, on the house.

In fact, Elinor had become ill just when the rose she'd last grafted seemed to be thriving. She had taken one of Rebecca's old roses, a variety found only in Unity that was said to wither if gazed upon by human eyes, and crossed it with a magenta climbing hybrid she had been developing for several years. At present, the new rose didn't look like much. Should any thief wander into her garden, he would surely bypass the scraggly shrub near the stone wall, protected from storms and scorching heat, in favor of what were clearly the showier specimens, so carefully pruned, so worthless to Elinor. Whether or not Elinor would last to see this crossbreed, she had no idea. Brock had refused to give her odds, even when she pressed him for statistics.

A tree could fall on us right now, he had said. *Lightning could strike us, then what would happen to all of those careful statistics?*

Elinor often thought of Will's mother, Catherine, how very quickly she went after her cancer was detected. Elinor hadn't cared much for the Averys, but wished them no harm. She certainly had never placed a rope with black feathers under Catherine Avery's mattress to curse the family when Will and Jenny ran off, despite what some gossips might have said. Anyway, that was so long ago, and looking back on the mismatch, Elinor understood there was no one to blame. It was the season had caused them to run off, pure, undiluted spring fever, a hazard for everyone. As a matter of fact, Elinor pitied Catherine having to raise a liar like Will Avery, although the younger boy, Matt, had turned out fine.

For fifteen years Elinor had hired Matt Avery to clear away deadwood and saplings felled by storms. Every once in a while, someone left a basket of mint and rosemary on Elinor's back porch, and she had a sneaking suspicion that someone was Matt, perhaps to repay her for the visits she'd made to his mother during her last weeks. All through the summer when Catherine was dying, Elinor brought her fresh roses, Fairy pink, not Elinor's favorite variety, but the one Catherine most preferred. After Elinor was diagnosed, she kept Catherine's courage in mind during her own treatment at Hamilton Hospital. Over the winter, she had gone through several months of chemotherapy, all the while keeping her business to herself.

But that had always been her failing as well as her strength; she refused to confide in anyone, or ask for help, or simply let on that she was human. By the time she had told Brock that her bones were

aching—not the usual arthritis, something deeper and sharper—
she had kept it to herself for too long. Now that there was a new
doctor over in Monroe, Dr. Stewart volunteered his time at the
clinic in North Arthur and the rest home near I-95; Elinor was his
only full-time patient. When the phone rang at night, it could only
be one person who needed him. A single patient, Elinor Sparrow,
and somehow he had failed her.

You couldn't have possibly known what I refused to tell you, Elinor had insisted, obstinate as ever.

Perhaps it was true; there had most likely been nothing he might
have done to save her. All the same, the doctor often awoke in the
middle of the night with his heart pounding, even when the phone
hadn't rung. He awoke thinking Elinor's name, as he had for years,
even before Adele had passed on, before his son, David, and his
grandson, Hap, had moved in with him. In the mornings, Brock
Stewart often had the urge to call and check up on her, but Elinor
never picked up her phone at that hour; she was out working, for
she had restored her garden in a way she had never repaired the rest
of her life.

She was there at work on the afternoon that her daughter came
back to town. It was a lovely day, and Elinor was wearing a mask and
gloves as she dusted the soil with fertilizer. All through the winter,
most of the plants in her garden appeared to be nothing more than
a fistful of sticks, but now those sticks were greening, sending out
new shoots, and would soon be in need of pruning. After the cold,
harsh months, the rosebushes were especially hungry for bonemeal
and fish meal and human attention. The little crossbreed against the
wall seemed quite insatiable, so today Elinor decided to cover the soil
around it with alfalfa filled with extra nutrients.

When she was done, Elinor went into the house, followed by her
old dog. The bones in her ankles and knees were particularly bothersome, with a sharp pain that often made her dizzy; lately, she'd be-

come dependent on a cane. Elinor Sparrow, the woman who leaned on no one, now relied on a stick.

Bonemeal, she thought as she walked to the house. *That's what I am.*

She'd make a paltry sample of that, given what the cancer had done to her. She'd seen the X rays; her bones looked like lace, a filigree as beautiful as it was deadly, much the way leaves looked when Japanese beetles were done with them.

Elinor washed her hands, then fetched her purse and car keys. She told Argus to stay, though he whined and followed her to the porch. The dog was still watching when Elinor got into her Jeep, which was rusted out on the side panels and the floor, and in need of a new transmission. It was mud season and Elinor wove in and out along the driveway in an attempt at avoiding the worst of the ditches. She'd been meaning to ask Matt Avery to level off the driveway for the past five years, but had never gotten around to it. Mud splashed up, dashing against the fenders of the Jeep, coating the wheels. There were still patches of ice in the woods, even on this fine day, and dozens of snowdrops growing nearby. There were those who believed that the Angel of Sorrow had long ago turned snowflakes into snowdrops, the first wildflowers to bloom every year, as consolation to anyone who had passed through the desolate reaches of winter. Personally, Elinor Sparrow had her doubts about this. As for snowdrops, she considered them to be little more than weeds.

Still, the appearance of these wildflowers reminded her that spring had indeed arrived. Elinor rolled down her window and breathed in the fragrant air. Yes, it was definitely here. Before evening, some rain would fall, much needed in the garden, but for now the dampness was caused by the lake air; the horizon was filled with the sweet, green light that arose at this time of year, especially near the shore of Hourglass Lake. When she gazed in her rearview mirror, Elinor could see Argus, still on the porch, loyal as ever. She hadn't even wanted a dog, but one day Argus had arrived in the backseat of Brock Stewart's car. The doctor had found the mutt by the side of the road, and his son, David, a widower who had moved into Brock's house with his own son, was allergic to dogs, as was Elinor's daughter. But Elinor's daughter hadn't been back for years, and the puppy needed a home.

"Just take him for a week," Dr. Stewart had suggested. "If you don't like him by then, I'll find another place for him."

Never agree to take a puppy for a week, Elinor knew that now. A week was all the time it took to be won over completely, despite the messes on the carpets and the shedding, the chewed slippers and shredded books. She hadn't really known she was going to keep him until there had been a thunderstorm, which had terrified the puppy. Elinor had been forced to sit on the kitchen floor of her big, empty house to comfort him. When she reached to pat him, she could feel his heart pounding. She never called Brock Stewart to pick up the dog, and when he next came to visit, Argus was already sleeping in Elinor's room, keeping guard by the door.

Today it was Elinor who was the one to stand guard there on the platform of the Unity train station. It was a small, serviceable depot, built in the Gothic Revival style out of brown granite by a work crew from out of town, ornate, with a brass clock which rang on the hour, loudly, positioned in the center of the pitched roof so that high school students on the other side of town often claimed to be disturbed by the chiming during exams. The noon train, which had left Boston's South Station at 10:45, was late, which was no great surprise. When the train did finally pull in, there was a big rush. The passengers must be gotten off quickly so that service would continue on to Hamilton. Eli Hathaway, surely one of the oldest taxi drivers in the Commonwealth, was honking his horn, offering the services of his ancient blue station wagon that had UNITY'S BEST AND ONLY TAXI SERVICE scrawled on the side in black paint. Sissy Elliot, as old as she was mean, was slowed down by her walker—far worse than a cane,

Elinor was delighted to note—and had to be helped into the coach car by her daughter, Iris, which held up the process of unloading entirely.

Elinor recognized Sissy Elliot, her neighbor to the west to whom she hadn't spoken in twenty years, yet on this day she didn't recognize her own daughter. Of course, she had been expecting an obstinate girl of seventeen, a girl so foolish she had run off two months before her graduation from high school. Jenny had been accepted at Brown and at Columbia, but instead she'd gone off to Cambridge and gotten a job at Bailey's Ice Cream Parlor, where she fixed hot fudge sundaes and raspberry lime rickeys in an effort to support Will at Harvard. Elinor was looking for that girl, the one who'd made one mistake after another, someone ruled by her own cravings who didn't know the first thing about love. She was searching the crowded platform for an individual with long black hair, wearing jeans and a pea coat, but instead there was a woman of more than forty, her hair still dark, but shorter now and pulled back, dressed in a perfectly ordinary camel-colored raincoat over a black suit. But some things had remained the same: there were the same distrustful, luminous eyes, as dark as Rebecca Sparrow's. There were the high cheekbones, the cool demeanor. There was her daughter, after all these many years.

Alongside this woman was Elinor Sparrow's granddaughter, a duffel bag in her arms, a backpack slung over her right shoulder, for her left, the one broken at birth, ached on damp days such as this. She was a blonde, and that was a surprise. The Sparrows had always been dark and moody, tragedy-prone and sorrowful, but Stella seemed cheerful as she gazed around the platform. She was tall, with fine features, and she was clearly a quick study, for she had already spotted her grandmother, though they had never before met. Right away, she began to wave wildly.

"Gran!" Stella cried. "We're here!"

Perhaps fear was the reason Elinor Sparrow couldn't move from her place on the platform, or perhaps it was the look on Jenny's face when she turned to see her mother. It was the same exact expression of disappointment that Jenny displayed back on the day when the curse was broken and the bees returned to the garden, when she was already convinced it was too late for her mother to make things right between them.

Luckily, Stella had no such fears. She ran to Elinor and hugged her. "I can't believe I'm finally here."

"Well, you are." Elinor appraised her granddaughter: here was a forthright girl who wasn't afraid to speak her mind. Here was a girl who wouldn't slink around resenting a person until it was too late to make amends.

The woman in the raincoat approached more cautiously. She was wearing expensive leather boots and a splash of color on her lips, but in some ways she looked the same, just as worried and fretful an individual as she'd always been.

"The train was late," Elinor Sparrow said to Jenny. The first words she'd said to her daughter in nearly twenty-five years and they had formed as a complaint. She sounded far more put out than she'd intended.

"Are you implying it's somehow my fault?" Jenny was just as cold as ever, and now her hackles were raised. "I suppose I'm responsible for the train keeping to its timetable. Is that it?"

Stella stepped between them, anxious to terminate this particular argument before it got started.

"All she said was that the train was late. Mere statement of fact."

Frankly, Stella sounded far more adult than either her mother or her grandmother. Silenced, Elinor and Jenny stared at each other. It was difficult to say who was more shocked by the other's appearance. The well-cut dark hair, the fine lines around the eyes and the mouth. The white hair twisted into a knot, the cane, the withered spine. Twenty-five years, after all. A quarter of a century. It took a toll.

"Stella is right," Jenny agreed. "You're doing me a favor. I'm not going to fight with you." She began to walk toward the parking lot. Just being in Unity gave her the chills, and Jenny buttoned her rain-coat; she wished she'd worn a scarf. "I presume the dilapidated Jeep is yours?" she called over her shoulder.

"Was she always this nasty to you?" Stella asked as she and Elinor followed Jenny through the lot. She wanted her grandmother to slow down. She wanted all the time she could get with her. Stella had that fizzy feeling in her head and she was a bit breathless in the damp air. At the moment she'd spied her grandmother on the plat-form, she had seen how it would end, with snow and silence on a brilliant afternoon. She had seen they only had until the winter, and that wasn't nearly enough.

"Not until I disappointed her." Elinor was furious at herself for being so slow. It took ages for her to traverse the parking lot. Jenny was already getting into the front seat, and they weren't even halfway there.

"That's no excuse for her behavior." Stella liked her grand-mother, and she liked their secret history, the phone calls Jenny never knew about, the times she had turned to her grandmother for support and advice. "Everybody gets disappointed."

When Elinor got into the Jeep, she found Jenny had rolled down the windows. "It smells like an old dog in here. I'm allergic. Not that you'd remember," she said to her mother.

Stella was still out back, tossing her backpack and duffel bag over the rear gate of the Jeep.

"How was her birthday gift?" Elinor said to Jenny.

"Her gift," Jenny said in a clipped tone, "is to be a normal thirteen-year-old girl who has no family nonsense to ruin her fu-ture."

"I meant the model of Cake House I sent."

"And that's another thing, you may have sent it, but that house was mine. It wasn't yours to give."

"Well, if she did get anything else, some family trait, I hope it was something better than knowing other people's dreams. That didn't work out too well for you."

Elinor could tell right away, the remark had stung. Jenny glared at her with those same dark eyes Elinor remembered so well, always reproaching her for one thing or another. Well, she might as well give Jenny something to be angry about, hadn't she? She might as well tell the truth.

"Like knowing who's a liar and judging them for the rest of their lives based on one or two mistakes? Would you say that's a preferable talent, Mother?"

Stella pulled open the back door and climbed into the backseat.

"Fighting?"

Immediately, Elinor and Jenny fell silent. One was the lion, one the lamb, but which was which, it was impossible to tell.

"I've got a great idea," Stella announced. "Let's all go out to lunch together."

"We can't," Jenny was quick to respond. "I want to get you settled and get back here to catch the three o'clock train to Boston."

"I can settle myself. What I need is food. Gran?"

Two against one, Jenny could see that well enough. They clearly planned to gang up on her whenever possible. There was no choice but to stop at Hull's Tea House, where they ordered Lapsang sou-chong tea, egg salad sandwiches, and scones with cream and jam. Their waitress was a high school girl named Cynthia Elliot, who worked weekends and after school. Cynthia was Elinor's neighbor and the great-granddaughter of Sissy Elliot, that imperious old lady who thought nothing of holding up an entire trainful of people so that she could get onboard and make herself comfortable. Elinor, however, didn't seem to recognize their young waitress.

"Hey, Mrs. Sparrow, I'm Cynthia." Cynthia Elliot had on black nail polish and her hair had been braided into dozens of tiny red braids. "I live next door to you."

"How nice for you," Elinor said, cleaning a spoon that was smudged, not in the least bit interested.

"Hey," Cynthia said to Stella, sensing the possibility of a kindred spirit.

"Hey," Stella said uncertainly.

"Do not pal around with that girl," Jenny said when Cynthia went to place their order. Cynthia was clearly a few years older, and several years more experienced. "Do you hear me?"

"Just because I hear you doesn't mean I'm listening to you." Stella turned to gaze out the window which overlooked Main Street. The linden trees were greening and the warblers were calling. Everything looked hazy and sweet and ready to bloom. The tea house lawn was filled with snowdrops, a field of what had once been sorrow.

"I love this town," Stella said. "It's perfect."

Jenny was so startled by this announcement, and so very uncomfortable with the notion, that she shifted in her chair, and the table, perched on the uneven floorboards, was shaken. The water in Jenny's tumbler spilled and her knife fell onto the floor with a clatter. Elinor couldn't help but recall what her great-grandmother, Coral, had always proclaimed: *Drop a knife and a woman will visit. Drop it twice, and she's bound to stay.*

"Well, don't get too comfortable here," Jenny advised her daughter. "You're only in Unity until things get straightened out with your father."

"Do you expect that to happen any time soon?" Elinor asked.

"You'll be here through the end of the school term at most," Jenny went on, ignoring her mother, as she had hundreds of times before. "Don't forget to tell your teachers that. This isn't permanent. You're just a visiting student."

They had their lunch without much conversation, then were waylaid by desert.

"Oh, look at that!" Stella had her eye on a tray of tiny iced cakes and tarts the proprietor, Liza Hull, was bringing over. "They're so pretty."

"Jenny Sparrow," Liza Hull said as she delivered the complimentary tray. "I can't believe it! I never expected to see you back in this town. I guess all birds really do come home to roost."

Liza and Jenny had been in the same year at school, but they'd never been great friends, and there seemed no point in pretending to be so now. "I'm just here for the day. My daughter, Stella, will be staying a little longer."

"I love this place," Stella declared for a second time, but now with even more conviction. "I love this town. I love this tea house. I love these cakes. Did you bake these?" she asked Liza, sneaking a bite of a petit four.

"I'll bake you more any time you'd like them." Liza had been such a plain girl no one noticed her, but as it turned out, she had a lovely smile; she seemed far more comfortable in her own skin now. "I see your daughter has Will's coloring and his yellow eyes. Lucky girl." A smile played at Liza's lips. "He used to stop by now and then when his mom was so ill. He always ordered apple pie."

"Did he?" Without ever once mentioning any such visits to Jenny, naturally.

"Oh, sure. Will Avery's a hometown boy even if he did go to Harvard and marry you." Liza turned to Stella. "Glad you're going to be around for a while. Want to see the kitchen?"

"Sounds like Will was sneaking around here even while his mother was dying," Elinor said when Stella had gone off for her tour of the bakery. "I told you he'd be nothing but trouble. He was a liar from day one."

"Look, Mother, I don't have to listen to your opinion anymore. I appreciate the fact that you're taking Stella in, but, believe me, I wouldn't have asked if there were any other alternatives."

"Oh, I know that," Elinor said. "You'd rather have her living with lions in the zoo."

"Why should I trust you to take good care of her? You never took care of me. You're right, I'm not thrilled about her being here, any more than I was to learn about the phone calls you made to her. I want Stella to have more than I did."

"I see." Elinor put down her teacup. She felt quite hot, really. Absolutely feverish, which wasn't uncommon for some people at this time of year. "But you've been the perfect mother?"

"I didn't say that."

"Good. Because Stella doesn't say it either."

This always happened; it went too far too quickly: sticks and stones, needles and pins, words too painful to remove, like a splinter, like thorns, like slivers of glass.

"At least I tried."

"And of course you were the only one who did."

Stella had been given a bag of scones by the ever-generous Liza Hull, and she now turned to their table and waved. Stella looked happy, even Jenny could see that. Clearly, she'd been hoodwinked by Unity; she'd been taken in by the birdsong, the pale green spring, the forsythia beginning to open, those branches of undiluted light right outside the window.

The tea house, Stella had been informed on her tour, was the only building other than Cake House to withstand the fire of 1785, when the rest of the town had burned to ashes. Leonie Sparrow had worked at the bakery then, a lucky happenstance, for Leonie was the one who toted leather buckets of water from Hourglass Lake to pour over the roof of the tea house, thereby protecting the shingles and straw from bursting into flames. Leonie enlisted the aid of half a dozen customers, creating a brigade, then went home to Cake House, where she continued to battle the fire long after anyone else would have been overwhelmed by smoke. In doing so, Liza announced, Leonie started the Unity volunteer fire department.

"They call the fire truck *Leonie*," Liza told Stella. "They're about to get a second truck they plan to name *Leonie Two*."

"Are you coming up to the house?" Elinor asked Jenny, as she paid the bill.

"I don't think there's time." It was nearly two. Time to go, time to find her way out of town before she, too, was drawn in by the green light and the forsythia. "I think I'll just go on back to the station. And, Mother," she added, in a tone that made it seem as though she were about to swallow poison, "do you think it's possible for us to stop fighting while Stella's staying with you? For her sake?"

"Of course it's possible." It was possible for people to walk on glass, after all, to go without sleep, to judge a liar, to find what had been lost, to dream what they never could have imagined in their waking life.

"Then it's also possible for you to keep her away from anything to do with Rebecca Sparrow while she's here. I don't want her hearing all those ridiculous stories."

Jenny got up from the table, in a hurry to leave. If she missed the train, she'd be trapped. If she missed it, she'd have to walk up Lockhart Avenue to Cake House, making the turn by the big oak tree that some people swore was the oldest in the Commonwealth. She grabbed for her purse and her raincoat. That was when the second knife fell to the floor. Hearing it bang against the hardwood, Elinor felt her heart lift.

Drop it twice and she's bound to stay.

Let Jenny do her best to avoid the path where Rebecca Sparrow pulled the arrows from her side. Let her kiss her daughter good-bye and hurry to the train station, ignoring the trill of the peepers, avoiding the snowdrops on the lawn. Let her run down Main Street, if she must, to catch the three o'clock train to Boston. Let her try to stay away, but it was clear enough now that she couldn't run fast enough. It was absolutely certain. Birds always did come home to roost. Before too long, Jenny Sparrow would be back once more.

II.

THE WEEK BEGAN with warm weather, too warm for the wool sweater Stella had chosen to wear for her first day at Unity High School. For the first time Stella wished she hadn't skipped a grade. Perhaps if she were enrolling in the Hathaway Elementary School, grades K–8, fear would not be rising in her mouth as it was now, a black stone she couldn't seem to spit out as she walked along the lane. This was the same route her mother had taken when she was in high school. Stella wondered if there had been blue jays swooping across the lane back then; if there had been the scent of bay laurel, planted by the colonists to protect against lightning, growing wild ever since.

Today, there were huge cumulus clouds in the hazy sky, and Stella felt the sultry dampness in the air; it was already frizzing her hair. Everything at Cake House was faintly wet, the blankets and the carpeting. All night long, Stella had heard the peepers on the shore and the whisper of reeds. She'd remembered that her science teacher at the Rabbit School had told the class that a cloud was a floating lake. Just think of it: all that water contained above rooftops and trees, a lake above our heads. Stella had lain in her bed, with its sodden bedsheets, trying her best to sleep in her new room. She had not been given her mother's bedroom, but instead she slept in an alcove on the second floor, dusty, closed off for years, but with a pretty view of the lake. Still, with all those peepers calling, it had been impossible to doze off. At a little after midnight, Stella had gone downstairs, to the phone in the parlor, where she'd called Juliet Aronson.

"I can't believe I'm here," Stella had whispered to her friend. She was curled up on a musty love seat; the upholstery was so damp, the grosgrain fabric had turned green.

"I can't believe you left without telling me." Juliet had abandonment issues on a good day; she was very up front about that. "I was in a panic looking for you the next morning. How could you leave like that?"

"It wasn't exactly my idea. It was my mother's. What does she think she's protecting me from?"

"Life," Juliet had murmured.

This indeed was the reason that Jenny had directed Elinor Sparrow to rid the house of any current newspapers. Poor Stella hadn't a clue as to what was happening in regard to the murder case. So it was Juliet who now read aloud from the articles in the *Boston Herald* and the *Boston Globe*. Both referred to Will Avery as a suspect. Stella didn't like the way those words made her feel, as if anything might happen next. As though she might lose her father and not get him back. Such things happened, even in the most stable of lives. Stella's mother had been three years younger than Stella was right now when she'd lost her father, hadn't she? She might have been in this very room when she heard the news. She might have been looking out the same window, listening to the twittering of the peepers, unable to sleep. From where she sat on the love seat, Stella could see the branches of the forsythia outside, glowing in the dark. Beyond that it was pitch, nothing but shadows and trees.

"Are people at school talking about me?"

"You can't think about that kind of stuff. But, trust me, there are a lot of words that rhyme with jail. They're all idiots at school, Stella. You know that."

"Right." Stella was relieved she didn't have to deal with her classmates. Maybe in Unity people would be kinder. In fact, they might not know about her father's current situation; they might treat her as though she were an ordinary girl, an unremarkable individual who lived down the lane with her grandmother. An average ninth-grader who had troubles with math but loved science; a loyal friend, a good listener, whose best feature was her long blond hair. "If I wasn't worrying so much about my father, I'd actually be glad to be here. Away from my mother. Away from all the Hillary Endicotts of the world. Free."

"Free to do what?" Juliet had asked. She was a city girl, through and through. "Wander through the woods?"

"There's a town, Juliet. This isn't the outback. We have stores."

"Is there a shoe store?"

"Not that I've seen," Stella admitted.

"In my opinion, any location without a shoe store is not a town. It's the countryside. Yuck."

Now, on her way to school, Stella was traversing the muddy lane, a thoroughfare so narrow the branches of hawthorns and lindens met overhead to create a dark tunnel. She admitted to herself that Juliet was right, yet again. It was the countryside, no horns honking, no traffic, no one else on the road. It was desolate, really, for a girl used to Beacon Street and Commonwealth Avenue. Stella shook the bell on her birthday bracelet; she tried whistling a tune, but she didn't feel any more secure. Starting a new school was never easy, and she actually had the chills when she reached the end of the lane, where it turned onto the paved road of Lockhart Avenue. She noticed a wooden post on the corner onto which someone had nailed a hand-printed sign, black paint scrawled on the wood: DEAD HORSE LANE. Oh, lovely. A countryside filled with deceased animals.

"Supposedly there's a dead horse at the bottom of the lake," someone said to her, a boy's voice, one that startled her. Stella turned to find a tall boy beside her. He was a year or so older than she, with clear, blue eyes. He was grinning at her, as though they'd already been introduced. "It's not exactly a scientific assessment. The lake is bottomless, it's one of those glacial lakes fed by an underground spring.

Supposedly, in the time of our great-great-great-grandparents, some idiot insisted on riding his horse down the path you're not supposed to go on, the one where nothing grows. The horse spooked and the rider wound up getting thrown and breaking his neck. People say the horse never stopped running. It ran across the water so fast it didn't sink until it reached the center of the lake. That's where it drowned. But it's all a bunch of bullshit, so don't let it scare you."

"Scare me?" Stella and the boy were in step now, walking down Lockhart Avenue. "I don't scare that easily."

A car came barreling by, too close to the shoulder of the road, forcing Stella and the boy to jump into a patch of nettle.

"See ya, Hap," a teenaged boy yelled out the passenger window.

"Count on it, asshole," Stella's newfound companion called back. "Jimmy Elliot and his friends," he explained once the car had sped down Lockhart. "Jimmy's a total idiot. I tutor him in English and earth science, so I ought to know. We've got a lot of morons around here."

"There were plenty of those in my old school," Stella said. "Except they were all girls."

"You went to an all-girls school? That sounds worse than Unity."

They introduced themselves then. He was Hap Stewart, Dr. Stewart's grandson, who lived on the other side of the woods, past the Elliots' property.

"I'm living with my grandmother," Stella said. "Over at Cake House."

"Oh, I know." Hap grinned that huge grin of his. "I know everything about you. Well, maybe not everything," he amended when Stella seemed displeased by this notion. Still, he admitted they hadn't met accidentally. He'd been waiting for her on the corner. "My grandfather said you might need help getting settled."

"Well, I don't." The last thing Stella needed was someone feeling sorry for her.

"The real reason I came was because I wanted to meet you. You're our closest neighbor—all you have to do is cut through the woods, go round the poison ivy, avoid getting any ticks, and walk five miles and you'll be at my door."

Stella laughed. "Lucky me."

"I thought you could use some friendly advice on the way things are around here. Like for instance you might want to let people get to know you before they find out who you are."

A school bus went by, and in the wake of its smoky exhaust Stella felt that fizzy feeling in her head. Was this boy telling her to hide her identity? Did he think he was doing her a favor by letting her know she wouldn't be accepted?

"It's because of my father," Stella guessed. There were several groups of kids on their way to school farther up Lockhart, all turning onto Main Street at the intersection where the oldest oak tree in the Commonwealth had stood for over three hundred years.

"Your father?" Hap said.

"It's because he's in jail."

"Is he? Wow. I don't know if anyone from Unity has ever been in jail before."

Now Stella felt even more of a fool. She'd defended an unhappy fact of her life that Hap hadn't known about. She was overdressed, a nervous wreck, and now she had broken into a sweat. Stella wondered if she might have to breathe into a paper bag, the way her father sometimes did when he was anxious. She slipped off her woolen sweater and stuffed it into her backpack.

"He's not guilty of anything. He'll be out on bail soon."

They walked along in silence for a while. In truth, Stella was grateful not to be approaching the high school on her own. They were passing the old oak, around which the brick sidewalk was buckling; the overgrown roots stretched out for most of an entire block, braided through brick and asphalt and grass.

"What were the charges against him?" Hap asked.

"Murder." They both leaped over the twisted roots of the oak.

Several older people in town had tripped at this very same spot, and they cursed the tree each time they went by. But the elementary school children planned field trips to the oak; they circled round and danced on the first day of spring. "He was only picked up for questioning," Stella added.

"I see." Hap was obviously impressed.

"But he didn't do it," Stella informed Hap.

"Of course not."

The girls at the Rabbit School would all be jealous if they could see Stella now, walking down the road with a tall, handsome boy, discussing dead horses and murder as if such things were an everyday occurrence. She couldn't wait to report back to Juliet Aronson. Hap Stewart's best feature? Definitely his height.

"I just want you to know that there are people at school who always believe the worst. Especially when it comes to Cake House. Some idiots have offered a hundred bucks to anyone who walks the path where nothing grows and survives to tell the tale. Jimmy Elliot made it halfway down. He swears he saw the dead horse. It was more likely marsh gas. Maybe it was gas from Jimmy. He is definitely full of it."

They laughed at that, and Stella felt more relaxed.

"Why doesn't anything grow on the path you were talking about?"

"That's where Rebecca Sparrow's blood fell. There aren't even any weeds now. That's how strong her blood was."

So it wasn't her father's history Stella needed to hide. Now she understood: it was Rebecca Sparrow's.

"She's the reason I shouldn't tell people who I am."

Hap nodded. "The witch of the north."

"Absolute bullshit," Stella said.

Hap looked at her and grinned. "Absolute and total crap," he agreed.

They had reached the high school; once they went past the crest of the hill on Main Street, it rose up from the athletic field like a mirage. Several school buses idled; masses of students streamed inside the building.

"It's a lot bigger than my old school," Stella said. *Yikes*, she thought. *I'm a goner. I can sneak out at lunch and run through the woods and take the three o'clock train back to Boston.*

"You'll be fine."

"Promise me that." She tried to laugh. No use.

"Just remember it's all bullshit," Hap advised.

He had a way of saying things that made them sound as though they were true. And, in truth, she was fine, at least until lunchtime. As Stella waited on line in the cafeteria, a room that appeared to be larger than the entire Rabbit School, several boys behind her began to whistle and make obnoxious tweeting noises. The song of the sparrow, Stella presumed. Absolutely juvenile.

"Hey, Miss Bird Girl. Let's see you fly," someone called out as they waited in the lunch line. There were a few chuckles and several people stared to see what Stella's reaction might be. Her response: she fervently wished the boys taunting her would fall into Hourglass Lake, headfirst.

The wiseguy approached her. "Seen any dead horses lately?" he asked.

"Only in the burritos," Stella said evenly. She herself had bypassed the burritos, opting for salad, and now she smiled at the wiseguy's full, meaty plate. "Watch out. You might choke on that," she warned.

A second boy, quite handsome, a few years older, with black hair and a bad attitude, came forward. Jimmy Elliot. "Are you threatening him?"

"Me?"

That was a laugh. Stella had spent the entire morning getting lost in hallways that appeared to be endless, trying to make up notes for the half of the semester she'd missed, borrowing loose-leaf paper and pencils from students who hadn't given her the time of day. At least she'd been partnered with Hap Stewart in earth science for a field project, a good thing, since Stella had never attempted research in the real world before. Now she glared up at the boy with the dark hair; she recognized him as the one who'd called out the window of the car that had nearly run her and Hap off the road. Thankfully, she didn't see anything about this boy's future, no death, no tragedy, only his dark eyes.

"Let me guess. You're a moron who needs tutoring in English and science? You like to offend people and run them off the road? You must be Jimmy Elliot."

Instead of stalking away or lobbing back an insult, Jimmy Elliot smiled. He seemed surprised and somewhat pleased by her response.

"Good one." He nodded approvingly. "I guess you do take after old Rebecca."

Stella had no idea if this comment was meant to be an insult or a compliment. "I'm just a good judge of character," she informed Jimmy, feeling more flustered than she would have liked.

"I don't think so," he told her as he grabbed a serving of burritos. "You're talking to me."

INSTEAD OF SETTLING DOWN to her homework when she got back to Cake House in the afternoon, Stella made it her business to find some answers. Her grandmother was preoccupied with a delivery of mulch, which gave Stella the freedom to search the house. She rattled through the pantry, examined the contents of dresser drawers, mucked about in the overstuffed hall closet that was piled high with old rain gear and boots. Still, after several hours, Stella had found nothing worthwhile. Or at least she hadn't until she came to the parlor. There was so much dust in the room it filled up the streams of light which filtered through the green-tinted windows with small, linty whirlwinds. Stella went to the corner where the bookshelves were. Here, there were editions the library would have loved to place on display, but the books hadn't been opened for a hundred years, the leather bindings were cracked, the gold letters faded, the crumbling pages gave off the powdery scent of beetle dung and mold.

Stella ran a finger over the spines of the books, then took down an old seashell. She held it to her ear. No sound. No far-off seas. Only spiderwebs and a few dead flies within. She replaced the shell and turned to the draped piece of furniture to her right. The embroidered shawl that cloaked the case was decorated with a thatch of hand-stitched weeping willows and nesting birds, in black thread and brown, surrounded by a border of red cross-stitching, red for protection, and loyalty, and luck. Stella pulled off the coverlet and stood where her father had once been stopped cold, back when he was a wild boy, shocked by what he'd found. Stella rubbed off a circle of grime with the palm of her hand. On a yellowing piece of parchment a date had been written: 1692. In beautiful, curling script were the words: *Saved so that we remember Rebecca Sparrow.*

Stella rubbed a larger circle in the glass, then took the wool sweater she had tied around her waist and cleaned the rest of the case, not caring if her sweater turned black from the dirt. She saw the arrowheads set in rows, just as they were in the little house she'd been sent as a gift. The only real difference was that here the tenth arrowhead was missing. But at some point it had clearly been in place; time had edged its shape onto the satin where it had once been.

A silver circle, an old compass, was in the north corner of the case. A tarnished bell, much like the one on Stella's bracelet, was displayed in the south. It may have been the rising dust that caused

Stella's eyes to burn, but most likely it was the sight of Rebecca Sparrow's hair, the single black plait tied with a frayed strand of ribbon. Now she understood why these relics were kept behind glass. She understood why her mother had run away from Unity, as fast as she could. Jenny couldn't bear to know what had happened; she'd do anything to stay clear of their family history. But Stella was nothing like her mother. For years, Jenny had watched her mother from behind her bedroom window without making a move herself. Stella, on the other hand, went directly to the garden, where her grandmother was raking mulch into a tall pile.

"Tell me about Rebecca Sparrow," she said.

Elinor didn't even glance up. "Out of the question. I can't do that."

"Can't or won't?"

Elinor was exhausted from raking and worn out from the constraints of a houseguest. All the responsibilities of family life she'd given up so long ago had arrived on her doorstep along with Stella; she had to get groceries from the market, and make certain there were clean towels and sheets; she was forced to converse when all she wanted was peace and quiet—all the niceties she'd never paid attention to when Jenny was a girl. Naturally, Jenny had no faith in Elinor's caretaking abilities and had therefore mailed out a written list of instructions denoting Stella's care: no sugar, no TV during the week, no newspapers until the mess with Will was settled, no late nights, no fried food, and absolutely, positively, no Rebecca Sparrow.

"I can't tell you because your mother asked me not to."

Elinor took the opportunity to sit on the bench Brock Stewart had given her, earlier that month. Why, she hadn't even thought there was anyone on earth who knew when her birthday was, and then the bench had been delivered on the day itself. She'd been ungrateful; she'd told Brock the bench was an unnecessary luxury. Why, she never stopped working once she walked through the garden gate. But, lately, she'd come to realize it was a fine bench, beechwood, with a delicately carved back. Lately, she'd found she needed to rest.

"My mother," Stella scoffed. "My mother was four years older than I am now when she ran away to get married, but she treats me like a baby. I want to know the family history. Maybe she was afraid to find out the truth, but I'm not."

"Don't you have history at school? Isn't that enough?"

"The Colonial period. Today we made a time line charting the journey of the *Mayflower*. Not what I had in mind. I want to know about Rebecca." Stella sat down across from her grandmother, balancing on one of the tumbled-down stone walls. "Just tell me a little bit. Tell me what her gift was."

Elinor looked into her granddaughter's sweet face. She wasn't about to lie to the girl, despite Jenny's instructions. "The worst one there is. She couldn't feel pain. And don't you dare let on to your mother that I told you."

"Isn't not feeling pain a good thing?"

Dusk had begun to fall in waves, first gray, then green, then inky blue. Today, in earth science, the teacher had noted that the sky began at the earth's surface, but no one ever thought about it that way. It was just plain old air to most folks. They never noticed they were walking through the sky, just as they never recognized the lakes above them, formed out of vapor. Here, in the garden, the air was especially fragrant and damp. Rose petals that were doused tended to mold, leaves watered directly became mildewed, and so Elinor had rigged up an elaborate irrigation system, one that slowly leaked lake water into the soil. It was lake water, Elinor believed, that made the difference in her garden, the nutrients of all that muck: the frog waste, the insect larvae, the murky water from the depths, so cold the roses shuddered on the hottest days of August and gave off clouds of scent.

"Every gift comes with a price. Haven't you found that to be true?"

Stella nodded. "Mine's a burden."

"How so?" When Stella wouldn't say, Elinor insisted. She was curious, too. Here was the bargain: if she were to give out information, she wanted some in return. "Go on. I won't be shocked, whatever it is."

"For one thing, I know you're not well." Stella began to braid her hair, a worry habit she'd recently begun. "It's some organ . . ."

"Pancreatic cancer." No one in Unity was aware of Elinor's illness, let alone its exact nature, except for Brock Stewart. Elinor Sparrow looked closely at her granddaughter to see how Stella might have guessed her secret. All she saw was that there wasn't a single lie inside the girl. "You can tell me when," she declared.

"People shouldn't know when they're going to die," Stella said mournfully. "If you knew when, you'd never accomplish anything. You'd just sit there and wait for the terrible day to come. Maybe you'd even go crazy knowing—every day of waiting would be torture. You'd never read books or build buildings or fall in love. It would just get you in trouble, like what happened when I told my father and he tried to help someone."

"It would be different for me. I wouldn't mind knowing." Ever since Elinor had finished her treatment and been told there was nothing more that could be done, she'd been waiting. For her, it would be a relief to have a timetable, something final at last. "I'm old. I'm not putting up buildings. I'm not falling in love. I can know when the time will be, Stella, and it won't hurt me. I have nothing to lose. Tell me."

"It won't be any time soon," Stella allowed. "It will happen when there's snow falling."

Did Elinor now feel a dread of snow when she heard this prophecy? Most people with her strain of cancer did not last but a few months. She might have considered herself lucky before to have any more time; had that changed? Now when winter approached, would she try her best to flee, to find some place on earth where snow could never touch her, a southern vista where she might live forever? Or would she go to her window when the first flakes fell, grateful for one last glimpse of the cold white sky?

"I'm sorry. I didn't want to see it and I probably shouldn't have told you. It's so much better not to know."

Elinor understood that the gift someone was given was often the one most difficult to accept. Now, as it turned out, after a lifetime of searching for the truth, Elinor had told a lie herself, for she did indeed have something to lose, and she had already fallen in love with this child.

"I might as well teach you one thing about Rebecca Sparrow. Something it can't hurt to know. As long as you don't tell your mother."

Stella followed her grandmother out of the garden, down toward the lake. The air was mottled and cool, fish-light, March-light. The sky was tumbling down, making the lawn appear endless and deep, a lake of new grass, dusky and brown at the edges. Soon enough, they reached the path Hap Stewart had described, the one where nothing grew. The woods on either side were filled with wild cherries and gooseberries, chokeberry and huckleberry, and several of the wild peach trees said to have floated ashore from a shipwreck, which bore the sweetest fruit in the county. Yet on the path they took nothing grew, just as Hap had said. Not swamp cabbage nor milkweed, not nettles nor common grass.

"Is this where the horse panicked?"

"That horse was bit by a fly and ridden by an idiot," Elinor told Stella. "And it was after Rebecca died, so they can't blame her for that."

They had reached the muddy shore where the snapping turtles laid their eggs. The branches of the weeping willows dipped into the shallows; swarms of mosquitoes drifted over the water.

"Stand right here. My grandmother, Elisabeth, taught me this." Elinor pointed to a spot on the muddy shore. "Arms straight out. Now close your eyes and don't move. Don't even blink."

Stella heard them before she saw them: the fluttering of feathers, the chirrup so close to her ear, the sound of the wind, as though the sky were wrapping around her, so near it was falling onto her skin.

"Stay absolutely still," Elinor advised.

Stella felt one bird land, then another. One lit on her left shoulder. One on her right arm, then a dozen or so more. By the time she opened her eyes, something was vibrating in her chest, a bird beating against her rib cage. The sky that began with her and went upward was teeming with sparrows. Her new science teacher had told them that the sky only looked blue because moisture mixed with dust and made it appear that way. In truth, without the blue light, without the dust, space was empty. People saw what they thought they saw, not what was actually there. They made up their reality out of water and dust.

That was what happened when the three boys from town saw Rebecca standing in this exact same place on the shore, with dozens of birds perched on her outstretched arms. The frightened boys decided what they were seeing: something unnatural, that was their fatal estimation. Something as impossible as a sky that wasn't really blue. Rebecca was only a girl, given over to the washerwoman when no one else wanted her, a child whose hands were ruined by the time she was ten, cracked by lye and grease. The shopkeepers didn't like her in their stores, touching the silk or the biscuits, for her hands often bled from the work of doing their laundry. Girls her own age looked right past her, as though she were nothing more substantial than a pile of the ashes from which she made her soap. Men gazed at her and thought she'd be a pretty thing someday, if she had the chance to grow up without first being felled by fever, or hunger, or the thousand sorrows she'd be prey to before she was a woman.

Women pitied her, but went on their way; they had their own troubles to attend to, and mercy was a scarce commodity.

But to those boys who were crouched down in the chokeberries on that day in March so long ago, it suddenly seemed that Rebecca was something more than a washerwoman's girl. With her long black hair flying and her eyes shut tight, she looked as though she were dreaming, as though she were ready to rise up from the shoreline of the lake that was bottomless, as endless, some people said, as the sky up above. Soon there were so many birds, the boys could barely see Rebecca. She'd all but disappeared right in front of their eyes. Up to then, she'd had no name but Rebecca, given to her by the town fathers when she appeared out of the wilderness not speaking their language, wearing her silver star. Now, the boys gave her a second name. *Rebecca Sparrow*, they whispered, naming her then and there.

It was fearsome in some deep way to see her poised there, so unafraid. Other girls in town ran away from sparrows, as they did from bats and crows; such things, after all, were bad luck, bound to get tangled in your hair and bring death to a household. The girls in Unity didn't go barefoot, as Rebecca did; the soles of her feet hardened by stones. Their hands didn't bleed at the end of a day. They couldn't call creatures out of the sky, without a single word, without a sign.

The boys began to whisper what all this might mean, first among themselves, then to anyone willing to listen. Gossip spread like fever, before there was time to take precautions. Soon enough, every boy in town had hidden in the chokeberries to watch Rebecca wash laundry, and every one swore he had spied a thousand birds perched on her shoulders as she hung yards of homespun and linen out to dry. Before long the women in town said a prayer whenever Rebecca brought baskets of clean, starched clothes to their back doors. They called her Rebecca Sparrow right to her face, and she didn't seem to mind her name, not any more than she minded that her feet had been hardened or that her hands were so rough she could reach into pots of boiling water.

Rebecca took on her name the way she accepted the rest of her fate, and she never once complained. In time, she hoped to leave this place where the boys spied on her and threw rocks, where everyone thought they were better than she. One day, she might just fly away, and then they'd all be surprised. If she were fortunate, if she didn't give up hope, if her wishes all came true, she might truly feel nothing at all.

III.

MATT AVERY had lived alone for eleven years, ever since his mother died, far too early, everyone agreed, for Catherine Avery was a kind soul who deserved an easier end to her life. There wasn't a day that went by during her last miserable weeks when Catherine didn't have at least one visitor, a neighbor, a ministering angel from down the street or across town who had brought over a pan of macaroni and cheese or a chicken potpie along with their warmest regards. These kind folks—Eddie Baldwin and his family, the Harmon brothers, Iris Elliot and her half-sister, Marlena Elliot-White—all insisted Matt take the opportunity to go get himself some rest while there was someone else to watch over Catherine. Matt would gratefully sink into his bed for a few hours of a deep sleep so crammed with realistic dreams—dreams of bread and butter, of washing his hands, of mowing lawns—that he sometimes awoke thinking he'd dreamed up his mother's illness as well. But, no, there she was when he went back to the living room, still in a hospital bed, still in pain, doing her best to appear cheerful, insisting to Matt that she was fine, when it was clear she was dying.

Elinor Sparrow came to call once a week. Then, as time wore on and Catherine's health disintegrated further, she stopped by more often. She brought bay laurel, which grew wild around Cake House, and bunches of Fairy roses; she brought a book of fairy tales, which were the only stories Catherine wanted read to her. Catherine's mother had read such tales to her when she was a girl, but now the stories came alive for her. As it turned out, Elinor Sparrow, who had never bothered to read to her own daughter, had a talent for voices. She was as believable a fox as she was a sheep. An excellent princess, a wonderful shepherd, a witch so convincing Catherine had to be given an extra dose of morphine in order to get to sleep after certain tales were read.

It was an unexpected friendship, considering the women's history. Both were grandmothers of a granddaughter they never saw, both had lives which had been trampled by Will. Matt was frankly shocked at how much his mother looked forward to Elinor's visits. He thought it might be the roses Elinor brought, or the stories, or perhaps it was their shared regret. He guessed the women spent their time together discussing Will and his many failures, or were they reminiscing about the Unity they had known growing up, a smaller, slower town than the one they lived in now? Then, one day, Matt peered into the living room during one of Elinor's visits, now a daily occurrence, the primary event of Catherine's day, and he saw they weren't discussing anything at all. Elinor was holding Catherine Avery's hand, seeing her through her agony.

I'm here with you, he heard Elinor whisper to his mother. *You don't have to hide your pain from me.*

Ever since, Matt charged Elinor half what he should when he collected fallen wood from her acreage, which he chopped into neat fireplace-sized logs. Not that Elinor Sparrow would ever notice this courtesy or ever think to thank him. Still, Catherine had shown Elinor something she couldn't reveal to her own son: how hard it was for her to die, how much she wanted, even on the worst of days, to hold on to a world where there were roses, and neighbors, and a boy who had grown up to be a man like Matt Avery, someone who knew when to back away and when to step forward. Someone she could depend on.

Will returned to town a few times that year, quick visits that clearly took a great deal out of him. Jenny never accompanied him; when asked, he told people Jenny stayed in Boston because Stella, then two, needed her at home. But the truth was, he never bothered to tell Jenny about these trips to Unity until they were over. She would have been one more burden, one more person whose feelings he had to consider, one more pile of stones, dragging him down.

It came as no surprise that Will wasn't comfortable with illness. The sojourns to see his mother were predictably brief. He had always run from any problem, and that behavior didn't stop now. He was so unused to giving of himself, so unable to place another's needs before his own, that he broke out in hives whenever he approached the town line. This was what he didn't want Jenny to see: the red welts on his skin. The panic he held close. The way he'd break into a sweat when he drove down Main Street, so that all the damned bees in town would gravitate toward him and he'd have to keep all the car windows closed, or risk being stung, which, because of his allergy, would surely put him in shock.

How do you do it? he'd said to Matt when he came to visit their dying mother. *How do you sit here and watch her die without going crazy?*

Several times, Will had stopped at Hull's Tea House, where he fortified himself with caffeine and sugar and a few kind words from that good-natured Liza Hull, who always gave him a slice of apple pie, made from a secret family recipe that had won a prize at the county fair on two separate occasions. But in the last month of Catherine's life, Will didn't even bother to stop at the tea house. He didn't come to town at all. He missed every visit he vowed he would make. The last time that he phoned with his regrets, he'd given Matt such a flimsy excuse—some nonsense about music exams and a flurry of snow that had been predicted—that Matt had let his brother have it. Had he not a shred of mercy for their mother? Not an instant of kindness? He called Will every name he could think of and then he just stopped. He had no more curses left inside, and no understanding of Will. Matt had every reason to be angry, left to be the one to tell his disappointed mother Will wouldn't be coming by, yet again, when there might not be a next time. Every day was measured into hours, then minutes, then seconds ticking by. But Matt had actually stopped raging because he'd taken pity on his brother. No one would want to be that selfish, not if they could prevent it, not if they had a choice in the matter.

In the end, Matt had told Will, *It's all right if you don't drive out. She understands.*

And perhaps she did. Kindness had come easily to Catherine, after all. And kindness, Matt grew to understand during the course of his mother's illness, came in many forms. The neighbors, for instance, many of whose names he couldn't recall, who brought over so many casseroles that the food lasted for months, long after the funeral. The single women in town still laughed about how full the freezer at the Avery house was; each and every one of them had thought they might have a chance with Matt once he was left on his own. Matt had dated a girl from Monroe for a while, and he had a girlfriend in New York that he visited on weekends, but that all stopped when his mother fell ill. Even when she had passed on, Matt was distracted; not that he was heartless, but his heart was taken up with something and had no more room for anyone else. He was big, and handsome, and half a dozen women in town would have taken him home, even if it was just for the night, but there was no way to win over a man like Matt Avery. Not with love that lasted a few hours, not with home-cooked meals; he liked things simple, a can of soup, some beans and toast, a bowl of noodles, lukewarm and covered with cheese. He preferred staying away from whatever could hurt him most. He'd become a bachelor, set in his ways, interested in his studies. If he wasn't pleased with his solitude, he was comfortable with it all the same. If he hadn't settled for his lot, then he'd come to accept a life that was nothing like the one he once wished to have.

Whether or not he was living in accordance with his true nature, he had no idea. He had simply followed fate to this place: meals taken alone, nights at the library, mornings in a house where the only voice he heard was his own as he chatted with the birds outside his window. He was supposed to go to NYU, but that was years ago, when his mother first took ill, and his plans hadn't worked out. Instead, he attended the state college in Hamilton, taking night classes, eventually earning his bachelor's degree. Soon, he would have his master's in history, if he ever finished his thesis, a study of Colonial life in Unity. Matt was well aware that the state college wasn't Harvard, but he'd be willing to wager that he knew a hell of a lot more about their hometown than his brother ever would, despite Will's high-priced education. He knew, for instance, that those peach trees which had naturalized all through the county had initially been shipped to Farmer Hathaway, along with two bolts of silk and a silver-plated mirror. All of it had been carried on an ill-fated ship called *The Good Duck*, which went down fast after hitting a stretch of rocks in the marshes in the days when there was still deep water and sturdy docks as far as a man could see. There were plum trees from China onboard as well, and rosebushes bound in twine; there were bales of green tea left drifting over the mallows and pickerelweed. One thing Matt knew for certain: his brother wouldn't know a peach tree from a plum, black tea from green, truth from self-serving dishonesty.

Matt had gone up to Harvard once, to visit Will and Jenny after they'd married and moved into an apartment in Central Square. He was a junior in high school, and Will and Jenny had seemed so much older, so sophisticated, cut off from their families and living on their own. Most college students, even when married, lived in the dormitories, but not Will. Will, who'd been accepted despite his laziness, due to phenomenal SAT scores, was a spoiled brat in Matt's opinion. He needed his space; his lifestyle demanded better. He had a grand piano he'd finagled from Lord knows where, and such a thing would never fit in student housing. Even back then, Will's neighbors complained about him, whether he was practicing Brahms or letting go with some boogie-woogie at 2:00 A.M.

What Matt remembered most about his visit to Cambridge were the hours he spent in Bailey's Ice Cream Parlor, where Jenny was working. He'd gone back, years later, but the place was gone, and he couldn't quite recall exactly where on Brattle Street it had been. What Matt did remember was that even though Jenny had only been a year and a half older, she had seemed like a woman, while he was still a boy. She'd already been promoted and was the manager at Bailey's, and was therefore free to fix Matt complimentary ice cream sundaes all day long. He had them for breakfast, for lunch, and for dinner. Butterscotch, hot fudge, strawberry, marshmallow swirl. He couldn't get enough. After two days of this diet, he was shaking from the sugar, yet he couldn't seem to stay away from Bailey's. He'd set out for the Fogg Art Museum or Blodgett Pool, but he'd always wind up walking back to Brattle Street. He had usually followed Will and Jenny around back in Unity, but it wasn't until the visit to Cambridge that he realized why this was so.

"I think you're addicted," Jenny had teased him, and of course she was right, although ice cream wasn't his problem. These days, he never touched the stuff, not even a plain dish of vanilla bean. At the tea house, Liza Hull always swore he was her only customer who preferred bread and butter to cake and pie. Matt grinned whenever Liza kidded around, but he kept quiet, and he continued to order bread and butter for dessert, for the truth was, that trip to Cambridge had cured him of the urge for sweets.

Matt liked to lose himself in hard work, but lately he found himself thinking about history the whole time he was landscaping, wondering if Farmer Hathaway or one of the other founding fathers of the town, Morris Hapgood or Simon Elliot, perhaps, had walked exactly where he now stood, or if Rebecca Sparrow had sat in the woods he was clearing of brambles and poison ivy, there to watch the light as it filtered through the trees on the Elliots' hillside, where the air was by turns green and gold. In the evenings, Matt always stopped at the library on Main Street on his way home. Beatrice Gibson and Marlena Elliot-White, the librarians, most likely would have put in a call to the police if he ever failed to show up, that's how regular his visits were, that's how dependable Matt Avery was.

By now, Matt had read through all of the journals in the historical research room under the stairs. He had grown so used to twists and turns of the founding fathers' script he could read what to any other man might look like chicken scratch or loop-de-loops. Each time he walked along Main Street, or reseeded the grass on the village green, or thinned the ivy that was choking the linden trees near Town Hall, or relocated a hive the honeybees had set up in the roof of the courthouse, Matt had the distinct feeling that he was walking through time. He thought of those who had lived their lives in Unity and died there, too, every time he went out his own front door and saw the grove of wild peach trees which thrived in an empty lot across the way. Matt Avery believed that history was made of the smallest details, the letter written, the list dictated on a deathbed, the ingredients of the dinner cooked with care, the variety of trees that had been chopped down, and those which had multiplied.

On the town green there were several memorials, testaments to the men from Unity who had died in war. Matt always stopped by the stone erected in honor of the four boys lost in the Revolutionary War on his way home from the library. Michael Foster, Seth Wright, Miller Elliot, George Hapgood. Not one of them had been more than twenty. Each had worn a bounty coat, one of the more than ten thousand woven by New England women, each tagged with the maker's name inside, the mark of hope for those boys who were brothers and husbands and sons. An angel had been carved into their memorial stone, tears pouring from her eyes. Matt might be the only man in town who knew that a local stone carver named Fred Bean, who had lost his own young son to diphtheria, had spent six months working on the black stone, a hard slab of granite brought down from the north country. There wasn't a day that went by when Matt didn't think about that angel's tears. That was history, in his opinion: that sorrow was unalterable and ever present. That tears could be preserved in the hardest granite.

Sometimes, the ink from the journals of those who'd recorded their daily existence in Unity rubbed off on Matt's fingers. Sitting there with these personal accounts written so long ago, he always felt as though he held a life in his hands. Perhaps this was the reason the thesis he was writing had grown to three hundred pages. The dissertation had come to focus on the Sparrow women, as if the thesis had a mind of its own and had chosen the topic despite what Matt might prefer. Whenever the Sparrows were mentioned in one of the old record books, the scent of lake water arose off the paper, green and sweet and unbelievably potent. Perhaps this was what had led Matt to them. Perhaps this was why he couldn't seem to stay away from the facts of their lives. Deep down, Matt had an addictive personality. He had begun to understand that he was not as unlike Will as he would have liked to have thought. He was loyal and dependable, true, but there was something more that drove him, an intensity he liked to deny because it made him uncomfortable. Whatever he desired most inched under his skin and it stayed there, like a bothersome pebble he did his best to ignore.

People in town used to wonder when Matt was going to get married, but they'd given up on that notion. Now, they asked when he was going to finish his thesis and get his degree from the state college instead, just as unlikely a proposition it seemed. Some folks had gone so far as to have taken bets, with *Never* being the resounding favorite, not that anyone wished him ill. Matt's neighbors liked and respected him as much as they distrusted his high-and-mighty brother. It was well known that Will Avery never did a favor for any man in town. He never made a move that benefited anyone other than himself. But blood is blood, and trouble is trouble, and early one Monday morning Matt drove into Boston to join Henry Elliot—whom he'd known all his life, but who was still charging him big-time for his legal fees—for a meeting with Will, whom Matt hadn't seen since that New Year's Eve so many years ago, when they'd tried to kill each other out on the street.

It was difficult to find parking in downtown Boston, especially with Matt's huge old pickup truck, dented, rusted through with salt, too big a vehicle to parallel park on narrow streets that long ago had been cow paths. Still, he made it to the courthouse on time. He greeted Henry Elliot, whom he worked for occasionally, and whose own son, Jimmy, was known to be a hellion. It was only then, after he and Henry had discussed the fact that Jimmy had been picked up on possession of marijuana charges over Christmas vacation, then released pending community service, some of which was to be spent as Matt's assistant during the big spring cleanup of the village green, that Matt realized the man standing next to Henry was his brother.

Last time they'd met, Matt's fury had been unleashed by too many boilermakers mixed with champagne. He had walked into the kitchen at exactly the wrong time during a sloppy, crowded New Year's Eve party. Because of this, he'd caught Will making out with one of his students, a beautiful young girl who couldn't have been more than twenty. Will had her up against the wall, hand down her pants, right next to the high chair where Jenny gave their daughter her breakfast every morning. He didn't seem to give a damn if people went in and out of the kitchen, looking for ice or another cold beer, as long as Jenny had no idea of what was going on. And she didn't, not a clue. The topper was, he had grinned at Matt when he caught sight of him, always the show-off, the liar, the big brother with a huge appetite for whatever he could beg, borrow, or steal.

Now, Will didn't even look like the same man. He seemed rung out, his complexion sallow, and he'd lost a good deal of weight. There was a tremor in his hands, the sign of a man who needs a drink badly and hasn't had one in days. He'd aged, that was it, and he'd done so badly.

"Hey, Will." Matt gave a noncommittal but not unfriendly greeting. He was wondering if Will had looked this wasted at their mother's funeral. Matt couldn't quite remember that day. All he knew was that after the service, Will and Jenny hadn't come back to the house, leaving straightaway from the cemetery, despite the casseroles arranged on the dining room table and all of Catherine's many friends who were bound to stop by. Will backed away, insisting he and Jenny had to get home to Stella, left at the last minute with a baby-sitter they didn't know well.

Go on, Matt had called after him. There were neighbors watching, but he didn't care. *Run away, you cheap bastard,* he'd shouted as Will walked to his car, another one that he'd manage to wreck before too long.

Today Matt had brought along a check made out to the Commonwealth, as Henry Elliot had instructed; all they would need to do was add the amount at which bail was set.

"Hey, brother," Will said, clearly amused at Matt's discomfort in the courthouse. Not that Will fared much better in his appearance; he had a terrible haircut and was wearing the same clothes he'd been arrested in, his usually pressed slacks and white shirt now wrinkled and sour-smelling, but a surefire step up from the uniform of the Boston city jail.

Matt moved to the left, to get a little breathing room. This was his brother, but Will was a stranger as well. He'd been gone since Matt was in high school, and even before that, he'd always been slippery. Someone who can't trust his own brother is naturally self-contained, cautious to a fault, suspicious if pushed. Matt turned to Henry Elliot, grateful that there was someone other than Will to talk to. "Parking was hell," he told Henry.

"Get used to it, bud." Henry was distracted, looking through his notes before they came in front of the judge. "You're in the city now."

True enough, Matt felt hulking and out of place in the courtroom, even though he'd thought to put on his one good suit. He was wearing his work boots and a tie that he'd had since high school. The courthouse certainly hadn't been made for people over six feet tall; Matt guessed it had been built in about 1790, perhaps even earlier, when most people were still fairly short. At that time, the accused would walk through the side door across from the judge's chambers, unwashed and underfed, shackled at the hands and the feet, possibly repenting, no matter if he was guilty or innocent, in the hopes of a less harsh sentence, or perhaps saying nothing at all, as Rebecca Sparrow had done at her trial. Matt had memorized the reportage of her final words in Hathaway's kitchen, uttered to the judge brought down from Boston. *There is nothing left for me to say*, Rebecca had told them. *You have taken my voice from me.*

Henry Elliot, a pessimist by nature, had insisted there was very little evidence against Will, other than the fact that he'd reported the crime several days before it had occurred. Still, bail was set high, due to the nature of the crime. It was everything Matt had been left by his mother, his entire savings, his nest egg cracked in two for the likes of Will.

"Don't worry," Will assured him. "I'm innocent. You'll get your money back."

They all went round the corner to a coffee shop once Will had been released, with the stipulation he stay in town in case further questioning needed. Will insisted a decent cup of coffee would help calm the tremors in his hands, a nightmare affliction for a musician that he hoped would be cured by a double espresso.

"Your landlord isn't so easily convinced when it comes to payback," Henry Elliot said.

Henry still seemed distracted. It was his manner and his fate to worry and fret, and although his character served him well in matters of law, he had no control over his own family. His wife barely spoke to him and his daughter, Cynthia, a good girl at heart, was busy painting her nails black and staying out all hours. But it was Henry's son, Jimmy, who was the real worry; he reminded Henry of Will, back when they were in high school, always looking for a shortcut, always thinking of himself. In fact, Henry had warned Jimmy about Will Avery, a cautionary tale, a disaster waiting to happen. The guy with everything, who winds up with nothing. *Don't think the same thing can't happen to you*, he'd told his Jimmy. *Don't think you're above failure.*

"You've missed paying rent, so you've been kicked out of your apartment." Henry had the papers in front of him. "And the music school? They phoned my office to ask that you not report back until your legal matters were settled."

"To hell with them." Will ordered another dose of caffeine, not that he had any cash on him. But someone was bound to pay the bill, so he got himself a croissant as well.

"This has always been his attitude," Henry Elliot said to Matt. "He was like this in high school. He would copy my homework and wind up getting a better grade than I did."

This past fall, Matt had been hired by Henry's wife, Annette, to put in a Zen garden, something the family thought that terrible old lady, Henry's grandmother, Sissy, would enjoy. There were a fair amount of bees on the property, always a sign of good luck. Matt himself never worried about stings, since the bees ignored him, always attracted to his brother, who was deathly afraid of bees, due to his allergy. Matt was thankful to have the bees share the landscape with him; he enjoyed the thrum as they went about their business and he worked away.

He had used natural rocks and sand from the marshes for the Elliots' garden; he'd planted bamboo in stone containers, but the matriarch of the Elliot family had trouble making it down the stone path because of her walker. When she got there, she scoffed at the notion of planting bamboo.

That's a weed, she had announced. *It may be from China, but it's still a weed.*

Sissy Elliot hated the garden, and now Henry said he was the only one to use it; he went there to escape from the troubles of the world. He'd probably head there that very evening when he got home.

"I think we might want to hire a detective," Henry told the Avery brothers. "Maybe find out something the police have overlooked. At least see if there's someone out there with a motive of some sort. It's in your best interest to clear your name," he told Will, who appeared bored. "No one's buying that crap that your daughter told you the victim was going to die."

"Is that what he told them?" Matt asked. Henry Elliot nodded grimly. "What an idiot."

"Stop talking about me as if I wasn't here. I am here, and I'm listening. Stella was the one who told them that, not me. But if you want to get a detective, be my guest. . . ."

Henry looked at Matt. Will didn't seem to understood this undertaking would demand money. "Sure, go ahead," Matt said, thereby agreeing to foot the bill. "Sounds like a good idea."

"How about a lift?" Will said when it came time to leave. Henry had an appointment, so it was left to Matt. They walked round to his truck. "This is what you drive?" Will laughed and took note of the rust and the dents. "Good old Matt. No BMWs for you."

He was referring to the way he'd spent his own inheritance from their mother. He stopped working full-time, took Jenny and the baby to Paris, where they'd fought bitterly, and bought that damned car, the BMW, which had flipped over on him when he was driving on the beach at Duxbury after a few too many cocktails with a woman whose name he didn't remember. Something with a *C*, Charlotte, perhaps, or Caroline, or, God help him, Catherine, the same as their mother's name. In the end, Will had sold that lemon of a car for next to nothing and he'd regretted the trip to Paris. Matt, he supposed, had invested his half of their mother's life savings wisely and was now fairly well off, in spite of his rust heap of a truck. Plus, he'd gotten the house, now worth double what it might have been eleven years ago. At this point, he probably had thousands piled up in the bank, an old miser of a bachelor with no one to spend his money on.

"Where to?" Matt said when he pulled into traffic. People liked to honk their horns at you here in Boston, he'd noticed that. In a few more minutes he'd be rid of his brother, at least for the time being, so he might as well keep his temper.

"Marlborough Street." Will grinned. "When all else fails, there's always Jenny."

They drove there in silence. Although he hadn't been back since that awful New Year's, Matt remembered the way. Why, he could have found it in his sleep, blindfolded, tied up with rope. He recalled exactly what Jenny had been wearing that night—a black sweater decorated with glitter and pearls, and a red skirt. *Too festive?* she'd asked him right before the party. *Do I look like a Christmas tree?* He thought he'd never seen anyone quite so beautiful. *No. Wear it*, he'd told her, and she had. *Wear it*, he'd said, when all he'd really wanted was to undress her, right there in the living room, with the guests already at the door.

"Want to come up? For old times' sake?" Will suggested when they pulled alongside the apartment building. "Rest your bones before you head back to the old homestead."

Matt shook his head. No way was he going inside.

"And by the way," Will told him, "I never minded that Mother left you the house."

"She didn't think you'd want it. So she gave you the larger share of cash."

"Did she?" Will was surprised by that. "You're saying I got more?"

"I was the executor. I ought to know. She wanted things to be fair."

"Fair." Will was surprised. He really didn't know the first thing about his mother, the way she thought, how she could have continued to love him despite his selfish ways.

"Let me guess," Matt said. "Your share's all gone."

"You want to think the worst of me, be my guest."

"Just tell me."

Matt suddenly felt entitled to something. If not to Jenny, if not to a life, then at least an admission. But he never got it. Will never managed to say, *I got more. I admit it. I was granted the larger portion time and time again.* A bee had found its way into the truck and it banged against the windshield.

"Jesus." Will panicked. "Get rid of it."

Will was rightfully frightened of bees, so Matt guided the intruder out the window with a newspaper. It was a gut reaction; protect Will once more, no matter the cost or the consequence.

"Now you're safe, brother. But one question. And I want you to answer this time." Matt had fought the urge to set the bee onto his brother's skin. "What makes you think she'll take you in?"

"Jenny?"

Will got out of the truck, then leaned back in through the opened window.

"It's in her nature."

It was the time of year when the magnolias began to bloom all over the Back Bay, on Commonwealth Avenue, on Beacon Street, here on Marlborough; even the tiniest patch of yard could be home to a huge magnolia tree. The light was altered when they bloomed, pink-tinged, hopeful, brighter somehow.

"I really do appreciate what you're doing for me," Will said. So he did understand that lawyers had to be paid, that bail money came not from the stratosphere, but from somebody's savings, that detectives wanted cash. "Don't think I'm not grateful."

Matt looked out at the pink street, a much poorer man than he'd been that morning. There was a lot he could say, but he kept his mouth shut. He didn't look up at the third-floor window, though he knew that was where their apartment was. He supposed it was in his nature to keep what he felt to himself. If he made good time on the highway, he'd be home in a little more than an hour, and that's what he intended to do. Some histories were meant to be forgotten, and others were fated not to begin in the first place; they remained where they belonged, in the hazy universe of lost possibilities, in the world of never-had-been.

"I mean it, brother," Will called as Matt was leaving. "I'll pay you back."

Matt laughed as he pulled back out into traffic. "Like hell you will," he said.

IV.

STELLA AND HAP STEWART had decided to test local bodies of water for possible toxicity as their earth science project, which meant they had to track through the woods all over town, in search of ponds and inlets, any body of still water, each and every larva-ridden puddle. They tromped through nettles and poison ivy, wild blackberries and duck grass. They had passed by so many peach trees beginning to flower that they soon grew hungry for peach cobbler, peach jam, and peach pie.

All of the water samples were bottled, labeled, and brought over to Cake House. Hap knew his grandfather came here often, but he himself had never been any farther than the driveway. Unlike Jimmy Elliot, he'd never gone swimming in Hourglass Lake; he'd never seen the mist people vowed was a dead horse rising from the weeds, or done battle with one of those ferocious snapping turtles.

Jimmy Elliot had the tip of one finger missing from an encounter with one such turtle, or so people said; the notion had so terrifed his fellow students in earth science class that no one dared walk past the old turtle kept in a tank at the rear of the room.

"Come on," Stella said when Hap balked at the steps to the porch of Cake House. Stella's back was aching from the heavy bottles of water stowed in her backpack. "My grandmother doesn't bite. And we can get some food. I'm starving."

They were covered by mosquito bites, and brambles had caught in their hair. Frankly, they'd had a perfect afternoon, and Stella had learned her way around town. Due to a teacher conference, they'd had an early release day and had been gathering samples since noon; they'd skipped lunch and Hap had to agree his stomach was rumbling.

As soon as they came into the house, Argus approached and let out a deep woof. "Whoa, boy." Hap backed up against the wall, hands up, as though he were about to be mugged.

"Argus won't hurt you. He's ancient," Stella assured Hap. "He's a pussycat."

"Uh huh." Hap carefully petted Argus's head. The wolfhound was as big as a lion, though his eyes, true enough, were cloudy, and his teeth worn to nubs.

Standing in the front hall of Cake House, Stella and Hap kicked off their muddy boots and wet socks. Hap took note of the woodwork and the threadbare carpets that felt like silk under his bare feet.

"I hear your grandmother doesn't like visitors," Hap said when Stella suggested they go fix themselves something in the kitchen. Actually, he had heard trespassers often found onions riddled with pins nailed to their doors, a curse on both the present and the future.

"Oh, don't be silly. Come on."

Stella went to the kitchen, and Hap had little choice but to follow; he didn't take his eyes off Stella's pale hair, which reminded him of the snowdrops that appeared in the woods so early in spring they were easily mistaken for snow.

Argus padded after them, then situated himself beside the table, where he waited politely for crusts from their peanut butter and peach preserves sandwiches. After lunch, they searched and found the perfect place to store their water samples, in the scullery where potatoes and onions were kept. As they sorted the bottles, their hands touched accidentally. Of course, they acted as though nothing had happened, but afterward Stella wondered if Hap might be something more than a friend. Shouldn't her hand have burned at his touch? Shouldn't she feel her heart in her chest when she was with him? Shouldn't she know for sure?

Last night Stella had sneaked down to the parlor at a little after midnight to call Juliet Aronson. She didn't realize she was talking nonstop about Hap until Juliet had asked if she thought she might be Hap's one true love.

"How would I know?" Stella had laughed, embarrassed.

"Ask him who he would want to have with him on a desert island and see what he says."

"That's hardly conclusive evidence."

"Just try it." Juliet had sounded so wise and so sad, she'd sounded as if she'd done everything there was to do in this world and had been disappointed each and every time.

Now, in the kitchen, Stella wondered what Juliet would make of Hap Stewart. He was feeding Argus a spoon of chunky peanut butter.

"Look at this guy," Hap said cheerfully. "He loves this stuff. It's full of protein, so it can't be bad for him."

It was when she'd spoken to that nasty Jimmy Elliot in the school cafeteria that her heart had been pounding. That couldn't be love, could it? That couldn't be destiny. Not possibly. Not ever. A reaction like that had to be some sort of illness, heartburn at worst, spring fever at best. For spring was everywhere in this corner of Massachusetts. The alewives were running in brooks, as they always did at this time of year, and the toads had begun to sing, that sorrowful, deep song that speaks of water and starry nights and mud. Out in the garden, Elinor Sparrow's hands were bleeding as she worked at her early spring cleanup. She was pruning, cutting back old growth, never a pleasant task, particularly when it came to roses with their sneaky thorns, some so tiny they were impossible to avoid, invisible until they pricked through the skin. Still, she'd heard the blood of a gardener always made for an early blooming season. The blood of a murdered woman, on the other hand, killed everything in its path, as it had when Rebecca walked to the lake on the day she was drowned, so that nothing remained but clods of earth and black stones the size of a human heart.

April was quickly approaching. Elinor could smell it in the musk of the wild ginger in the woods; she could tell by the regularity of the rain that had begun to fall in the late afternoons. Before long, there would be sheets of green rain of various different consistencies: fish rain, rose rain, daffodil rain, glorious rain, red clover rain, boot polish rain, swamp rain, the fearsome stone rain, all of it washing through the woods, feeding local streams and ponds. This was the time of year when Elinor usually began grafting floribundas with Chinas and damasks as she searched for her true blue rose. She knew it was foolish, an all but impossible task, and yet she had continued. No wonder they talked about her at gardening clubs all up and down the Commonwealth, as far away as Stockbridge, as nearby as North Arthur. Didn't Elinor Sparrow know that genetic tinkering was the only way to make something brand-new, the single possible method of ever forcing a blue rose into being? Didn't she know that fools such as herself had been trying to devise a blue rose for centuries, always failing, always facing disappointment?

And yet, Elinor was convinced that spindly seedling in the north corner might surprise everyone. No one would have expected that a garden could contain one of the native swamp roses that were only found in Unity, odd vines that were spied even when the first settlers arrived. *Invisibles*, people called them, for the swamp roses were said to wilt once seen by human eyes. But this one had flourished in the garden; if that could happen, then perhaps Elinor would have her blue rose at last. Perhaps all those other fools who had tried and failed before her would travel to this section of the Commonwealth, in awe of what had grown despite all odds, ready to sink to their knees and kiss the earth.

The possibility of success felt like a cherry stone in Elinor's mouth, real and hard and true. For the past few months she'd had the impression that time was rushing past her, as though she were walking through a wind tunnel, with years streaming by on either side, days and night disappearing in a white blur. When it came right down to it, what did she remember most of her lifetime? The woods when she was a child, the way they seemed to breathe, as if they were a single green creature with one heart and mind. Her mother, Amelia, whose hands eased pain, sewing quilts in the winter. *Love's Lost. Honor's Gone. Dove in the Window.* The moment when she first spied Saul in the library of the state college where she'd been a student and he a new teacher, an instant when the whole world stopped on its axis. Her little girl, Jenny, seeing snow for the first time. The smile on her granddaughter's face when she waved to Elinor at the train station. The rose she had always dreamed of, always blue, always unattainable.

When a rain shower began, Elinor went back to the house. She had in mind her granddaughter's insistence that she wouldn't die before snow began to fall. Was she relieved or terrified by this decree? Was she glad to know this timetable, or did she regret having asked for a date? Possibly the girl had been right: it might indeed be better to wake every morning without knowing what the day would bring, how the story would end, at what hour night would fall. Elinor was so preoccupied by these notions she hadn't even realized she had blood all over her clothes until she went into the kitchen and noticed the look on the face of the boy who was, for reasons unknown to her, sitting at her table.

"You're bleeding, Gran," Stella said in a perfectly reasonable voice. There was quite a lot of blood, actually; some of it was still leaking from a cut on Elinor's arm. The boy at the table looked as though he might faint, but not Stella. She had no fear of blood; in fact, she found it quite interesting, a strange and mysterious elixir. She brought her grandmother to the sink, where she ran cold water over the places where the thorns had gouged out pinpricks of skin, then went to the scullery for some bandages.

"It's nothing," Elinor insisted. She would have to tell Brock Stewart how the blood hadn't bothered Stella in the least. How quickly the girl had reacted, as though caring for someone came to her naturally. In that regard, she clearly had not taken after her father.

"What's he doing here?" Elinor nodded to Hap. "Shouldn't you be in school?"

"We had half a day. Anyway, it's four o'clock now. And this is Hap Stewart, the doctor's grandson. I'm sure you know him, Gran."

"We're using a toxicology kit I ordered from the Fish and Game Department to test local water."

Once he began to speak, Hap couldn't seem to shut up. He couldn't quite believe he was sitting in the Sparrows' kitchen in a house that some people in town said had been known to rise above its stone foundation, especially on windy days.

"We've either found some pretty interesting microorganisms or a lot of fish poop," Hap went on.

Elinor narrowed her eyes, but the boy still didn't seem familiar. Interesting, but she could see that the boy didn't have a single lie in him. A very rare condition, especially for the male of the species. In this way, he certainly resembled his grandfather. Of course, she had known Brock Stewart was lying to her that one time, when he came to tell her about the circumstances of Saul's death. Elinor could see through an honest man as if his soul were a windowpane. Why, when old Judge Hathaway was still on the bench and Elinor was a girl, he'd often call her down to the courthouse to get her opinion, particularly in issues of domestic disputes. *This girl knows her liars*, the old judge would say. *Try telling her a tall tale and see where it gets you.*

And, indeed, she knew Brock Stewart was lying when he told her Saul was alone in his car at the time of his accident. Things were different back then, people listened to doctors and held high their opinions in all matters, not merely medicine. Dr. Stewart must have convinced Chip White, then chief of police, and several members of the Boston Highway Patrol to go along with his story. For they had all conspired to leave out a single fact: one of Saul's colleagues, a woman new to his department, had died along with him in the crash. Once Elinor picked up the doctor's lie, she phoned the college, but even they wouldn't give out any information. Still, she understood now why Saul had often been late coming home in the evenings, why the telephone rang and, when she picked up, no one was on the line. How had she, of all people, not known of his disloyalty? Saul had never quite lied, that was the thing; he had only not told her the truth, and even Elinor Sparrow could not decipher emptiness and evasion.

Ever since the accident, Elinor had wondered if Dr. Stewart's lie had forever bound them together, tied their fate into one strand with invisible thread. She remembered exactly how cold the day was. How the doctor's breath had turned to frost as he lied. It pained him, she could tell, but he lied anyway. There was snow, the swirling sort that never stuck to the ground, and Elinor went through the snow into the garden, where she could feel the weight of the lie the doctor had told, the lie she had been living when she was so certain she was the one person in town who could divine the truth. She left it to the doctor to tell Jenny, even though it was her duty to do so. Elinor was in so much pain, she couldn't think straight. She was bleeding from the inside out, and unlike Stella, Elinor had never been able to stand the sight of blood, especially her own.

Even now, she couldn't bring herself to examine the red marks left by cutting back the roses. If Stella hadn't been there to see to her wounds, Elinor would have surely ignored them, such was her habit and her inclination, even though she knew whenever someone ignored what hurt her most, she'd wind up in grave circumstances. Ignore love, she now understood, and a person might bleed forever, even if no one could tell.

Elinor wondered why this boy, the doctor's grandson, was hanging around, grinning, eating peanut butter. The motive might be water samples and fish excrement, but it might be something more. So often love was invisible; sometimes only two people could see it, and everyone else was blind. The women in the Sparrow family never looked before they leaped; they were easily pulled into the sort of desire that wouldn't let go. Unless Elinor was mistaken, Stella was wearing lipstick and some sort of black gunk lining her eyes. Well, the girl was growing up, wasn't she? And even if Elinor didn't see Hap and Stella as well suited, who knew where their friendship might lead. The cat, after all, was most definitely away. Jenny phoned every night, but her attention was taken up with Will Avery. He had returned, trapped in Boston by a court order; he had nowhere else to stay and Jenny hadn't the heart to turn him away. Well, Jenny certainly wasn't close enough to hear the bell chiming on her daughter's bracelet as Stella went out walking into the rain with Hap Stewart. She thought she still had a child as a daughter, but she had something entirely different, someone who had turned thirteen.

As Stella walked along the driveway with Hap, she wished she could predict the weather. She wished she could stay underwater the way Constance Sparrow was said to have done, in which case she could take water samples from the depths of Hourglass Lake. How much better it would be if she could ease someone's pain, or find what was lost, or tell a liar from an honest man. Instead, all she could see was that Hap Stewart would break his neck when he was thrown by a horse. She had seen this shadow the first day she met him, but she hoped it would disappear. Now as she walked closer beside him, shivering in the rain, she looked at him again. His death was still there.

Stella had already seen that Cynthia Elliot, who worked at the tea house and was two grades ahead, would die of pneumonia in her eighty-second year, and that Mademoiselle Marcus, who taught French I and French II, would be felled by a stroke. She had seen that the wiseguy who had stood behind Jimmy Elliot and teased her in the school cafeteria would be in a car wreck when he was a freshman in college. The way she saw the future of such people was as real to Stella as anything else in this world: a mockingbird, a table, a chair, the smile on Hap Stewart's face as the rain fell down on them.

There was no way that Stella was going to allow Hap to be thrown from a horse. He was her only friend in town.

"Do you like horses?" Stella asked as they walked along. Having pulled their wet socks and muddy boots back on, there was no need to avoid the mud puddles in the driveway.

"Does this have something to do with the dead horse in the lake?" Hap asked. "You know I don't believe in that."

"Just wondered if you liked to go riding. That's all."

"Nope." Hap grinned. "I'm not exactly a cowboy. Anything else you'd like to know about me?" The rain was pouring down now, but neither one cared.

"Maybe. Let me think." Perhaps she should try Juliet's test. Perhaps she should feel more about Hap; he was perfect for her, after all. Anyone could see that. "Who would you most want with you if you were stranded on a desert island?"

"Living or dead?" Hap said thoughtfully.

"Either."

"Male or female?"

"Either." Stella felt sillier by the moment. Her hair was wringing wet and her clothes were drenched. They were passing by the lake where the rain fell like stones into the still water. They stopped by the shore to watch as lily pads floated by.

"I guess it would be you," Hap said.

For a moment, Stella thought she'd misheard. Maybe her pulse had drowned out his words. But, no, she had heard him correctly. He was such a good person, so careful and thoughtful. He knelt down near the shallows to take a water sample from the lake and he didn't spill a drop. She knew she should feel the same way, but as Hap closed the last sample of cold, green water and tadpole eggs and algae, she had only one person in mind, the most unfortunate, horrible boy in town, the one she couldn't stop thinking about, even when she tried.

IT WAS NOT as though Jenny was about to take Will back, despite what her landlady and the other tenants in the building might think. Naturally, they would all be against a reunion of any kind, for each and every resident, from the first to the fifth floor, despised Will Avery. These neighbors did not care if Will was handsome, if his eyes were flecked with gold; they did not give a damn if he knew by heart every tune Frank Sinatra had recorded and could play Scott Joplin rags in his sleep. These were the same people who'd been forced to hear him going at the piano at all hours when he'd lived in the building before: Dylan songs in the middle of the night, "Idiot Wind" or "Tangled Up in Blue." Louis Armstrong in the afternoon, when most hardworking people had better things to do. Repetitive practicing of four-octave scales when he really wanted to let his neighbors have it, right at dinnertime, played fiercely, without mercy.

They all knew Will was the one who was too lazy to throw the bags down the chute to the incinerator, that he picked through other people's magazines left out in the entranceway, that he sang in the shower, that he slammed doors. Most of the other tenants were also well aware that Will had had an affair with Lauren Baker, previously of 2E, who wept for weeks after he broke up with her and then moved to Providence to start a new life. All of it, the recriminations and the crying that echoed through the air ducts to 3E and 4E, had gone on right under the nose of his wife, who now seemed to be taking him back, though she denied it. Not that anyone believed Jenny. For there Will Avery was once again, thankfully without his piano, which remained in storage, but still making a nuisance of himself all the same, leaving garbage in the hall, stealing people's morning newspapers, blaring the TV when his wife went off to work, trying his best to flirt with Maureen Weber who lived in 2D, and who'd been warned never to invite Will Avery into her apartment, not unless she wanted trouble on her hands.

While it was true that Jenny Sparrow made dinner for Will, she was used to cooking for two. She did his laundry, but she was washing her own clothes anyway; it was no bother to throw his shirts and underwear in with hers. Here was the thing Jenny most wished to share with her nosy, disapproving neighbors: their official divorce papers had come through. Briefly, she considered nailing the document to the lobby wall. She imagined standing in the hall to shout out that Will was sleeping on the couch. This was no reunion; no forgiveness was involved, no hot, greedy kisses in the kitchen while she fixed macaroni or beef stew. Jenny had gone so far as to invite the landlady, Mrs. Ehrland, up for tea and lemon pound cake, just to show that the couch in the living room was made up with blankets and sheets. Only a few months earlier, Jenny had accompanied Mrs. Ehrland to Mass General Hospital, and she'd sat in the waiting room all morning while the landlady had her cataracts removed. But Mrs. Ehrland could not be swayed or convinced that Will's stay was only temporary. When she saw Will's clothing piled up on a chair, and an overflowing ashtray he'd left on the floor, she clucked her tongue disapprovingly.

"You are making a huge mistake," the landlady told Jenny. "Now you'll never get rid of him."

It would have been nice if Will had thought to help out, go food shopping or vacuum, or perhaps be kind enough to pack away the dreadful model of Cake House, still set on the hall table, but Will had other things on his mind. He was in constant contact with Fred Morrison, the detective Henry Elliot had hired, even though Jenny reminded him that his brother was surely being billed for every one of those phone calls to the detective. Jenny had tried to phone Matt several times, to thank him and touch base, since they seemed to be in this mess together, but no one ever seemed to be at home.

"He's probably sitting in the library," Will guessed. "Hard at work on the thesis that will never be finished."

"He's writing a thesis?" Jenny herself had always regretted not going to college, a mistake she thought about every weekday when she was forced to revisit a job she despised. Working in a bank she had realized that money had an odor, a mix of mothballs and sweat, and it had a texture as well, somewhere between silk and flypaper. She'd become quite allergic to the stuff, so that it often left a raised rash on her hands; she tended to tell waitresses and cabdrivers to keep the change, and when she came home from the bank, she washed her hands three times.

"I thought you knew about Matt's endless academic studies. History. The state college. He got his bachelor's degree, which took about ten years. A master's should take about twenty."

"Really? Well, say what you will, he's the only one among us who managed to get a degree." Jenny thought history would suit Matt, or the Matt she used to know, always so cautious, so very serious. If she remembered correctly, he was a big fan of butterscotch sundaes. "A degree in history is nothing to sneer at."

Of course Will would be jealous, having never finished his class-work. Why, he'd never even begun his senior thesis at Harvard.

"Well, knowing Matt, it's probably the history of the lawn mower. He's still cutting down trees and taking care of people's lawns, so don't give him the Nobel prize yet."

As the days wore on, Jenny felt more and more ill at ease over the way Will had been settling in. He left toothpaste in the sink, he charged booze on her account at the liquor store, he watched TV wearing only a towel wrapped around his waist. Once, she came home from work and smelled some sort of perfume. Jasmine, she thought, definitely. A bottle of wine appeared to be missing from the pantry. And Coltrane had been on her CD player, perfect for seduction.

"Did you have someone up here?"

Will had taken to watching *Oprah* at four in the afternoon and was therefore always engaged when Jenny came home from the bank. "Up here?" Will said, puzzled.

Jenny's feet were killing her. She'd stopped at the deli and bought all the ingredients for mushroom risotto, fool that she was.

"You bastard," she said. "You did."

"Am I not supposed to have friends in the apartment?" Will followed her into the kitchen, where she was proceeding to throw the groceries into the fridge. "Because you never mentioned that, Jenny. You never posted the frigging rules."

"Friends, fine. A fuck while I'm out working, in my apartment, in my bed most probably, no!"

To hell with him, she thought. She'd be damned if she made him dinner. Let him eat Swiss cheese and crackers, rat that he was. Let him go hungry instead.

"I won't do it again," he said later, when he brought her a sandwich, a rather lousy attempt, but an attempt all the same, consisting of old bologna and a dab of relish on a hard roll. "I'm in your debt," he admitted.

They had been together for so long, he was part of her family. So she let him stay, as she would an untrustworthy cousin she was doomed to assist, like it or not. They phoned Stella together every evening, and were properly cheerful, but more than ever, Jenny felt unmarried, and although Will spent a good deal of time sleeping, he was still the same dreamless creature he'd always been. Was it always this way: what attracted you most to someone was the trait that disappeared first? Only once did Jenny pick up a snippet of Will's dream: a man was standing on the grass, weeping, lost and forgotten, his clothes stripped away, leaving him with nothing but the sound of his own cries. Afterward, Jenny knew she had to let Will stay for as long as need be, despite her misgivings and the nasty notes some of their neighbors had taken to stuffing under the door.

They went together to meetings at Henry Elliot's office on Milk Street, and met with Fred Morrison, the detective, who had found out a great deal about the victim's life. She'd been born in New Hampshire and had been fairly new to Boston. She'd been teaching third grade in a public school since the previous September. She'd had several boyfriends, past and present, but only a handful of women acquaintances in town. She was quiet and pretty and law-abiding and her landlord swore she always kept her window locked at night. Whoever had killed her had most likely been let in through the front door. Thankfully, none of the fingerprints matched Will's. DNA testing was being done, but with no clear suspects emerging, Will had better pray.

Will, however, had never been one to leave well enough alone. He did more than pray, he did exactly what Henry Elliot had advised him against: he talked to a reporter. He didn't bother to mention the encounter to Jenny, not any more than he'd ever explained the scent of perfume in the apartment, a favorite scent of Ellen Paxton, a fellow teacher at the music school who was surprisingly good in bed. In fact, Jenny found out about the interview with the reporter from one of the tellers at work, Mary Lou Harrington, who'd always resented Jenny for becoming a bank officer, and who was happy enough to show the article in the *Boston Globe* around. Eventually, the article made its way to Jenny's desk. There, on the front page of the Metro section, was a photograph of Will Avery, a rather good one that showed off his handsome profile as he stood on the steps. Unfortunately, the photo also showed off the number of their building, which was clearly displayed.

Some of their neighbors were already phoning Jenny at work, leaving outraged messages. How dare he drag everyone into his mess by publicly displaying the address? Hadn't he any sense at all? Will's interview was the reason Bill Hampton, Jenny's boss, called her into his office; considering the publicity and the squeamishness of the bank's trustees, it might be best if she left her position, Hampton informed her, with two weeks' pay, of course, and another two weeks' vacation.

"They fired me," Jenny announced when she got home. "Just like that. After twelve years."

Will had the TV on and was already deeply engaged in *Oprah*; by now, he'd already had his second drink of the day. He was keeping count of his alcohol intake now, at least until he got to the fifth drink. Hearing Jenny's news, he was quick to be outraged. "We'll sue. They can't just fire you for no reason."

"No reason?" Jenny laughed, but the sound was brittle. "You're the reason. Why would you let yourself be photographed right in front of our building?"

"I had to take a more positive stand against the false claims that had been made against me. Didn't I? That's what any self-respecting innocent man would do."

"No, that's what an idiot would do, Will. Did you ever stop to think that whoever did murder that poor woman now knows where we live?"

"Shit." All at once Will seemed crushed. There were other people in the world, he'd forgotten about that. His daughter, for instance. His ex-wife. "I hadn't thought of that."

"Yeah, well it's a little late for second thoughts."

Jenny sat down next to him on the couch. She felt exhausted.

"They're doing makeovers," Will said of the *Oprah* show. "It'll take your mind off the *Globe* article."

Will's psyche worked that way; just cover up the facts and everything would be fine. Overlook what's right in front of you, hope for the best, enjoy yourself, and don't waste a moment worrying about what's out there, lying in wait. But how could Jenny ignore the fact that with their address made public, they were now prey to all sorts: thrill-seekers, murder buffs, and, of course, the person responsible for such a cruel and heartless crime. Even if Jenny were able to find a school willing to take Stella at this point in the term, bringing her back to this apartment was clearly out of the question. No, Stella would remain in Elinor Sparrow's care, but the least Jenny could do was to be there as well.

She packed that night, taking only what was necessary, and the next day Will had the decency to help her carry her luggage out to the cab.

"Don't worry about me," he told her.

"It's the apartment I'm worried about. Don't forget to turn off the oven. Put out your cigarettes. None of your women in my bed."

"I'm not going to cook and I'm about to quit smoking, so stop worrying." Jenny noticed he didn't mention anything about other women. "It's good you're going. You can counteract the old witch's influence. Keep an eye on Stell."

"My mother always said you were the wrong man for me. That's why you hate her."

"She was probably right about that," Will admitted. "I'm a waste."

The magnolia in front of their building was about to open. The photo in the *Boston Globe* had been black and white; it hadn't shown how rosy the buds on the tree were, how the air itself seemed diffused with pink light. Jenny got into the taxi, headed for the noon train at South Station. She could see the pink light all the way down the street. It sifted through the bars of the wrought-iron gates; it caught in the window glass, making it difficult to see straight.

Jenny dozed on the train, and was surprised by how short the trip was. Her hometown always seemed a million miles away, but here it was, so very close. People used to city life were always surprised by how quiet Unity was, especially once the noon train pulled away from the station in a rush of smoke and noise. There was a drizzly rain falling and the birds were attacking the hundreds of worms that had wriggled to the surface of the new grass. Jenny remembered that her mother had invented dozens of names for the varieties of rain that fell at this time of year. The air was filled with birdsong and a cloudy mist. What sort of rain was this? Jenny could hardly remember. She had forgotten what the rain was called, just as she had forgotten there were no taxi stands at the station. People who needed a ride to the airport had to call a limo service in Hamilton; locally there was only Eli Hathaway, who offered the one livery service in town. Jenny spied a station wagon idling at the curb, but she remembered Eli was old and strange even back when she was a girl. Given the choice of getting into his famously smoky car or calling her mother and swallowing her pride, asking to be picked up as though she were still a child, Jenny decided to walk in spite of the rain.

She had a large roll-along suitcase, her overloaded purse, and an overnight case. The rain was light enough not to be bothersome. Daffodil rain, that's what Elinor always called it, Jenny remembered now, as opposed to rose rain, which was a sudden downpour in a dry season; or fish rain, a torrent of greenish water falling in buckets so that any right-minded person would run for cover. Jenny cut across the town green, where the war memorials stood. As a girl, she had often come here; she'd waited for Will to meet her in the shade of the plane trees, lying in the grass, looking up at the flat, wide leaves above her. She had never paid much attention to anything in town except Will, but now she slowed down. She had no choice, really, what with the suitcase and the overnight bag to tote along.

The Civil War monument, a soldier astride a great horse, was in the center of the green. It was modeled, some people said, after Anton Hathaway, the son of the mayor of Unity at the time, killed in a Pennsylvania battlefield. On the far side of the green was the black granite memorial dedicated to those who gave their lives in the Revolution. Jenny was out of breath by the time she got to that one, so she didn't bother to examine it. Instead, she stopped and let the daffodil rain fall down on her. Funny how you could grow up in a place and never notice certain things. Jenny, for instance, had never realized that the plane trees had been planted in rows, or that the steeple of Town Hall was decorated with two golden birds, or that rain could smell so fresh, precisely like new daffodils.

Jenny was about to go on, past the green and toward Shepherd Street, when a car honked at her. It was one of those cute little SUVs, the kind she'd wanted to get after Will wrecked the BMW, and after their next car, an old Ford, was stolen from the parking lot behind the Hornets' Nest Restaurant. But they'd never had enough cash for a down payment, even for something secondhand.

The SUV pulled up and the driver rolled down the window. It was Liza Hull from the tea shop.

"Come on. I'll give you a ride."

Jenny threw her luggage into the back, then came round and got into the passenger seat.

"Thanks. I forgot you need a car out here."

"Where's yours? Break down?"

"I don't have one." Now that she was out of the rain, Jenny felt a chill in her bones. April was like that, sneaky sometimes, appearing to be mild as could be, until your teeth began to chatter. "No job either. Actually, I have nothing."

"Untrue. You have your daughter." Liza wasn't one for self-pity. She explained that she'd been married and divorced and currently lived alone, no children, no pets. "Unencumbered" was the way she chose to characterize her situation.

"You're right." Jenny appraised Liza Hull. Back in high school she'd never taken the time to get to know her. "I do have my daughter. Even if she doesn't speak to me very often."

"Stella comes in to the tea house pretty regularly. I think she's going through every dessert on the menu."

Jenny laughed.

"I told her that one of your ancestors used to work for one of mine. Leonie Sparrow, the one who saved the tea house and started the fire brigade in town? Actually, I think I was named for her, and for another one of the Sparrows who was famous for her cooking. I guess it would be your great-grandmother, Elisabeth. My full name is Elisabeth Leonie Hull. If you're staying around for a while, maybe you'd want to work for me. Continue the tradition."

"Me? I'm not a baker."

"You don't have to be. I need a shop manager, which means waiting tables and balancing the books. Cynthia Elliot comes in after school and on weekends, but I really need someone else."

"I couldn't make you any promises. . . ."

"Good," Liza agreed. "I won't make you any either. Unless you think it's demeaning to take people's lunch orders and wash a few dishes."

"Nothing's beneath me. I married Will Avery."

Jenny had expected a laugh, but Liza's expression was dreamy. "Will Avery. Man, oh man. I had the biggest crush on him."

They had turned onto Lockhart Avenue, where the big oak stood. Jenny had met Will a hundred times or more on this corner, for it was exactly halfway between his house and hers. The old tree was on the record books, if she remembered correctly. More than three centuries old, part of the ancient-growth forest, all of which had been chopped down by the colonists, all of it replaced by farms and fields, save for one single beloved tree.

The rain had eased off, leaving the air glassy. It was still humid, and the sweet smell of mint lingered, as it had so long ago on the morning of Jenny's thirteenth birthday. There was a droning sound that reverberated, much like the buzzing of a thousand bees, the sort of hum that could wake even the drowsiest individuals and boil their blood. When they went a bit farther down Lockhart, Jenny saw that the noise was caused by a chain saw. Orange cones made for a detour around the base of the old oak, which had been ailing in past years, and now seemed to have finally died. The town council had voted to have the whole thing cut down before a storm could shatter the trunk, leaving limbs free to fall and strike electric wires and street signs.

"Hey, there!" Liza had opened her window so she could shout at the man on the ladder. There was a big, rusted truck parked across the street. "Think I can put in an order for some of that oak for firewood? I just love that tree. It kills me that it's being chopped down."

The man nodded and waved. He was tall, with fair hair and broad shoulders; he wore earmuffs to cut down on the sound of the saw. Watching him, Jenny felt something lurch inside of her; perhaps it was seeing him up on that ladder, for she had a fear of falling. Or it might be the way he was looking at her, as if he had already fallen. He hung on to one of the dying branches and watched them drive away.

"Who is that?" Jenny asked as they headed toward the dirt road everyone in town called Dead Horse Lane.

Liza was the one to laugh now. "You don't know?"

"Should I?"

Maybe she felt queasy because of the ruts in the road and the way the SUV lurched over ditches, past the swamp cabbage and the wild peach trees. Or maybe it was because she could now see Cake House through the trees, its many architectural details thrown together to form a whitewashed wedding cake, one that was tilted on its foundation and covered with vines.

"It's Matt Avery." Some people didn't see what was right there in front of them, even if they had twenty-twenty vision. Some people needed to be led by the hand or they'd miss the most important facts of their own lives. Liza shook her head as they turned into the driveway. "That's the man who's in love with you," she informed Jenny Sparrow.

PART TWO

THE GIFT

I.

*T*HREE WOMEN IN THE SAME FAMILY FIXING A meal in one kitchen could only mean trouble. Even at breakfast, problems were sure to arise. Someone was bound to prefer hard-boiled eggs to fried. Someone was certain to resent a comment that veered too close to criticism. Someone could be counted on to slam out the door, insisting she was no longer hungry or that she never ate breakfast anyway, and hadn't for years. In the Sparrow household, there was the sort of civility that was far worse than yelling and screaming. It was a cold curtain of mistrust. When people related by blood were so careful with each other, when they were so very polite, there was soon nothing left to say. Only niceties that meant so little they might as well have been spoken to a complete stranger. *Pass the butter, open the door, see you after school, there's rain again, it's sunny, it's cold. Has the dog eaten? Has the window been shut? Where are you going? Why is it I don't know you at all?*

Such statements did not add up to anything like a

family, and yet Elinor Sparrow had hope. True, she and Jenny had spoken less than a mouthful of words to each other since Jenny's arrival; they had sat down together at the dinner table on a single occasion, and then only because Stella forced them to do so—an attempt which, having been met with nothing but awkward silence and lukewarm asparagus quiche, had not been repeated. Still, you never could tell. Especially when it came to family. You thought you were done with someone, and they'd reappear when you least expected to see them. Who, after all, would have ever imagined Jenny Sparrow would be living at Cake House again? No one in the town of Unity, that was certain. No one in the entire Commonwealth, Elinor was willing to wager. And yet here was Jenny, sleeping on the best linens, hand-stitched and presented to Amelia Sparrow from Margaret Hathaway eighty years earlier, in gratitude for easing the birth of her newborn son, Eli, a gentleman now so old patrons had to repeat themselves twice whenever they got into his taxi, and, even so, they still had a good chance of winding up at the wrong address.

Elinor had used the best of everything to make up Jenny's room. She'd swept the floor herself, so there were no spiderwebs or mouse droppings; she'd opened the windows, to ensure fresh air. On the bureau, she'd left a vase of branches from one of the peach trees on the hill, well aware that Jenny would not have wanted anything that grew in her mother's garden. It was a good choice; when the forced blossoms opened, the room smelled like peaches and had filled with the dense heat of summertime.

Luck came in threes, or so Elinor's grandmother had always said. First there had been Stella's arrival, then Jenny's, wouldn't it make sense for something equally impossible to follow? Of course, Elinor could not expect a reversal of her medical condition—she found herself weakening more each day, needing more sleep and less food—but perhaps the rose in the north corner of the garden would indeed be blue. It was no less unlikely an event than her daughter's return. And there was Jenny, in the flesh, washing her face with cold water in the mornings, for the hot tap never quite worked at Cake House, fixing herself a cup of strong coffee, the beans hand-ground, for the electric grinder was on the fritz, before she headed down the lane to the tea house, where she'd taken a job.

Was a blue rose any more a fantastic notion than the idea that Elinor's granddaughter, whose first thirteen years she had missed entirely, now helped out in the garden on sunny afternoons, laughing at the birds who followed closely as she raked mulch, waving away bees that drifted through the damp April air. If the blooms did turn out to be blue, Elinor would feel that she had completed something: a single act that had left its mark, that's what she wanted. Another, more impatient woman might have cut open one of the buds on the hybrid and taken a peek, but Elinor knew that a blossom that hadn't yet opened was an untrustworthy measure. Yellow climbers could appear to be orange, snowy floribundas might be streaked with a pink tint that would disappear as soon the petals unfolded in the light of day.

We know what we need when we get it, Brock Stewart had once said. Elinor understood this to be true whenever she heard Jenny in the hallway, when she looked up from her work in the garden to see a light burning in the kitchen. She knew it when the kettle on the back burner of the stove whistled, when the back door opened and shut, when the house she lived in wasn't empty. She hadn't understood how alone she'd been until she was no longer alone. She had cut herself off, not unlike those invisible roses which could not bear the weight of humankind.

Elinor had begun to seriously doubt every one of her decisions, and this uncertainty had led her to do a very foolish thing; she had allowed Dr. Stewart to drive her to the hospital in Hamilton for her most recent oncology visit. There had been one condition: he was not to discuss her case with her oncologist, Dr. Meyer. He was not to treat her like a patient once they crossed over the Unity town line.

You know me well enough to know what I'll do if you ask me not to butt into your life, Dr. Stewart had said.

And, yet, when Elinor came into the hall after her appointment, there he was, conferring with Dr. Meyer. *Hopeless,* she'd heard someone say. Or was it *hapless*? Or was it *blessed,* or was it some entirely new language, one she had no prospect of ever understanding?

You promised me you wouldn't treat me like a patient, she had said to Brock Stewart when they left the hospital. She was so angry and so disappointed by his untrustworthy behavior, she could hardly catch her breath. *You heartless creature. How could you lie to me?*

Maybe that had been what was said in the hallway. *Heartless.*

I don't lie, Brock Stewart had said, wounded.

What had surprised Elinor most of all was that she hadn't seen his deception. Gauging an honest man had come so easily to her, like breathing in and breathing out. But now breathing itself hurt, and she'd been blindsided by Brock, just as she had been by Saul. She might have taken the train home, she might have never spoken to the doctor again, if she hadn't been so damned exhausted. To salvage some of her pride, she walked ahead to the Lincoln, got in, and refused to look at him.

I never said I wouldn't talk to her, Brock Stewart reminded her when he got in the car. He had turned the key, but he let the old Lincoln idle. *You know me well enough to know I could never do anything to hurt you. But you are my business, Elly.*

She knew this was true as soon as he said it. It had been true for some time, but she had ignored it. They knew each other better than they knew anyone else in this world, but they had never before admitted what they meant to each other. Elinor didn't look at the doctor on the ride home, but when the Lincoln pulled up in front of Cake House, she turned to him.

How dare you give me hope at this point?

Ever since, her optimism had surfaced unexpectedly and unbidden, at a time when surely it would have been far wiser to have given up completely. Anyone would understand if she'd chosen to draw a quilt over her head. If she'd closed her eyes and taken a double dosage of the morphine she had saved for the evening. She should have burned anything that smacked of hope in a red-hot fire; she should have swept up all the ashes. Instead, she let it rise up within her. She let it wake her in the morning, and help her to sleep at night. She let it fall down in the rain, and wash down the green lawn into mud puddles where the snapping turtles laid their eggs at this time of year, as hopeful as she was, eager for the arrival of what they cared about most in this world.

AS FOR JENNY, no matter what she did in Unity, she was bombarded by two simultaneous sets of images—whatever she was currently doing, washing the dishes in the old soapstone sink, for instance, was overlaid with something she had done years earlier, climbing out the window above that same sink at midnight to meet Will, or arguing with her mother, or watching her father rake leaves into huge piles near the stone wall one brilliant autumn afternoon.

Each morning, when she heard the clock in the hall chime, Jenny was both rising out of bed to wake Stella and getting ready for school herself. She felt her old jeans slide up against her body when she slipped on a pair of black slacks. Her black hair fell to her waist when she combed out the strands that had been cut well above her shoulders. Her reflection in the mirror was more trusting than it would later become, as though she were still convinced love would win out, still certain the path she chose was the one she was meant to follow.

In the shadows of the laurels, in dark corners of empty rooms, she could see the girl she'd once been trailing after, flicking her long, black hair over her shoulders, waiting for time to pass so she could grow up. She'd been in such a hurry, she'd never taken a minute to think things over. Now she wished she would have opened her eyes and considered her options instead of spending so much of her time dreaming, other people's dreams at that, those worthless things. Indeed, there was a reason why she'd been happy enough to avoid her own dreams: hers were always dreams of mazes, intricate traps formed of hedgerows or concrete or stone. In her own dreams she tried her best to find her way, but each night she was lost once more, deeper in the maze, making an even more pathetic attempt to escape.

She understood what she was telling herself: her life had gone wrong, her choices had all led to dead ends. A job would do Jenny good; it took her away from Cake House, it gave her a reason to set her alarm and pull on her clothes and walk across the lawn while the birds were still waking, calling in a glorious ribbon of unending song. She left the house before Stella, and maybe that was a good thing as well. Better to leave well enough alone now that they were under one roof. Better to skip breakfast, keep quiet, stay away from any topics that might cause dissension, which at the moment included just about everything, so that only the weather seemed safe conversation, and even then, there were often arguments about what the day might bring.

Surely, Jenny's first shift at the tea house was incredibly long. No one could debate that. She had no idea so many people in town stopped by on their way to work, or came in for lunch. They all were so persnickety about what they ate: mayo with this, mustard with that, tea with lemon, coffee with cream. By late afternoon her head was reeling. But at least she had not once thought about Will Avery, left to his own devices in her apartment, inviting his girlfriends up, no doubt, using every dish in the house, leaving the back burner of the stove switched on while he took a leisurely nap. At least she had not thought of Matt Avery, either, or at least not so very often. The vision of Matt's cutting down the tree, waving at them from atop the ladder. It should have been a foolish image, ridiculous, almost, with that saw droning on, and all those bees floating around him. It should have been easy to chase Matt Avery out of her head right alongside his older brother, what with all the work that was at hand and so many tea house details to consider—fizzy water or tap water, knife or fork. But there he was, like a line of heat across her skin, a bee caught between glass, humming along no matter what the circumstances.

"There are women who have thrown their aprons on the floor and flown right out the door after their first day of working here," Liza Hull announced once the teatime crowd had cleared out and the end of the day was in sight.

Liza presented Jenny with a plate of lemon chess pie and a hot cup of coffee. Jenny never ate pie, but Liza's recipe was a mixture of tart and sweet that wasn't easy to refuse. Some people vow that when someone feeds you well, you have to be honest with them, and Jenny was no exception to this rule. She asked the question she would have been most mortified to recite at any other time.

"Were you serious when you told me about Matt?"

"Come on, Jenny. Didn't you ever notice the way he followed you and Will around? He was like a dog, checking out your every move."

"He idolized Will."

Liza Hull snorted. "He thought Will was a moron. He told me so himself. The way he saw it, Will had been granted everything a man could want in his lifetime, and he'd thrown it all away."

"A quote from twenty years ago," Jenny said dismissively.

"From last week, Jenny. He was in here for tea. And bread and butter—that's his favorite, for some reason. Just like you are." Liza grinned and Jenny could see how someone who knew Liza well could think she was pretty rather than plain.

Jenny had been warned that customers often arrived just at closing, and sure enough, at ten minutes to four, Sissy Elliot was helped inside the tea house by her daughter, Iris. A light rain was falling and they tracked in puddles of mud. In the kitchen, Cynthia heard the scratch-scratch of the walker and put a hand to her forehead as though she were in pain.

"Don't tell me. It's my granny and my great-gran. Why can't they go to the Pewter Pot on the highway?"

Cynthia immediately started pulling the tiny braids out of her hair, which she had died a hennaed red the color of a stoplight. She threw on a long white baker's coat to hide how short her skirt was, although there was nothing she could do to conceal her multicolored leggings and her thick-soled black studded boots. Cynthia set to work rubbing off her dark lipstick, then wiped the black liner from her eyes.

"I'll wait on them," Jenny said. "Relax."

"Thank you, more than you can know. My great-gran hates me. I'm like the missing link to her, less than human, more than a bug."

"She can't be that bad," Jenny insisted as she grabbed some menus. Liza and Cynthia stared at her. "Can she?"

Iris Elliot, who was Henry's mother, and Cynthia and Jimmy's grandmother, was a pleasant woman who looked embarrassed when Jenny handed them their menus. "Hello, dear. Sorry to come in so late. We won't be a minute. My mother just wanted some tea."

"Jenny Sparrow," Sissy said thoughtfully. She was ancient, with a sharp face and cloudy blue eyes. "Aren't you the one whose husband is in jail for murder?"

"That's me." Jenny recommended the lemon chess pie and the homemade shortbread, although what she really felt like serving up was a plate of nails.

"Well, don't you worry," Sissy went on. "Iris's boy Henry will get him off no matter what awful thing he's done. But it must be a horror to have a husband like Will Avery. Even before he committed that murder, he must have worn you down. It shows in your complexion, you know. Pallid."

"Ex," Jenny said. "We're divorced. And he didn't commit anything."

"What about your poor mother?" Perhaps Sissy could no longer hear. Certainly, she was unable to listen. "How is she? Still as bitter as ever?"

"My mother," Jenny found herself saying, "could not be better. But I'll be sure to give her your regards," she said as she went for the sugar and cream. "You're right," she told Cynthia and Liza in the kitchen. "She is that bad. She had me defending my mother. I never thought I'd see that day."

"Spit in her tea," Cynthia whispered. "It would serve her right."

When Jenny brought out the pot of English breakfast tea and two orders of pie, Sissy Elliot still hadn't let go.

"So many people are getting divorced I can't keep track. Of course, it's not always a moral failing, more like an epidemic of bad judgment. Anyone could have told you your life would be ruined if you married Will, and here you are, waiting on tables. Speaking of that, where is my great-granddaughter? She's on the same downward spiral. Cynthia!" she shouted.

Cynthia Elliot stuck her head out of the kitchen. "Hey, Grans. I'm doing dishes."

Iris Elliot waved. "You go right ahead," she called to her grand-daughter. "Don't let us interrupt."

"What has she done to her hair?" Sissy wanted to know. "It's monstrous. And why is she washing dishes? She never does anything at home."

"They pay her, Mother," Iris Elliot said. "It's her job."

Out in the kitchen, Cynthia Elliot angrily added more soap to the sink. "What a bitch," she said of her great-grandmother when Jenny returned. Cynthia was good-natured, but now she was all riled up, and her hair was stuck straight out, like a porcupine. "Is it all right to say that about someone in your family? Lightning won't come through the window and strike me dead, will it?"

"It's fine," Jenny assured her. "You won't be punished for your thoughts. And she really is a bitch." Why, Sissy Elliot made Elinor seem like a darling, a notion that was entirely disconcerting for Jenny.

"It's not very compassionate to be so judgmental," Liza Hull told them both. "When there are ashes around, then you can be sure something has burned."

"What does that mean?" Cynthia and Jenny both wanted to know. They couldn't help but laugh to visualize Sissy Elliot pushing her walker through a pile of ashes.

"It means when somebody's that nasty, it's because she must have walked through fire. Those comments you're getting are flying off her like sparks without her even knowing she's all burned up inside."

"I think Liza's saying *we're* the bitches," Cynthia whispered to Jenny.

The back door opened and Stella peeked inside. "Is that your great-gran out front?" she asked Cynthia. When Cynthia nodded, Stella said, "I thought we should probably avoid her. I've heard she cooks up babies for lunch."

"Only on Tuesdays." Cynthia grinned. "The rest of the time she eats lemon chess pie."

"Ooh," Stella said. "Pie." She grabbed a slice for herself. "Is that who Jimmy takes after? Your great-gran?"

"She refuses to sit down at the table with him. Even at Thanksgiving. She calls him 'the delinquent,' right to his face."

Although Cynthia was two grades ahead, she'd taken Stella under her wing at the high school; the two often had lunch together. Cynthia's brother had tried to join them on several occasions but Jimmy had been told, in no uncertain terms, that his presence was not appreciated. For this Stella was eternally grateful, for something strange happened to her when he was around, and she hated herself for whatever wicked thing she felt. It was during these lunches with Cynthia, with Jimmy glowering at them from across the room, that Stella had heard all about Sissy Elliot, who was known to keep a pile of rocks by her front door, ready to throw if anyone was foolish enough to walk across her lawn.

"Where's your partner in crime?" Cynthia joked. "I thought you and Hap were always together."

Stella opened the door wider and there was Hap Stewart waiting for her on the back porch. Hap leaned his head through the door and asked for a piece of pie-to-go, if that wouldn't be a bother. He was ill at ease in Jenny's presence, but he had that grin you couldn't help but respond to, a sort of goodness that shone through.

Stella came to stand next to her mother as Jenny wrapped up some pie for them. "So you made it through your first day."

"Barely," Jenny admitted. "I never worked so hard in my life."

Stella had a heavy backpack over her shoulder, always favoring that side that had been broken at birth. She wore jeans and boots and an old rain slicker that Jenny thought she recognized as her own from years ago. Stella's hair streamed down her back, rain-soaked and pale. All the same, she looked more solid since she'd moved to Unity.

"But you made it through." Lest she sound too complimentary, Stella added, "Now I can say my mother's a professional pie-server. I'll be home late. We're still working on our science project. Can I have another piece of pie in case I run into my uncle?"

"Your uncle?" Jenny had a light-headed feeling, surely brought on by standing on her feet all day.

"He's cutting down that big old tree on the corner of Lockhart. I met him there one day. He's great. But it's so weird—he's nothing like Dad."

"No," Jenny said. "He wouldn't be."

"Call me later," Cynthia reminded her new friend as Stella and Hap left through the back door. Cynthia and Jenny finished cleaning up the kitchen, allowing the more compassionate Liza to collect the bill from the grans. Let her be hit by the sparks of old Sissy's comments. Let her put out the fire.

"I think I will spit in your great-gran's tea next time she comes in," Jenny confided to Cynthia. She wished she could feel as at ease with Stella as she did with this child with the scarlet hair.

Cynthia laughed. "I wish my mother was more like you." Annette Elliot was a lawyer like her husband, Henry, and Cynthia hadn't spoken to her in a month. "Nothing I do is right."

"Maybe everyone wishes her mother was like someone else."

"Especially my grandmother, I'll bet," Cynthia said.

Jenny had thought, *Especially me*, but in light of Sissy Elliot's dreadful behavior, she didn't feel she especially deserved anyone's sympathy. She was now completely exhausted; all the same, she decided the walk home would do her good, the fresh air might revitalize her. The rain had eased off and was little more than a sprinkle, so she turned down Liza's offer of a ride home.

"Get a bike, like me," Cynthia called as she zoomed past the porch of the tea house, spraying Jenny with water from the damp road. "It will take you where you want to go."

But where was that exactly? Jenny was far too old to be taken in by the green light of spring or by the way she felt when she breathed in the humid air. She was certain Liza Hull was mistaken. She and Matt weren't even the same people anymore. She would assuredly never have recognized him if Liza hadn't informed her of who he was. He was just a good-looking man hired to take down the oldest tree in town, waving good-naturedly, someone she used to know, nothing more.

BECAUSE OF THE RAIN, the oak on the corner of Lockhart Avenue had been spared one more day. Matt had been taking the tree down slowly, in pieces, the top limbs first, and he didn't want the trunk to split on him, as it was a sure target for lightning. In fact, Matt had been in the library ever since noon, having lunch in the historical collections annex, able to enjoy the sandwich he picked up at the market by special permission of Mrs. Gibson, who didn't usually allow food in the library, but was willing to make an exception for one of her favorite patrons.

Matt especially liked the collections room when it rained; he felt as though he were in a fishbowl, swimming toward knowledge, diving into the journals of the Hathaways and the Elliots and the Hapgoods. Today he had been working on his favorite topic, charting the effects of the Sparrow women on the town of Unity. Constance Sparrow had begun the lifesaving station, out on the tip of the marshes where the lighthouse was later built, initially set up because her husband was a sailor, so often at sea. Coral Sparrow, who predicted the weather with amazing accuracy, rang the bell at the meetinghouse to warn of storms, thereby evacuating half the people in town during the hurricane of 1911, an incident which began the weather service stationed on the far end of Lockhart Avenue, still in operation and far more accurate than those meteorologists on TV. Most people in town knew that Leonie Sparrow began a brigade that was later to become the volunteer fire department. But few people knew that Amelia Sparrow was the first midwife in Unity, and if not for her ability to see a mother through the most difficult of births, there'd be no Hathaways in town, including old Eli, for Margaret Hathaway would have died during labor before producing a single heir.

"Still fooling around with those Sparrow women?" Mrs. Gibson said when Matt brought the key to the research room to her desk at the end of the afternoon. She and Marlena Elliot-White exchanged a look. Neither had figured out why none of the girls in town had managed to snag Matt. Mrs. Gibson's own daughter, Susan, who had changed her name to Solange and was dating a married man up in Boston, an alleged artist who treated her cruelly, when here was Matt, all alone in the library nearly every day, free as a bird.

"Hopefully, I'll be done by the end of May," Matt said. "That's when my thesis is due."

Mrs. Gibson lowered her voice. "I heard about your brother." She looked over her shoulder to make sure that Marlena, who always reported everything back to her mother, Sissy, and her half-sister, Iris, wouldn't overhear. "I've heard he murdered some woman in Boston."

"I'm the one who told you!" Marlena called, not in the least tricked by her coworker's whisperings. "And it's not exactly a secret. There was a full report in the *Boston Globe* and the *Unity Tribune*."

Matt had a soft spot for Mrs. Gibson, even though they'd all been terrified of her back when they were kids. *No talking!* the boys in town would scream at the top of their lungs when they saw Mrs. Gibson on Main Street or in the market, but Matt had never resented the fact that she wanted books cared for properly or that she insisted upon peace and quiet.

"My brother had nothing to do with it. Murder takes some kind of effort unless it's accidental, so you can count Will out. You know he never applies himself at anything. This is one time he's innocent."

"Well, that's nice." Mrs. Gibson was headed off to the research room, where the founding fathers' journals were stored in a metal cabinet that had a separate humidity control. "I'm glad it wasn't Will. To tell you the truth, I always hoped he'd find his way. If only for your mother's sake."

Driving through town on his way home, Matt thought about how easy everything had been for his brother. Good fortune stuck to Will like glue. He didn't even have to try and he came out a winner. On that night when they'd dared each other to sleep beside Hourglass Lake, the payoff had been that whoever chickened out first was bound to be the other's servant for an entire day. But for all Will's bravado, Matt had always wondered if his brother had in fact been too scared to sleep that night. Matt had woken early, his bones aching from the damp ground, to find Will watching him, his sleeping bag thrown over his shoulders like a cape, his expression bleary. The boys blinked at each other in the cool, laky air.

"I've been keeping my eye on you," Will had said. "I've been waiting for you to bolt and run. Why don't you go ahead and run right now? I can hear that horse underwater. He's coming after you."

They had spent the night so close to the shoreline they both smelled like water weeds. But obviously the dead horse had not yet risen, although the other boys in town swore that when the demon surfaced it would chase them into the lake, forcing them to run until it wasn't solid ground beneath their feet, but floating lily pads. So far, that hadn't happened, and Matt had experienced a fairly good night's sleep.

A bee buzzed around him, and Matt waved it away, mindful of his brother's allergy. "Well, keep waiting," he'd responded. "I'm not running."

The air was green, filled with pollen. It was the first warm day of the season, and the mayflies had already begun to hatch. Matt swore he could smell a dead horse, not that he was about to change his mind. The stink might be nothing more than skunk cabbage in the ditches.

Matt usually deferred to Will, and his sudden defiance made Will laugh. "Okay, little bro. We'll see who wins."

Well, who always won? Who walked away with everything? All the same, looking back, Matt was fairly certain Will had been terrified by their night at the lake. He'd never admit it, Will would lie till there wasn't a breath left in his body, but Matt had seen the haunted look in his eyes; he'd seen Will huddled beneath his sleeping bag, peeking out like a rat from a burrow in the field.

Matt knew only too well that courage was an elusive companion. All he had to do was look at his own life to see what could happen to a man who didn't step up to the plate. He'd been so afraid of coming in second-best, so sure he'd be repelled and rejected, that he'd never even tried. Not at anything, not really. He just drifted through, until here he was, a grown man, with nothing of his own. Driving along Main Street, his files and books in a jumble behind his seat, he wondered if he'd have half the courage of some of the old-timers whose journals he spent his afternoons looking through, those men who walked into uncharted territory, those women who suffered a hundred losses.

He had read in Simon Hathaway's journal that the figure on the horse of the Civil War memorial was indeed modeled after Simon's own son, Anton. But it was only through reading Morris Hapgood's diary that he knew the truth beyond the facts and was aware that Anton's mother, Emily, visited the monument each and every day until she died. Snow or sleet never stopped her. Why, she didn't even look up; she didn't once see the sky again after her son died. All that had mattered to Emily in this world had been buried in the ground, and there were people, Morris Hapgood's wife, Elise, among them, who believed that the lily of the valley that grew at the base of the monument arose from her tears.

Although Matt's thesis centered on the Sparrow women, he had yet to find a single word written by any of them, other than a few slips of Elisabeth's recipes. Everything he knew he'd learned from the journals and diaries and letters of the men of Unity, a stew of fact and possibility, salted with gossip. As for the women, they left behind journals filled with shopping lists and newspaper articles, birth announcements and obituaries, specific details anyone would have guessed would have been lost to time. But when it came to Rebecca Sparrow, most of the facts of her life were still unknown. Some history wasn't just hidden, it was buried, locked away not only to protect the innocent but also to obscure the guilty, and thereby relieve the descendants of both from the burdens of the past.

Matt always slowed down when he passed the town green, as a mark of respect to those citizens who'd come before him. He'd done so even back when he was a boy riding his bike, delivering newspapers. But now he stopped altogether. He put on the brakes and switched on the wipers to clear off the windshield. He had pretty good vision, so he assumed he was seeing straight. He could feel a chill settle on his skin as he rolled down his window.

"Jenny?" he called.

She was standing near the *Commemoration to the Men Who Fell in the Revolution*, Matt's favorite monument. Though forbidden by law, Matt had come down here one evening with several large sheets of white paper and black chalk. One of the chalk rubbings he made was now framed, hanging over his bed, an angel to keep watch while he slept.

Matt left his truck idling and got out. It was definitely her.

"Jenny Sparrow?"

Jenny turned when she heard her name called. At that moment, her head was filled with peach pie and dirty dishes and tallies in which the numbers didn't add up. Minutiae, true enough, but a big relief from obsessing about Will, or her mother, or Stella. She narrowed her eyes as a man walked toward her, waving his hands as though he knew her. It was that tall, good-looking man that Matt Avery had grown up to be. It was the person she'd forced out of her mind.

"Hey, there," Jenny called back uncertainly. "Matt?"

Matt grinned and hugged Jenny before he could stop himself. Then he took hold of his own stupidity and backed away.

"You look exactly the same," he told her.

"No one looks the same after all this time, Matt."

Still, Jenny was flattered. Could it be she never noticed the way he looked at her, that he had been following her, not his brother? Not that Jenny put much stock in anything Liza Hull told her. Love wasn't like that, was it? Just sitting there in a back drawer for all these years, like a shirt you'd never bothered to try on, but which was still there, neat and pressed and ready to wear at a moment's notice. At any rate, he couldn't possibly think she looked anything like she used to. Hadn't he seen that her hair was much shorter, that there were lines around her eyes and across her forehead, that she was a woman and not the same headstrong girl she once had been?

"I heard you were in town. I met Stella, and I was going to call you at your mother's, but I didn't know if you wanted to hear from me. I thought you might hang up."

Jenny laughed. Funny how Matt seemed so completely changed yet so thoroughly familiar. He'd always been worried and cautious, thinking about others, second-guessing himself. "Why? Because of that fight a million years ago on New Year's Eve? Whatever happened, I'm sure Will deserved it."

"Oh, he did."

Matt's face had grown moody at the mere mention of his brother. Stella had been right in her assessment, he was nothing like Will. He was thoughtful to a fault, carrying his regret around with him as though every mistake he'd ever made was lashed to his back.

"Well, it was years ago," Jenny reminded Matt. He looked so adrift, Jenny had the urge to reach out to him, but instead she took a step back and nearly stumbled over the black granite monument.

Matt put out his arm to steady her. He had thought about Jenny Sparrow every single day since that New Year's Eve when he last saw her. Now he supposed he was staring. He'd been staring that day he was on the ladder, trying to puzzle out if it really was her.

"Actually, I tried to call you," Jenny told him, just to say something, just to stop him from staring. "But you were never home. I wanted to thank you for paying Henry Elliot's fee and putting up the bail money."

"Don't forget the detective. I'm paying for that, too. Good old Will," Matt said forlornly. "He can make a pauper out of anyone."

"I'm well aware of that. Whatever you do, don't lend him your truck. Not ever. Not if he tells you there's a pile of gold over the border in New Hampshire, and all he has to do is pick it up and you'll both be filthy rich. Although I don't think even Will could do much damage to that old thing."

Jenny nodded to Matt's battered warrior of a pickup and they both laughed. *Something very odd is going on here,* Jenny thought. She felt that line of heat across her skin. The rain had started up again, but neither one had made a move to leave.

"Good old Will," Matt said.

"Not that he killed anyone."

It was probably the humidity that was making it difficult for Jenny to breathe. All this country air, the pollen, the dampness. She wished she had a paper bag to breathe into. She wished her nerves were steadier.

"We got a report from the detective that there were fingerprints in the victim's apartment." Why did he keep talking about his brother? God, was he his brother's keeper, his apologist, his second-best? "But they weren't Will's." Matt hadn't spoken this much at one time for years, except to Mrs. Gibson. He finally shut up and drew a breath. "You smell like sugar," he said, and immediately thought to himself, *Idiot.*

"First day of work. Over at Liza Hull's Tea House."

"Liza's a great girl." At the moment, Matt couldn't quite remember who Liza Hull was. Had he always been so dumb in Jenny's presence, startled into stupidity? "You must be tired. Do you need a ride?"

"Oh, no." Jenny took another step backward. She tripped over the granite once more, but this time she salvaged her clumsiness by sitting down on the edge of the memorial. The granite was cold right through her clothes to her skin, but Jenny didn't care. For some reason, she was burning up. "I'll walk. It's good exercise after being cooped up all day."

Matt realized there was a scent other than sugar. Jenny Sparrow gave off the odor of lake water, the same seductive scent there had been that night when he and Will camped out on the Sparrows' property, listening to the chorus of the peepers.

"I'll be in touch if I hear any more news about Will's case," he told her.

That damned Will again. Couldn't he leave his brother out of the conversation for a minute? What he really wanted was to kiss Jenny Sparrow, right here on the town green. It was what he thought about every single time he drove past, only now she was here, sitting on the edge of the memorial, looking up at him.

"Because I hear from Henry Elliot about Will pretty much every day."

At this point, he would have liked to kill Will. Matt made a note to himself: erase this most irritating word, this vilest of names, from his vocabulary, starting now.

"Oh, Henry. I work with his daughter, Cynthia. She's sweet, but mixed up. I'm so glad I'm not a teenager."

Matt, on the other hand, fervently wished that she was. He wished he could reel back time so that he'd been the one who'd gone inside Cake House and Will had been left in the yard, crouched beside the forsythia. He wished he could go back to the moment when she came across the lawn toward them, barefoot, her long hair tangled from sleep.

"Rosemary Sparrow could run faster than any man in town," Matt said. Immediately, he was embarrassed by his non sequitur. He tended to do this—use his storehouse of historical information to lead him away from anything resembling emotions or regret. He was terrible at conversation, a little better if he could recite a few facts.

"Excuse me?" The rain was falling in earnest now, but Jenny still felt hot. Daffodil rain could do that to you. It could turn you inside out. Jenny unbuttoned her jacket and fanned herself. "Did you say she could run?"

"She was a relative of yours. A great-great-great-great-great. Revolutionary War. She could outrace a deer, that's what people said, at any rate. When the British were sweeping through, she ran all the way to North Arthur. She got there in time to save close to a hundred boys, who would have been ambushed by the British, and who took off for the woods instead to do a little ambushing themselves."

"Wow." Jenny laughed. "How do you know all that?"

"The library. Good old Mrs. Gibson."

"Mrs. Gibson! I think I still owe her money for an overdue book. I never returned anything in those days. God, I was thoughtless. She probably has me down on a most-wanted list."

"No. Not Mrs. Gibson. She's a softy. She doesn't have a list."

The clock on the tower at Town Hall chimed, and they both turned, startled. Six o'clock. Darkness was falling through the leaves of the plane trees, along with the rain. Yellow rain, light rain, the daffodil rain that made people do foolish things.

"You should come over for dinner sometime."

From the look on his face, Jenny wondered if she'd said something wrong. He appeared panic-stricken, as though he might turn and run himself, faster, perhaps, than Rosemary Sparrow.

"You don't have to. I wouldn't be offended if you didn't want to." She offered him a polite out. "Not many people are fond of my mother. I understand that. Believe me."

"I am. I'm very fond of her."

"You are? Well, then, some time next week?"

Matt nodded and headed off across the green.

"Next week," he said, having at last avoided including his brother's name in a sentence.

He walked right through puddles and didn't even notice. His boots were soaking, but what did he care? He had left the window of his truck open and now his files would be damp, but he wasn't concerned about that; he'd dry the papers later, beside the stove.

Jenny stood up and waved. Unlike dusk in Boston, always so slow to envelop the streets, here in Unity there was a curtain of night. One minute you were standing in daylight and the next you were completely in the dark.

"Check out the memorial behind you," Matt called as he got into his truck. "It's my favorite."

He honked his horn as he drove away, and the sound echoed across the green. Jenny felt as though she were drowning somehow. What a strange and rainy place this was. How green and dark and quiet. She turned to inspect the monument she had been using as a bench. She had never once bothered to look at it, not once in all the years she lived here. The past was the past, it was what she had always wanted to run away from. It was the future she'd been interested in, so she'd never noticed the angel carved into the black granite; she never knew that the angel she had seen so many years ago on the morning of her thirteenth birthday had been here all along, the solid twin of what before had only been a dream.

II.

THE CLINIC in North Arthur was on Hopewell Street, at the very edge of town where the urban landscape blended into muddy, useless fields, overplowed and left to wither. The only other building for nearly half a mile was a barnlike edifice used to store the county's school buses. Dr. Stewart wondered if the North Arthur town council had chosen this location as a way of keeping disease at bay, or perhaps they merely wanted to hide the fact that many of the patients were farmworkers who arrived to pick strawberries in June and apples in October. All the same, the clinic had a first-rate staff and a good, level parking lot, something Dr. Stewart especially appreciated, as there was always plenty of space for his huge, old Lincoln Town Car.

Hap sometimes accompanied his grandfather to the clinic, and this time he'd dragged Stella along. Today there were several physicians from Hamilton Hospital, giving freely of their time along with a nurse practitioner, two RNs, a resident who staffed the small ER room, and a secretary named Ruth Holworthy, who all but ran the place.

"Hey, Doc," Ruth called out as they entered the clinic. "I see you brought a couple of freeloaders along with you."

"That's right, Ruth," the doctor said cheerfully. "My entourage. You two can sit out front and help Ruth," Dr. Stewart told Stella and Hap. "Do whatever she tells you to do."

"Good. No dealing with sick people." Hap was pleased. Out in the waiting room an elderly man was coughing and there was a little girl who yowled as though she'd been stuck by a pin. "I can't believe you came along. This place is not exactly a laugh riot."

They were alphabetizing the Medicare forms Ruth had given them, sitting cross-legged on the carpet in the rear of the office, beside the filing cabinets. The fluorescent light flickered and the yowling in the waiting room kept up, rising like a mini-siren.

"I'm not afraid of sick people," Stella said. "That's the difference between you and me."

"I didn't say I was afraid. It's just that they're so impossible to fix." Everyone expected Hap to be a doctor, but he didn't have the heart to deal with the frailties of human beings. "Being a physician is like working on a machine that keeps breaking down, time after time. It's like a toaster than burns everything no matter what you do. Or a car that won't start even if you jump the battery every single day. It's a pointless battle if it's one you can't ever win."

Clearly, Hap was thinking of his mother, who had died when he wasn't much more than five. Hap had told Stella what he remembered most was picking violets with his mother, the scented kind that grew on the stretch of property between the Sparrows' acreage and his grandfather's house, beneath tall pine trees. A single image, that's all he had left of her. *Purple stars*, Hap had told Stella one day when they were exploring Rebecca Sparrow's laundry shed. They could see a bank of violets from a window which had never contained glass. *That's what they looked like.*

"Some people are fixable," Stella said stubbornly. "Plus, they're more interesting than toasters."

All the same, this discussion brought to mind the image of her grandmother covered with snow, unmoving in the garden. Stella shivered just thinking about it. People died, Hap was right, and so often there was nothing you could do about it. No cure could be given, no antidote was available. You simply had to give up hope when it came to some people. But not Hap. Stella wasn't about to let anything happen to him. If she couldn't be in love with him, she could at least protect him. She thought of the way he had confided in her while they sat close together in Rebecca's shed, the look on his face when he spoke about violets. She thought about the way he'd been waiting for her on the first day of school, the way he'd grinned at her when she'd appeared round the corner, walking right toward him. Hap had told her he wished he had his camera with him at that moment; her expression, he swore, was that of a bird that had been trapped and could think only of how she might best escape.

That's what Hap was interested in, photography. He had set up a darkroom in his grandfather's basement, and wherever he went, he carried his camera along in his backpack. He had it with him now, an old Leica, that he used to take a shot of Ruth Holworthy.

"Cut that out," Ruth called. "I'm working."

"You'll be happy when you see the print," Hap called back.

"You should tell your grandfather you don't want to be a doctor," Stella advised. "Then he'll stop dragging you here."

Hap looked at her helplessly. "I can't hurt his feelings."

"Just tell him! He won't break when he gets the news."

There was a ruckus out in the waiting room, never a good sign.

"Shit," Hap muttered. "I smell tragedy."

"You kids stay right here," Ruth Holworthy said in the no-

nonsense tone of someone used to being obeyed. But Stella had no such intentions and she did no such thing. Instead, she trailed along behind Ruth, ignoring Hap as he grabbed for her arm and reminded her, "That means you."

Out in the parking lot, there was an ambulance and several police cars. There had been an accident over on 95, a bad one, and the Hopewell Clinic had been the closest emergency stop. The paramedics came rushing through the waiting room, so that Stella was forced to jump back, out of their way. All the same, she had seen what was before them, the tragedy of the day: a young man on a stretcher, covered with blood, limbs mangled, who would die, not because of any of his obvious wounds, but because of a lacerated liver. And she had seen something more: as they were racing by her, Stella had looked into the young man's eyes. For an instant, his eyes had focused and met hers.

Without thinking, Stella began to follow the paramedics into the examining room. Ruth Holworthy put a hand on her shoulder. "You're not going in there, kiddo. No possibility. No way."

But Stella pulled away and went through the doors on the heels of the paramedics. She had a buzzing feeling in her head, so she had barely heard Ruth admonish her, and even if she had heard Ruth cry out behind her, she would have paid no mind.

When Stella slipped into the examining room, a resident was taking the young man's vital signs. Everyone was too busy to notice Stella, until Dr. Stewart came in.

"Good Lord," he said, when he spied her. She was right there by the door, watching one of the residents from Hamilton Hospital labor over the now unconscious young man. "Stella. Go back to the office."

But Stella stayed where she was. She could feel the young man sinking, like a ship out on the ocean. Even she could tell that the resident was not up to the task before him.

"That doctor can't help him. He has a lacerated liver."

"Did you overhear someone mention a diagnosis?"

The young man on the table was shivering uncontrollably, the way patients with internal injuries often did. His color was ashen and he hadn't responded when the nurse practitioner hooked up an IV.

"It's what's wrong with him," Stella said grimly. She sounded so sure of herself that Dr. Stewart forgot about shooing her out. "Is it something that can be fixed?"

"That all depends."

When he approached, the resident said, "I think I've got this covered." All the same, Doc Stewart examined the injured man's abdomen. It was bloated and he could feel fluid inside. The pulse rate was dangerously low and Dr. Stewart didn't like the looks of the whole situation. The resident was taking all the appropriate steps, but sometimes that wasn't enough. Sometimes there had to be a leap of faith. Brock Stewart had seen it before, a nurse or a doctor who somehow knew what was wrong before any tests were taken. He'd had those gut feelings himself; he'd acted on impulse, he'd taken a risk, when waiting would have meant the possibility of sacrificing a life.

He signaled the nurse to phone the medevac; they'd need a helicopter. Dr. Stewart would call ahead to Boston so that X rays and surgery could be arranged.

After the patient had been moved, airlifted out in less than twenty minutes, there was a stunned silence in the clinic. A good deal of blood had washed through the waiting room, a trail that led out through the hall and into the examining room. Ruth always used a mixture of bleach, vinegar, and club soda to remove such stains.

"I'm better than a professional carpet cleaner," she declared. She turned to Stella. "Next time I tell you to stay, are you going to listen?"

"Probably not," Stella admitted.

"You're just like the old doc." Ruth shook her head; in her opinion, there were some people in this world too stubborn to ever toe the line. "You do as you please."

Hap and Stella were both quiet on the drive home. Hap was sitting up front with his grandfather, with Stella in the backseat. She was studying the shape of Hap's head. He had fine brown hair, but when she narrowed her eyes, it looked as though some sort of light was streaking through in radiant bands. *Say it*, Stella thought. *Let him know who you are.*

"I'm thinking of not becoming a doctor." It was ridiculous how hard this was for Hap to say out loud. It took all his strength and once it was said, he leaned his head against the car window, drained.

The day itself was sunny and mild, though you'd never know it while working in the clinic, where the fluorescent lights flickered and the shades were always half-drawn. There was silence for a while after Hap's proclamation; the old Lincoln turned off the service road and they headed toward town. Light filtered through the leaves of the plane trees. Green and yellow. Shadow and sun.

"Not cut out for it?" Brock Stewart finally said.

"No, sir."

"Well, Stella, what do you think? Should I draw and quarter him? Should I send him into exile for not following in the family tradition? Should I never speak to him again?"

Hap blinked, confused. He had been so nervous about telling his grandfather about this decision, he thought he might not be hearing correctly. But Stella laughed out loud. After all this worry, the doctor was letting Hap off easy. She leaned forward, elbows on the seat behind Hap.

"Your grandpop's joking," she whispered, before she turned to the doctor. "Definitely a beheading. But first can we order pizza? I'm starving."

"Pizza it is," the doctor agreed.

They drove to the doctor's house, which he had helped to design and build fifty years earlier, when he was newly married to Adele. He had wanted a house which was completely different from his family home, a cottage he had donated to the town. The Stewart House was the first edifice to be built in Unity after the great fire; it was now a dark and rather moldy gift shop where imitation Revolutionary War trinkets were sold to tourists who happened by in summer and fall, looking for a piece of the Freedom Trail. The doctor's current house had a great deal of glass and overlooked a vista of rhododendrons and azaleas that bloomed pink and white and purple. There was a stockade fence between the driveway and a rolling field on the other side. Once the car had been parked, they all trooped in to the kitchen, exhausted, mud on their feet. Hap called the pizza place in town, to order the delivery of a large pie with everything, while the doctor went to wash up.

David Stewart, Hap's father, was a tall, rumpled man who had just gotten home from work. He was in the den, fiddling with the TV, searching for the Red Sox game, when Hap brought Stella in to meet him.

"So you're Stella," David Stewart said when they were introduced. "Well, well. You're nothing like your mother."

Since Stella had always believed being different from her mother to be one of her primary goals in life, Mr. Stewart's comment should have pleased her. Instead, she felt her face color. Somehow, she felt insulted.

"Your mother had all that dark, beautiful hair the Sparrow women are known for. Guys at school used to follow her around. Everybody was crazy about her, but she wasn't interested in anybody but Will Avery."

If Juliet Aronson had been there she would have probably said, *Oh, yeah? Well, I'm sure you were the guy she was least interested in, Mr. Stewart, you punk, you skunk. You're an idiot even now.* Stella, on the other hand, merely stood there smiling, politely frozen and deeply taken aback by the comparison with her mother. So she was nothing, invisible, a pale imitation of the real thing.

"My father's kind of a jerk," Hap said apologetically when they went outside to wait for the pizza delivery van. "I think he was a disappointment to my grandfather. He sells pharmaceuticals and he does okay, but he was supposed to be a doctor. Kind of like me."

"You're nothing like your father." They both laughed at that echo of David Stewart's assessment. Still, Mr. Stewart's comment stung. Stella was less than her mother, that's what he'd been telling her. The sort of girl no one in his right mind would follow around. "My father's kind of a jerk, too. But a nice one. He listens to me. At least, he tries."

The face of the patient who'd been in the accident kept surfacing in Stella's mind, even now, hours after the event. As she gazed at the rhododendrons, as she brushed a strand of hair away or spoke about her father, it was that young man's face she was seeing. It was the look in his eyes. Something had passed between them that could never be taken back or denied. Perhaps that was all there really was in this world: seeing someone, if even for a moment, looking inside to the deepest core.

A breeze had come up and there was the scent of loam in the air. Hay and fertilizer. Sweet grass and wild ginger. April. Stella was just starting to relax from the intensity of the day when she noticed something in the field. The thing was eating leaves off a hazel tree. It looked like a camel in reverse, the kind of creature that only existed in dreams, made up of pieces and parts, hoof and head and tail.

"What is that? Is there some sort of animal out there?"

"It's Sooner. My grandfather's horse."

Stella felt herself grow cold, even though the day was still mild, the sunshine bright. She had seen an image of Hap being thrown from a horse on the day she met him; he was in the air, falling much too fast with no one nearby to catch him.

"They supposedly hate each other, but they're stuck with each other. Look at Sooner's back. Ever see such a swayback?"

"You didn't tell me you had a horse. Jesus, Hap. You should have told me. We're supposed to be such good friends, and now this comes out. What else have you kept hidden?"

"I don't have a horse." Hap was surprised by how upset Stella was. "I told you, it's my grandfather's."

Dr. Stewart had taken in the horse as a favor to a farmer in North Arthur who'd been his patient for decades, despite the many times he couldn't pay the doctor's fee. The old farmer was dying, he hadn't anyone in the world he cared about, except this huge, ancient horse, dusty brown with white markings on its face that formed the shape of tears.

He won't live long, the farmer had vowed. *He'll be dead sooner than you can turn around. I promise you. Just let him live out his last in that field of yours. He'll eat grass and take care of himself if you just throw him a bale of hay when winter comes along. He'll lay himself down and bury himself, too. I swear. You won't have to do a thing for him.*

When the old farmer died, Dr. Stewart went down to his worthless acreage. He'd realized he'd forgotten to ask if the horse had a name. *If you're going to die sooner or later, it had better be sooner*, the doctor had said aloud as he stood by the fence, at which point the horse pricked up its ears. It was a cold January afternoon and the doctor had come directly from the farmer's funeral. He rubbed his hands together and wondered what on earth he'd agreed to. He could count the horse's ribs. He could see that it had mange. But when it came close, the horse's breath was surprisingly sweet, like apples.

I've been assured this creature will be dead in no time, Brock Stewart told Matt Avery, who borrowed a trailer from the Harmon brothers, which he attached to his pickup on the day he delivered the horse to Unity. Doc Stewart had already paid Matt to fence in the field and build a lean-to, so the horse would have shelter when there was lightning and thunder.

Don't count on it. Matt had grinned. *Something tells me he's sticking around.*

So far, sixteen years had passed and the horse seemed unchanged, no older, no closer to death. The vet, Tim Early, had guessed that Sooner was thirty-five or more, from the wear on his teeth, but all the doctor knew was that over time he was out nearly ten thousand dollars, if he included the fencing, the barn, and the feed. As it turned out, Doc Stewart and Elinor Sparrow had the two oldest pets in town, although if anybody dared to call Sooner a pet, the doctor hit the roof. *He's an albatross. He's a hay bag. He's no pet.* That's what the doctor told anyone willing to listen. *He's the price I'm still paying for one idiotic moment of mercy.*

"He should have called the horse Later." Hap laughed. "Or Forever. Or maybe Ten Grand."

Stella had a queasy feeling, bad timing because the pizza delivery van had pulled in and was heading along the driveway.

"Maybe your grandfather should have him put down." Stella looked sideways to see Hap's reaction. Right away, he got that furrow on his forehead that appeared whenever he was worried about something. "It would be an act of kindness, really, to put him out of his misery. He's probably in pain with that back of his and all."

"Sooner is as happy as can be. He spends his days eating and shitting and we do all the cleaning up."

The delivery guy honked, and Hap went over to pay and collect their dinner. Exhaust drifted from the tailpipe of the idling van and the distance looked hazy and blue. From Stella's vantage point on the porch, Sooner seemed like a horse in a dream. He moved slowly as he searched out the tender new grass. He disappeared behind the leaves of the hazel tree.

"Nobody rides him, do they?" Stella asked when they took the pizza inside.

"Stella, he'd collapse if they did. You've seen him. Mr. Swayback."

"Well, promise me you won't."

"Why?" Hap had opened the lid of the pizza box and steam rose between them. A pie with everything in Unity meant sausage, peppers, and mushrooms.

"Because I have good ideas." Stella hoped that she sounded more lighthearted than she was. "I'm known for them."

Stella had taken some plates from the cabinet, but she wasn't certain she could bring herself to eat.

"Really?" Hap grinned. "What about the onion?"

Stella couldn't help but laugh. Cynthia Elliot had told her that her brother, Jimmy, had been telling people to stay away from Stella, announcing that she came from a long line of bad luck and twisted genetics. As if Jimmy Elliot knew anything about genetics. He had failed earth science twice and was now repeating the class. Plus, he was a liar. Cynthia had told Stella that the fingertip he always swore had been bitten by a snapping turtle had really been torn off by a lawn mower he didn't know how to start properly. The girls all swooned over Jimmy for some reason, but he seemed intent in following Stella around, or at least watching across the cafeteria at lunchtime.

One afternoon, Cynthia and Stella had broken into Jimmy's locker and they'd left a peeled onion stuck with a single pin atop his books, none of which appeared to have ever been opened. It was a joke, but Jimmy had gone around insisting that Stella had put a curse on him, and that she'd done so because she wanted him, badly. It was just a matter of time, Jimmy said, before Stella begged him to go out with her.

"Oh, please. Jimmy Elliot is such an idiot. Who's afraid of an onion?"

Stella felt more cheerful after this discussion, and she wound up eating three slices of pizza after carefully picking off the sausage. Hap's father ate in the den, in front of the TV, and Dr. Stewart was on the phone and didn't come into the kitchen until Hap and Stella were washing up.

"Go ask your dad if he wants some coffee," Dr. Stewart suggested to Hap, and when Hap had gone off to the den, the doctor came to stand beside Stella at the sink. He could tell that she was a girl who looked straight at death, and he appreciated this trait in a person. It was good practice to stare into the abyss, rather than turn and run the way so many did.

Brock Stewart had seen more people die than he could put a number to, and it always amazed him to see how individual the process was. Strong men he'd expected to go easily called for their mothers and wept. Honorable people whispered they were ready to sell their soul to the devil if need be, in exchange for one more day, a single hour longer, a breath or two more of this life they held so terribly dear. Then there were the deaths he had dreaded, sorrowful, untimely endings, that had turned out to be smoother than expected, like a stone thrown into still water, like a sigh. That baby Liza Hull had given birth to nearly fifteen years ago, born prematurely with a heart defect so tragically irreversible the neonatal unit at Hamilton Hospital had told Liza from the start the child had a matter of months at the most. Liza was already divorced from her husband, one of the Hathaway cousins from Boston who joined up with the Merchant Marine, and so Dr. Stewart had gotten in the habit of stopping by and keeping an eye on the baby's decline.

Liza called him when the end seemed close. She wanted her daughter to be at home when it happened, and that's the way it was, the three of them in Liza's bedroom in the little apartment above the tea house as dusk fell through the trees. Dr. Stewart had tried to prepare himself on the drive over. He assumed this would be one of the toughest deaths, a new life cut off almost before it had begun, a young mother left with nothing, but in fact the night turned out very differently from what he'd expected. Brock Stewart thought he had seen everything, but he'd never experienced a silence and a beauty of the magnitude he was privy to in Liza's apartment. The way Liza held her baby close and let her go at the same time, the way their breathing settled into a single rhythm, so that the only way he knew the baby was gone was from a subtle shift of air, and then a sob.

In Dr. Stewart's experience, the moment of death was always accompanied by an expulsion of breath that was unlike any other. It was as if the spirit arose from the body to join with the air, as if the essence of an individual could no longer be contained by mere flesh and blood. This was the moment when Liza Hull bent her head and kissed her baby's lips, and the spirit appeared to move into her. For an instant it did, indeed, seem as if they were one being.

The doctor sat there with Liza all night long. He figured this poor woman was owed at least that: a night without sirens and ambulances, without death certificates. She deserved those few extra hours of peace when the world stood still. In the morning, when light was just beginning to crack open the sky, Doc Stewart phoned down to Hamilton Hospital and gave the hour of death as 5:30 A.M. When the time came, Liza draped a blanket over her child; she was ready when the ambulance arrived.

Thank you, she said before she left, going downstairs by herself, the baby in her arms. *You were with me when I needed you.*

Brock Stewart had already been a physician for many years at that point. He'd seen it all: cancer, heart failure, the slow withering of disease, the utter surprise of accidental mortalities, including two boys who fell through the ice in the marsh and froze to death holding hands. But the night Liza's baby died, he went out to his Lincoln, the car that could get through anything—mud, or snow, or floods—and he cried. In Liza Hull's bedroom something had happened, a sort of acceptance the doctor had never experienced before. All this time he'd been fighting against death, his enemy, his dragon, invincible, unbeatable. Now he saw he'd been mistaken. It was as if he'd seen only one stone, but not the river that rushed around it. Death was his constant companion, he understood that now. It followed him into houses, arm and arm, there beside him every time he walked through the streets, as much a part of what he did as the lives that were saved, the babies born, the fevers broken.

Thank you, he said to Liza Hull, as he sat in his parked car and watched the ambulance go slowly on its way to the morgue at Hamilton Hospital.

That was why he'd wanted Hap, whom he loved so, to be a doctor. He wanted his grandson to know what that moment had felt like, what it was like to be sitting in your parked car as daylight opened up the night, as the sky shone silver; how it felt to be with someone at the most important hour in their life. Well, the boy clearly wasn't cut out for it, but this girl Stella was another matter entirely.

"They got that patient to Mass General in time," he told her as she dried the dishes. "You were right. Laceration of the liver. He lost a huge amount of blood, but the prognosis is excellent. They're very hopeful. Good call."

Stella tried to keep her excitement in check. If she had seen a death and it had been reversed, then wasn't she only seeing a possibility rather than certain fate? Could it be that the deaths she had seen were uncertain, easy enough to change if given the right circumstances?

"I'd been looking through some anatomy texts in the library," she told the doctor. "I just put the symptoms together. It was a lucky guess."

"It was more than lucky, it was smart."

Stella was so thrilled by the compliment she didn't trust herself to speak.

"I go down to the clinic every Saturday." The doctor was casual, so as to avoid any pressure. He'd already done that, with Hap and with his son, David, and it hadn't worked out. "I make rounds at the nursing home out on the highway, too, if you're ever interested. You've got a feel for medicine."

"Sure." Stella had liked being in the clinic; she'd felt completely at home there. Why, she hadn't even noticed there were little drops of blood on her boots. "Thank you. I'd like that."

She was so pleased by the turn of events—the young man with an excellent prognosis, the potential for a person's fate to change until his last moment—that she threw her arms around the doctor before she headed for the back door. "I'd better get home. Tell Hap I'll see him in school."

Stella went down the driveway, stopping when she reached the field. She felt an odd sort of joy within her, as though all of a sudden she mattered. Giddy, she waved her arms at Sooner, but the horse only stared back at her, peacefully eating grass in the fading April light. Some horses panicked at wind or passing clouds, they spooked when birds took flight, when field mice skittered through the grass, but not Sooner. He'd seen too much to be startled; he'd lived too long to be alarmed.

"I wish you would die," Stella told the horse. "Go on," she urged. She raised her arms to the sky as though magicking away the future she'd seen for Hap, thrown from a horse with no one around to ease his fall. "Die," she commanded the old swayback.

Sooner stayed where he was, chewing. But there was someone else around; Jimmy Elliot had come up the driveway, and he'd heard every word. He was wearing jeans and a black shirt which allowed him to fade into the shadows as the light shifted. Now he came to stand beside Stella.

"That can be arranged," he said.

"Please." Stella laughed. She should have been surprised to see him, but she wasn't. "What are you going to do? Shoot him? Or maybe you'll just throw an onion at him. That can be pretty scary."

"Hah. Very funny." Jimmy had actually saved that onion, it was in the back of his closet in a zip-lock plastic bag. "What's wrong with this horse? Why would you want him dead? He looks harmless. Kind of pathetic, actually. Like your good buddy, Hap."

The truth was, Jimmy didn't know what he was doing there. He'd seen Stella and Hap driving through town with the doctor one minute and the next thing he knew he was walking down the Stewarts' driveway, stopping to hang on the fence, looking at some old mule.

"He's a menace." Stella thought about what Hap's father had said, how her mother had driven all the boys crazy, how Stella was nothing like her. She looked over at Jimmy and noticed his puzzled expression. It seemed that Mr. Stewart was wrong. "Just like you."

"And you can tell that by looking at me?" Jimmy laughed, and when he did, he didn't even sound like himself anymore. When he coughed to clear his throat, he felt his heart hit against his ribs.

"I told you before. I'm a good judge of character." Stella leaped away from the fence and took off running. "Race you to the road."

But Jimmy stayed where he was, watching her, although she was disappearing fast. For some reason he couldn't take his eyes off Stella, even if that meant letting her win.

"I don't think so," Jimmy Elliot called after her. He grinned when she reached the road. Just as he'd hoped: once she had won, she didn't ignore him. Instead, she turned back to wave. "You're still talking to me."

III.

THERE WAS NO ONE to tell Will when to wake up; he had no job to go to, no wife to complain about his lazy and slovenly ways. Therefore, he rose at noon. No one was around to tell him to clear his dishes away, so they piled up in the sink until they reached a monumental height, a free-form of forks and spoons and chili-encrusted bowls and congealed spaghetti, all of it balanced upon Jenny's favorite teacups, which were cracking beneath the weight of pots and pans. The other tenants in the building had given up expecting their complaints would force Will to toe the line. Why, he no longer even bothered to carry his overflowing bags of garbage into the stairwell, let alone hoist the bags into the trash chute. Instead, he let it pile up in the hall, and although Mrs. Ehrland had consulted her nephew, an attorney with the housing authority, there was no way to get rid of Will Avery, not even when people began to complain of mice in the hall.

On weekends the tenants had a bit of a reprieve, thank goodness, for Will often spent Friday and Saturday nights at the home of Ellen Paxton, who wore jasmine perfume, the aroma Jenny had previously detected in their apartment. Ellen taught voice at the music school, and although she wasn't a great beauty, she supplied Will with some decent meals and good after-dinner sex, if he hadn't had too much to drink, that is, at which point he often fell asleep on her couch, where he served as a pillow for Ellen's cat, a shedding Burmese Will despised.

With Jenny gone, Ellen had become hopeful that her relationship with Will was going somewhere, and Will didn't particularly want to dash these hopes until he had a little more ready cash. No need to give up Ellen's dinners or the loans she occasionally handed over when Will was flat broke. Certainly there was no need for her to know that he was also sleeping with Kelly Butler, a waitress at the Hornets' Nest, who was only twenty-three, young enough not to be disturbed by the mess in Will's apartment or the fact that he never took her anywhere.

The truth was, it was Stella he missed most of all; Stella's trust in him, Stella's faith. His daughter often left messages on the answering machine, since he always seemed to be out or asleep when she phoned. She missed him; she wanted him to come to Unity for a visit. But the bail agreement insisted he stay in Boston. Boston, his ball and chain. Boston, a cruel and thoughtless city if an individual had no money and no dreams. All those shops and cafés on Newbury Street, Symphony Hall, with its near-perfect acoustics, the Ritz with its glorious view, what good was any of it to a man who had no money and no prospects? Will was broke, and weakened by disappointment; at night he couldn't sleep without several drinks to help him drift off, and even then his sleep was restless, a dreamless deep he couldn't escape. Often he woke with the shudders, as though he'd dived into the coldest waters and could barely drag himself ashore. He sputtered and needed several cups of coffee, and still he was shivering.

Now when he walked across the Common he stared straight ahead, not wanting to see the men on the benches, the homeless stretched out on wooden planks as if they were in their own beds. Jenny had told Will these men most often dreamed of slices of apple pie and beds with clean sheets; they dreamed that someone loved them and was waiting at the door, and of all the hundred small things that were slipping away from Will now. Since his piano was being held hostage at his previous address, and his hands were shaking anyway, he spent most of his time watching TV. He'd begun to have a whisky along with his second cup of coffee, just to get him revved up. In fact, he was a little buzzed on the afternoon when a reporter managed to get into the building, with no one to stop him before he managed to locate the Averys' door. Occupants' names were listed in the front hall, so Will hadn't been especially difficult to find. Right beside his name several rude comments had been scrawled by his fellow tenants, in Magic Marker, in ink that wouldn't wash away: *Go get a fucking job. Ever hear of rats? Throw your damned garbage away!*

"I've got to ask you to leave," Will was quick to say when he opened the door to a stranger who quickly introduced himself as a reporter. Will was still wearing the clothes he'd slept in, so he'd thrown on a sports coat in order to look presentable. "I don't give interviews since my last debacle. I always say too much."

"I know," the reporter agreed. "That's how I found you. Posed in front of your building with the number showing. Major bad idea."

Will laughed. "I'm full of those." He felt a certain kinship with this fellow who'd tracked him down.

The reporter looked Will up and down and took measure of his situation "Look, I won't print anything you don't want me to. And that's not all." The reporter coughed, embarrassed. He gazed around the empty trash-strewn hall with something that resembled pity. "I'll pay for the interview."

Frankly, Will's stomach was growling and he felt somewhat dizzy from the caffeine and whisky he'd already consumed. There was half a cold pizza in the fridge and that was pretty much it. He was on the verge of having to call Jen and ask her for money. Or maybe Matt would come through, yet again. Henry Elliot had told him in no uncertain terms not to speak to another reporter, or to anyone else for that matter, in regard to the case. But Henry had always been a self-righteous ass and Will had never put much stock in anyone's advice.

"How much?" he asked.

"Two hundred bucks."

"I don't know." Will tried his best to look thoughtful. He did have to support himself, after all. "How about a thousand?"

"Five hundred. It's the best I can do." The reporter took out a billfold and counted out five hundred-dollar bills. "Nobody will pay more."

"Why argue?" Will took the money and folded it into his jacket pocket. He grinned and opened the door wider, allowing his visitor inside, just in time, as Mrs. Ehrland was on her way up the stairs to once again complain about the trash and the late-night TV blaring out the window. By the time Mrs. Ehrland knocked on the door, Will had already brought the reporter into the living room. He ignored the rapping and took off his jacket, which he flung over the desk, littered with unpaid bills. That was what Mrs. Ehrland was probably blubbering about, the unpaid rent.

"What paper did you say you write for?"

"The *Boston Herald*. I'm Ted Scott. And I won't keep you long. Everyone says that, but I really mean it."

Will gathered together the magazines and newspapers strewn about on the couch and the easy chair. Frankly, it was something of a relief to finally talk to someone. It felt good to get it all out, rather than bottle everything up the way Henry Elliot, a tightass even back in school, had advised. Besides, everything Will said in this interview concerning Stella was off the record: the fact that she had been the one to suggest he go to the police, that she'd somehow seen the death of the woman in Brighton.

"Could I talk to her?" the reporter asked. "For a minute or so?"

"Good lord, no. She's at her grandmother's. A big old house in the woods. Miles out of the city. Safe as a bug in a rug."

"What else did she see?" the reporter asked. "Did she see the circumstances? Could she make out what the killer looked like?"

Will had poured himself another whisky. He loved the way it burned and made him feel something inside. "Off the record," he reminded his guest. "All she saw was that the poor woman's throat was slit." Will was thinking about the five hundred bucks and how he would spend it. He could go to the Hornets' Nest every night, once he paid up his bar tab, maybe even treat Kelly Butler to dinner. He'd nearly forgotten what it was like to eat a good meal. He'd all but forgotten how hungry he was. "I'm just going to grab myself something to eat." He started for the kitchen. "Want anything? A beer?"

"A little early for me," the reporter said. "Thanks anyway, but I'm all set."

Will retrieved a slice of pizza from the crumpled cardboard box. There were no clean plates around, so he snagged a paper towel, and got himself a beer. Last one in the six-pack, but he'd soon remedy that.

"I'll just be a minute," Will called. "I'm looking for hot peppers. Pizza is worthless without hot peppers, in my humble opinion."

He carried everything out to the living room, bumping the door open with his hip. "You're sure you don't want anything?" he asked.

But as it turned out, Will was talking to himself. The chair where the reporter had been sitting was empty. A breeze came through the open window and ruffled the newspapers that Will had tossed on the floor. Ted Scott was nowhere in sight.

"Shit," Will muttered. He tossed the pizza and the beer onto the coffee table. He stood there for a moment, chilled, then he went over to the desk and picked up his jacket. He slipped a hand into the pocket. The money was gone.

The door of the apartment had been left open and the hallway was empty. Just some garbage bags Will had left in the hall that morning, toppled when someone hurried past. There were his empty beer bottles rolling along the floor. He never bothered to recycle; he couldn't think that far in advance. His mother had warned him that the ease with which he lived his life would be his undoing in the end. When he'd last visited her, she had grabbed on to his hand and apologized to him.

"For what?" Will had laughed.

"Maybe I should have made things harder for you," Catherine Avery had said. "Maybe I shouldn't have applauded everything you did."

That was the sort of woman she was, always ready to blame herself, even for his ruined life.

"Mother," he'd said. He had bent down close to her, even though she smelled like death and he had always been put off by such things. Her breathing was labored and he realized all at once he had never asked her a single question about herself. Why, he didn't even know how she'd voted in the last election, or what films she had liked, or if she read novels late into the night, when she was up worrying about him, unable to sleep. "You did an excellent job," he told her. "Any screwup is entirely my own responsibility."

"Oh," his mother had said, with a last burst of energy. She had grabbed his hand so tightly that he'd pulled back, frightened. "I loved you so," she said.

If he hadn't been such a greedy fool, his radar might have been out about this Ted Scott individual. It took one to know one, isn't that what people said? Well, not this time. This time he'd been blinded by a few dollars. He phoned the *Boston Herald* and he wasn't surprised when the editor of the Metro section told him there had never been a Ted Scott on staff. He called the tabloids then, but no one had ever heard of Scott.

Every con man gets conned himself eventually, and Will couldn't believe he'd let the five hundred dollars out of his sight. He was losing his touch. He gazed at himself in the hall mirror Jenny had found in an antique shop on Charles Street when they first took the apartment. He was losing his looks as well, he saw that plainly. Someone else might not have noticed, but they wouldn't have inspected him as carefully as he monitored himself. There was a bloating in his face, a darkness around his eyes; his skin was sallow, and this time he couldn't blame his pallid complexion on the terrible lighting in jail.

"Idiot," he said to his reflection.

Had he thought it would be easy forever? Had he imagined he'd never have to pay for all the shortcuts he'd taken in his life? He thought of those men on the benches in the Boston Common, and their dreams of what had been stolen from them or what they'd thrown away. Lately his fleeting murky bits of dreams had been of the very same things: clean sheets, true love, a woman who didn't care what he looked like or how much cash was in his wallet.

For the first time in a very long while, Will looked past his own reflection. There in the mirror, right in his sight line, was the trestle table where Jenny kept the mail, where she had left Stella's bagged school lunches, where she used to tack notes for Will, reminding him of his domestic responsibilities, errands and tasks he was sure to shirk. It was now he realized that the model of Cake House, which had been there earlier, good for nothing but collecting dust, was gone. He could tell because the empty space where it had once been seemed polished, where everything around was covered with a film. The old house in the woods, given over like a gift, free of charge. The location of his daughter, a witness before there'd been a crime.

The phone rang, but Will didn't answer it. His stomach felt like hell now. It might be Henry Elliot calling him, or, worse still, his brother. He wasn't ready to talk to anyone. He needed a moment before he could admit what a mistake he had made. Now whoever wanted to find Stella would have something far better than a map. He would have a model, and it wouldn't take long before he managed to find the real thing, the address where the forsythia was not made of felt, but of flowers, tumbling into bloom. Before long he would be at the front door that was full-size, where the hedge of laurel was so tall this season no one would ever see if someone were hiding there, breathing in the scent of laurel, surrounded by the hum of bees.

IV.

IT HAD BEEN MORE THAN thirty years since the last dinner guest had been invited to Cake House, that colleague of Saul's who had arrived late, so that even before it began, dinner had been ruined. Their guest had been attractive, with chestnut hair and arched eyebrows, black as crows. *Who can find these little towns?* Their guest had laughed, not bothering to make excuses for her tardiness. She'd been overdressed, lost without a map; while Saul went to the parlor to fix them drinks, their guest watched Elinor finish up the salad. She'd asked too many questions about Saul: what his favorite foods were, did he work in the garden on Sundays, watering the seedlings, wearing a straw hat? Or did he take the paper up to bed, and was it the sports page he looked at first or was it the news? Their pretty dinner guest wasn't lying, not exactly, which made her especially difficult to read. She just wanted to know Elinor's husband better; she just wanted him for herself, that was all.

For thirty years there had been no visitors other than Dr. Stewart occasionally stopping by for a bowl of vegetable soup or some gingerbread near the holidays. Why, the silverware had grown tarnished in its velvet case and needed to be polished, the decent china was dusty and had to be rinsed, the ashes were swept from the fireplace, and a new fire was lit, for although it was April, and the fields were filled with trillium and trout lilies, although jonquils were blooming in the lane, the dining room was as cold as a tomb.

"You don't have to be involved," Jenny told her mother. Elinor prowled about the kitchen, useless, as Jenny cut up leeks and onions for a chicken dish she'd decided upon, not too fancy, not too plain, a recipe that wouldn't reveal how hard she'd been working simply because Matt was coming to dinner. In fact, she'd been up at six, planning the menu, before rushing off to North Arthur to the farmstand where the vegetables were always so fresh.

"Of course she has to be involved," Stella called from the scullery. She'd reached behind the bottles of pond water for the oldest cookbook in the house, the one that had belonged to Elisabeth Sparrow, and was now thumbing through the grainy pages stained with suet and jam. "Gran and I are making dessert. I found it!" Stella declared as she returned to the kitchen. "Bird's-nest pudding. Isn't that perfect?"

"Perfectly awful," Elinor replied.

"Actually, I have to agree with your grandmother." A shock for them both, a first, perhaps. All the same, Jenny was pleased by Stella's interest. Anything other than stomping out of the room was a definite movement forward. Here they were, three women from the same family in one kitchen, and trouble had managed to stay away, at least so far.

"It's custard poured into apples." Stella tied back her hair and set to work coring the apples. "We can make vanilla or butterscotch. Elisabeth preferred vanilla," Stella informed her grandmother, whom she'd set to work beating eggs. "I wish Juliet could see me now. She wouldn't believe I could cook."

"Juliet?" Jenny's radar went up.

"My best friend," Stella reminded her mother. "Ever hear of her?"

"Well, well," Elinor said, not exactly pleased by the obvious rift, but glad to see a chink in Jenny's alleged perfection, grateful for human nature. "So you don't know her best friend."

"I know her. I just don't think Juliet is the right sort of person for Stella to spend time with."

"At least Juliet's mother went to college. She went to Smith. She didn't give up her whole future to support some man's education."

"That man was your father. And are you comparing me to the woman who poisoned her husband? You don't have to go to Smith to do that."

Elinor noticed that the custard was cooking too fast on the back burner of the stove, boiling over, in fact. In no time, the filling for the bird's nest would be singed, a faint rubbery skin formed at its edges.

"Well, now I have a parent who's been in jail, too. Does that make my friendship with Juliet all right, Mother? Is she good enough for me now?"

"You take everything I say and turn it around."

"I don't need to! You turn it around yourself! You always think you're so damned right!"

"Well, I am about some things! Not that you can ever admit it!"

They faced each other across the table, the cored apples turning brown between them, the leeks cut to pieces, the pudding boiling over.

"Everything was perfect until you got here," Stella declared. "Everything was absolutely fine."

"This is clearly none of my business, but the pudding is on fire," Elinor announced.

Stella grabbed a tea towel and ran to lift the heavy pan from the flame. In the old cookbook, Elisabeth Sparrow had recommended stirring for fifteen minutes, but this pudding was ruined, scorched beyond use.

Stella threw up her hands and ran outside, so it was Elinor who placed the pan in the sink and ran the cold water. Billows of steam rose and fogged up the kitchen window. In the reflection of the old green glass, thick as a bottle, Elinor could see that Jenny had sunk into a chair, her head in her hands. The chopped leeks and onions made the room smell like spring, a sweet, rainy scent. Elinor stayed where she was, by the soapstone sink. A long time ago she had known how to comfort someone, she had rocked her baby in her arms, but she had lost the knack for consolation. She really hadn't a clue of what to do next.

"Don't worry about the pudding," Elinor said briskly as she scoured the burned pan. "Everyone in town knows Matt Avery doesn't eat desserts. He's a bread-and-butter man."

"He used to love sundaes. I guess he gave them up." Jenny blew her nose on a paper towel. "Good old easygoing Matt."

"Somebody had to be."

To Elinor's surprise, Jenny laughed. Elinor felt a tinge of pride at having cheered her daughter when Jenny went back to fixing the meal; at least her daughter had the ability to get on with things, to pick up the pieces, to adhere to the task at hand. By the time Matt's truck pulled up, the casserole was browning in the oven, the rice was made, the salad was on the table.

Matt had brought along a bottle of wine and some caraway cakes, the kind his mother had liked for him to pick up at Hull's Tea House.

On the porch, Argus woofed at him and ambled over, back legs dragging due to arthritis.

"Hey, old man." Matt patted the dog's head, then opened the white bakery bag. He took out a caraway cake, freshly baked. "Don't tell anybody about this," he said as the dog gratefully gulped down the cake.

Stella had watched the encounter from the garden, where she'd been sulking. She smiled when she saw her uncle dust crumbs from the wolfhound's beard.

"You made it," she called as she walked over through the damp grass. Little frogs skittered out of her path, leaping into the bushes.

"I did, but I'm not sure I'm really welcome."

"My grandmother might put a curse on you and my mother might poison you with her casserole, but if you're not afraid of them and you don't mind vegetables, come on in."

"Did you say casserole?"

"Oh, yeah, she's been cooking all day."

"Really?" Matt thought that over, pleased by her interest, yet reminded of the time when the women in town filled his freezer with turkey-noodle lasagne and lima bean pie. "A casserole, you say?"

Stella was already through the door.

"Are you coming in?" she said when he paused.

Matt had stopped so he could take the time to look around. He might never be invited back, and he wanted to experience Cake House. The only other time he'd been inside was the dreadful day when he'd sneaked in to defend Will against Elinor.

"I saw you when you were born," Matt told Stella. Argus, usually standoffish and dignified, followed along, nose twitching, in the hope another caraway cake might be tossed his way. "Actually, it was three days after you were born. I brought my mother with me, your grandmother, Catherine. We both agreed that you were the most beautiful baby in the world."

Stella smiled. Her uncle was the sort of person with whom it was easy to feel comfortable. "I made you bird's-nest pudding, but I burned it."

"My loss, I'm sure. Although honestly, it sounds revolting. Were there beaks and feathers?"

Stella laughed. "Pudding and apples."

"Equally bad. I hate sweets."

Elinor had come into the hall. Although she looked displeased to see a guest in her house, she accepted the bakery bag, into which she peeked. "Your mother's favorite," she said.

Matt was impressed that she would have remembered. Though he'd worked for Elinor for years, he couldn't say he knew her, and when people in town asked what she was like, he kept mum. All he knew was that she refused to pave the driveway, which he often suggested, and that she didn't want to bother leveling off Dead Horse Lane.

Now, standing here in the hall, Matt realized that although he'd only been in the house once before, he'd dreamed of it many times. In his dreams, it was always the original house, before the additions were added on like frosting. It was a house made of wood and mud and straw. Everything smelled like smoke and water lilies in his dreams, and he thought he detected the scent now, although it was quickly replaced by the aroma from the pan of rolls Jenny brought out of the kitchen. The rolls were from a package, but Liza Hull had advised that if sprinkled with butter and a few sprigs of rosemary, they'd appear to be homemade.

"Well, here you are," Jenny said cheerfully. She fanned herself with the tea towel; holding on to the pan of rolls must be causing her to burn up. The scent of rosemary made her feel somewhat intoxicated. "Our first guest ever."

Matt had recently read in Emily Hathaway's household journal that some fools in love used to believe that the mere act of buttoning a shirt could reveal whether or not they had a chance with their beloved; evens and odds would predict the outcome. The same was true for plum stones found in a tart. Odd meant sorrow. Even, love.

"You can take your wine home with you. We don't drink," Elinor said.

"Some of us do," Jenny said as she took the bottle of Chardonnay from Matt. "Of course, if Will were here he'd insist upon whisky. And only the best. Johnnie Walker, isn't that what he drinks?"

Once it was said aloud, Will's name sat there on the carpeting, an unwelcome toad.

"Good old Will," Matt Avery said.

In studying her uncle, Stella saw that he was her father's opposite in every way. If the brothers were placed facing each other, it would be as though one were shadow and the other substance. Only which was which?

"Aren't genetics fascinating?" Stella said as they proceeded to the table. She was wearing the silver bracelet her father had given her and the bell chimed softly as she reached for the salad to pass to Matt. "The variations. The mutations. That's why I'm going into medicine," Stella informed her uncle. "Anything's possible."

Matt was seriously impressed. When he was in ninth grade he was too busy dreaming to think about his future. His idea of a plan had been to walk over to North Arthur to the movie theater on a Sunday afternoon.

"What are you into?" Stella asked.

"You've seen what I do. I cut down trees. I also mow lawns. Plow driveways when there's snow. Try to talk your grandmother into paving her driveway and trimming back some of that laurel."

"Never," Elinor said.

"And he studies history," Jenny added. "He's an expert on Unity."

"Oh, really?" Elinor put down her salad fork. "Tell me something I don't know."

He could tell her that her granddaughter looked nothing like the other Sparrow women, with her gold eyes and hair the color of snow. She looked like the women in the Avery family, however, like Catherine and her sisters and her aunts, although no one among the Averys smelled like water lilies. Instead, he told Elinor that her grandmother, Elisabeth Sparrow, was said to be unable to taste, a lucky trait during the Depression years, since she could make do with next to nothing. This trait was said to be the basis for her excellent cooking.

Elisabeth Sparrow, Matt went on, made a soup out of water lily pads that was surprisingly filling. Some of the other women in town at the time, including Lois Hathaway, had noted that Elisabeth also made a supper of local ingredients, water parsnip, parsley, and a few secret items, that she called nine-frogs stew. Before long, people in town who were out of work lined up on the porch of Cake House, too hungry to be prideful. Eventually, Elisabeth set up a kitchen in what was now the community center, and some people say that over the years she served over twenty thousand meals to those in need, including the men who'd been hired to build the train station. Liza Hull's grandmother had eaten there nearly every night when she was a girl.

"That's how Liza managed to get hold of Elisabeth's recipe for lemon chess pie," Matt said.

Stella ran to get Elisabeth's cookbook. "It's the original," she told Matt, who was clearly impressed. Stella flipped to the last page and there it was, written down, the recipe for nine-frogs stew. "Ooh. It says to strain the water to get out all the mud and mosquitoes. Yummy. But there are two ingredients I can't read."

Matt took a look at the cookbook. "I can't make out the first one." The handwriting was slanted, and the lettering was a pale orange, as though the ink had been made from lilies. "The last item on the list looks like sage."

Jenny applauded Matt's knowledge of their family. "I told you he knew everything."

Matt stared at Jenny across the table in a way that made her uncomfortable. "I don't know everything," he said. "Not by far."

"Well, maybe you know why they keep the glass case in the parlor," Stella said to her uncle. "Maybe you can tell me why no one in this family has ever thought to throw away those horrible things."

"Should I check on the casserole, or will you?" Elinor asked Jenny.

"I will," Jenny said, grateful to her mother for changing the subject. "I'm sure it's done by now."

Stella turned to Matt. "Do you see what they do?" In the fading light, he could see there was already a frown line across her forehead. He recognized her place in the family, for he'd been there himself: the worrier, the one who sees what others deny, the responsible one left to clean up the messes made by others.

"Would you like to show me the case?" Matt had always been curious. There wasn't a day that went by when he didn't wish he hadn't been left behind to wait for his brother, breathing in the humid air that was so thick and green with pollen.

Stella pushed her chair back.

"We're in the middle of dinner," Jenny said. "Stella, please!"

Ignoring her mother, Stella led her uncle to the parlor. It was the center of the base of the wedding cake, a room with a wall of windows; but the glass was old and the light coming through was murky. Argus lay at the threshold to the room, and Matt had to step over the dog. He had been waiting all these years to come back here, he hadn't had a chance to look around when he came to rescue his brother, and now he wasn't disappointed. He recognized the beams that crossed the ceiling as cherry, which gave off a mild, fruity scent. He noticed the bookcases had been built out of walnut. Stella brought him to the corner and pulled off the cloth which Matt knew had been embroidered by Sarah Sparrow, Rebecca's daughter, and her own daughter Rosemary. There was a red heart, broken in half. There was a willow tree weeping black tears. The ground was covered with snowbells; the sky filled with birds. Every stitch had been carefully made; it had taken three winters, and a magnifying glass had been needed to see the thin silk thread. Matt barely breathed as he studied the contents of the case. What the historical society wouldn't give to place these artifacts on display for a single afternoon. Why Mrs. Gibson would be all but delirious if anyone managed to smuggle a single one of these mementos over to the library. The silver compass alone would be thrilling. The braid of hair almost too much to absorb.

Matt saw that his niece had a fearless nature, unusual in an Avery, but far from uncommon among the Sparrows. "These are the arrowheads shot at Rebecca Sparrow by some local boys. The Frost boys later admitted to it, and I think there may have been a Hapgood and one of the Whites involved, too. People said she didn't feel pain, so these boys decided to put the theory to the test. Even if she didn't react, it seems that she may have gotten peritonitis, because after being struck by these arrows, she walked with a limp."

Jenny had followed, but she stayed on the far side of the threshold. She had always thought of the glass case as their personal museum of pain, keepsakes to remind them not to trust anyone, never to forgive. Now, she wasn't so sure.

"That's the thing those boys didn't understand," Matt told Stella. "Just because you don't feel pain, doesn't mean you don't experience it."

He reached into his pocket and took out the tenth arrowhead. He had been carrying it around with him for more than thirty years. He should have brought it back immediately, but he had feared getting Will in trouble, and so the arrowhead had served as his lucky piece for all this time. Not that it had ever brought him the slightest bit of good fortune. Not that it hadn't made him think of Jenny each and every day. All the same, without the arrowhead he'd probably be lost for a while, but he'd felt like that before.

"I can't believe it!" Stella let out a laugh. She'd noticed one of the arrowheads was missing, and had wondered what had happened. "Where did you get that?"

"It was misplaced," Matt said. He'd found it in Will's dresser drawer years ago. "Now it's back."

From where she stood in the doorway, Jenny recalled that she had left Will alone in this room on her thirteenth birthday. It had only been for a moment, long enough for her to argue with her mother, long enough for him to steal the arrowhead. If Jenny had been more cautious, she would have noted that Will had rubbed his fingers together that day, as though he were itchy, the sure sign of a thief.

"Rebecca's story has mostly been written up by a fellow named Charles Hathaway. Pathetic guy, really. Had the first land grant, then lost almost all of it and wound up with his own son despising him."

"Is that her hair?" Stella asked of the dark coiled plait. *Rebecca*, she thought. *Show me a sign.*

Matt nodded. "I'd say it is. This town treated her badly, Stella. If you want to know the details, come down to the library."

"Sorry it's been such a horrible dinner," Jenny said when Matt had left Stella in the parlor, allowing the girl a bit of privacy as she carefully replaced the missing arrowhead.

"Not horrible. Not for me." He would not have cared if she'd served lily pad soup and the nine-frogs stew Elisabeth Sparrow perfected. He would have eaten tree bark, leather, snowdrops sautéed and served on a platter of rice. Food wasn't what he was hungry for.

"I'll bet you hate casseroles, anyway."

"I wouldn't say that." Matt was standing near enough to be made light-headed by the scent of lake water. *Was it on her skin?* he wondered. *Could this be the case with every Sparrow woman? Was it in their blood?*

"What would you say?"

Jenny was a little too close to Matt Avery. She had grown reckless, that green sort of abandon spring brought on, even though it was no longer March. Could it be she was maddened by all the rain, daffodil rain, rose rain, fish rain, all of it pouring down in this part of the Commonwealth.

"I guess I would say I wish things had turned out differently."

"Well, most people would say that, wouldn't they?" Jenny felt itchy under her skin. It was the rosemary she'd sprinkled on the rolls, most probably. "Given the wrong turns a person can make, wouldn't anyone feel the same?"

Elinor had come to call them to finish dinner, but she'd noticed something in the yard. She peered out through the glass panel beside the front door, then signaled to Jenny by tapping her cane on the hardwood floor. "There's someone out there. Someone's walking down the driveway."

Jenny went to have a look. The glass was bumpy, riddled with air bubbles, difficult to see through. All she could make out were shadows and the hedge of laurel. "There's no one."

"Do you realize you never agree with me?" Elinor said. "If I said it was noon, you wouldn't care if the sun was in the center of the sky. You'd tell me it was nighttime. You'd want to argue no matter what. He's right there! Look!"

Jenny looked again, and this time she squinted and went so close to the window her nose touched glass. Sure enough, the figure of a man had turned off Dead Horse Lane and was headed up the rutted driveway, stumbling a bit as he went. The sky was still blue, but the road was already dark. There was a humming sound, from the bees in the laurel.

Matt came and opened the door for a better view. At any other time he would have been distracted by Jenny's presence, but now he paid attention to the man on the road. He would know that walk anywhere. He knew it as well as his own.

"It's Will." From his tone anyone might think he was referring to a demon or a dog rather than his own brother. "He's jumped bail."

"Well, I hope he likes cold food," Elinor said. "At this rate, that's all we're going to have."

They could see now that Will was carrying a gym bag, clearly stuffed with clothes, as though he fully intended to stay. He strayed through several mud puddles, and by the time he got to the house, his shoes were covered with muck, his slacks were wet to the knee.

"Jesus. This road," he said. "It's worse than ever."

"I don't want you in my house, but if you insist on coming in, take off your shoes," Elinor directed.

Will leaned against the porch railing and removed his shoes.

"Someone could say hello," he suggested.

Matt and Jenny exchanged a look.

"Is something going on?" Will asked, puzzled.

"You tell us," Jenny said. "Haven't you been ordered to stay in Boston? And while we're at it, why haven't you called Stella? She phones you daily, and you're never home. Is there ever a time when you don't think solely of yourself?"

"How about you?" Will said to Matt. "Anything you'd like to berate me for?"

"You still have mud all over you," Matt said.

"I screwed up," Will admitted.

The sky was pink in the farthest horizon, mixed with a pure shade of blue, the sort of blue Elinor had been searching for, the color she believed she might have found at last. From where they stood, the air closest to them was all shadows, ink poured from the well.

"The house is gone," Will said.

"I sent Mrs. Ehrland the check for this month's rent. She can't kick you out," Jenny said. "Though I'm sure she wants to."

"No. No. Not the apartment. The little house. Someone stole it."

Will looked ragged standing there, shoeless, with mud on his pant legs. He looked like a man who'd come to beg for his dinner, a seeker after charity, hopeful that his luck would change, but fairly certain it wouldn't. From the way his brother was babbling, Matt wondered if he wasn't suffering from the DTs, perhaps he was going cold turkey. But, no, Matt could smell whisky; Will had recently had a drink, perhaps on the train. The evening train from Boston had been known for its bar car even back when they were boys, along with a bartender who never asked for ID. Sometimes, Will would ride the train back and forth to Boston all day, throwing back whisky sours, gin, and ale till he couldn't crawl in a straight line, let alone walk.

Stella, having heard her father's voice, ran out from the parlor. She threw her arms around Will. "Why didn't anyone tell me you were coming?"

"I'm not actually here," Will said. "And this isn't a real visit. Just a slight problem."

Matt recognized his brother's tone, the voice of disaster, of failure, of borrowed money and fights in the street, of getting fired, quitting school, screwing the downstairs neighbor, walking away from a dying woman because it was too hard to look at her, too depressing, too desperate, too real.

"Of course there's a problem. You haven't any shoes." Stella glared at her mother, as though it were Jenny's fault that Will was standing there in wet, muddy socks riddled with holes. "Are there slippers?"

"Front closet," Elinor said. "With or without pom-poms."

The light was fading so fast now that the pink laurel blossoms shone in the spreading pool of dark. There was the lazy end-of-the-day drone of bees who had drunk their fill. With the door opened, one large bumblebee mistook the front hall for the open air. It buzzed inside and landed on Matt's hand. When he waved it away, the bee rose from his skin slowly, reluctant, it appeared, to depart. Jenny stared as the bee continued to circle, drawn to him still. It was cold with the door thrown open, yet another trick of April, warm days, cool nights. All the same, the air was thick with spring fever. It was still the season of rash decisions, of bravery where before there was none, of vision, of blazing white heat at the coldest of times. Proof of love could be found in a single blade of grass, in what was kept and what was thrown away. Jenny thought about the bee that hadn't stung and the black carved angel on the town common. She thought about the fact that there had been two boys standing on the lawn on the morning of her thirteenth birthday, with only one dream between them.

There was a faint buzzing sound inside Jenny's head. That was the way it had all begun on the morning of her birthday. Once upon a time she had been absolutely sure of whom she was meant to love. She had seen what she wanted to see, not what was before her. She hadn't stopped to turn around twice. Patience, that was the illegible ingredient in nine-frogs stew, that was what Jenny had missed entirely.

"Someone stole it?" Matt said to his brother. He had just realized the impact of this theft.

Will knew what his brother thought of him. It had been clear since that horrible New Year's party, when he'd been too drunk to think straight and had gotten involved with one of his students. Well, Matt had every right to his disdain, but it was Jenny whose disappointment Will dreaded. Oh, they were over, he knew that, but she was due some consideration after all the years she'd put in. He fully expected her to be furious. She had every right to be. He had allowed a stranger into their house, he had put his needs first, selling his daughter's safety for five hundred dollars that he had only possessed for an instant. The payoff had evaporated in his greedy hands, like smoke, leaving nothing but ashes.

Will looked at Jenny and for the first time he hid nothing from her. They'd been together so long, he owed her this at least: a single moment of honesty.

"Baby," he said, the enormity of his failures crashing down on him as he stood beneath the laurel in his wet socks. He could see his reflection in the glass panels on the side of the door to Cake House: he appeared to be underwater, a drowning man with nothing to hold on to but a single shred of truth. "I made a mistake."

"I understand completely," Jenny told him. "So did I."

THE CURE

I.

*H*AVING LIVED IN ONE PLACE FOR THIRTEEN years, Stella was now forced to move yet again. They had all agreed this was the best course of action; with the model house stolen and fears raised, it was decided that Stella must leave Cake House. But where would she go? An Avery cousin in New York was an option, or boarding school in Rhode Island or Connecticut. But Stella refused to leave Massachusetts. She was not about to enroll in a third school in a single year. No matter the circumstances, she planned to finish ninth grade at Unity High School. Let there be flood or famine, parental anxiety or real danger, she was staying put. For the first time in her life she was earning all A's; she enjoyed going to the clinic and the rest home with Dr. Stewart. And there was her personal life to think of. What would Hap do without her? Who would Jimmy Elliot follow around if Stella left town, whose window would he throw pebbles at late in the evening, when darkness was falling and the warblers began to sing the last of their songs?

"I'll be no trouble to anyone," Stella said. "I'll be a mouse," she vowed.

There were few people in town the Sparrows could turn to; those who believe the best neighbors are those who don't speak to each other have few allies to call upon in times of trouble. But Liza Hull was known for her big heart. When Jenny phoned to ask if Stella could move in with her, Liza didn't hesitate. In a matter of hours, Stella was ensconced in the guest room above the tea house. Oh, scent of vanilla, of soapsuds, of Assam tea. Oh, room with privacy, with a lock on the door, with a view of the plane trees. If this was charity, it was fine with Stella.

Liza hadn't even asked any questions, she'd simply made up the bed with clean sheets, then showed Stella how to regulate the water in the tub, which had a tendency to be too hot or too cold. Stella was down to a few treasured possessions—just enough to fill her backpack and a shopping bag—still, she was given an old oak dresser to use, one that had belonged to Liza's grandmother, the one who as a girl had written down Elisabeth Sparrow's best recipes.

"I'm going to love having you as a guest," Liza announced after Stella was all moved in. She hugged the girl, and although Stella wasn't much for such shows of affection, it was hard to dislike anything about Liza. As for the tea house, it was a fine place to live, except in the mornings, when a steady stream of customers began to arrive at 7:00 A.M., so that Stella could not sleep, even with the quilt over her head. There was no way to avoid the sound of dishes rattling or water running through the pipes every time the dishwasher was turned on. Perhaps it would have been impossible to sleep late anyway, all those pain-in-the-neck warblers chattering in the lilacs outside her window, the bravest coming to perch on the window ledges, tapping their beaks against the glass, drawn to the tea house in the hopes of crusts and crumbs.

Soon, there was the weekend to look forward to. Stella and Juliet Aronson had made plans, none of which Stella had mentioned to her mother, who had never approved of Juliet. True, Juliet was always surprising; she wasn't like other people and she had no desire to be one of the crowd. The last time they'd spoken, for instance, Stella had confided she was confused about which boy in town was her heart's desire. Did she follow her brain, her heart, her overheated pulse rate?

"Stick a pin in a candle and light it," Juliet had advised. "When the flame burns down to the pin, your true love will walk through the door."

Stella had laughed. "Very scientific." Preposterous, of course. Still, it might be worth a try. Perhaps just once. "What sort of candle?"

"A plain old candle and a plain old pin. It works every time."

Stella had found a candle and an old brass holder in the kitchen; these she kept in the tea house dining room, ready to light should there come a time when she wanted to try Juliet's silly game. But what if Jimmy Elliot was the one who walked through the door, would it mean she was bound to him? And if it was Hap, would she be disappointed?

At last it was Friday, the day Juliet was set to arrive. Juliet would be cutting classes at the Rabbit School and arriving on the three o'clock train. Thankfully, Jenny would not be working on the weekend; she had the time off, but still would be busy, for there was plenty to do at Cake House now that Elinor was failing. Who would have ever imagined it would be just the two of them in the house by the lake? That there'd be so many errands to run? Food shopping at the market in Hamilton, laundry to do in that horrid old washing machine in the scullery, chicken and rice to cook for Argus, whose stomach was more and more sensitive.

By Friday, Jenny was simply wiped out. Her feet hurt from standing most of the day, her hands burned from the soapy dishwater, and she found herself shivering when the wind blew through the open window beside the cash register. It was a dark, rainy morning, which usually meant a brisk business at the tea house. People wanting to put off going to work, lingering over another cup of coffee or tea, something to warm them against a day of wind and chill, puddles and hard work. *Stone rain*, Elinor called it, the sort of cloudburst that didn't care about the state of humanity, with sheets that poured down so hard it hurt, enough precipitation to flood side roads and gutters and lakes. The rain had kept Jenny up half the night, hitting against the old slate roof. She kept thinking of Matt Avery, even when she didn't want to. She was sleepless over him, bound up with some sort of dumb yearning she couldn't seem to put a stop to. Even when the sun rose, there'd been little difference in the slate-gray sky. The one bright spot of the morning was that Stella had stopped at the counter for a quick breakfast before rushing off to school.

"This brioche is great," Stella said as she happily munched and poured herself a cup of tea.

Drinking tea was something new. Favoring brioche over cinnamon rolls was, too. Jenny had the sense that with each move away from her, her daughter grew happier. Stella glowed in the dark dining room, brighter even than the candles Jenny had lit on the sideboard.

"Liza! Your brioche is the best thing in the world," Stella called when Liza came into the dining room with two blackberry pies for the display case. Before going back to the kitchen, Liza came to give Stella a dish of butter and some of her homemade apple cider jam.

"Did you tell your mother about your weekend plans?" she asked.

"I'll talk to her," Stella assured Liza, fingers crossed behind her back.

"Talk to me about what?"

Jenny had returned from taking a breakfast order from that

ill-humored Eli Hathaway. "Don't give me any health food," Eli had demanded. The old taxi driver looked about a hundred years old in the murky dove-colored light. "Strong coffee and two jelly doughnuts. That's what I want," Eli had said. "Don't try to talk me out of it."

There were no jelly doughnuts, and Jenny sincerely hoped the raspberry strudel would suffice. Eli's vision was failing and he probably wouldn't even notice the difference.

"Talk to you about my helping out here on weekends," Stella said.

Thankfully, Liza had gone back to the kitchen and Stella did not have to actually admit to Juliet's impending visit. But lies weren't so easy to tell for a novice, and Stella began to cough as the words stuck in her throat. Jenny patted her daughter's back and poured her a glass of water.

"Not necessary," Jenny said. "School's more important."

"But Cynthia works here."

Stella and Jenny exchanged a look.

"Let me guess." Stella's expression had soured so that she looked a bit green around the edges. "Working here is good enough for Cynthia, but it's not good enough for me. You never like my friends, do you?" Stella grabbed her backpack and headed for the door.

"I do like Cynthia. I just think she's troubled, that's all."

"Everybody's troubled," Stella informed her mother. "Including you."

Here was the argument, about to fall harder than the stone rain outside, about to hurt just as much, maybe more, causing wounds that might or might not be permanent. But just as their argument was about to become a full-fledged fight, the strangest thing happened, and as it did, their disagreement fell away as though it were a shadow. For there on the highboy, beside the sugar bowls, one of the lit candles flickered high into the dark air. There seemed to be a bit of silver, a radiant light. Outside, the stone rain fell harder, but here there was a brilliant spark. The pin Stella had stuck in the wax.

"Where'd you get the candles?" Stella had a panicky feeling, as though she worked a charm all wrong.

"In a drawer behind the napkins. It was so dark when I first got in. There'll be a dozen turtles in the driveway today when I get home."

Jenny had stopped wiping down the counter. She had noticed the spark as well. The rain fell like a river of rocks, a thousand hard drops that were as clear as the first ice that covered Hourglass Lake in winter. Stella was holding on to her backpack and her umbrella and a yellow rain slicker Liza had lent her. The rain hit against the screen door and splashed drops at her, cool and sweet and unforgiving.

When the light touches the pin, your beloved will walk in. Close the door, you need not see more.

"That's how you'll know it's true love," Juliet Aronson had told her. "You'll know for sure."

The fire had reached the pin, but nothing had happened. So far no one had appeared, and maybe that was just as well. Stella couldn't control who would walk through the door any more than she could choose whom she would fall in love with. At least she could now tell Juliet she had tried the silly game.

"I'd better go," Stella said.

"I could drive you." Jenny wrote out Eli Hathaway's bill. She'd been right; he hadn't complained about the strudel.

"No. You're working. Don't worry. I can take care of myself. I won't drown."

Still, it was dark as night, the parking lot illuminated only by the headlights on a truck pulling in. Matt Avery ran through the rain, in his old duck-weather jacket and his leaky work boots. That oak had another reprieve, it seemed. This was no day to cut down a tree.

Matt let the door slam behind him, and he stood in the threshold, wiping the rain from his face.

"Hey, there," he said when he almost bumped into his niece. She was standing right there, mouth open like a fish's. The flame was burning the pin and she saw the way Matt turned to look at her mother.

"See you." Stella was actually embarrassed; she could use a dose of the cold, windy weather. She opened the screen and let the rain splatter into the tea room.

"Do you need a ride to school?" Matt said.

"You've got more important things to do," Stella told her uncle.

He laughed. "Such as?"

"Whatever. But good luck. You'll need it."

"Teenagers," Matt said when he took a seat at the counter.

"They're crazy," Jenny agreed. She poured Matt a cup of coffee, but she didn't meet his eyes. She felt quite crazy herself, in the dim tea room light with Matt staring at her and Eli Hathaway clinking his spoon against his water glass as a way of calling for another slice of raspberry strudel.

"Come on, girl," Eli called. "I'm starving to death. I'll have another jelly doughnut."

Girl, Jenny thought. She laughed at the notion. "I thought you had diabetes," she called back to Eli. Eventually, she'd have to look at Matt, so she did so now. Outside, a chorus of frogs called from the puddle beside the steps. The only other sound was of the rain falling, the sort of rain that occurs in dreams, endless, invisible, the pulse of the universe.

"How's your brother?" Jenny said as she cut a last piece of strudel for Eli and handed Matt a menu.

"Ah, Will." Matt added cream to his coffee. "Always Will. We can never seem to get away from him, can we?"

They both thought this over as Jenny delivered Eli Hathaway's order. Will, it turned out, had moved in with his brother. He and

Henry Elliot had gone to the judge and explained the theft of the little house. Will had cooperated, of course, and had described the individual who had claimed to be a reporter and might easily be a murderer, so that an artist could draw a likeness. Now, Matt informed Jenny that the judge had decided to allow Will to live in Unity while the case was pending, in his brother's custody.

"So you are your brother's keeper?"

"There's no place else for him to live."

That rain could make you dizzy, it really could. Matt recalled that in Anton Hathaway's diary, sent to his mother after the boy fell in battle, Anton had noted that the thing the men in his troop dreaded most was rain. That's when they were most homesick; there were those who had bravely faced down blood and bullets who would call out their mothers' names when the thunder began and torrents of rain began to fall.

"I paid the rent." Jenny was livid. She sent Matt's order for rye toast and eggs, over easy, to the kitchen with the new fellow Liza had hired to wash dishes and take out the trash. "I don't understand. I sent a check long before the first of the month."

"You sent it, but Will cashed it. Apparently, the model house isn't the only thing he's managed to lose. The rent money's what he's been living on. I went over there to collect some belongings. Mrs. Ehrland said to say hello."

"Oh, great. Lovely."

Jenny poured herself a cup of coffee. The Harmon brothers, Joe and Dennis, came in, waving, stomping the mud off their boots. Jenny had been in class with Joe Harmon all through elementary school. She could not believe that she had been at the tea house long enough to know both men's breakfast orders by heart: one bagel, one rye toast, two cheese omelets, cooked through.

"Did Stella seem a little odd to you today?" Jenny asked as she put in the Harmons' order.

"Maybe she has a test. High school's got its pressures."

Every time Matt was in Jenny's presence he had the feeling that he was dreaming, still asleep in his bed, far from the customary emptiness of his waking life. Jenny, on the other hand, so accustomed to dreaming other people's dreams, had begun to have her own dreams as well. Just last night there was a maze of green hedges that went on endlessly, so that she'd had to run, breathless, ready to fall.

Matt had begun to talk about his day—he had to drive into Boston to collect Will's belongings, now stored in Mrs. Ehrland's cellar. Hopefully, he would get back to work on the old tree by the end of the week. If it wasn't rain that had slowed him down, it was errands, other jobs, and then, of course, there was a hive of bees inside the trunk, honeybees drunk on the pollen of spring from the field of red clover behind Lockhart Avenue. By then Jenny was staring at Matt. In last night's dream there had been bees in the hedges, on every single leaf.

"Are you okay?" Matt said when he saw her expression.

"Oh, yeah." Jenny got his breakfast and watched him eat. The food disappeared. He was almost through and she was still curious about something.

"The other evening when Will came back, you were standing on the porch. A bee settled on you, but you waved it away. You weren't the least bit worried."

"Bees don't usually sting you if you're polite to them. On the other hand, if you curse at them, they'll come after you. I've seen it happen."

Jenny laughed. "I cursed them once. To keep them out of my mother's garden. It worked till she got wise to what I'd done. She concocted some brandy cake and they all came flying back. Double what I'd sent away."

Matt loved the sound of her laughter; it reminded him of that day on the lawn, when everything was green and he fell in love with her. He wanted to give her something, but the only thing he had was his knowledge of the town. He turned to local history, searching for a tidbit Jenny might appreciate. "If you have a wedding, you're supposed to offer the bees some cake as well, for luck. Elisabeth Sparrow did it on her wedding day, and she stayed married for sixty years."

"Now you tell me," Jenny said. "After my marriage is over."

They stared at each other. The candle had burned down, past the pin, past the point of returning to the way things had been.

"Maybe that was luck."

He was becoming a compulsive talker, like that foolish Farmer Hathaway, who blamed himself for what happened to Rebecca. Charles Hathaway could never stop talking about his mistakes, so that in time everyone in town who kept a journal took note of how they'd come to avoid him. Matt gulped the last of his coffee and put on his jacket. The one thing he didn't want to do on a murky April day when the roads were sure to be flooded was to drive his brother into Boston and back again.

"I think I've just worked in so many gardens in this town that the bees know me," he told Jenny as he set out to leave. "That's why I've never been stung." It was Will who had the fear of bees, who'd been prey to allergic reactions, Will who all the same had gotten everything he'd ever wanted. But in this one circumstance, Matt had been the lucky one, and standing there at the counter, watching him duck into the rain, Jenny couldn't help but wonder why she hadn't seen it was him all along.

II.

THE TRAIN WAS ON TIME, but Stella had been asked to clean up the science lab, and so she was late. She had to run all the way to the station, splashing through puddles, winded by the time she arrived. The rain had eased to a drizzle, but the sky was still as dingy as steam. Juliet Aronson sat on one of the green wooden benches out on the platform, smoking a cigarette and sipping from a cup of coffee she'd bought at the vending machine inside the station. Juliet had her hair pulled back and her lipstick had worn off; leaving the city for parts unknown made her nervous, and she'd been biting her lips. She was wearing a black dress she'd borrowed from her aunt's closet and a silk blazer that was too lightweight for the day's cool, damp weather.

"Finally," Juliet announced when she spied Stella. "I'm freezing my ass off."

Juliet tossed her cigarette away and the girls hugged each other. Then Juliet held Stella at arm's length in order to examine her. "Oh, my God! You're a country bumpkin."

Stella looked down at her yellow rain gear, her heavy lace-up boots, her waterlogged jeans. Her hair had frizzed up in the humidity and she hadn't a touch of makeup on her pale face. She had strapped on a backpack filled with books and test tubes to collect more water samples.

"Bumpkin sounds like a bad thing."

Juliet laughed. "Don't worry. We'll fix you. Although I seriously can't believe you actually live here." Juliet grabbed her overnight case, Gucci, stolen from Saks. "Good gracious. You have trees out here."

The trees had leafed out after the past week of drenching rains. Now, when the girls looked upward, the sky itself seemed green. Stella usually slopped through puddles, but Juliet Aronson was wearing good leather boots, so they avoided the common and walked through town. Stella had homework, but she didn't care. She felt lit up inside. It was Friday and Juliet was finally here and the rain was ending.

Juliet sniffed and wrinkled her nose. "It smells like something around here."

Stella laughed. "Mud?"

"Ah, mud. The bumpkin perfume. We have got some changes to make in this town."

They went to the pizza place and ordered four slices, then sat across from each other in a red vinyl booth. Juliet leaned her elbows on the table. Stella hadn't noticed before that her friend had a nervous tick above her eye.

"Did you try the love-foretelling thing?"

"It didn't work." Stella recalled the look on her mother's face when Matt walked into the tea shop. *Close the door, you need not see more.* "At least, not for me. I think I screwed it up."

"That just means you haven't decided who it is you want to be in love with you. So when do I get to meet the famous Hap, so brilliant, so fascinating? I can compare him to the infamous Jimmy, who sounds like a dimwit."

Stella hadn't exactly imagined Juliet meeting anyone in town. Rather, she'd thought of this visit confined to a bubble, rising above the rooftops and trees so there was no real contact with local residents and fewer occasions for Juliet to critique her life.

Juliet had dropped her voice to a whisper. "Is that guy staring at us?"

It was the pizza delivery guy. Stella recognized him from the night he'd made a delivery to the doctor's house. He must have been fairly new at the job, because Jessica Harmon, married to Joe, the older of the Harmon brothers, and who managed the shop, was going over a map, giving the deliveryman directions.

"I swear he was staring at us. Yuck. He's probably thirty years old. Don't look at him," Juliet hissed when Stella turned to gaze over her shoulder. "We have other things to think about. Tonight we can look through your wardrobe and toss out everything that doesn't work. That ought to debumpkin you."

"I don't have a wardrobe. I have three pairs of jeans, four T-shirts, and four sweaters. Oh, and some socks."

Juliet grinned. She reached into her overnight case and pulled out several packets of Rit dye. "Black," she said. "Don't leave home without it. By tonight, you'll have a wardrobe."

Hap Stewart caught up with them soon after they'd been to the pharmacy, where Juliet had managed to swipe a tube of long-lash mascara and a pair of hoop earrings.

"Always in style," she said when she pocketed the earrings.

"It's not the same here," Stella informed her friend as they walked down Main Street. "Everybody knows everybody else. You can't just steal."

"But I just did." Juliet made a face. "Little Miss Honesty."

"Hey, wait up." It was Hap loping across the common.

Stella had a sinking feeling as he approached. Two universes were about to collide, and she could guess which one would come out on top.

"Hap Stewart." Juliet looked him up and down, considering.

Stella noticed that Hap looked like a bumpkin as well, wearing an oversized brown jacket and muddy work boots, with his hair curling foolishly and that huge grin of his. For no reason at all, she thought about the expression on Jimmy Elliot's face that day they watched the doctor's horse, how puzzled he'd seemed, how he'd made her want to laugh out loud.

"You've just turned fifteen, you plan to go to Columbia University, if accepted, not that you're worried because you can always go to the state college. You're interested in biology, but your real dream is to become a photographer. You're six-two, your hair is brown, but it looks blond in the sunlight. You don't like the sight of blood, you have a great smile. Hapgood was your mother's family name." All of the information that Stella had slowly revealed to Juliet over the past few weeks had now been reeled back out in a single whoosh. Juliet turned to Stella, who seemed stunned. "Did I get everything?"

"Pretty much." Stella couldn't bring herself to look at Hap, who now knew how much she had confided in Juliet. Would he feel betrayed? But, no, this release of information worked two ways and Hap was still grinning.

"Juliet Aronson." They continued on across the green, and now that they were with Hap, Juliet didn't seem to mind that her boots were soaked by the wet grass. "You'll be fifteen on July twenty-seventh. Your mother's in Framingham Prison for Women, and you're not certain what you believe constitutes a crime of passion. You like black clothes, cigarettes, gold earrings, older men. You're far smarter than most people give you credit for. You're beautiful."

Stella looked up; that last part was Hap's own observation.

"In regard to the older-man reference? That's not always the case."

Juliet grinned as well. Stella noticed there was no mention of bumpkins now that Hap was around. Stella glanced over at him. He actually had a blade of grass in his mouth. How much more of a bumpkin could anyone be?

"I like her," Hap confided when Juliet was out of earshot, stopped by a parked truck to peer into the side-view mirror as she tried out her newly stolen mascara.

"Do you?" Stella said coldly. "Well, great."

After Hap had taken off for home, Stella and Juliet walked toward the tea house. "What a strange person," Juliet said of Hap. "I like him." She must have then noticed Stella's cool expression. "For you, I mean. God, not for me."

They had reached the corner of East Main. Liza had lit a fire and a plume of smoke rose into the damp air. Everything was gray, and perhaps that was why Juliet didn't notice Jimmy Elliot on the corner. He'd biked over with his sister, but had stayed on after Cynthia had begun her shift, the way he did most days, acting as if he were looking at something important, when the only thing out in front of him was the foggy air.

Stella had already decided. If Jimmy was there, she would not mention his presence. She would not say *See that boy over there, the one with the dark eyes? He spends a lot of time staring at me, and for reasons I don't understand, I'm staring back.* For the first time, she didn't want anyone's opinion but her own. She opened the door for Juliet, and waited until Juliet went inside, before she quickly turned and waved. Spotted, Jimmy sped down the street, right through the deep puddles on East Main.

"Very Hansel and Gretel," Juliet said when they hung up their jackets inside the tea house. There was the spicy scent of the apple turnovers that Liza had recently baked. "I'll bet if you walk into this place, you never walk out. You're charmed into staying for the rest of your natural life."

Thankfully, Stella's mother was already gone for the day; Stella had wisely been watching the clock to make sure they didn't arrive until after 4:30. Her mother needn't know her every move, her every friend, her every desire. She needn't know anything at all.

When they went into the kitchen, only Liza was there to greet them. Liza was wearing a white cook's jacket over her blue jeans and sweatshirt; her hair was tied back and she wore a kerchief. "Too bad! You just missed your mom."

Stella and Juliet looked at each other and tried not to giggle.

"Rats." Juliet had the ability to sound sincere in the most frivolous of times. "And I was so looking forward to seeing her."

"Instead you've got me." Liza smiled and had them sit down for a snack. "You can be my test cases. New recipe. Actually, old recipe. One of Elisabeth Sparrow's."

"My great-great-gran," Stella explained.

It was curds-and-cream with raspberry sauce, which the girls deemed delicious, although they suggested the name be changed if Elisabeth's dish was added to the menu. No one liked the notion of curds these days. Pudding, perhaps, or, better yet, mousse.

"Have you heard about your father?" Liza asked. "He's moving in with Matt." Liza slipped off her kerchief and ran her fingers through her hair, which once had been auburn but had faded to a dull brown. "He's probably already there. Moved in to his old room."

"Yippee," Stella said. "I'm so glad he's staying. He's wonderful," she told Juliet. "I want you to meet him."

"Then let's go over there tonight. We can get ourselves invited for dinner. I never got the chance to meet him in Boston. He was never around."

They began to plan their evening, forgetting that Liza was there until Juliet elbowed Stella. *Look*, she mouthed. *Lovestruck.*

"Why don't you come with us?" Stella asked Liza. "You could show us the way. I've never even been to my uncle's house."

"Oh, no." Liza grew flushed. She wiped at her eyes as though she'd had a bit of curd in the corners that caused her to tear up. "I couldn't."

"But you know what we should do first?" Juliet Aronson knew a fair share about being vulnerable. She knew that people's emotions showed in their faces even when they didn't think they were giving anything away. "We should dye your hair," she told Liza. "I'll bet you used to be a redhead."

"That was a long time ago," Liza demurred.

Juliet reached into her overnight case. Along with the black clothing dye, she had brought along several boxes of Egyptian henna. You never could tell when someone might need a makeover, as Liza Hull certainly did. Why, she had pastry flour streaked through her hair. She probably hadn't worn lipstick for years. Anything they did to her would be an improvement.

"Oh, please, Liza," Stella begged. "And if you don't like it, it can always be undone."

Actually, it would take a good three months of shampooing to get the color out, but Juliet nodded in agreement. "It's perfect timing. It will just be us and Stella's uncle and father. And who cares what they think?"

It was a simple trap, but one that Liza fell right into: Juliet grinned when she saw that Liza's complexion grew even more florid. Yes, indeed, there was definitely something there. When they'd finally talked Liza into trying the henna, and had left to race up the narrow twisted stairway for some shampoo and towels, Juliet Aronson was chortling. She loved it when she was right.

"Ten to one Liza is in love with your uncle," she crooned. "Ah, love. No one is immune."

Stella stopped on the narrowest section of stair and allowed Juliet to go first. Standing there in the dim stairway, she understood why Liza would allow them to pour henna all over her hair and change her utterly. It was true and lasting and unrequited love that was at the bottom of all this, the sort of ardor for which some people said there was no remedy, but which others believed could be turned around in an instant, so that someone like Stella might find herself looking out her window before she went to bed each night, furious when she spied Jimmy Elliot sitting out there beyond the plane trees, but even more disappointed on those occasions when he failed to appear.

III.

AT THIS RAINY, green time of the year, the snapping turtles had already laid clutches of eggs in every muddy hollow in the driveway and the lawn. Jenny had even found some beside the kitchen door, which she'd covered with handfuls of grass in the hopes that the opossums and raccoons wouldn't have those poor kitchen eggs for dinner. Jenny had already found such sorrowful leftovers on Rebecca Sparrow's dirt path; some animal had gotten to a clutch of eggs and left only the rubbery cases, split in two, emptied and shimmering like pearls. Poor mother turtle. Jenny had wondered if she would know what she'd lost when she returned. Would she tend to the ruined eggs, hopeful still, or would she have already moved on, back to the depths of the lake, back to the water lilies and the duck grass and the reeds?

Every night, Jenny went to the bedroom where Stella had been sleeping before she moved over to Liza's apartment. She hadn't changed the sheets because Stella's impression had been caught in the creases of the pillowcase, and her scent was there as well, a mixture of resentment and water lilies. Some people swore that when you let a daughter go, she was sure to come back, like the sparrows which perched on the window ledge, begging for crumbs, for crusts, for kindness. But Stella wouldn't even come to the phone when Jenny called over to the tea house. She was busy, Liza was quick to explain, but Jenny had heard Stella's muffled voice in the background. *Just tell her I'm not here.*

She had wanted the opposite of what she'd had with her own mother, but somehow it had turned out the same. The same words unspoken, the pain held on to, all tenderness invisible, like ink that has drifted off a page to leave only a blank white sheet. Just last night, Jenny had gone for a walk. It was lonelines that got her walking, and perhaps it was loneliness that drew her to the Avery house, although the path might have come naturally to her, for she'd taken this route so very often as a girl. Past Lockhart Avenue, past the old oak, the most rotten section of which was now held down by wire, like a captured giant that might take to roaming the streets if it were ever freed.

As a girl, Jenny had always felt expectation rising within her as she walked to the Averys'; now she felt it again. She crossed the common, passing the black angel that was Matt Avery's favorite. Thinking about him, even for a moment, made it difficult to breathe. It was so silly that she tried a child's trick to ward off whatever was happening to her and began to count to one hundred. She tried not to think about Matt. For reasons she didn't understand, she imagined a pin, silver, shining. She imagined she was falling right through the dark, her way lit by a candle, when in fact all she was doing was treading across the town green. There was a faint breeze and the scent of the plane trees rose into the air, spicy and damp.

In town, the shops were closed except for the Pizza Palace, whose blinking neon light cast pools of blue and yellow onto the sidewalk. In Jenny's day there had been an ice cream parlor in its place, Grandpa's, run by the Harmon family. There had been cardboard tubs of vanilla bean and butter pecan, and Jenny had worked there for three summers, good practice, it turned out, for the manager's job at Bailey's when she moved to Cambridge. Before she could stop herself, she thought about Matt sitting at the counter of Baileys, watching her work, ordering sundae after sundae when he'd preferred bread and butter all along. She thought about the look on his face when he'd walked through the door of the tea house on that rainy day when the rain fell in sheets, the stone rain that filled all the gutters and the streets.

She hadn't been back to the Averys' for more than twenty years; it looked smaller than she'd remembered. But there was the old slate path, the white fence, the perennial boarder in which Catherine had taken such pride, a collection which Elinor Sparrow had always dismissed as the typical hodgepodge of the unsophisticated gardener, a jumble of phlox and daisies and snapdragons. Jenny stopped beside a holly tree Catherine had planted to ensure there would be green in her garden all year long. She could see inside the window; there was the exact same furniture, the love seat where she and Will had kissed until they were burning up, until they had no choice but to go further, which they finally did one summer evening when Catherine was out at her bridge club. There was the table under which they'd made love one night when there was a terrible thunderstorm. Catherine and Matt had been home, asleep in their beds, and Jenny was so terrified she and Will would be caught that she'd broken out in hives.

Now, there were dinner guests, quite a large gathering. Jenny stepped closer to the window, edging through the straggly phlox. Matt and Will were at dinner with a red-haired woman and two girls. Jenny had her nose pressed against the glass before she realized it was Stella and that horrible friend of hers, Juliet Aronson. Will was at the table, offering up a toast. He'd had a haircut and he'd shaved, but he still looked tired and far too thin. He looked nothing like the boy she used to wait for in this very place. She would remain here, hidden, until at last he appeared and they could sneak out to Rebecca Sparrow's shed, or, when the weather was fine, to the cool, flat rock formation called the Table and Chairs, which they rested upon in order to look up at the stars, kissing until the stone beneath them grew so hot mosquitoes lighting on the granite burst into flame in an instant.

The red-haired woman in the dining room at the Averys' was Liza Hull, although she looked quite changed. She looked pretty in the candlelight; prettier still when she threw back her head to laugh. Maybe it was the vantage point which altered things, or perhaps the night air, the dark, the scent of phlox, the aroma of something old and new twisted together. Liza had brought a cake, and there was a bottle of white wine. Even the girls had splashes of wine in their glasses. They were most likely toasting Will and his return; they were actually applauding him. Only Matt stood in the background, leaning against the hutch that had belonged to his grandmother. It was here that Catherine displayed her prized Minton pottery. There was a dish which resembled stalks of asparagus, a plate which appeared to be made out of starfish and mollusks, a pitcher that seemed to be lily pad after lily pad, with a frog for a handle. Matt looked up, past the dining table, past the celebration, out into the yard where Jenny stood beside the holly.

Perhaps a branch moved, perhaps it was something else that caught his eye. Whatever it was, Matt seemed to spy her, and as soon as he did, Jenny took off. She ran because of the mistakes she had made, because she'd been so foolish as a girl and so dead wrong as a woman, because she hadn't known one dream from another, because she had finally fallen in love. She ran until she was forced to stop, then doubled over to catch her breath before jogging the rest of the way home, through the common that now seemed far too dark, through the shadows the plane trees cast into twisted shapes on the walkways, all the time thinking: *I've thrown it all away. Now I have nothing at all.*

ON SUNDAY, when Stella had gone off to walk her friend Juliet to the train, and Cynthia Elliot had pedaled off on her bicycle to write her final English paper on her chosen poet, Sylvia Plath, due the following morning, Liza Hull closed the tea house and locked the doors. The handyman didn't work on Sundays and neither did Jenny, and that was just as well. Liza Hull was embarrassed by what she was about to do, although not so embarrassed as to put the thought away. She drew the curtains and then she sat down at the counter and took a photograph of herself with one of those Polaroid cameras she'd picked up at the pharmacy.

She breathed lightly while the film developed right before her eyes, magicking her into existence. Was that really Liza Hull? The woman with the red hair, the shining eyes, the smile that transformed her face? Where was her white coat, her kerchief, her stained clothes, her sacrifice, her sorrow? None of it had developed on this square of film. There was only a woman smiling on the first day of May. It was Liza, it truly was. Liza, who had fallen in love.

Liza Hull's grandmother had operated the tea house until her ninety-second year; she had known Elisabeth Sparrow when she was a little girl and Elisabeth Sparrow's hair had already turned white. Granny Hull had once told Liza that, long ago, baking bread was referred to as a "mystery." Mystery it was, much the same as turning straw into gold. Flour and water and yeast became sustenance. One thing became another, transmuted, as Liza Hull now understood she herself had become. It was alchemy, nothing less: pieces to a whole, straw into gold, flour becoming bread, she who was ordinary made beautiful, overnight.

Liza went upstairs to her bedroom and opened the closet. There was a full-length mirror hung on the back of the door, one she'd always avoided in the past, artfully draping scarves and shawls over the glass. Now she removed all of the fabric. She took off her clothes and stared at herself. She saw the mystery of one thing becoming another right there in the glass.

Liza reached for a green dress that had always made her think of spring, and slipped it on. She had always been resigned to her own bad luck, but that was about to change. She knew it Friday night, when Will had walked her and the girls home from dinner at the Averys' house. The girls had run on ahead, giggling, racing toward the common. Liza had told Will he should turn and go home; an escort wasn't necessary, not in Unity. But Will had insisted; the walk would do him good, and besides, he joked, this way he could leave his brother with the cleaning up. As they strolled, Will didn't bother to try and charm Liza. He was too tired for that, and he was comfortable with Liza Hull. He'd known her forever, after all, since kindergarten, not that he'd ever paid her the least bit of attention. She was simply there, good old Liza; why, he'd never even noticed that her hair was red until tonight.

"I made a right mess of everything," he said.

They were walking toward the old oak, the one that would have to wait to be cut down, since Matt had already begun spring cleanup for most of his customers. They stopped and looked at the huge branches; the ones wired to the trunk so they wouldn't crack off in a storm looked especially sad.

"They call these trees of mercy," Liza said.

"Really?" Will looked over at Liza, ready to make a joke, but, no, she was serious.

"Maybe if you ask the tree to forgive you, you won't feel so bad."

"Forgive me?"

Liza had smiled and nodded. She'd come here often; she knew what it was like to feel that you'd done everything wrong.

Will approached the tree. He was sure he wouldn't do such a foolish thing, it just wasn't in his nature, but then he looked over his shoulder at Liza. He got down on bended knee. "Forgive me," he said. "Forgive me for being a fool, for placing myself above all others, forgive me for all of my lies."

He realized that Liza had come to kneel beside him. They were on the concrete sidewalk, on the corner of Lockhart and East Main, but it was as dark here as any woods. There was only a sliver of moon in the sky. They could hear the girls up ahead of them, making whooping noises as they ran across the green. It was a starry night, and although Will never noticed such things, he noticed now.

"You are forgiven," Liza said. "At least by me."

The external world had maps and signs, but none of these would do for a man who'd lost his way as thoroughly as Will had. A man like Will needed absolute faith, in something, in someone. He needed peace of mind and someone to believe in him, and that was not so easily found.

"I'm forgiven?" He tested the words to see how they might feel in his mouth. He'd never even looked at Liza Hull, and now he couldn't get enough of her. Now, he believed every word she said.

Out on the green, Juliet was sneaking a cigarette. The orange light of the ash burned with every intake, a single firefly. "Well, I was wrong. Your uncle's not the one Liza has the hots for. It's your father."

The girls had perched on the Civil War monument.

"You think Liza's in love with my father?" Stella had laughed out loud. "Oh, my God, you are so wrong. Liza? She's like his exact opposite."

"Thereby proving nothing. Opposites attract, honey pie. Don't you know that? It's some scientific fact, like the way magnets work."

"Polar opposites." Stella could feel the cold of the monument right through her jeans, dyed black that very afternoon in the tub in Liza's bathroom, along with all the rest of her wardrobe. Even her underwear was black now, along with her socks, her T-shirts, her flannel bathrobe.

"Exactly. That's why they're drawn to each other. Each makes up what the other lacks." Juliet had stubbed out her cigarette on the ledge of the monument, leaving Stella to clear away the ashes with the palm of her hand.

Stella was still thinking about polar opposites on Sunday, while Liza was studying herself in the mirror, while Juliet smoked the last cigarette in the pack taken from her aunt's purse. Stella and Juliet were headed to the train station and for once they hadn't much to say.

Polar opposites. Definition: a magnetic force that was uncontrollable. Stella knew that magnetic fields could affect human behavior; there were cases of unusual strength during storms, for instance, of women who lifted cars off their baby's carriages, of men who picked up ponies and carried them to safety when rivers rose. But could such things affect love? Or was it another case of the pin and the candle, a foolish test to measure a phenomenon that could never be understood?

Stella recalled a case Hap showed her in a science journal, the story of a man who could set things on fire with his breath. He was tested again and again. Each time he held a cloth to his mouth and breathed, the fabric would burst into flame. Were some people made of fire, others of water, or earth, or air? Were there those a person was drawn to, no matter how much she might fight her attraction, and others that repelled, no matter how they might try to please?

"This is truly one of the bumpkinest places I have ever been to," Juliet decreed. She was looking down the road. Hap Stewart had said he would try to meet them, but he hadn't showed up. "It wins the prize for most hicks contained within a square mile."

They could hear the whistle of the train in the distance as they approached the station. Juliet fished her return ticket out of the bag. There was still no sign of Hap. For once, the sun was shining. The air was so clear it nearly hurt to breathe.

"I'll bet good old Hap thought I was a freak," Juliet said.

"No. He liked you. He told me so."

"Yeah, sure." People had started to congregate on the platform, and Eli Hathaway's taxi pulled up to deliver Sissy Elliot and her daughters, Iris and Marlena, all headed for the ballet in Boston. "Actually, I am a freak," Juliet said quietly.

"So what? Hap likes freaks. He once showed me an article about a man who could set fires with his breath," Stella said. "Isn't that crazy?"

"That's one really bad case of indigestion."

Juliet and Stella started to laugh.

"The worst ever recorded," Stella gasped.

They laughed so hard people could hear them inside the station, but when Stella stopped, Juliet didn't. In no time her ragged laughter turned into tears. Stella took a step backward. She hadn't even been sure that Juliet could cry, and now here she was, sobbing.

"This isn't about leaving, so don't think it is." Juliet wiped at her eyes; black eye pencil and mascara had begun to leak. She was tearing little chinks out of her train ticket. "I don't even like this place. I'm a city girl."

"I know. You are. Completely."

"I'm happy to leave. I'd go nuts in a place like this."

In all the time they'd known each other, Stella had only been to Juliet's apartment once. It was a one-bedroom, so Juliet slept on the couch. Here, Liza Hull had made up a bed for her with clean white sheets scented with lavender. She'd slept till noon on Saturday and said she couldn't remember sleeping so peacefully before.

Stella hugged her friend. "Maybe next time you can stay longer."

"Don't forget about me," Juliet whispered, close, so that Stella could feel the heat of her breath.

Once she'd gotten on board, Juliet probably couldn't see Stella out on the platform, waving, but Stella stayed anyway. She lingered until the train had pulled away, until the whistle was so far off it echoed past the corner of Lockhart and East Main. Juliet had confided that she had left her aunt's apartment without so much as a note; she suspected that when she got back to Boston her aunt wouldn't have noticed her absence.

It was the worst of fates, to be forgotten. On one hand there were those who became part of history, their birthdays celebrated, their lives remembered; on the other, there were those who had been erased. At dinner the other night, Matt had been talking about his thesis to Liza; Stella had overheard him say that the Sparrow women had written the town's history in invisible ink. All he was doing down at the library was holding certain pages up to the light.

Hap was running toward the station, cutting across the common, a rain poncho flapping out behind him. He looked worried; he looked as though he'd been running for miles.

"What happened to you?" Stella asked, angry on Juliet's behalf. "Where the hell were you?"

"It was the horse. He's sick or something. I had to wait with my grandfather for Dr. Early, walking Sooner around in circles. I've got to go back and keep on walking him. I just came to say good-bye."

"Well, you're too late."

"Shit." Hap looked down the tracks.

Stella probably should have been jealous; instead she felt a wash of relief. "Does this mean you're in love with Juliet?"

"Don't be an ass." Hap turned to leave. He didn't want to talk about this. He didn't want to talk at all. "I've got to go walk the horse so his stomach doesn't clinch up."

"Maybe it's time for him to die."

"You really have a morbid hatred of equines."

Stella laughed and waved as Hap took off. "Just don't ride him," she called.

The rain had begun in earnest, sure to be fish rain, for it was already spilling over the rooftops. It was because of this torrent that Stella ran across the common and ducked into the library. By the time she entered the front vestibule, her shoes were soaked, so she slipped them off and left them under the coatrack. Outside, the whole world was wet, and the wind was moving across town in fits.

When Stella hesitated at the threshold, the librarian, Mrs. Gibson, signaled for her to come in.

"Looking for your uncle?"

It was very odd indeed to live in a town where most people knew your family history better than you yourself did. What Stella wouldn't give to know more about her ancestors. She went where she was directed, past the stacks to the reading room. The glass door was marked UNITY HISTORICAL SOCIETY. It was here all town papers, diaries, newspapers, announcements, journals, medals, and trophies were stored, along with Anton Hathaway's uniform, an ink-colored homespun that was dyed with a mixture culled from the indigo reeds that once grew beside Hourglass Lake.

Matt Avery was at the table inside, typing the last page of the last chapter of his thesis. Because Matt was a pet of Mrs. Gibson's, he was allowed to eat an orange, which was set out in neat sections, along with a cup of tea Mrs. Gibson had fixed herself, black, no sugar, with a sliver of lemon affixed to the rim. The oak tree would have to wait another day before it was taken down. Most of Matt's scheduled spring cleanups, the Elliots, the Quimbys, the Stewarts, the Frosts, would have to wait as well. Why, Matt was so set on his thesis, he hadn't even begun the plantings on the town common; usually, at this time of year, he had put in most of the annual beds, dozens of marigolds and zinnias and petunias. He had the past on his mind, and it took up a great deal of space. He wore a set of headphones, he liked to listen to Coltrane or Dylan as he worked—his musical taste being the single thing he had in common with his brother. He was so engaged in finishing, he hadn't even bothered with his orange or his tea. If he hadn't been imagining the last moments of Rebecca Sparrow's life, he might have heard Stella open the door.

Stella herself had a strange cold feeling, the same sort of shivers she'd had whenever she and Juliet stole makeup or jewelry from Saks. Is this the way badness was formed? A cold pebble that begins as a tiny speck? An impulse that couldn't be resisted? A desire that can't be denied? Stella didn't think, she didn't plan; it was like reaching for the sparkly hoop earrings behind the counter, like holding her breath and diving underwater. One minute she was standing there watching her uncle type, and the next instant she was folding the thesis into her backpack.

She tiptoed out, closing the door carefully; she waved to Mrs. Gibson, then hurried to slip on the soaking pair of shoes she'd left beneath the coatrack. Doing something so bad made a person hot: a coal in the palm of her hand. An arrow set afire. All her life, people had been hiding things from Stella, but not anymore. The rain was slowing, fish rain good for nothing but the old catfish in Hourglass Lake, for when such a rain dissipated there would be clouds of mosquitoes and mayflies. As Stella jogged through puddles she thought about the cancerous growth she had seen on Mrs. Gibson's lung; if Dr. Stewart was alerted, and treatment was given, perhaps Mrs. Gibson would die of old age rather than of cancer; she'd pass on while asleep in her bed, or surrounded by the books in the library.

Since the accident when the young man on the highway had survived liver damage, Stella had become far more hopeful, even though Dr. Stewart had told her that there was no cure for some ailments. Hope was a good thing in most cases, but when it came to Elinor Sparrow, hope was out of the question, no more likely than snow in May, and that in itself was a good thing, since that was what Stella had seen, a snowy blanket covering her grandmother, drift after cloud-white drift. Thankfully it was too warm for anything like snow. The last of the rain sizzled when it hit the pavement. Stella darted inside when she reached the tea house. She hung up her jacket and kicked off her shoes, which were downright squishy. Her blond hair was drenched, like sleet falling down her back.

"You've been gone so long," Liza called. "Did Juliet get off all right?"

"The train was late," Stella lied. Perhaps she did take after her father, after all. Lies seemed to come easily. She'd been lying to the new handyman all weekend; he'd given Stella and Juliet the creeps. He lived in North Arthur and yesterday he'd offered the girls a ride to the North Arthur mall.

"Oh, yeah," Juliet had said after Stella had demurred, with a polite lie, thanking the handyman for his offer, but assuring him there was plenty to keep them busy in town, activities such as dyeing everything in the closet black and fixing bird's-nest pudding in Liza's kitchen at 3:00 A.M. "Like there'd be anything in the North Arthur mall that would interest us. Doesn't he realize we're Saks girls? What a loser."

"I liked Juliet," Liza told Stella when she'd returned from the library and had come to fix herself some hot tea. "Tell her she's welcome here anytime."

Stella had her backpack slung over her bad shoulder, the one that had been broken at birth and which throbbed on rainy days. Stella's father had told her a bedtime story when she was little, a tale about a girl who'd been born with one wing. After being repaired by the doctors, the only sign that she had ever been different was an aching shoulder. Anyone would think all Stella would remember were the many times her father had disappointed her, but that wasn't the case. He always said, *Ssh. No flying away tonight* when the story was done and it was time for bed. Even now, what had happened wasn't his fault. She should have never told him what she saw in the restaurant on her birthday. She should have kept it to herself. It was her fault Will Avery was in trouble.

"Did my father tell you anything about that murder case in Boston? Has he heard anything at all?"

Will had told Liza that Henry Elliot had filed a motion to have all of the charges against him dropped, due to lack of evidence. But the charges weren't what Will worried about. It was the little house that had been taken that kept him up nights; when he closed his eyes, all he saw were its white gables and its wedding-cake form, its satin flowers, the carved front door. It was his daughter's safety he worried about most of all.

"Nothing yet. But don't worry," Liza said protectively to Stella. "Your father's a good man, deep inside."

No one had ever said such a thing about her father before, at least not in Stella's presence, and as she went up to her room Stella wondered if perhaps Juliet Aronson was right. Perhaps Liza was in love with her father.

Stella took off her black jeans and her black T-shirt; they were so wet they leaked dye; Stella had to wring them out in the tub. She slipped on her black flannel bathrobe and flopped into bed. She was exhausted. All the same, she reached for her backpack; she didn't bother to switch on the lamp or reach for the flashlight she kept in a night-table drawer. The greenish tinge of the last pitter-patter of fish rain was light enough to read by. She took Matt Avery's thesis out, all of it there but the very last page that he'd been typing today, and opened it. The pages smelled like water, she noticed that right away, and something that reminded her of water lilies.

Invisible Ink, An Account of the Life and Death of Rebecca Sparrow.

The rain was coming down one lazy drop at a time, and Liza, still down in the kitchen, was listening to Sam Cooke, whose voice could take anyone's troubles away. *Darling you send me* was the echo that filtered up the stairs. *Honest you do.*

Matt's thesis began with the first lines of Charles Hathaway's journal.

I was the man who was at fault, whose guilt was never known until these words were written. And even then, who will ever read these lines and know these words to be the truth?

It was cold in Stella's room tonight, so she grabbed a blanket and tossed it over her shoulders. She had the bad habit of chewing on the ends of her hair when she was nervous, much the way her own mother bit her nails. Now, Stella had taken up her bad habit without thinking. She could no longer hear the rain or Sam Cooke or the cars on the street. She skipped over Matt's introduction: the founding of the town by Hathaways and Hapgoods and Elliots, the encounters with native people, the bear that was killed in the middle of town beneath the old oak tree, the number of horses and cows and sheep that were owned, the shipments from England of spices and tea and mirrors and ink, and, on rare occasions, bolts of blue or crimson silk.

For so long Stella had wanted to know everything. Now she had a funny feeling in her stomach. Now the book was in her hands. She took a breath, the way a diver might, as though the pages and the print were deep water, deep as the lake beside her grandmother's house, deep as all time.

IN THE YEAR OF 1682 the winter was so cold the ice froze solid in Boston Harbor, and it stayed that way until the middle of March. On the morning when the ice finally melted, a fierce blue day when the wind toppled some newly constructed birds' nests from the trees, a child of seven or eight years old walked out of the woods, up on the hill that overlooked Hourglass Lake, near the rock formations the settlers dubbed the Table and Chairs. This was the place where some people said invisible roses grew, the sort that disappeared in the blink of an eye. No one was surprised that a person could just as easily appear, one who spoke a language no one understood.

She arrived on the day when the first snowdrops appeared, growing right through the melting ice, there to remind one and all of the gifts of the Angel of Sorrow. Who saw her first was a matter of debate, but it wasn't long before the whole town knew that a child had wandered out of the wilderness, coming down from the north where there was far more ice than there were snowdrops. Before most people saw her, they already knew that the roses that withered when seen by the citizens of Unity were said to flower in her presence. It may have been Charles Hathaway who first reported that he had seen the child whistle and call the sparrows to her; these birds, people vowed, had brought her berries and sweet clover, and on this she had survived during her time in the woods. She spoke only gibberish, and she didn't even know how to pray. Her black hair was tangled with brambles. In her possession she had three things, brought from whatever cold country from which she had appeared: A silver compass. A golden bell. A star on a chain. People looked at these things and whispered. They peered at the soles of her feet, turned green and tough as leather from walking so far, and they wondered who indeed she might be.

Which generous neighbor among them would take her in, a child of not more than eight? Unity was a town built in the sight of the Lord, but where was the charity that was so often preached when the minister traveled the winding roads from Boston? None of the families wanted her, not even the Lockharts, who raised pigs and sheep on the far edge of town. The child was pretty enough, with a bright countenance, but when she was brought to a meeting on the town common, called to pray for guidance and rejoice in the salvation of a human life, she didn't even know to get on her knees. She looked right at the heavens, prideful, questioning, and that was worrisome indeed.

John Elliot was the first to take her in, not that he wanted to. It was his wife that suggested they study compassion, but on the very first night the child was with them, the family heard the bell ringing. They couldn't sleep, not a wink, so they brought the girl back to town. The Hapgoods took her next, but she refused to take off the star she wore around her neck; she was neither pious nor obedient, so they took her back as well. It was then that Charles Hathaway had no choice but to take her. He was the richest man in town, granted his acreage by the king, and he saw it as his duty to succeed where other men failed.

Hathaway had a son of his own, Samuel, nearly the same age as the lost child, as fair as the girl was dark. Hathaway accepted no nonsense from his own flesh and blood, and he took it upon himself to train this child from the northern woods and teach her the ways of civilized people. When the bell rang and woke everyone in the house, Hathaway beat Rebecca with a switch cut from a hazel tree. When she took the compass and wandered through town, he brought her back and beat her again, this time with a switch from a hawthorn tree. When she would not take off the star, he tore it from her neck, then beat her with a switch made of oak.

Already, the girl and Hathaway's son were inseparable, united, perhaps, by their hatred for Hathaway. One night the children disappeared. Guided by the silver compass, they found the place where the girl had first been spied, on the far side of the Table and Chairs. Hathaway discovered them late that night, asleep on the Table, their arms locked around each other. He got rid of the girl the very next day. He took her down to the washerwoman, who lived at the edge of the lake, an old woman who had an eye for worthwhile things.

It was said the washerwoman could tell the difference between homespun and silk at a distance of a hundred yards. Although the washerwoman's name was never recorded, it was she who decided to call the girl Rebecca, after she who'd been found in the wilderness. This was the name anyone passing by the lake would hear, at any given hour of the day: *Rebecca, come here! Rebecca, where are you now?*

For there was a great deal to be done on the shore of the lake. A girl must be smart if she was to learn not to burn herself when she added hot grease to the ashes in the making of soap. She must be strong if she were to wring out heavy bolts of wool. She must be sweet so that she would never complain when her fingers bled from the toxic lye. She must be quiet, so she would not say a word when her hands ached from the harshness of the starch made from potatoes. She must make certain to bide her time.

SOMETHING SOUNDED against the window. Stella thought it was only the rain, so she ignored it. She was consumed by Rebecca Sparrow's history, but there was the sound again, more insistent this time. Pebbles were being thrown against the glass, a rain, it seemed, of stones. It was just past twilight, the murky hour when everything turned blue. Outside, blackbirds flew across the sky and disappeared into the shadows. Stella opened her window and peered down, past the lilacs, past the plane trees, past the blackbirds taking flight.

There was Jimmy Elliot.

Stella couldn't see his face exactly, but she knew it was him from the way he stood there, as if he'd just happened by for no particular reason. As if one minute he was minding his own business, and the next he'd found himself throwing rocks at a window he didn't even know was hers.

He'd been more and more underfoot lately. Arriving where he was least expected, happening to stop in when Stella and Cynthia went to the pizza place or standing beside Stella's locker at school with that same confused look on his face, as though he'd been lost, as though he needed a map in order to find his way through his own hometown. Now, on this evening, he was making his presence known and something more: he was daring her to respond.

Stella never backed down from a dare. She got her key from her backpack and threw it down to the sidewalk. Whether or not this was the reaction he expected, Jimmy immediately picked it up. He went to the locked door of the tea house and before long Stella could hear him on the stairs. She hoped Liza wouldn't notice, that she was still in the kitchen, busy with making out the week's grocery list. Because Stella felt a churning in her stomach each time she saw Jimmy, she wondered what her own response would be when he came through the door. Did she want him here, did she not? She realized she was only wearing underwear and a T-shirt under her bathrobe, so she quickly pulled a quilt over herself.

He came into the bedroom and closed the door behind him. The room seemed quite unreal to Stella with Jimmy Elliot there at the foot of the bed. She could feel him, as if particles of his essence were filtering into the air. He smelled like rain and something Stella couldn't place.

"Did she hear you?" Stella whispered.

"Liza? She's in the kitchen listening to music and singing along."

Sure enough, Stella could hear Liza's muffled voice. They both tried not to laugh. "Natural Woman" was the tune Liza was singing. Aretha. Will often played her CD. The Queen of Soul.

"What's with the blanket?" Jimmy said. "You look like one of those old ladies who never gets out of bed."

"Don't make fun of me." Frankly, Stella felt a little sick to her stomach right now. She felt that churning. She wished Jimmy Elliot wasn't so good-looking. She wished he didn't look so confused.

"Grandma, what big eyes you have."

"I mean it. Shut up."

Jimmy stared at her. It was growing darker. "Fine," he agreed. He threw himself down on the bed beside her, grabbed a corner of the quilt and pulled it over himself. The only thing between them was Matt's thesis. "What's this?"

Stella quickly grabbed the manuscript and stuffed it under her pillow. She was wearing the bracelet her father had given her, and the bell made a small, shining sound. "Nothing."

"It's something."

He kissed her then. Right away, Stella's lips began to burn. She thought of the candle and the pin and the way love walked into a person's life, uninvited. She could feel Jimmy's hip against her own, and she burned there, too. Wherever he touched her, wherever he was. So this is what it was, this burning up, this wanting something you knew you shouldn't have.

"Maybe we shouldn't do this," Stella said after a while. By then her lips hurt, not that she wanted to stop. All the same, she had a panicky feeling inside her chest.

"What should we do? Read?"

Stella laughed in spite of herself, then muffled her laughter, for they could hear Liza's tread on the stair. *You make me feel*, Liza sang, off-key, but with feeling. *You make me feel.* Stella put her hand over Jimmy's mouth so Liza wouldn't hear him laughing. Even his breath against the palm of her hand burned. She thought of the man Hap had told her about, who was able to breathe out fire. When she leaned her head against Jimmy's chest, she could hear what a strong heart he had. Was that what attracted her? That she saw his death when he was a very old man; that when she was with him she didn't have to worry about what terrible fate might be waiting around the next corner?

"Turn around and don't look," Stella told him when it was time for him to leave. She got out of bed, slipped off her bathrobe, and pulled on a pair of jeans. When she turned back, he was definitely looking. "Well, that was trustworthy." She was still whispering.

"What about you?" Jimmy reached for the manuscript beneath the pillow. "Are you trustworthy? Isn't this your uncle's thesis?"

Stella leaped to grab the pages.

"I won't tell anyone," Jimmy said. "I swear."

He'd gotten off the bed; his boots had been muddy and now he dusted off the quilt. Oddly enough, she did trust him on this. He could keep a secret; he wouldn't tell. They went downstairs together and she let him out the door. It had rained hard and the air was clear. Now it was she who watched him; she who couldn't look away until he was all the way down the road, past the lilacs, past the shade trees where the blackbirds slept, all in a row.

IV.

AS THE DAYS GREW LONGER, there were more hours for Elinor to work in her garden. She felt greedy for the ever-expanding twilight, greedy for most everything, especially time. Her knees were bad, oh, embarrassment of age, but oddly enough when she knelt in the garden she swore she could feel the interwoven roots under the soil, the pulsing of the cicadas in the weeds, the beautiful heart of the world. She could feel the growing things quicken her own blood and she felt young again. Once, she fell asleep in the middle of the day, back against the old stone wall, just like Argus, and that was the way Brock Stewart found her, curled against the stones like a bird which had fallen from the sky, or a star that was burning, or a coil of roses without the protection of thorns.

Elinor and her old dog hadn't heard Dr. Stewart's Lincoln come sputtering up the driveway any more than they'd heard the warblers in the trees. Brock Stewart leaned on the garden gate. He thought about everything he'd learned from Elinor Sparrow. Why he knew that the wild roses in Unity were said to be invisible, that they tended to wilt and fade right before a person's eyes, if one was lucky enough to ever spy them. This local variety refused to grow in gardens, in backyards, in nurseries, and yet Elinor had managed to persuade one specimen to take root and then she'd crossed it with a variety she favored. Even now with summer so close, the hybrid was still covered by a cone of burlap, which allowed sun in, yet protected against wind and bad weather, like the stone rain that had fallen last week, battering down some of the more fragile roses, until they broke in two.

The doctor came into the garden and sat on the bench he'd given to Elinor. When a person accepted a gift from someone, she was accepting the way the giver felt about her as well, any fool knew that. So what did it mean that she was sleeping on the ground, rather than using what he'd given her? He watched her breathe, and each breath was a precious thing. *One more day*, the doctor thought, as greedy as anyone, greedier than Elinor by a mile. *Maybe two.*

"Hey, girl," Dr. Stewart said when at last Elinor opened her eyes.

She had been dreaming that she was walking down the lane, under a bower of green. Then she saw Dr. Stewart and he looked so handsome, the way he looked when he came back to town after medical school, that she wondered if she had woken at all.

"Hardly a girl," she was lucid enough to remind him of that.

Elinor's eyes were filmy; her vision was failing and she felt a weakness in her legs. She thought about the various ways in which a flower faded, some petal by petal, others all at once, torn by wind or circumstance, or merely by time.

"How's our blue rose?" the doctor asked.

"Not ours. Mine. The burlap's the only thing that's yours."

Brock Stewart laughed.

"If you really want to know, I feel sorry for the poor thing," Elinor went on. "All wrapped up that way. I'm starting to think there's no point in being a rose if you're tied up and covered with burlap."

If he wasn't a doctor, if he hadn't seen it many times before, would Brock Stewart have noticed the darkness around her eyes, the faint plumlike tinge? Would he have seen that her skin was sallow, truly yellow in full light. By now, he knew, the pain in her spine must be unbearable; he'd checked with the pharmacist on how often she filled the prescription for morphine. Perhaps that was why she had been sleeping on the ground, with milkweed pods scattered all around her, dreaming of roads that led home.

"You wanted a blue rose," Brock said. "Didn't you? Wasn't that the whole point?"

"Doesn't everyone want what they cannot have?"

"Here's what I think: it's the quest that matters. Just my humble opinion."

Elinor laughed. "You're not humble. You're a know-it-all."

"Me?" the doctor said. "Know-nothing's more like it. Don't know the first thing about roses, so don't ask me what I think."

Elinor was gazing at Cake House. At this hour of the day, the white painted wood took on a blue hue as the sky darkened directly above.

"I made a wrong turn somewhere," Elinor said.

She thought about her dream, the long green road, how single-minded she'd been all these years. Now, she could force a thousand blue roses into existence, just when it wasn't at all what she wanted.

As for Brock Stewart, he couldn't even remember when the way he felt about her had begun. Was it the day he walked up the ice-covered path to tell her about Saul? Or the day after, when he'd found her in the garden once more, barefoot and frozen right through, so that when he brought her home and sat her in front of the fire, the ice on her clothes melted into puddles on the floor? Was is yesterday or twenty years ago? "I'd be lost without you."

"Well," Elinor said sharply, "you'd better get used to it."

It sounded as though rain had begun, but it wasn't any sort of rain Elinor could identify. Not rose rain, or fish rain, or stone rain, not daffodil rain, only the sound of water. It was the doctor, crying. It was all but over, now, now that she knew what she wanted.

"Let's have a secret." Elinor could feel the heat of the stone wall against her back. She could feel the little earthworms in the soil and the roots of her garden beneath her, a plaiting so interwoven it would take an ax to cut through. "Let's have something no one else in the world knows about."

Dr. Stewart wiped his eyes with the back of his hands. Ever since Liza Hull's baby's death, he'd stopped trying to hold back his tears. Once or twice he'd cried in front of the residents at the clinic. They'd all turned away, embarrassed, from what they clearly perceived to be an old man's failing. He'd kept quiet then, but what he'd really wanted to say to all those new residents, so blindly sure of themselves, so convinced that the only way to cure was to deny certain parts of themsevles: *This is what it is. Watch me. This is what it's like to be human in this world.*

"We'll move the rose," Elinor had decided.

Brock laughed. "Why is it that your ideas always include physical labor and a wheelbarrow?"

But once they began, it wasn't very difficult to dig up the little rosebush. They lifted the seedling, still in its burlap, set it in the cart, and then it was up to the doctor to push the wheelbarrow. Trout lilies and trillium were blooming and the woods they approached were dark, except in those rare places where the sunlight came through strong as a spotlight, illuminating swirling mayflies and silvery dust motes. The scent in the air was of mud; there were layers of it: red mud, gray clay, fishy lake mud. Swamp cabbage grew thickly here, and in a clearing there was a lady's slipper orchid. Dr. Stewart stopped to gaze at the remarkable plant. The orchid was the shape of the human heart, but paler, and like the human heart, it was surprisingly strong, especially when you stopped to consider how fragile it appeared to be, how very many ways there were for it to break.

They went on until they came to the place where people said Rebecca Sparrow had first appeared. She had walked out of the woods one evening as though she were walking out of a dream that had ended, there beyond the flat rocks called the Table and Chairs. Brock Stewart used to come here with Elinor in the weeks after Saul's death, just to sit here, nothing more, although time after time he'd thought of kissing her. But he'd put the thought away, he was married, happily, really; it was just that this was something more. This was everything he felt inside.

Argus had followed along at a slow pace. Now, the wolfhound stretched out to watch as Dr. Stewart hacked away at vines in a spot that Elinor had deemed sunny enough. After expending all that energy, the doctor took a break, taking a seat on one of the Chairs, but the granite was cold, and brought little comfort, and Elinor was toting away the vines herself. After he caught his breath, Brock began to dig in the clearing with an old wooden-handled shovel they'd brought along. There were cinnamon ferns growing wild, and yellow iris that had escaped from Colonial gardens, jumping fences, growing underneath hedges. There was jack-in-the-pulpit, and dozens more swamp cabbages, which gave off a sulfury scent if brushed up against. It seemed unearthly quiet here in the woods, but for anyone who listened carefully, there was actually endless sound. The hum of the mayflies and the mosquitoes, the drone of the bees as they visited the wild dogwood, which had come into full bloom, the chattering of catbirds, the song of the warbler, the trill of the sparrows, who had lit on every branch.

When the doctor had dug a deep enough hole, Elinor removed the burlap from the rosebush; she folded the rough fabric and tossed it into the wheelbarrow. As she worked, she was careful not to look too closely at the little plant, lest she frighten it into invisibility. It was a foolish folk tale, surely, but perhaps not completely without merit. Things withered, after all; they fell away. But some things went on even when no one was looking; unseen, unknown, they grew.

"Do we mark the path with stones so we can find it again?" Brock Stewart said as he turned the wheelbarrow around.

"We can never find it again." Elinor had come to stand beside him. She hooked her arm through his, and rested her hand on the wheelbarrow. "That's why we brought it here."

The way back was tough going, through the underbrush, past the swamp cabbage. Before long the doctor was confused. Perhaps they should have marked the path. "Damn," Brock Stewart said, for every dogwood tree looked like every other and every stand of yellow iris appeared to be no different from the next.

The doctor was sweating, he was tired from working so hard, and there were blisters on his hands. *Look upward*, he had told his son, David, when David was a boy, so very long ago. *When you're lost, remember: the sun always sets in the west and you're sure to find your way.* Now, the doctor wasn't even able to see the sun through the tangle of trees.

"I'm not sure where we are," he admitted.

"That's good." Elinor was so close it was possible to feel her warmth, her certainty, her breath. "If we can't find it, no one else will. That's what we want, Brock."

They might have stood there together forever, lost in the woods, in the dark, on that ridge where Rebecca Sparrow first appeared so many years ago, from the north, people said, although no one was sure, but luckily the dog knew the way home. They had to trust Argus and walk blindly on; it had grown foggy and there was a pale, light rain that made for mist. It was the last of the season's daffodil rain, the sort that falls for no reason, when the lawns and the hedges are already green enough, but the sky just can't stop from falling down.

At the edge of a clearing the doctor stopped and picked a bunch of yellow iris. His fingers turned green with their sap and his senses grew dizzy with their redolent, golden scent. He could walk here endlessly, never growing tired, never feeling thirst. What initially drew him to anatomy he felt once again on this leafy path: the sheer abundance of life, the heat of it, the connection of things, the mat of roots under the soil, so like blood and bones, the wild potato vines like arteries, the honeybees' hive, so like a heart. If he could take one thing with him to eternity, it would be the way he felt right now. Their feet were wet and the going was difficult. It was ridiculous for people their age to be wandering around in this manner, and still the doctor didn't wish it to end. Elinor was feverish, he saw that clearly; a flu, perhaps, easily caught in her weakened condition. He saw clearly, too, they would indeed never come this way again.

Walk slower, he whispered, because by now the iris he held in his hand lit their way, globes of light in the dark. *I don't want you to go.*

That night, Elinor dreamed of the rose they had brought into the woods, and in her dream the petals weren't blue, but silver. A broken mirror reflecting the sky up above. She knelt to pick a single flower, but it came to pieces in her hands: it shattered once, then twice, then a thousand times. Down on her knees, in a panic, she tried to put the pieces together again. She heard someone say, *You have it now*, and she thought, *How ridiculous. I have nothing at all. I've lost everything.*

Her hands were bleeding from all that glass. She could see herself in the shards, but she was only a girl. How strange that when she stood up she was still that girl, the one with the long black hair, lost in the woods where the brambles grew. Above her, in the inky sky, the stars were moving too fast, like a child's wind-up toy. She recognized some of the constellations: Leo, which always accompanied spring. The Herdsman in search of his lamb. Blue-white Vega, the brightest star in Lyra. It all looked like snow, caught in a globe. Shake it, and it falls to pieces. Shake it, and it covers you.

Jenny arose when the sky was still black, awakened by her mother's dream. She sat up with a gasp. The girl with long black hair had walked over glass and had never even cried. Jenny's own face was hot and wet. There was the dawn chorus of the wood thrush peeping through the dark. There was a line of sparrows on the window ledge. A sob escaped from Jenny's mouth, and it seemed to fly out the window, chasing the sparrows away. But not too far; they perched on the branches of the laurel and fluttered into the damp grass.

Jenny got out of bed and went to the window. She half-expected to see the girl with black hair standing out on the lawn, dressed in a white nightgown of the sort Rebecca Sparrow was said to have worn when she first walked out of the woods. Night was rising from the grass the way steam lifted from a mirror. Jenny threw on her robe and went down the hall. The floors were cold on her feet; light fell in through the leaded panes of the hall windows so that the dust motes seemed like living things, circling in little whirlwinds.

It was so early the wasps were first waking, the bees were just beginning to visit the garden, the stars were fading, one by one, until only Venus was left in the sky. Jenny found her mother's bedroom door ajar. If she'd ever thought to ask, she would have found that her mother had a great fear of sleeping alone, and had ever since that night when the doctor came to tell them Saul was gone. She had the ability to spot a liar, except for the lies spoken by someone she loved. That's what had caught her up; she'd been distracted by love, which seemed, at least at the time, to be the truest thing in the world.

Argus always slept beside the bed. Now, he lifted his head when Jenny came into the room; he gazed at her, but Jenny could see from the pale film over Argus's eyes that he was nearly blind. Why had she not noticed that before? Why hadn't she taken note of how cold her mother's room was, or realized that it hadn't been painted in such a long time that the white walls had turned cream-colored, yellowing with age. Why hadn't she realized how very ill her mother was until this very moment, this instant when the birds were waking, when the sky was clearing into a milky opaque light, when there was suddenly and surprisingly everything to lose.

On the nightstand were a handful of yellow iris, the ones picked in the woods, musk-scented, set out in a vase that was familiar to Jenny. It was, in fact, one of Jenny's first art projects, made in third grade, snaky ribbons of clay, painted brown and blue. She remembered bringing it home one afternoon when the rain was torrential, far beyond fish rain. It had been hurricane rain, plain and simple. Jenny had tucked the vase into her coat. With every step she wished for only one thing: *Don't let it be broken.* She was surprised to see now that her mother had kept it, that she had it still, so nearby.

Jenny's feet were freezing, so she stepped over Argus, pulled back the quilt, and got into bed beside her mother. Elinor had awakened when she heard someone come into the room. She had always been a light sleeper, but her vision had begun to fail her, and she thought if Argus hadn't barked, perhaps it was best for her to be silent as well. She felt the bed shift. There was a woman beside her with black hair who appeared to be her daughter. Could that be real? Wasn't that an impossible thing, no more likely than a dish that could grow legs and run away over the moon or a roomful of straw spun into gold?

"I'm dreaming," Elinor Sparrow said. As she spoke, her words evaporated, the way words evaporate in dreams, leaving only a scrim of language, the core of something it's impossible to understand.

"Maybe I am, too," Jenny said.

They could hear the call of the wood thrush from the lawn. Outside, morning had broken into bands of yellow and green. What was a dream but a way of knowing what was inside you? After all this time, they forgave each other on this morning in May when the world was green, when bees circled the laurel, when words didn't need to be spoken, when anything that had been lost could still be found.

IN THE MORNING, Stella called good-bye to Liza, grabbed her backpack, and left as though it were an ordinary day. But when it came time to turn onto Lockhart, and head toward the high school, she went the other way.

"I'm not going to school," Stella said when Hap caught up with her. "Take notes for me in science."

"I'll come with you," Hap said, ever grateful for an excuse to miss classes on such a clear, fine day as this.

"No." Too abrupt. Hurt feelings. Could he tell she'd been kissing someone last night? Did it show in the light of day? Could he figure out she wasn't quite as trustworthy as she appeared to be? "I mean, it's a family matter."

"Sure." Hap was looking at Stella as though he had just realized something. Perhaps he didn't know her as well as he'd thought. "You do what you want."

Stella went down Dead Horse Lane, and took the cutoff when she came to Rebecca's path. The day was warm and mayflies circled over the shallows. Long ago, there were so many turtles living here it was impossible to count their number, even though scores of their eggs were collected and made into soup. There were wild turkeys in the thickets and the brooks were filled with alewives, a bony fish that swim inland from the salt marshes every spring. By the time of Rebecca Sparrow's thirteenth birthday—celebrated on the day when she first walked out of the woods, set in the very center of March—the town of Unity was twice as big as it had been when she first appeared. No one who met her would guess she hadn't spoken a word of English when she was found, but anyone could tell in a second that her livelihood was laundry, for her hands were chapped and raw, with fingertips the color of plums and nails broken to the very quick. The old washerwoman had died of a pox, leaving Rebecca her house, her kettle, and her secret recipe for barley soap.

When Charles Hathaway saw Rebecca Sparrow walk over the shattered mirror on the morning of her thirteenth birthday, he knew he'd done right to keep his son away from her. All the same, there was just so much a father could do. When local boys began to shoot arrows at Rebecca for sport, Samuel was the one who chased them away. It was Samuel who visited Rebecca in the evenings, paying no mind to the mosquitoes that hovered over the lakeshore like a black curtain, ignoring the snapping turtles that sank into mudholes, ready to bite through the toughest pair of boots. He went to see her even after his father insisted he marry one of the Hapgood girls in town, Mary. Even after a son was born to them, he remained loyal to Rebecca, if loyalty meant she was the one he couldn't wait to be with. He went to the lake no matter the weather; he used a salve of swamp cabbage to keep mosquitoes away, and he knew his way through the dark, past stones and turtles, past the old oak tree where the beehive held honey so sweet bears came down from the woods and refused to be chased away by smokers or muskets.

When Rebecca was close to her seventeenth year, she gave birth to a daughter on the first day of March, Sarah Sparrow, a calm child who seemed to need no sleep at all. That was the year when the mosquitoes swarmed in huge, dank clouds, and anyone who came too near to stagnant water took ill with a high fever. Samuel was the first to die, and after his death the sickness spread out in a circle, one family to the next. But down at the lake, Rebecca Sparrow was healthy as could be, though she cried for weeks over Samuel. People took note of how her baby thrived. If that was not suspicious enough, Mary Hathaway, Samuel's widow, had seen Rebecca and the child she held with their arms stretched out, covered by birds, as if they were both made of feathers, not flesh, as if neither one was entirely human.

It seemed reasonable to question Rebecca about those who'd fallen ill. Soon enough she was brought to the meeting hall, where she was watched carefully for signs that might reveal if the town itself were being put to the test. God worked in mysterious ways, it was true, but so did the devil. Wasn't that the reason why upstanding men often craved things they had best stay away from? Why women often strayed to vanity, and children needed to be guided, lest they stumble and fall? The town fathers took from her the silver compass she kept in her pocket and the star around her neck; they removed the gold bell that kept the baby occupied, and paid no attention when the poor thing began to wail.

There were those, such as Mary, who'd had suspicions all along, but now the town fathers agreed there must be a test. Everyone knew a witch felt no pain, so pain was the method they employed. A hot coal was placed into Rebecca's boot, and the townsfolk were even more certain they were in the right when Rebecca didn't cry, although clearly her foot was burned, the skin smoldering. They stuck pins beneath her nails, and still she didn't say a word, though her fingers turned scarlet, and several of the nails dropped off. They added whole acorns to the stew they served her for dinner, and she didn't spit them out. At last the good women in town were instructed to sew stones into the hem of Rebecca's dress, and her cloak, then they filled her boots with rocks as well, before they brought her back to the lake.

It was afternoon by the time Stella got to the terrible part, the part that took place not ten feet from where she was now hunkered down, beneath a blue sky that was overcast then. They dragged Rebecca Sparrow along this path, which was overgrown with brambles in those days, not caring that her feet were so torn from the rocks in her boots that blood began to seep through the leather. It was January, far too early for the snowdrops to appear, yet everywhere Rebecca's blood fell snowdrops grew. Everything else was burned away. Grass never grew there again, even thistle would not sprout here, not milkweed, not even thorn apple. The men's breath billowed out in smoky clouds. There seemed to be no color in the world on this day: the skies were leaden, the reeds, dull brown, the hay in the fields, pale and flaxen, sprinkled with frost.

They had held off, waiting for the ice to melt, but every day was more frigid than the last. But when one of the Hapgoods took to his bed and two of the White cousins died, they decided they could wait no longer: a group of boys were sent to chop a hole in the ice. Hours had been spent in discussion of what strength of rope to use. As she read, Stella wondered if Rebecca would have escaped if she could. In a footnote, Matt suggested that the idea that witches could fly at night might have been due to hallucinogenics. Flying ointments had been around forever, Matt noted; even Francis Bacon had suggested a toxic concoction that included hemlock, nightshade, saffron, and poplar leaves.

Many of these poisonous ingredients were easily found in the fields surrounding Unity, but what would an individual see if she were high above town? Wouldn't she miss everything that was truly important if there was so much distance between herself and the rest of the world? Rebecca was grounded, tied to the village by the presence of her baby daughter, left in the care of the Hathaways. She didn't even try to run, let alone fly. She had nothing, yet she was weighted down by devotion. Everything she owned in this world had fit into a single basket: the bell, the compass, two dresses, several bars of barley soap that could wash away any stain, be it tar or gravy or blood. Some of the women were handed shears and told to cut off her black hair. Though it was winter, the sparrows sang as if it were already spring. The turtles moved beneath the ice, floating below the surface as though they were logs.

Many of those in attendance couldn't understand why Rebecca refused to say a word, and several referred to this fact in their journals. But from reading Charles Hathaway's recollections of the day, Matt knew that her last words had already been said, in Hathaway's kitchen, where Samuel's widow held tight to Rebecca's baby girl, though she clearly preferred her own child.

I forgive you.

They had to listen carefully, and even then were unsure, for afterward Rebecca was mute. Not that her promises or lies were needed. If proven innocent, she would be asked to take her place among the good wives who had sewn rocks into the hems of her clothes. But she who survived a drowning was never deemed innocent, not with stones to weigh her down. She'd been burned and pricked, she'd stepped on glass and been struck with arrows, and she hadn't felt a thing. When her boots were removed, they were so full of blood the snowbank turned crimson. As they sent her beneath the ice the first time, they could hear gulping sounds from deep within the lake. The sparrows set to chattering and the ice groaned. They pulled her up with the rope they had decided upon, the strongest of all, and asked her to confess. When she would not, they sent her back below. Perhaps her lips had frozen shut, perhaps she lost her voice from the cold. They dunked her twice more, but on the next attempt, when they pulled the rope, it came to them too easily. Nothing was attached but a bundle of weeds.

The bell and the compass and the star and the braid of dark hair were locked away in Charles Hathaway's desk drawer, but at night Hathaway could hear them, even with the drawer shut. No matter if he was safe in bed, they spoke to him. Before long, he couldn't hear anyone's voice but Rebecca's, he couldn't discern his wife calling to him or the thunder on stormy days and he often was found wandering through town. He had grown so fearful of water that he would not wash his hands or face. He stank and grew filthy and even his own horse shied from his presence; his wife and his daughter-in-law and his grandson would not sit at a table with him.

Sarah Sparrow was raised by the Hathaways, but when she turned thirteen she opened the desk drawer where her mother's belongings had been stored. She had heard Rebecca calling to her just as surely as her grandfather had. She looked around the Hathaway household and remembered that she didn't belong. Hathaway went after Sarah when she ran off, for she was his natural granddaughter, but as he neared the lake, he heard Rebecca's voice again. He'd never really stopped hearing it, it had merely grown quiet. Now it was roaring loud. Maybe it was this voice that spooked his horse, which took off running from the very spot where Stella was now sitting, the place where nothing grew, where clouds of mosquitoes still rose at this hour, where the sky fell down in blue waves. Stella put away Matt's thesis; it was too dark to read, and she had mostly finished, anyway. Now that she knew what had happened, she had the urge to keep the thesis. Why should it be shared with the town that had done this? Stella packed up and headed for Dead Horse Lane. She could hear the catkins move in the wind, and the hollow reeds rang out, like bells. The lane was inky with shadows, and even though Stella's mother and grandmother were less than five hundred yards away, in the big old house, it was lonely out here. She thought about Rebecca, in her bloody boots. She thought about Sarah, raised by a woman who despised her. She thought about the horse that had bolted and ran right over the water until it sank, somewhere in the center of lake, which people said had no bottom.

It was a relief to turn onto the paved road of Lockhart Avenue. Soon Stella heard an echo on the asphalt, a van behind her, sending out blinding pools from its headlights. Stella scrambled to the side of the road, narrowly missing a patch of nettle that would have left her legs stinging right through the jeans that Juliet had helped to dye black. She'd jumped aside so quickly that her head pounded. She could feel the thrum of her pulse when the van pulled up alongside.

"Hey, there. Want a ride?"

Stella stopped and blinked. All she could see was a shadow behind the wheel. She thought of that woman she'd seen at the restaurant in Boston and the way she'd died, and her pulse actually hurt. You had to be careful in this world. You had to look twice at what came your way.

"I don't bite," the driver assured her.

Stella recognized the van: the pizza delivery truck. Now she recognized the driver as well.

"You almost ran me over," Stella said, relieved to know who it was who had stopped.

She saw the driver's fate hanging over him: a traffic accident somewhere in Maine on a hazy summer day. She wouldn't get in the car with him for any reason. Not if her life depended on it.

"I've got to get the pizzas out while they're hot. So do you want a ride or not?"

"No, thanks. I like to walk."

Stella stood there breathing hard, even though it was only the pizza delivery guy who waved and drove off.

"Slow down," she called after him.

The moon had appeared in the sky, an arc of white surfacing. The crab apples were in bloom, and as Stella walked on, she counted the many kinds: there were the ones with white creamy flowers, the ones edged pink, the ones with dark red blooms, the color of the human heart. Tonight, it seemed as though the whole world was breathing; everything was alive. The gnats in the air, the peepers in the ditches, the leaves of the poplars and the ash rustling, like a breath in and out.

Stella couldn't help but wonder if this was the path they had taken from town on that cold day when Rebecca's blood fell on the ice. Was that why Stella felt so nervous? Was that why she had the urge to run? She made a promise to the dark night: if she reached Liza Hull's safely she would make a sacrifice in Rebecca's name. All she needed was a sign. Another car passed by, slowing down, but Stella looked straight ahead. Cynthia Elliot had told her that four years earlier a girl was hit by a car on Lockhart Avenue, and they never did find the driver. She said the body was left on the corner of Lockhart and East Main, with a blanket thrown over it, so that it seemed the girl was sleeping, there in the gutter.

Stella counted her steps to the old oak tree, then took off running. Juliet Aronson had once suggested that if you counted your steps in the moonlight, when you reached home you'd have the first letter of your true love's name. But Stella didn't actually have a home at the moment, and she knew whom she loved despite what common sense recommended, so she counted for counting's sake. When she reached the tea house she hightailed it upstairs. Liza came to stand in the hall, but all she had time to do was call out a greeting as a streak of lightning fled to the second floor.

"I'm supposed to be giving you three meals a day. Don't you want dinner? It's beef stew. Your father will be here."

Every day proved Juliet Aronson's assessment to be correct. Will Avery was hanging around the tea house like the blackbirds who waited for crumbs.

"Not hungry," Stella called back. "Thanks anyway. I'm just so tired. I'm going to bed."

"It might be that flu that's going around," Liza said.

When Stella was safe at last, up in her single bed, made up with clean white sheets that very morning, she was still thinking how easily people could disappear. She thought about sparrows and roses and invisible ink and girls who were left in the road. She kept Matt Avery's thesis under her pillow and all through the night the pages rattled, like the leaves of the trees. Some things are given and some are taken away; some things stay with a person forever. Stella dreamed of lakes and stones, of girls with black hair; she dreamed the same dream as her mother and her grandmother and all of the women in her family who had come before her. When she awoke in the morning she had already decided what her sacrifice would be.

Long before Liza took the stairs down to the kitchen to begin the day's baking, before her mother reported for work, before her grandmother went out to her garden, Stella went to the bathroom and locked the door. She shook out her hair and looked at herself in the mirror. Pale as a star, invisible unless seen against the darkness. Thankfully, Juliet had left a shopping bag of everything she had stolen during her weekend in Unity, and that included several boxes of hair dye. All the while Stella was bent over the sink with the water running, she was thinking about that day when ice was covering the lake, when the water below was so cold it could turn a woman to stone, when the fields were dark with crows and a thousand sparrows came to the shore and refused to fly away, even when they were chased with sticks.

In less than an hour, Stella's best feature, her long blond hair, which Juliet Aronson had always advised she wear loose so that it fell down her back like a handful of stars, had been turned black. She used a pair of nail scissors to cut it short, above her ears, exactly as they had chopped off Rebecca's hair on the morning of her drowning, a single braid of which Charles Hathaway kept in a drawer along with the compass and the star and the bell and, when he found them in his son's belongings, the ten arrowheads lined with Rebecca's blood. There the possessions stayed until Rebecca's daughter returned them to where they belonged. That was the first thing Sarah Sparrow did when she left the Hathaways': she built the case where the mementos were still stored. She insisted on remembering. The glass wasn't added till later, but the casement itself was carefully made from oak and hawthorn and ash. Sarah needed no sleep, so she stayed up all night, working until the job was through. Only then did she give a few strands of her mother's hair to the sparrows who were waiting so patiently. Each strand was quickly woven into their nests in the reeds, where it called out on windy days, spooking horses and frightening local boys, murmuring to anyone who might be brave enough to walk down the path where nothing grew, but where long ago there were snowdrops before it was the season, growing through the hardest ice, a gift from the Angel of Sorrow.

THE CHARM

I.

I T WAS THE SEASON WHEN PEOPLE IN UNITY put in their gardens, when winter's fallen maples were culled and chopped into firewood for the year to come, when the peach trees bloomed and spring fever was at its height. Usually, at this time, Matt Avery would be working overtime, but this year he had stopped answering the phone. Even the old oak tree was still standing, though it was leafless, and people said it wailed whenever the wind blew through. Matt didn't care about the tree; he was a man who had always risen by 5:30 A.M. without having to bother setting his alarm clock, but now he couldn't get out of bed. He heard his brother rattling around in the kitchen, fixing coffee, chatting on the phone with Liza, and there Matt would be, quilt over his head, convinced that getting dressed or brushing his teeth or even breathing was far too much of an effort.

Matt had fallen victim to the flu, a potent spring-time variety that boiled the blood and made for light-headedness, an illness that left him suffering with aching bones and a cough that rattled his ribs. Perhaps he was so afflicted because his resistance was down: in losing his thesis, he appeared to have lost everything. The world no longer interested him. Everything he'd ever tried in his lifetime had gone wrong. Now it was Will who was the early riser; he who used to wake at noon now concocted protein shakes at dawn. He who favored Scotch and gin gulped bottled water. As unbelievable as it seemed, Will Avery had taken up running. He left the house at six and didn't return until eight, when Matt would once again hear him, whistling like a madman as he showered, some prelude of Chopin's that could set a person's teeth on edge if all he wanted was peace and quiet.

Will had begun to give piano lessons on their old Steinway, the one they'd both learned on so long ago, although Matt had been tone-deaf and Will had a natural aptitude. Their teacher had actually told their mother that Will flared with talent, whereas Matt . . . well, Matt was a lost cause. Indeed, it was true. And now he had misplaced his thesis to add to his many failures. Gone was the project he had been working on for so many years, due to be handed in at the end of the week. To be sure he had notes and the first drafts of six of the ten chapters. He had the very last page, the one he'd been revising when the damned thing disappeared. But what sort of fool did not have a copy of the finished product? A fool such as himself it would seem, a man who had taken twenty years to complete his education and who couldn't seem to get to the end even then.

Whatever Matt Avery wanted slipped through his fingers like water. If he couldn't have love, if he had no hope, then at least he could teach, or so he had believed. The chair of the history department at the state college, Brian Lewis, had proposed Matt teach a night class for the fall, an offer that would surely be retracted when it became known that Matt's thesis was AWOL. Thinking about his fate, Matt couldn't help but consider Charles Hathaway's last days, how he'd taken to his bed when his granddaughter left and went back to live at the house by the lake, how he'd suffered with fevers and delusions, even though his wife brought him chamomile tea and poltices made from poplar leaves. Charles Hathaway wrote in his journal that he'd dreamed of Rebecca Sparrow so often she seemed to be with him even in his waking hours, sitting at the foot of his bed, dripping with green water, slipping away from him whenever he tried to reach out.

When Matt did manage to get out of bed, for a glass of water or some Tylenol, he didn't bother to check the phone to see if he had any messages. He simply had given up hope. True, Mrs. Gibson had put up signs in the library, but a lost manuscript wasn't like a stray dog. It didn't come when you called; it wasn't taken in and fed by kindly neighbors; and it assuredly wasn't waiting in a cage at the pound, tail wagging. The phone calls were always for Will, anyway, for he seemed to have taken over the house. Matt wondered what the mothers of Will's students would think if they knew Will Avery had spent his entire adult life as a drunkard and a liar. But the fact of the matter was Will had stopped drinking completely. For all Matt knew, he'd stopped lying as well.

"Rise and shine, brother," Will would call through the wall before he went running, and why shouldn't good old Will be happy? All charges against him had been dropped, now that the murdered woman's dinner companion had come forward to say the victim had been considering taking out a restraining order against an old boyfriend, one who wouldn't leave her alone. The boyfriend had turned up missing, and Will had been the one to identify him, from a photograph, as the so-called reporter who'd interviewed him and stolen the model of Cake House. *Inside Edition* had already dispatched a reporter to interview Will right on the town green, and there was a rumor that the *Today* show would be sending a film crew on Memorial Day. Will had been asked to be the parade marshal. Will Avery, who hadn't visited his mother on her deathbed, who'd lied for sport and cheated on his wife, who'd frittered away his talents and had been the sort of father available only for birthdays and special occasions, would be running alongside the mayor's white convertible Cadillac on Memorial Day, his music students following along, tossing Tootsie Rolls and lollipops to the crowd.

Will hadn't mentioned to anyone—except for Liza, in whom he now confided everything—the reason he'd taken up running. It was a reaction to the fear that arose inside him when he went into the station house in Boston to pick out the photograph of the man who'd stolen the model house. When Will got back to Unity, he was concerned enough about Stella's safety to go and talk to the chief of police, Robby Hendrix, who had been three years behind Will in school. Robby had assured Will that Stella would not be in any danger, but as far as Will could tell, the most difficult case the Unity police force had dealt with, prior to tracking down what was possibly a cold-blooded murderer, was ridding the neighborhood of a family of rabid raccoons that had to be trapped up in the Elliots' attic.

Will had little faith in the Unity police department, however well intended it was. And so he had taken up running. He had become the ears and eyes of the town, and by now he knew most people's habits quite well. Henry Elliot, for instance, headed out to Boston at a quarter after six each day. Eli Hathaway was usually the first customer at the gas station on the corner of Main. Enid Frost opened up the doors to the train station at 6:30 exactly. On fair days she swept off the platform; when it rained she used a mop to clear away puddles.

Will found he could cover most of the town in two hours, making a loop that led around the common, down Lockhart, past the library and the elementary school and the shops on Main Street, all the while looking forward to the moment when he'd pass by the porch of the tea house, where Liza Hull was often waiting to cheer him on. Lately, Will had felt as though someone had drained the poison out of him; without alcohol, without the weight of his lies, he was light-headed and light-footed, faster than he'd ever imagined possible. Another runner he'd met, Solange Gibson, the librarian's daughter, had shown him a few stretches to prevent his legs from cramping up. Sometimes, when he was out on his appointed route, he'd meet up with one of his piano students and their families and they'd all be so pleased to see him Will had at first thought such people had mistaken him for his brother, someone else entirely, a well-respected man who cared about more than how easily something came to him or how little work he had to put in to get by.

When he heard that Jenny had come down with the spring flu, Will was so penitent he actually picked some of the phlox in his mother's perennial garden that always bloomed early, an unexpected burst of white in the midst of all that May greenery. He ran over to Cake House one morning while Matt stayed in bed bemoaning both his future and his past. The wisteria was blooming and the whole town smelled sweet. Even the muddy lake, best known for its drownings, had a spicy aroma, more like cinnamon than its usual muck.

"I know you hate me," Will said when Elinor opened the door. Elinor blinked when she saw Will, surprised to find him on her front porch. "I'm just here to visit Jenny. I won't steal anything."

"You're not planning on getting back together with Jenny, are you?" Elinor wanted to know before she allowed him inside. She eyed the flowers, pathetic stalks of half-bloomed phlox. Catherine would have been embarrassed by such a paltry bouquet from her garden.

"Oh, no," Will assured Elinor. "We're through."

Elinor's ability to spot a liar seemed to be failing her; either that, or Will was actually telling the truth.

"Liza told me Jenny had the flu. I thought it was only polite to stop by."

"So now it's Liza." Elinor opened the door wide. What a relief to know he'd finally moved on. "You should have said so."

Will took the staircase two steps at a time, then wandered down the hall to Jenny's room. Jenny used to sneak out her window at night to meet him, climbing down the twisted wisteria which grew along the roof so that she smelled like flowers and often made him sneeze. He was so allergic, Liza had convinced him to carry an Epi-Pen in his pocket when he went out running, in case he met up with a bee. He ran fastest when he passed that oak on Lockhart, for inside, where the wood was dead, a huge hive was nestled. Will could hear them humming as he ran past and he made sure to quicken his pace. Some people commuting to work in the city or over to North Arthur didn't even recognize him as they drove past: he was a blur, nothing more. A man who was running from everything he'd ever been.

"You look terrible," he said when he found Jenny in bed. She was feverish, her nose red, wearing flannel pajamas though the day outside was fine.

"Thanks so much." Jenny tried to run her fingers through her knotted hair. She'd been working on a watercolor propped up on her knees. She'd taken up painting again.

"Nice landscape," Will said.

Jenny laughed, then blew her nose. "There's a tiger on the hillside. If you bother to look."

" 'Tiger, tiger burning bright.' But not, I suspect, on the hillsides in Unity. I didn't know you could paint."

"What did you know about me?" Jenny couldn't resist that dig even though Will was arranging the flowers he'd brought in her water glass.

"Not much. I didn't know much about my mother, either. I had no idea she was a gardener, but apparently she was. This stuff is all around the house."

"Phlox," Jenny informed him. In spite of herself, she had picked up stray bits of gardening lore from her own mother, though she herself had never grown so much as an avocado plant from a pit. "It naturalizes. It may even do better when there's no one around to tend it."

Jenny narrowed her eyes when Will started tidying up her bedside table. He moved the bell that her mother had left so that Jenny could ring if she needed anything. A ridiculous notion, truly. Elinor herself wasn't well and could hardly be anyone's nursemaid, and when had she ever been so? Not when Jenny was a child, not on the day Jenny phoned Dr. Stewart herself, when her fever reached 104 and her throat felt like sandpaper, and her mother was out in the garden, heedless when it came to anything that existed beyond the gate.

"Isn't this from the glass case?" Will said of the bell. It made a sweet sound when he held it up and shook it. "Didn't it belong to Rebecca?"

Jenny took the bell from him and put it down beside her water glass filled with phlox. His fussing was making her uncomfortable. "Why are you here? What do you want? Frankly, I'm amazed that my mother let you in the house. Especially after it turns out you stole that arrowhead the very first time I brought you here."

"That was terrible," Will said sadly.

"Yes. It was. So what do you want now that you've returned to the scene of your crime?"

"I want your forgiveness."

Jenny laughed, even though her throat hurt. Then she looked at Will. He wasn't kidding. "And I should do this because . . . ?"

"Because we'll be better parents if we're working together."

Jenny stared at him, shocked. "And when exactly did you have this revelation?"

"Actually, I didn't come up with this idea myself," Will admitted. "I was helped along."

"A woman's influence," Jenny guessed. "Marian Quimby?"

Marian had always been jealous; she had wanted Will for herself.

All through high school she'd called Jenny the dead-horse girl and the whore of Cake House. She'd traipsed around after Will, not that it did her the least bit of good: in the end, Marian went to law school and now had a practice in North Arthur.

"Marian?" In point of fact, this Marian had been the first girl that Will had sex with, on a couch in her parents' basement. The summer after eighth grade. "Good God, no." An awful thought possessed Will. "You don't think Stella's fooling around with Dr. Stewart's grandson, do you? You don't think she's sleeping with him?"

"Of course I don't think so. And we were talking about you, so don't try to avoid it. Who's the woman?"

"It's Liza."

"Liza Hull? My Liza?"

Jenny pushed her watercolors away. Will was staring right at her, when usually he couldn't meet anyone's eyes. He was rangy-looking; he'd lost weight, Jenny realized, and his color was better. He was drinking bottled water and wearing running shoes, not at all his style. When was the last time he'd had a Scotch, told a lie, ruined someone's life? How had this happened without Jenny noticing?

"It's definitely Liza," Will said.

The plainest girl in their class, Jenny's boss, a woman who gave more thought to the ingredients of a piecrust than she did to her own appearance. Until recently. Several times lately, Liza had asked Jenny what she thought of an outfit, some dated pantsuit or dull, serviceable dress, and just last week Jenny had caught Liza gazing into the mirror above the buffet table, studying her own reflection, lips pursed, as though, all of a sudden, the way she looked meant something.

"And you reciprocate this . . ." Jenny had to search for the word. "Feeling?"

"Liza's an amazing woman. She knew I was innocent long before the charges against me were dropped. Did you see her on *Inside Edition*? She was right there with me."

"Well, fancy that. So now you want me to forgive you?"

"Pretty much. We've been through so much together, Jen. All of our adult lives. It would mean a lot to me."

What had Liza Hull done to Will? Put a spell on him? Helped him find his inner self? Or had she simply believed in him?

"Then tell me one thing. That day you and your brother came here on my birthday, you said it was your dream I was describing."

Will nodded. "The black angel, the bee who wouldn't sting, the fearless woman."

"Yes. That's the one."

"I wanted it to be my dream, but I was too scared to sleep that night. You know me, on a good night I rarely dream, but back then I was terrified that the dead horse might rise. I was biting my nails. My brother told me the horse belonged to Charles Hathaway, and that it reared when he tried to force it down the path where Rebecca Sparrow had walked. Matt was studying local history even back then, but who would have guessed he had a dream like that inside him."

People made mistakes all the time, and sometimes it was more than worthwhile to forgive someone, even if that person was Will. Even if the first words he'd ever spoken to her were lies.

"Didn't you guess it was Matt? You two even have the flu at the same time," Will said as he was leaving. "That should tell you something."

Was love catching, like a common cold? Or was it more like a virus that afflicted a person gradually, until the unsuspecting individual was sick with love, consumed by it, riddled by its aftereffects? Once Will had left, Jenny Sparrow realized that her blood was so hot it felt like burned sugar inside her veins. Was it possible that her light-headedness was as much caused by thinking about Matt as it was from her fever? Why was it so difficult for her to recognize her own heart's desire, a task not unlike stringing beads on a thread of smoke, or setting a fire to green wood, or finding her way through the dark without a lantern or a flashlight or a sliver of moon?

There was a knock on her door. Elinor came in, dependent on her cane, but carrying a tray all the same. She had heard the bell, rung when Will lifted it from the table, and here she was with the tea she had not brought to her daughter nearly thirty years earlier, the tea that was never made but had caused so much bitterness.

"What's this?" Jenny said, surprised.

"Elisabeth Sparrow's recipe for break-a-fever tea. Mint and lemon and lavender honey. I've also got some of that horrible stuff I mixed up. Bird's-nest pudding. It's supposed to be good for you."

There was indeed a bowl full of some unrecognizable pudding-like stuff poured into a baked apple. The last thing Jenny wanted was food, but she forced herself to take a taste of the pudding. To please her mother, she realized. *How odd,* she thought. *We're trying to make each other happy. How backward. How unlike us.*

"It's creamy," Jenny said. "You made this?"

Love was never a mistake, even when it wasn't returned. It was not unlike the phlox in Catherine Avery's garden, untended, ignored, but there all the same.

"I'm sure it's terrible," Elinor said. "You don't have to humor me."

"I thought you could always tell when someone was telling the truth. Or at least it always seemed that way."

"I knew a lie. That's different from knowing the truth. Isn't it funny; as far as I can tell, Will's stopped lying."

"He's in love with Liza Hull."

"Should we be happy for Liza or send her our sympathies?"

"Happy." Jenny nodded. "Definitely."

Elinor reached for the little watercolor of the tiger on the hillside. "How lovely. I dreamed that same image last night. That's the hill behind the lake."

"But there aren't any tigers in Unity."

"I know. I was dreaming of tiger lilies."

They both laughed at Jenny's error; she had seen a cat instead of a flower, a liar instead of a man who'd be true.

"I got it wrong yet again," Jenny said.

Elinor took Rebecca's compass from her pocket. "Maybe you need this."

"Isn't this from the case in the parlor?"

"What good does a compass do under glass? I thought you might put it to some use."

Jenny thought about what her mother said all that day as her fever raged. She thought about tiger lilies and cups of tea and the strange turns love took. In the evening, Elinor came back with some vegetable broth and a cold compress for Jenny's forehead, and not long after, Jenny's fever broke. One minute she was burning up and the next she was cool and refreshed, probably the result of Elisabeth's tea. Break-a-fever, break a heart, break every rule if you must.

Jenny took off her flannel pajamas and quickly dressed; she had a frantic desire for fresh air and for something more. When she stepped outside, there was the Archer, on the western horizon. There was Pegasus, high in the east. In the dark, the house really did look like a wedding cake, layer upon layer of white paint. She walked past the laurel, past the lilacs; she kept on until she had turned the corner by the old oak, half of which had leafed out and half of which was dry as kindling. She didn't quite know where she was going until she was almost there. She could feel the weight of the compass in her pocket, and before long, she saw the phlox, blooming like little stars in a row.

Jenny knocked on the Averys' back door, and when no one answered, she found the key under the mat, where it had always been stowed. The kitchen was dark—Will must be at Liza's—but someone was home, that much was certain. Jenny could feel a person dreaming. In the dream a man was lost on a long road. It was a lane that never ended, which repeated itself just when the dreamer thought he'd reached the end. Night had begun to fall for the dreamer, but the time frame was unnaturally fast, with so many stars racing through the sky it was impossible to recognize the constellations. Even Polaris, the most constant point of all, had changed its position.

He was lost, Jenny could feel that. She had reached the door to his bedroom, where he slept with all the curtains drawn. He was so deeply asleep he didn't open his eyes until she lay down beside him. Jenny thought about the first moment when she'd seen him following along as if he didn't matter, always in the background, two steps behind, but staring at her across the lawn on the morning of her thirteenth birthday, when she was too young to know any better.

After he'd woken, she put the compass in his hand. She could feel the heat of his body, the fever he'd had for thirty years. Jenny Sparrow took off her clothes; she didn't want anything between them. She felt cool, like a stone fished from the lake. She was so close, it was like a wave had come over him. He had convinced himself he was satisfied with his life; he'd stopped thinking about what he might have had or could have been. All the same, with Jenny in bed next to him, he was already drowning. That was what desire could do to a person. That's what it did to him.

"Am I dreaming?" Matt Avery said. "Did I lose my thesis? Are you really here?"

Long ago, there were women in Unity who wore summer's peach stones around their necks all year round, hoping for love. There were still people in town who believed it was this custom, rather than the shipwrecked saplings bound for Boston, which had caused so many peach trees to grow wild in backyards and all through the woods. Every time a new house was built, a bucket of peach stones would be found, and even children on their way to school knew that finding one meant luck, no matter the outcome: love forgotten, love gone wrong, love despite all odds, love ever after, love after all this time.

II.

JENNY WAS WORKING at the tea house on a Saturday afternoon. No one who saw her would have guessed that she had been a moody girl who couldn't wait to run away from home, unhappy most of the time, waiting for the worst to befall her. Today, she was cutting up a plum pie and thinking about Matt's kisses. She was halfway through this task, humming a song about love, when an odd-looking girl came straggling in through the door, with Hap Stewart tagging along behind with a somewhat mystified expression. Jenny, as a matter of fact, couldn't stop thinking about Matt. For the past two nights she had gone out walking after Elinor went to bed, only to find herself at his back door, knocking softly, so Will wouldn't hear. She had tiptoed through the living room as though she were a teenaged girl herself, somehow transported back to the time when a kiss meant something, when it could bring her to her knees.

Since she'd fallen for Matt, she'd been as irresponsible as a teenager, coming in late to work, failing to see her own daughter. Jenny was so distracted she paid no attention to the girl who'd come to the counter, only nodded to Hap, before going to grab a couple of menus. Liza came out with a tray of raspberry tarts as Jenny was setting the menus down on the countertop.

"Hey, Jen. Aren't you going to say hello to your daughter?"

Liza might as well have hit Jenny over the head with a sledge-hammer or tossed a handful of stinging yellow jackets into the crust of the plum pie she had recently cut into slices. Was it really possible that this outlandish girl was her wonderful child, her equinox girl, her baby, her whole world? Of all the changes in her daughter, what was the most distressing? The choppy black hair? The smudgy eye pencil she had taken to using? Was it how tall Stella was? Five-seven, a woman's height. Or was it how pale the girl was, more so it seemed than ever in contrast to that raven hair? Or was it simply the way she was staring at Jenny, as though her own mother were a stranger who didn't know the first thing about her? It was the exact same expression that had been on Jenny's face when she had glared at her mother on the day she ran down the driveway and threw herself into Will's car, ready for Cambridge and the rest of her life.

Lately, Will had been stopping by the tea house in the afternoon, and while he waited for Liza, he and Jenny had coffee and discussed their daughter, this shared worry, the one subject on which they could agree. Was she still seeing visions? Was she carrying on with Hap? (Will thought possibly, Jenny said no way.) Was she spending too much time trailing around after Dr. Stewart, visiting the dying and the hopeless? What sort of hobby was that for a young girl, anyway? When was the last time either of them had heard Stella laugh out loud? Wasn't it dangerous for her to come by and help her grandmother in the garden when her whereabouts were supposed to be kept secret?

"Is that permanent?" Jenny asked.

The girl with dark hair who resembled her daughter sat at the counter, sulky and ill tempered and ready for a fight. Ink, that's what the color of Stella's hair brought to mind. The sort that was far from invisible. She sneered, but failed to answer.

"Hey, Mrs. Avery, that pie looks great," Hap said with a nervous smile. You could cut the tension between mother and daughter with the plum-stained knife in Jenny's hand. Hap drummed his fingers on the counter. In one of his late-night conversations with Juliet Aronson, Juliet had told him most people had only one best feature, but he had two, his height and his integrity. "I guess I'll have to try some."

"It's Sparrow, not Avery," Jenny corrected. "I'm divorced."

"Is that why you're sleeping with my uncle?" Stella took a wedge of pie between her fingers and shoved it into her mouth. Plum syrup plopped onto the countertop. It looked like a blob of ink, like half a butterfly's wing, like a lie, twice-told. Jimmy Elliot had let slip that he'd seen her mother leaving the Avery house at 2:00 A.M., when he was walking home from the tea house. She certainly hadn't been there to see Will.

"What are you talking about?" Jenny flushed with color.

There was the lie.

"I'm not sleeping with anyone."

There it was twice.

"Uh huh." Stella cleared the blob of pie filling off the counter with her finger and sucked it off. "Neither am I."

Jenny stared at her daughter and had a single, horrible thought: *Jimmy Elliot.*

Stella looked straight back and traced an *X* on her chest. "Cross my heart," she said.

Lying could run in a person's nature, or it could spring up out of necessity and circumstance. But there were some individuals who merely stumbled into lying, honest people who fell before they knew it, only to find themselves drowning in a pool of words. It had happened to Stella, but perhaps seeing death would make a liar out of anyone. For instance, only yesterday Stella had told her science teacher, Mr. Grillo, that she would bring in her overdue homework on Monday when what she really wanted to say was: *Stop drinking, it's ruining your liver, you'll die of cirrhosis if you don't watch out.*

She clearly couldn't walk up to people and tell them whatever future she saw for them. Honesty was like a stone, dropped and ir-retrievable once it was spoken aloud. But a lie never stayed put, it spread in a slinky circle, a puddle of deceit. There were straight-out lies and crooked ones and ones left unsaid. There was the unspoken lie about taking Matt's thesis, and the veiled lie, for although Jimmy

Elliot threw rocks at her window most nights and he came up to her bed, she wasn't technically sleeping with him.

When Jimmy had told Stella about her mother wandering around in the middle of the night, Stella wanted to know if Jenny had seemed happy or upset.

"I don't know." They'd been under the quilt and Jimmy was burning hot. The last thing in the world he wanted to do was talk about Stella's mother, but he had only himself to blame for bringing up the subject. "She looked confused."

Confused, exactly how Jimmy himself looked when he stood outside in the dark, waiting for Stella to throw him the key. Confused when she kissed him, when she told him to go, when she said she never wanted to see him again, when she told him to come back. Stella knew what that was, which is why she left without bothering to say good-bye to her mother. One lovelorn individual per family was more than enough.

"DID YOU SEE HER HAIR?" was the first thing Jenny said when Will came by later. "I'm sick over it." Liza was closing up the kitchen and everyone else had left for the day.

"Where've you been? Everyone in town has seen her hair." Will helped himself to a bottle of water. "Just like everyone seems to know you're sleeping with my brother."

"That's not fair. Your brother is in crisis."

"The missing thesis, yes. Big deal. Actually, he's never seemed happier, Jen, so maybe that thesis of his was just a substitute for real life. Now he has what he's wanted since we were kids. You."

"Since you were kids?" Jenny leaned her elbows on the countertop, pleased. For a giddy moment, she forgot about propriety, lost manuscripts, daughters with dyed hair.

"It was his idea to sleep out by the lake that night. You knew that, right? He was crazy about you even back then. I had that goddamned bee allergy even then—I hated the countryside, but I couldn't let him win. Not at anything. Not at you."

As for Matt, he'd given up hope that his thesis would be found, and had finally set to work taking down the old tree. He might never get his master's, but his life had taken such an unexpected turn he didn't know what to think. Everything that had once been important barely mattered to him now. He understood now why people pinched themselves to make certain they weren't dreaming. Real life was much stranger than any of his dreams, on this Jenny Sparrow agreed. When she slept beside him, Jenny experienced his dreams of the history of Unity, the everyday details of a hundred, two hundred, three hundred years ago. He dreamed of his work, as well, of lilacs and lilies, of tangled bittersweet that was so invasive some of his clients had acres of their land covered by it, hiding evergreens and beech trees until they resembled camels cloaked with green fabric. Impossible to know what's beneath all that bittersweet. Nearly as impossible to get rid of it altogether.

On the day he began to work on the oak tree, Matt found himself whistling, for no reason or for every reason, he wasn't quite sure. The hive in the dead section of the oak was enormous; the bees were bound to be somewhat disturbed, but Matt hoped to take the hive out into the woods, or down to the dairy farm in North Arthur where the owner might be willing to let him set up in return for some of the honeycombs. There were fields of red clover in North Arthur, and half a dozen strawberry farms. Strawberry-clover honey would be a treat, and hopefully the bees would make the transfer to their new location without too much stress.

The two lowest dead branches had already been cut off and Matt had begun to saw the first of the huge limbs into manageable logs that he could cart away. He was supposed to have a helper on this day: Jimmy Elliot had been assigned to him to serve extra community service. It kept piling on, hour after hour, but Jimmy Elliot, it seemed, had other things on his mind. He continued to be drawn to the tea house. As he stood out in the road throwing stones at the window one night, Robbie Hendrix, the police chief, happened to be driving by in his cruiser. Hendrix, having forgotten all the trouble he himself had been in as a boy, had stopped and ticketed Jimmy. Public nuisance, that's what he was.

"What's wrong with you?" the chief asked as he wrote out the ticket for Jimmy, scratching out the twenty-five-dollar fine and writing in: *Public Works—10 hours. See Matt Avery.* "Are you out of your mind? Don't you know glass breaks?"

Well, of course Jimmy knew that. And if the truth be told, he couldn't quite explain what he was doing. He'd been snagged by love, when he was the last person anyone would expect to be a target. At any rate, Jimmy had never shown up at the appointed hour of his community service. Because of this, work on the old tree was progressing slowly. If Jimmy had been there, he might have been dizzy from the sound of buzzing or feared being stung as bees circled round, but Matt only paid attention to the wood. Oak was beautiful, one of his favorites, but he loved fragrant fruitwood as well. Peachwood stayed on a woodcutter's hands and he couldn't wash the scent away. Applewood looked pink in the center. Plumwood had a heart inside its trunk; strike it once, and the whole tree would fall.

Matt had received several requests for the cut logs from this old oak—Mrs. Gibson wanted to make a bookshelf out of it, Enid Frost had requested firewood for the woodstove in the train station, old Eli Hathaway came round in his taxi and had picked up a quarter-sized piece of wood which he vowed he would keep in his pocket so that he could always touch wood for luck. Cynthia Elliot stopped by on her way to work at the tea house, and as she watched Matt cut up the logs, she had tears in her eyes. Cynthia had recently turned sixteen but she looked like a kid with those dozens of braids in her hair, still riding through town on her bicycle, bemoaning the fate of a tree. She'd walked past it in kindergarten, after all. She'd tangled a kite in its branches one summer and watched, terrified, as her brother Jimmy climbed so high to rescue the kite she thought he'd disappear into the sky. She'd climbed it the first time she'd run away from home, and had spent the whole night in its branches, convinced she would never speak to her mother again. But in the morning she'd felt comforted; instead of hitchhiking to New York or Boston, she'd walked home.

"Your brother's supposed to be helping me out here, but I may just leave part of the trunk. It may still grow," Matt told Cynthia, when he shut off his saw, removed his goggles and headset, and saw she was crying. "The one side, at any rate."

Sure enough, half of the tree had unexpectedly begun to leaf out, weeks behind its season, but not entirely dead. Several grades from the elementary school had come on field trips to visit the oldest tree in the county. They'd practiced their cursive while writing letters to the mayor which protested the cutting down of the oak. The Friday before, the entire third grade had circled round the tree as Matt worked. The boys and girls had been holding hands as they chanted: *One, two three, don't make firewood out of me! Four, five, six, I'm more than a pile of sticks!*

Another man might have felled the tree completely, despite such pleas, certainly it would have been easier, but Matt had decided he would try his best to salvage the half that was still somewhat healthy. He worked late, and on the weekends. People in town got used to hearing a saw, just as they became accustomed to bees flying through the air, a buzzing cloud that hovered above backyards and along lanes. There was a great deal of yellow in the air when Matt noticed someone familiar walk by. He took off his goggles, thinking they were obscuring his vision, but, no, there she was. Rebecca Sparrow stood on the street corner, wearing jeans and work boots, a backpack slung over one shoulder.

"You're staring," she called up to him, and indeed he was, even though by now he had realized the girl on the sidewalk was his niece, Stella.

"You look, exactly like her." Matt climbed down from the ladder that rested against the oak. "Have you seen the portrait in the reading room at the library? There used to be a miniature, given to Rebecca by its painter, Samuel Hathaway, but that was lost somehow."

"Sorry. I haven't been to the library." That particular lie burned in Stella's mouth, so she accepted a Life Saver from the roll that Matt offered, even though she hated him at the moment. What would he be to her if he and her mother wound up together? An uncle? A stepfather? Nothing at all? Maybe she should burn that thesis of his that was right now in her backpack. Maybe it would serve him right. They stared up at the old tree. The air was filled with amber pollen and bees.

"That's an eyesore," Stella said. "What an ugly tree."

"Your friend Cynthia cries whenever she rides by."

"She cries on a regular basis. She's so sensitive she breaks out in a rash if she sees a sign for a lost dog. Everyone knows Cynthia is too kindhearted for her own good."

"Unlike her brother?"

Matt continued looking at the tree, but he could feel the heat of Stella's glare. All the same, he'd seen Jimmy mooning around after her. The last time Jimmy had been in trouble, the community service he'd been assigned was helping to clear the snow off the common. He'd been a taciturn and surly helper. Maybe it was just as well Jimmy hadn't shown up for work; if Matt remembered correctly, the only thing the boy had said in his three days of service was *Am I done?*

"Don't think you know the first thing about Jimmy, because you don't," Stella informed.

"Sounds like you do."

"Are we discussing our love lives?"

The glare was worsening; it was white hot, as a matter of fact.

"Do you want to talk about your mother and me?"

"Absolutely not." Stella took a step back. "Good God, no." As she thought that over, she had a most sour expression. Her mother in love? Just the idea made her head hurt. She looked up at the beehive. "There are too many bees. Aren't you afraid you'll be stung?"

"Watch." Matt went to a bee drowsing on the bark of one of the cut branches and snatched it up in his hand. When he opened his hand for Stella to see, the bee hovered there for a moment, stunned, then calmly flew off.

Stella laughed out loud. "You're nuts."

"You're the one with the black hair."

"I wanted to honor her," Stella said. For some reason she felt like crying. "I wanted somebody to remember Rebecca."

"So did I."

Stella was standing on a completely familiar corner, yet she felt impossibly lost. Could it be she and Matt wanted the same thing?

"I think you deserve this."

Matt reached in his pocket for the compass Jenny had given him.

"Your mother gave it to me. I guess your grandmother gave it to her. But I think it's meant to be yours."

"Are you trying to buy my friendship or something?"

"Nope."

"What are you trying to do?"

"Cut down an eyesore."

Matt went back to work and Stella watched for a while. The sound of the saw and the hum of bees echoed all through town. People had to shout at each other in order to be heard, and there were some folks who had a craving for honey when they weren't even partial to sweets.

After a while, Stella decided to try out Rebecca's compass. It showed true north and felt cool as the north in her hands. She walked for half a mile, and when she looked up, she was standing outside the library. That's where she'd been led.

Mrs. Gibson was locking up, but she agreed to let Stella run in and look for the bracelet she said she had lost. Mrs. Gibson more than understood. She wasn't judgmental; her own daughter Solange had tinted her hair blue when she was a teenager and run off to New York to be an actress.

Go on, Mrs. Gibson said, unlocking the door that was carved out of local wood, another huge oak, felled before anyone in town had been born.

Stella had told one last lie, but one which wouldn't hurt anyone. The bracelet her father had given her was around her wrist, as always. This lie told to Mrs. Gibson tasted plain in Stella's mouth, that's how close to the truth it was.

Two minutes, Mrs. Gibson called, but that was time enough for Stella to run in and leave her uncle's thesis on the table in the historical records room. Nearby was a case where important artifacts were displayed: the town seal of Unity, the land grants from the king, a letter from Lincoln to Anton Hathaway's parents, citing the boy's bravery and his sacrifice to his country.

"I see you found what you were looking for," Mrs. Gibson said when Stella came out of the library. Stella held up her hand and shook it so that the bell on her bracelet made a tinkling sound.

"Every time someone died in this town they rang the bell that's up at the old meetinghouse. But not for Rebecca. Matt wrote about it in his thesis."

"Did he?"

"The meetinghouse burned to the ground in the big fire. That's when the bell melted. Matt told me all about it."

Stella remembered a mention of the slight of the unrung bell in the last chapter of the thesis. She found herself walking Mrs. Gibson to her car, wanting to hear more about Matt.

"He's a good person and he'll be a good teacher. I'm glad he's going to get his degree."

"Why wouldn't he?" Stella said.

"My feelings exactly," the librarian agreed. "That thesis is bound to turn up."

After Mrs. Gibson got into her car and drove off, Stella stood there for a while, watching the exhaust from the car turn from black to blue to gray. When she left the parking lot, Stella took the long way back to the tea house. She passed the firehouse, which never would have existed without Leonie Sparrow, and the elementary school, founded by Sarah Sparrow, and the town hall, built a few years after Rosemary Sparrow ran so fast through the woods that she managed to save every boy fighting in the fields. The whole town turned blue at this hour, the white houses, the church with its steeple, Town Hall, the train station where the clock chimed the time. Blue as the shadows of the plane trees, the lilacs, the sidewalks, all of it blue as could be before the dark fell, a curtain of night so deep most people in town could sleep well, and the rest—the guilty, the lovesick, the aging, the sorrowful—would simply have to face whatever the night might bring.

III.

OLD ELI HATHAWAY had taken ill; the end, it was now abundantly clear, would come the way he always suspected it would, with his heart. First he was brought to the hospital in Hamilton, then taken to Boston to see the specialists, and just when he felt he had become a parcel that was undeliverable at any address, he was brought to the nursing home in North Arthur, at the very end of Hopewell Street. In spite of his age, Eli was strong; he'd had a series of cardiac incidents that another man wouldn't have survived. With a family history of cardiac trouble and early death, he had done his best to stay away from matters of the heart. He had never married, or had children, nor had he spent a cent of his family's money, which had increased over the years as the remaining properties from the original Hathaway land grant were sold off, acre by acre. Eli didn't need to work, he had chosen to drive a taxi; he enjoyed the fact that everyone in town knew him by name. As he aged, people in Unity decided he was charming rather than ill tempered. His neighbors brought him dinner and Christmas pies; Enid Frost, who ran the ticket office at the train station, had fixed Eli Hathaway coffee each day for the past twenty-two years without ever asking for a donation to the coffee-break fund.

Now, at the nursing home, Eli was grumpy, and who could blame him? All the nurses wanted to do was to prick his fingers with needles to test his insulin level or take another vial of blood to check his white count. He was dying, you didn't need a test to see that, and he was none too happy about it. A new driver, a fellow from Monroe, had bought Eli's taxi, dirt cheap, and he was probably already overcharging people that needed a ride home. Eli had never asked for more than five dollars and none of his passengers would have guessed that his account in the savings bank was so large that the bank president, Henry Elliot's brother, Nathan, invited him to Thanksgiving dinner every year. The bank oversaw all of the Hathaway investments, because Eli was convinced financial affairs took too hard a toll on the heart, and he had all that cardiac history to consider. All this time, he'd been a rich man who had driven a taxi, who considered a pair of shoes worthless if they didn't last a good ten years. But even if he had used his wealth, what difference would it have made? He would have still wound up in the nursing home, his life reduced to his most essential belongings: a bag of clothes, a shaving cup, a pair of eyeglasses that weren't much good, a straight-edged razor the nurses wouldn't let him use, and the silver star he wore on a chain around his neck.

When Dr. Stewart came to see him, Eli didn't recognize the doctor at first, even though he'd been Eli's physician for forty years. Eli thought the doc was some old boy from the next room who was roaming the halls, giving people checkups for the hell of it. Eli pulled the sheet up to his neck and told the doctor to get out, but he stopped cold when he noticed the girl. He recognized her immediately. Dr. Stewart leaned down to ask if Eli knew where he was, but Eli waved him away.

"Rebecca's here," he said. He felt his pulse thrum and there was a sweet taste in his mouth. "I must be dying if you're here."

Eli Hathaway closed his eyes and waited for heaven, or hell, if that's what was in store for him. When nothing happened, he opened his eyes again. There in front of him was Dr. Stewart and the girl with black hair, both peering at Eli as though he were a dancing chicken or a man from Mars.

Standing there, on a Saturday morning, at an hour when other girls her age were still in bed, Stella saw that Eli Hathaway would die in this room when a massive heart attack came; in less than twenty-four hours his eyelids would flutter and his breath would rise up, all at once. Another girl would have been afraid of Eli, of the scent of death that clung to him, of his crumpled body and the blue veins so very close to the skin, but not Stella. Here in the nursing home, death was everywhere; Stella had spied it in every hallway, in every room. Some of the deaths were so quick, they were easily missed in the time it took to blink. Others were long, drawn-out, not what you'd wish for anyone, not even your worst enemy. In the dining hall of the home, Stella had seen so much death, that one Saturday morning she'd been compelled to sink down onto the linoleum floor, overwhelmed not so much by the sorrow of it all, but by the human dignity, the almost supernatural ability to face the abyss and still order scrambled eggs and toast for breakfast.

In Eli's room, Stella looked over at Dr. Stewart and was certain he saw what was about to happen just as clearly as she did. Her grandmother had told her that Brock Stewart was the most honest man in five counties, but in Stella's opinion, he was a liar, just as she herself was. He'd lied on their last visit to the nursing home, for one thing. Stella saw the look on his face when an old woman, wheezing and spitting up blood, asked if she were dying. Dr. Stewart had brushed the question aside and talked instead about the patient's grandchildren and about the lush spring, brought on by the record rainfalls in April. *There are lilacs growing right in through the window*, the woman said cheerfully, setting her original question aside. *When I close my eyes I still see purple. I hear bees.*

You didn't tell her the truth, Stella had said when they were driving home.

There is no truth. I thought you knew that by now.

On this visit, Dr. Stewart pulled a chair up to Eli's bed. "It's Stella Sparrow who's visiting," the doctor told Eli. "Rebecca's been dead for more than three hundred years. If you're seeing her, my friend, you're seeing angels."

Dr. Stewart took Eli's pulse. Stella counted along with the doctor; slow as molasses. So slow he was clearly winding down. All the same, ill as he was, Eli paid the doctor no mind. He was convinced he recognized the girl in his room. "I knew I'd see you before I died. I knew you'd forgive me."

The doctor and Stella exchanged a look. Eli Hathaway would be dead by morning; they could both feel that. Hathaway signaled for Stella to come near and Brock Stewart marveled at the girl's grit. Even in medical school there were those who'd been repelled by an old man with tubes in his nose and veins, a fellow like Eli, who stank like a bedpan and shook with cold, though the heat was turned up to almost eighty throughout the nursing home, for the comfort of the patients.

"I've got something for you," Eli said.

With difficulty, he tried to open the top button of his striped pajamas. He'd always thought pajamas were a nuisance, and now they were giving him trouble on his last day on earth. Stella helped with the button. There it was, the silver star, the one Eli had worn every day since his own father had given it to him, on his deathbed, as every Hathaway had done since the time it was found among Charles Hathaway's belongings in the days after his horse had sunk into Hourglass Lake, however deep that bottomless place might be.

When Eli couldn't unfasten the clasp on the chain, Stella unhooked it for him.

"Yours." There was a great deal more Eli wanted to say, but his lips were dry, his throat parched; words were escaping him and he had to save them and cherish each one if he were to get out his last request.

All the same, Stella was touched by the gift. She felt like crying, but she didn't. Instead, she secured the star around her throat. Eli watched her carefully; he smiled even though he was dizzy. He looked at Stella and saw a bowl full of stars and endless, unfathomable blue. Of course it would be heaven, he believed that now, it would be stars, and light, and forgiveness.

"I'm leaving all my holdings to the town, but I want you to decide what to do with it," he told the dark-haired girl, the one he'd been waiting for all his life. "Get me a piece of paper," Eli demanded of the doctor. "You'll be my witness."

"Are you sure you want to do this?" Dr. Stewart said. "She's not of legal age."

"What does her age matter? How old were you when they drowned you?" Eli asked Stella, whom he continued to believe was Rebecca.

Having read Matt's thesis, now joyously in the possession of the history department at the state college, Stella knew the answer. "Seventeen and a half. It happened on the sixteenth of November."

"She wasn't of legal age when they did that to her, was she?" Eli said.

"Is he of sound mind?" Stella whispered to Dr. Stewart.

"What's the state we live in, old boy?" Dr. Stewart asked Eli.

"You don't know Massachusetts is a Commonwealth and you call yourself a doctor? Shame on you."

"He's sound," the doctor said. "He can make his own choices."

Stella went to the nurses' station for a pad of paper and a pen, then returned and wrote down everything Eli Hathaway said. His accounts in the bank, his investments, his real property, everything he owned in this world would go to the town, and Stella Sparrow Avery would be the trustee.

"Are you sure you don't want your name down as Rebecca?" Eli asked.

"Stella is fine."

Hathaway signed the document, although he was so weakened Dr. Stewart needed to help him hold the pen; then the doctor signed as well.

"Now I'm free," Eli said. "No more driving around town for me. There's a new fellow doing it and I hear he doesn't know his ass from a hole in the ground."

"True," Dr. Stewart said. "Sissy Elliot wanted to go to the supermarket and the new driver somehow managed to leave her at the Laundromat. She was stuck there for hours."

"But Rebecca knows what she's doing."

Stella was sitting on the ledge of the window. To Eli, with his vision so cloudy, she looked like a bird perched there. She looked like light in the endless darkness. As for Stella, she liked the cool sheen of the star necklace against her skin. When Rebecca walked out of the woods, she'd been wearing this amulet; now it was back where it belonged. In exchange for its return, Stella repaid the favor to the last of the Hathaways. She was glad she'd brought her backpack with her, for she had a great deal of algebra homework due and a dreaded essay to write for American history on Paul Revere. They would be here quite a while, but Stella intended to stay until the end. That was what she had to give Eli: She'd be here with him. She'd see him over.

She set to work while Dr. Stewart dozed and Eli Hathaway's pulse grew so slow it was nearly reversed, a clock unwinding, backward through time. When the light outside faded to dusk, Stella borrowed a lamp from the nurses' station so that she and the doctor could play hearts. Brock Stewart felt proud for Elinor that this was her granddaughter. He wished that Elinor was here with them, but he knew she needed rest. He wondered now if losing so many people had all been preparation for losing Elinor Sparrow. At night, he still called her, at eight o'clock exactly. It was the time he always looked forward to, when they could discuss their day, no matter how small or insignificant the details. Now he was afraid of that hour, and every time he phoned he felt a sinking dread: *What if this is the time when she doesn't answer? What if it's now?*

"This might take all night," the doctor told Stella, as he made himself comfortable in an easy chair after a good hour of cards, a blanket thrown over his shoulders. "I could call you a cab."

"I'd wind up someplace I didn't want to be. You heard what Eli said about the new driver. No. I'll stay."

It had taken three hundred years to get to this day, what was another few hours? Sitting in the darkened room, with both men now sleeping, Stella felt as though she were drifting through space. They breathed in, they breathed out, and then something else. Some time after 2:00 A.M., there was a myocardial infarction. Eli Hathaway began to have convulsions, and then his breathing altered; his color changed, and his eyes became so cloudy he couldn't see this world anymore. The ETs from Hamilton Hospital were called, and while the ambulance sped toward Unity, Stella remained at Eli's bedside.

"He's going," Dr. Stewart said.

Death was in the room with them at that very moment. If it was too much for the girl, she'd leave now. She'd make up an excuse, she'd get sick to her stomach or be desperate for fresh air. Instead, Stella held Eli Hathaway's hand, and Eli held her hand right back, with all the strength that he had. He was a good man, and he'd had a heavy burden; he'd been driving that taxi of his for longer than most of the town's residents had been alive. At night, he had dreamed of the lanes and roads of the village. Now he held tight, as though he'd never loosen his grasp. He did it until the girl leaned down, close, in order to whisper that it was all right, he could let go: He was forgiven. After all this time, he was free.

ONE MORNING, Hap went to the kitchen sink for a glass of water and then he stopped for no discernible reason. He merely felt that something had changed; a drop in air pressure, perhaps, a day that had begun quietly. It was early, and Hap was sleepy-eyed. Looking out at the field he thought he saw a huge pile of hay and leaves. Curious, he pulled on his boots and went out. There was his grandfather, weeping, sitting beside the horse, Sooner, who had died in the night. Already, the horse was cold to the touch.

"Didn't it seem like he'd be the one thing that would last forever?" Dr. Stewart had officiated at dozens of deaths; he'd broken agonizing news, held the hands of the widowed and the bereft, and now he found himself crying over a horse that had lived far too long. One he'd never wanted in the first place.

"Stella will be relieved. She was convinced I'd ride him and break my neck." Hap sat down beside his grandfather. The field was damp with dew, but Hap paid that no attention to the soggy ground. His grandfather, the strongest man he knew, was crying. "We'll have to hire Matt Avery to come in with his bulldozer and bury Sooner right here. I guess it wasn't sooner or later, it was forever."

Dr. Stewart nodded. His grandson was a smart, good boy; at least he didn't have to worry about that. Frankly, he felt connected to him in a way he never had to his own son, David. Maybe he was at fault for that estrangement; he'd been busy, he'd been young, somewhat self-important. The doctor patted Sooner's cold body and remembered reading somewhere as a boy that cowboys in the freezing pioneer West would kill their horses if need be, and crawl inside them, blood and bones be damned, for the warmth. Although the doctor had been sitting beside his horse for four hours, he had missed the actual moment of death. Now he wondered if a horse breathed out his last the way a person did at the very end, a short exhalation, a rising of the spirit. Was Sooner still here in the field, among the grasses and the stacks of hay? Was he in the air they were inhaling right now, entering into them, becoming as much a part of them as their own lungs and liver and heart?

Later in the day, the doctor and his grandson went down to Town Hall together. A meeting had been called to discuss Eli Hathaway's gift to the village, and the doctor, as the witness to the last will and testament drawn up in the nursing home, had been requested to attend. When they arrived, Hap sat in the hallway and read the *Unity Tribune* while his grandfather and Stella and the members of the town council went into the conference room. Mrs. Gibson was there, and Harry Strong, who owned the market, and Nathan Elliot, the bank president. Hap didn't mind waiting. He especially loved perusing the police log, the news section he always turned to first. A car had been broken into on Hawthorne Street. A dog, a spaniel named Mitzi, had bitten the mail carrier and neighbors. Jimmy Elliot had been picked up for throwing rocks at the tea house, and his community service had been extended by ten hours.

"I guess Jimmy Elliot is working for you again," Hap said to Matt Avery when Matt came by, uninvited, to speak on Stella's behalf.

"He was supposed to. Never showed up. What did they nab him for this time?"

"They got him for throwing rocks at the tea house."

"That's an asinine thing to do."

"I think he's in love."

"Ah." Matt nodded, sympathetic. Even Jimmy Elliot wasn't immune to such things. "I stopped by your grandfather's house and took down some fencing and left the bulldozer inside the field," he told Hap. "Tomorrow morning make your grandfather go out somewhere, take him to breakfast. I don't think he should be there when I'm digging the hole for Sooner."

"He's pretty broken up."

"Well, he spent twenty-five years pretending to hate that horse."

After Matt went in to the meeting, it was quiet in the corridor, and Hap got back to reading the police report. People inside the meeting room were surprisingly silent as well, in something of a state of shock as they listened to Dr. Stewart explain that Eli Hathaway had asked Stella to determine what would be done with his estate. At this point many members of the council were wondering if Eli Hathaway wasn't merely being spiteful in his choice of a teenaged executrix; this child now had the power to decide what to do with far more money than anyone had guessed Eli had possessed. They realized it was a huge bequest as Nathan Elliot read off the list of properties, securities, bank accounts, investments. Wasn't choosing Stella to oversee it all a joke on the council members and on the town?

But, no, as it turned out, this was no prank; Stella had already come up with a plan. A clinic was to be built on a lot of Hathaway land, and a doctor and nursing staff employed, for such was Stella's resolve; people wouldn't have to go all the way to North Arthur or Hamilton if they were ill. Not only that, but the Hathaway Recreation Center would be built across from the library. There would be tutoring and an afterschool program; in the summer, swimming lessons would be offered to one and all. This was well and good, this was excellent, as a matter of fact. The members of the town council began to relax, but then Matt Avery got up and he started to talk. This was something of a surprise as well, for Matt wasn't known for his oratory skills. All the same, after so many years of plowing snow and cutting down trees, after so much time spent being alone, he couldn't seem to talk enough. When he finally got in front of a classroom in the fall, he'd go on lecturing for an hour or two at a time, without stopping for breath or a glass of water.

It took Matt more than an hour to tell Rebecca's story; those members of the town council who hadn't been silently taking an oath against Eli Hathaway's memory were cursing him now. But when Stella stood up to thank Matt for his background for her most important decision, even the dissenters fell silent. Now the other shoe was about to drop, the bloody, stone-filled boot. Stella had on the silver star Eli had given her, the one Rebecca had been wearing when she'd been lost in the woods.

Stella informed the group that a dispensation from the mayor and the council would allow a memorial to Rebecca to be built in the center of town. A crew had already been approached and were carting a six-foot-tall slab of granite down from New Hampshire; an ironworks in Lowell had already been contacted. If anyone felt that such a memorial was a sacrilege, they didn't speak up on that day— there was the health center to consider, after all, much needed in town. There was the rec center, where their children would learn to swim—and so work was quickly begun.

If anyone expected letters of protest, they were sorely disappointed. To most people in town, Rebecca Sparrow was nothing more than a portrait in the library, one of the first settlers in Unity, a young girl with long black hair. Folks got used to the idea of Rebecca's memorial, just as they became accustomed to seeing Stella on the town green, sprawled on the grass on days that were fine and on those that were foul. Something that had taken so long now went up in no time, right in the very center of the green, surrounded by plane trees and lindens. Atop the simple granite slab there was a bronze bell which, when it was rung, would be heard for miles around. There would never be silence again, at least not in this town.

Elinor and Jenny came to the common on the evening when the

bell was set in place. It was a windy night in May, and Elinor and Jenny had both dressed up. It was an occasion, after all. Stella hadn't wanted a public display; no fireworks to announce the memorial's completion, no town sing-alongs. It was a family matter, first and foremost. Jenny did the driving now, and she helped her mother along the path that cut across the common. Stella had picked a handful of violets, which she'd set on the step of the memorial in a little glass vase.

"Did it turn out all right?"

Elinor was out of breath and chilled, but seeing the memorial was worth the trek she'd made from Cake House. She nodded her approval; it was, indeed, beautiful. She thought about everything that was invisible: courage, honor, pain, love. She narrowed her eyes and the memorial disappeared, just for an instant; then it was right there in front of them again.

"It's perfect," Jenny Sparrow said.

It was the hour when the light faded quickly, when it drifted down and turned everything blue, houses and steeples, fences and sidewalks. In the time when Rebecca Sparrow lived in this town, people believed blue could protect them from evil, and they often attached strips of indigo homespun to their undergarments and the hems of their skirts. They believed anything sewn with red thread could cure what ailed them, be it fevers or nightmares or fits of coughing, that bay laurel could protect a man from lightning, that helping a blind man would bring good fortune. They believed that remembering someone could bring them back to you long after they had departed, if you only concentrated hard enough, if you stood outside on a windy night and tried to count every star sprinkled across the universe like rice on a table or stones in a lake, like bones in a body or snowdrops in the grass.

IF A TRAVELER was without a map in this section of Massachusetts, he could easily grow confused. The villages blended together to any out-of-towner passing through, particularly when the view was surveyed from the window of the train. Look, and look again; white steeples, town halls, houses with black shutters. Farther out—malls, triplexes, parking lots—and farther still—green woods, streams, fields of black-eyed Susans and barley. It was a quilt without distinction, lilac here, green there, bordered by blurred faces, by rocks and clouds, by bricks and train tracks. Imagine the stations that go by: Concord, Lincoln, Hamilton, Monroe, North Arthur, Unity. The last of these had been built in 1930, out of brown granite, constructed by men from out of town, from Boston or New Haven, men so desperate for jobs they were willing to sleep on cots set up in Town Hall. There they dreamed of home and of trains and of the brown granite dust that fell everywhere whenever the stone was cut, dusting their faces, drawn into their lungs.

When Elisabeth Sparrow came to feed these men she brought pots of nine-frogs stew and over a hundred loaves of bread. Elisabeth heard these men crying in their sleep, she heard them praying for a familiar face, a kind word, supper set before them with care. She was that face, those words, that bread for an entire year. The train station was built with Elisabeth in mind; her name could be found etched into the granite in dozens of places, although an individual had to know what he was looking for in order to identify the lettering. On the whole, people in town didn't seem to notice; to them, the marks were all but invisible, dusty strikes, like a chicken's scratch, a pattern that was indeed impossible to make out if someone was standing too near.

Eli Hathaway used to be a common sight here, out in the parking lot in his taxi or chatting with the ticket-seller, Enid Frost. Eli himself had made a hobby out of counting the times Elisabeth's name appeared in stone, and at last count it was 1,353. But the days of Eli Hathaway's counting her name were over. Now, it was the new driver, Sam Dewey, from over in Monroe, who was parked at the station. Sam was an overly eager fellow who'd confide to anyone who got into his cab that he was trying to start a new life in Unity after his divorce. Indeed, he had a lot to learn. Ever since that incident with Sissy Elliot, when he left her outside the Laundromat, where she stood on the street for several hours, hoping for a neighbor to pass by to give her a lift, Sam had been studying local maps. He no longer had to ask his passengers for directions: *How do you get to Lockhart Avenue? What's the shortcut to the mall in North Arthur?*

On the seventeenth day of May only one passenger got off the early train. Sam Dewey had already begun to wonder if he'd be able to earn a living driving a taxi in this town, so he made a bet with himself on that day, not that he was a betting man, not since his wife had left him, claiming he spent more time at Foxwoods than he did with her. All the same, if the gentleman on the platform got into his cab, Sam would stay in town. If, on the other hand, the fellow who'd gotten off the train turned and walked away, or if a friend or relative came to pick him up, Sam would move to Florida. Just thinking about Boynton Beach, where he'd been once on holiday, and the sunny life that might be ahead, cheered Sam up mightily. But after he went to the phone and looked through the Yellow Pages, the man on the platform approached. He was a well-dressed individual in his thirties, dark hair, a good-looking man who wasn't bogged down by luggage, except for a backpack slung over one shoulder.

Walk on by, Sam started thinking, because after only a few weeks, he could already feel his body molding into the indentation in the driver's seat left by Eli's inert form, positioned in the very same place for so many years. But as it turned out, Boynton Beach would have to wait. Sam would be staying in Unity, at least for the time being. It seemed he had a passenger.

"Lucky you're here," the passenger said. He was a little out of breath and he wasn't as well dressed as Sam had first thought. It was an old suit, actually, but who was Sam to judge? He himself was wearing a frayed sweater and a pair of chinos stained with coffee. "I thought there'd be a car rental place," the fellow said.

"In Unity? You've got the wrong town. Wait a second, maybe you do have the wrong town," Sam joked, angling for a tip later on. "Who is it you're going to see?"

When the passenger said he was just passing through and thought he'd find a motel, Sam Dewey told him, once again, wrong town. The closest motel was the Night Owl in North Arthur, so if it were lodgings he wanted, his best bet was Laurie Frost's guesthouse. Laurie was Enid the ticket-taker's daughter, and quite attractive; Sam wouldn't mind if she felt grateful enough for this referral to say yes if he asked her out to dinner. Laurie's guesthouse was really a converted garage, but it looked fine to most people's eyes, and Sam waited as his passenger walked up the slate path bordered by hostas. He stood outside, leaning up against the taxi, where he smoked a cigarette and nodded as a man ran past.

"Slow down," Sam called out to the runner, feeling quite neighborly as Will Avery went by. Will was not in the least deterred by the fact that Laurie's house was at the top of a hill, but he didn't want to waste any energy in speaking. "Save your energy! Take a taxi!" Sam suggested, but Will only waved and kept on, as he did every morning on his sweep through Unity.

When Sam's passenger returned, he wanted to drive around a bit, see the town. He sneezed several times. "Damn it," he said as they headed back down the hill.

"It's the pollen." Sam cast himself in the role of local expert. "The lilacs, the grass, all the wildflowers. Pollen everywhere you look. My guess, you're a city boy."

The passenger described a historic house he'd heard about, one built like a wedding cake, and Sam Dewey assured him it wouldn't be a problem to drive over and take a look. Of course, without an address, Sam had no idea of where to go, so he drove around awhile, circling the town and wondering how much he could charge for this tour. He stopped for a minute outside Town Hall, ran in, and quickly scanned the map posted in the hall which listed points of interest. Cake House. The earliest surviving building in town. It had to be that.

They drove past the old oak, surrounded by orange cones, for the branches were now dangerously brittle on one side, down Lockhart, to reach what some people called Dead Horse Lane.

"Can't go any farther," Sam Dewey said. At least they could see the three chimneys from here, and a bit of the roofline as well. "My cab would never make it past the ruts they've got. Look at that one!" He pointed to a hole in the driveway so deep it was filled with water. What appeared to be a large stone, but was in fact a snapping turtle, was in the center of the mudhole. "I'd break my axle on that."

The passenger paid and got out. This time he told Sam not to bother to wait. He let Sam Dewey believe he'd checked into the guesthouse, when all he'd done was pick up the copy of the *Unity Tribune* that was on Laurie Frost's doorstep and stick it in his backpack. He didn't want to appear to be a drifter, although that, in fact, was what he was these days. He liked to walk, he told the nosy cabdriver, and that seemed to satisfy Sam Dewey and send him on his way. The passenger walked down the driveway, past the mud puddle. There was the white house that looked so much like the model he'd taken from the table in the front hall of the apartment on Marlborough Street. There was the very same porch, the windows with their funny bumpy panes of glass, the hedges of laurel that were so sweet the bees that hovered around the blooms were groggy, unlike the felt ones on the model's laurels, bees stuck on with glue, with wings that never moved.

One thing he'd said was true: he was just passing through. He'd need a place to rest though, so he turned into the woods. In fact, he wasn't a city boy as that idiot taxi driver had deduced. He'd been raised in the north, far up in New Hampshire, and there he'd stayed until his girlfriend had broken his heart and moved to Boston. In time he had followed her; he'd won her back, but she'd cast him aside again. Twice was once too many times to do that to him.

Now, stepping into the woods again, he felt at home. He kept going until he reached the Table and Chairs; amazed by the rock formation, fascinated by the many shapes nature invented, he took from his backpack the newspaper he'd swiped from Laurie Frost's doorway and the lunch he'd brought with him, a ham sandwich fixed by the maid at the motel in Medford where he'd stayed last night. In exchange for the sandwich, and a free room, he'd left the model of Cake House behind; it had been a gift for the four-year-old daughter the maid had no choice but to bring to work with her in the mornings, since she hadn't the money for a baby-sitter. Why shouldn't he leave it for the child? He didn't need the thing anymore; he had it committed to memory by now, every brick, every stone, every bit of glass.

When he was done with his lunch, he tidied up so that he wouldn't leave a trace. He always left the woods the way he'd found them; he liked the way things looked when there hadn't been human intervention. Frankly, he stayed away from human things. It was sheer luck that he stumbled upon the shell of the old laundry shed, the one Will had all but destroyed so many years ago. Still, the huge core of the chimney remained, and the fireplace would give him shelter. He stood inside of it and immediately felt at home. Seeing one of the bricks was missing, he put his hand inside and drew out a small portrait. There'd been a photograph in the hallway he'd noticed the day Will let him in. Her hair had been blond then but this was the girl he wanted to get rid of. He was sure of it. Once he dispatched this meddler who had seen what he was about to do before it happened, there'd be no one to connect him to the crime, not that his ex-girlfriend hadn't deserved it, not that they all hadn't got what was coming to them, not that he'd had a single restless night of sleep since she'd said her last words to him: *How can you do it? How could your love have come to this?*

THE KNOT

I.

*I*T WAS A BEAUTIFUL SATURDAY MORNING when it happened, so bright Will had woken at the very first light. He was off running earlier than usual, at a little after 5:00 A.M., when the town was still sleeping and only the birds were available to keep him company. At 5:30, the garbage trucks began to lumber through town, stopping first at Hull's Tea House, where the new kitchen helper had set out the trash neatly in barrels the evening before. Liza was awake, of course, baking blueberry scones, watching out the window for Will to run by at some point on his route, as he did every day, sometimes leaving a newspaper on her back step, sometimes a handful of violets in a paper cup, sometimes a note with a single word: *You.*

Elinor Sparrow was always awake at this hour. She didn't have much time to waste, and her sleep came in fitful periods of napping. Now, when she managed a few hours of restless sleep, she always dreamed of snow. Jenny, bombarded by her mother's dreams, had a whole series of snow paintings set out on her dresser and window seat. In the past few days she had gone through so many tubes of titanium white that Mavis Strickland, who stocked the pharmacy's small art supplies section, suggested Jenny order directly from the distributor.

But Jenny needed more than white. Snow could be blue, she had realized, or violet, or the palest pink. It could be an integral part of one's life: her love for Matt was like a snowstorm, sudden, insistent, leaving her breathless. Stella's hair when it was cut had most surely fallen like snow all over Liza's bathroom floor, in an endless blinding whirl. Snow was the flour in the kitchen at the tea house as it was sifted into a bowl or the laundry flakes when Jenny washed her mother's sheets; it was the rice pudding Jenny brought upstairs on a silver-plated tray, one of the few foods Elinor could still keep down. Stars like snow dusted the black night. Snow in the dust motes as rays of sun streamed in through the library window. Snow in the rattle of the last dead arm attached to the oak tree on the corner of Lockhart and East Main, a huge, rotten branch, still uncut, the paper-thin leaves shaking like the air before a storm, before the ut- ter quiet, before whatever came to pass. Snow gathered in the petals of the peach trees, which bloomed throughout town all at once, pink-white flower-ice that smelled of the summer that would soon arrive. Little wonder there were so many words for snow in some languages, the way there was a litany of possible expressions for love or sorrow, or the many varieties of rain Elinor had named.

There were endless sorts of lies, as well, and Stella Sparrow Avery told one more. A last little lie that wouldn't hurt anyone. Poor Liza had actually brought some oatmeal cookies and a glass of milk to Stella's room, for she had come to have a heart-to-heart. Upon hear- ing footsteps on the stairs, Stella had drawn the covers up to her neck, hoping to be left in peace, but Liza could not be dissuaded and Stella lay there, trapped, as Liza asked her questions about her feelings. Did Stella mind if Liza was involved with her father? Should they wait? Or perhaps they should see a therapist in North Arthur together and discuss the new configurations in their life?

"I'm fine with it," Stella was quick to say. If this wasn't a white lie, then at least it was pink, a love-tinged fib told to protect Liza. No, Stella wasn't happy that both her parents were dating. Weren't they supposed to be the ones who were old and sensible and she the one who went wild? But even if Stella wanted to resent Liza, it would have been difficult; Liza was simply the kind of person it was difficult to hate. But not difficult to lie to, so Stella smiled and said goodnight and thanked Liza for the cookies and watched her go out and close the door behind her.

Lie of omission, lie of a teenaged girl, lie of good-night before I climb out the window, lie of I'll explain it all to you in the morning if you find out I haven't slept in my bed, but of course if you never find out, then you really don't need to know. White lie, pink lie, black-and-blue lie. It wasn't Jimmy Stella was going to meet, but Hap Stewart, and it wasn't all fun and games either. Hap was angry at her, annoyed that their joint science project was late because Stella had been spending so much time with Jimmy. True enough, she had taken to meeting Jimmy at the Table and Chairs up in the woods after supper, where they kissed for hours even though Stella had a hundred more pressing things to do. She called him late at night at a prescheduled time just to hear his voice. He couldn't even pass a simple high school class—he was taking earth science for the third time, for goodness' sakes—but each time Stella saw him standing out on the road with a handful of pebbles to throw at her window and that confused expression, as though he'd been drawn to her without reason or forethought, she thought it would be perfectly fine if Jimmy Elliot were the only person in the world, and if all she saw was his face, nothing more.

To assuage Hap, ignored and now in danger of failing science himself due to their late project, Stella had come up with a plan. They needed one more water sample, something no one else in the class had, for them to make up for their lateness with the project. Hap had been the one to suggest Hourglass Lake, then Stella had said they should sleep out there and take the sample early in the morning, first thing. She brought along her backpack and a sleeping bag flung over her good shoulder and she climbed out the window of the tea house, down the trellis that would be covered with clematis in June. She also brought along six peanut butter sandwiches to sustain them, several glass sampling vials, and a flashlight. Hap, who met her at the corner where the oak stood, contributed a tent that smelled like a damp cellar, where it had been stored for fifteen years. The night was warm and humid and mosquitoes were hatching everywhere.

"That dead horse legend is such a load of crap," Hap said when they turned down the lane where the horse was supposed to have first spooked, carrying Charles Hathaway to his final destination. "But I heard a group of kids in the playground behind the school swearing it was true."

"It's total crap," Stella agreed.

They both laughed, recalling this had been their first conversation: their agreement of what was crap.

"Fear not," Hap said.

"I don't intend to," Stella told him.

One night, at dinner, Stella's father had told her and Liza about the night he and his brother had spent at the lake when they were boys, waiting for the dead horse to rise. Matt had fallen asleep like a log, Will had said, leaving him to shiver and watch the dark water alone. *Charles Hathaway*, he'd announced to the murky water. *I'm not afraid of you or your horse.*

"People made that up in the old days," Stella said, "when everyone was still afraid of stupid things."

"Right." Hap was thinking of Sooner, dead in the field, and the look on his grandfather's face. Now whenever Hap went past the field where Sooner had been for so long, he ran, spooked by the breeze or by the clouds or by the rustling of leaves. He'd been growing a lot in the past few months and he towered over Stella. He thought she'd seem like a stranger with her hair cut short and dyed, but she was still the same.

"Sometimes when you get rid of your best feature, you find out it really wasn't anything. Sometimes it turns out your true best feature is something else entirely."

Stella stared at him, surprised. "Have you been talking to Juliet?"

"Juliet?" Hap said. In fact, he'd been talking to her nearly every night, late when everyone else in his household was asleep. The universe had been made out of only two things at such times: the darkness and Juliet's voice. They hadn't meant to keep their conversations secret from Stella, but that's what had happened. Now, Hap was embarrassed, for reasons he couldn't quite comprehend. He was thankful that he was slow in answering, for the time for an answer seemed to pass; they had to concentrate now so as not to stumble in the ruts.

The air smelled like sap and mud and violets. It was the waning of the full moon, the milk moon, which had always told gardeners when to plant. They set up their campsite at the far end of Hourglass Lake. From here they could tell why it had been named so: in the middle, at the deepest point, the shoreline was equally indented, creating a narrow passageway that could fit two rowboats at most, such as the two that were hidden in the tall grass. Hap had tripped over one of the boats, then he leaned down to flatten the weeds. The boats hadn't been used for decades, not since Jenny went out fishing with her father, who called her little Pearl on these occasions, and who taught her that sitting quietly was more important than how many fish were actually caught.

"We'll go out into the dead center," Stella said. "We'll get our water samples from a location no one's ever been to before. Mr. Grillo will be so impressed he won't mind that we're a little late."

"We're already two weeks late, Stella. I thought we were waiting until morning." Hap stood there holding two oars he had found, chewed up by field mice and time, but still serviceable. All the same, he hadn't planned on night fishing. It was dark, in spite of the milk moon. And there was the dead horse to consider, after all, the one he wasn't worried about.

Stella began to drag one of the boats out of the grass. *Little Pearl*, it was called. "I wonder who little Pearl was."

Stella, of course, had no idea that her mother had been a girl who liked to go fishing and swimming with her father and who had once counted ninety-two water lilies among the weeds. The bullfrogs were croaking, and the sound of the water was soft as the rowboat was pulled into the shallows. Stella got in.

"Come on," she urged, and Hap lurched into the boat awkwardly, holding on to the glass sample vials; *Little Pearl* tipped with his weight and Stella laughed at her friend.

The reeds were tall and feathery, black in the night, like the strands of Rebecca Sparrow's hair when they chopped off her braid. They drifted a bit and could spy the wedding cake house as they neared the center of the lake. There was a light on in the kitchen. Someone couldn't sleep. Elinor, perhaps, was ailing; someone was most likely fixing tea. Still Stella and Hap were fairly certain they would go unnoticed. They both had the feeling that their friendship was about to change, not unwind, exactly, but shift. It had done so already, because of Jimmy Elliot, and now there seemed to be Juliet. Stella wasn't a fool; she sensed her two best friends were becoming closer to each other than they were to her. People were coming between Stella and Hap, mattering, if not more, than certainly differently.

Perhaps that was why they were out on the lake, steering toward the center where a good number of lily pads were sucked into the current created by the movement of their oars. Soon, the yellow water lilies would open, but now they looked like a mass of frogs, the pads greenish black and leathery.

There was a plashing sound and Stella stiffened. It was a moment when she suddenly felt they had no business being out here at this hour.

"Bullfrog," Hap whispered.

Stella, comforted, leaned back and looked up at the swirl of stars up above. " 'I wish I may, I wish I might,' " she whispered now. Unbidden, Jimmy Elliot came to mind.

A bullfrog hopped from one lily pad to another, scaring them for a moment.

"Jesus," Hap said.

The boat rocked back and forth, and Stella and Hap held on to the sides and laughed.

"Jeremiah." Stella recalled an old song her father sometimes played. The notion of a bullfrog with a name like Jeremiah set them to laughing again, although they tried their best to muffle the sound. For that instant they concentrated completely on not being caught, all they heard was the sound of each other's mirth, the laughter gulped down. They didn't hear anything else in the water until the second boat knocked into theirs. It was the boat they'd left behind in the grass, *The Seahorse*. Stella felt a wave of anger, thinking it was Jimmy following her, but Jimmy had been tossing rocks at her window and was only just turning down Lockhart on his way toward home, disappointed by her absence.

Stella thought "*Seahorse*" a second time, and then the anger turned to something else. She divided the word, and was left in that dark instant with a single terrifying syllable.

When the other boat hit against theirs, an oar was swung out toward them through the black night. Hap was knocked overboard so quickly, it was quicker than the leap of any frog. One minute he had been leaning over to dip a glass vial into the water, trying his best not to laugh at the bullfrog's antics, and the next he'd been swallowed whole by the dark.

The oar hit Stella when she turned to see where Hap had gone. It hit her squarely between her shoulder blades, the weakest spot in her body, where the bones had been broken at birth. At that instant of pain she arched her body away from the thing that had hit her. She might have gone overboard as well, but her bracelet, the birthday gift from her father, caught on the screw which held the seat of the *Little Pearl* in place. Stella tore at her wrist until the bracelet came free. It fell into the water, without a sound, as though it had been swallowed whole.

Stella was not thinking clearly; certainly, she wasn't thinking someone had tried to hurt them. It must be a branch, an obstacle they'd missed in the dark. All she thought of was Hap. Stella stood without thinking, so that the boat rocked back and forth and she shouted into the dark. The sound of her cry went across the lake and the lawn, through the kitchen window where her mother was making a pot of chamomile tea, down the lane to where Jimmy had kicked some papery oak leaves into a pile, before setting a match to the collection, trying his best to burn out his disappointment with himself for all of his blind, stupid actions.

Jenny Sparrow had been up most of the night with her mother, who was suffering with a fever. At first Jenny thought Elinor had caught the spring flu, but Dr. Stewart had assured Jenny this was not the case. It was the beginning of her unraveling, that was the only way he could describe what was about to happen, and it was best to make Elinor as comfortable as possible with blankets and hot tea. The fever made for terrible shivers, but Dr. Stewart did not mention that tea and blankets would not alleviate this condition. The coldness was formed inside: Elinor's blood was so thin it was as though ice crystals had formed. Brock Stewart did not tell Jenny Sparrow that he had ministered to patients whose last breaths were entirely made out of ice, so that their lips turned blue at the moment of their death, as the crystals which held their essence melted into the warm air.

Jenny had just set the teapot and cups on a tray when she heard the scream. She was wearing a T-shirt and a pair of sweatpants and she had no shoes on, but she took off running. Every mother knows her child's cry, and Jenny was no exception. She heard the screen door slam behind her, but she didn't feel herself push it open. She heard the bullfrogs in the lake, yet she didn't feel the grass under her bare feet. Up in Elinor's bedroom, Argus began to bark, and his barking sifted through his mistress's dreams. By then, Jenny had raced across the lawn where Will and Matt had once stood looking up at her window; she was halfway down the driveway with ruts so deep any one who wasn't aware of them would surely stumble. She could see the boats on the dark water, like coffins afloat. She could see Stella's form as the girl leaned toward the lake, too close, and then utterly gone as Stella slipped over the side of the boat, in a desperate attempt to search for Hap. At the same time, Jenny could hear a boy shouting from the lane—Jimmy Elliot, running like a madman in the same direction as Jenny, shouting for Stella, hurdling over clumps of weeds, paying no mind to the nettle and the swamp cabbage, the bloodroot and the water dragons with their fragrant white spikes that snagged on the legs of his jeans.

A man in one of the boats was standing. He saw Jimmy racing through the weeds and right away he thought he spied a demon. He had followed Stella and Hap in *The Seahorse*, the boat Jenny's father always said was the more unpredictable of the two, more difficult to row, more likely to tip. The man who'd never been aimlessly passing through town went over the side, and was grateful for the dark water. He had to get away before the demon came any closer, even though he hadn't managed to get to the girl. Mission not accomplished. He cursed himself and the demon running through the tall grass and everyone he'd ever known. If he'd been a better swimmer he would have gone after the girl, but as it was, he was lucky to get away before Jimmy Elliot got to the shore.

Inside the house, Elinor had reached for the phone. When she pushed 1 she was automatically connected to Brock. The doctor was used to Elinor calling at odd hours and in fact he always swore he slept with the phone on his pillow. Indeed, it must be true because he answered after a single ring and assured her he would phone the police and an ambulance. Elinor wanted to see for herself what was going on. But by the time she managed to get out of bed, Jenny had already reached the waist of the hourglass and dove in. Stella was difficult to make out from a distance; she was treading water, shivering as she tried her best to feel in the cold water for Hap. She cried at the same time she splashed around frantically. Jenny pulled her over to the boat.

"Stay here," Jenny told her daughter, and for once Stella did as she was told. "I'll go and get him."

On the shoreline, Jimmy Elliot pulled off his boots and his shirt. He couldn't see Stella, paddling around and crying on the other side of the *Little Pearl*, but he jumped in the water anyway. He was a lousy swimmer, but he made it there. He helped Stella into the boat, then looked round for Jenny as he spit out water that tasted like frogs.

Jenny was underwater, and when she came up, sputtering, there was grit and mud in her teeth.

"Stay with Stella and the boat," she told Jimmy. At that moment she had no idea who he was. A teenager with dark hair who looked frightened when he saw her. Still, he was there to keep an eye on Stella while Jenny went down to search again. The moonlight sunk into the water with her; it spread out in a crinkly silver splash, then disappeared, leaving only pitch. Jenny felt something spindly, a leg, perhaps, or the bones of the old horse, or the remains of Rebecca Sparrow. But it was only drifting root strands trailing beneath some water lilies, twisted into a braid. Jenny grabbed something heavy; she thought she had something, she thought it was Hap, but found it was only an old boot she'd brought to the surface, which she hurriedly threw back, before she went down for the third time.

Stella leaned over the edge of the *Little Pearl*, to put her cold hand in Jimmy's as he clung to the boat. He felt amazingly hot, even though the water was frigid. He felt alive. "She'll find him," Jimmy said. "Your mother's a good swimmer."

In the boat, Stella finished making the wish she had begun when they first rowed into the lake. When they drowned Rebecca Sparrow, everything had been white, blindingly so. Blinding sunlight, blinding ice, snow that fell like stars. Only the water had been dark, as it was now; it pulled Rebecca down and twisted around her like a sheet, with water weeds and the silky tendrils of the water lily roots threaded around her ankles, her wrists, her waist.

Elinor was at her bedroom window. A wind had come out of nowhere and it shook the leaves from the trees. From where she stood, Elinor could see her granddaughter in the boat on the lake. But she couldn't see Jenny. All at once she wondered what on earth she'd been doing all these years, why she'd needed a rose that might never bloom, why she'd allowed all those years to pass when she didn't see Jenny, why she'd shut the door against one and all. Love could do that to some people and they wouldn't even know how much they'd missed out on; they simply remained in the place where love had left them, while the whole world spun around.

In the water, something was pulling Jenny down; perhaps it was the weight of her own body, or the rush of her own descent. She thought he was a log at first because it was so dark, but she grabbed hold of whatever it was. Already, she thought she might not get back herself. There was no air in her lungs, but she could see the moonlight, and the surface of the water moving, and the shape of Jimmy Elliot reaching out to her as she dragged Hap Stewart along, gripping tightly to this boy who was meant to live even though he'd been thrown hard and part of his spine had been shattered. Hap was hoisted into the rowboat where Stella breathed life back into him: she refused to stop until he blinked his eyes open, until he could see the stars in the sky, not from beneath the black pool of water but from the safety of the boat as it bobbed up and down in the water, as the ambulance and the fire trucks came tearing down Lockhart Avenue, so fast the marks their tires made on the asphalt would last until October. Ever after, Lockhart Avenue would seem to have a white stripe on either side of the road, and there were people in town who would step on their brakes every time they took the turn off East Main Street, slowing down to consider just how lucky they were.

What was a siren but a call to your neighbors, a cry that would let them know that grief of one sort or another was coming through, as it did for someone every day, every evening. It had to be someone, and on this night it was Hap; on this night, when the wind picked up until the fair day was gone from memory. Running down the lane, muddy and wet, was the man who had killed his ex-girlfriend in Brighton, who had hit Hap with his oar, though he'd been aiming for Stella. Stella, who was too smart for her own good, just like his ex-girlfriend. No one would have noticed his ex was missing, if not for that girl and all the publicity her father had generated. His ex-girlfriend had no family and only a few friends; she should have already been forgotten. Instead, people had remembered. On the corner in Brighton where the victim's apartment building was located, neighbors had taken to leaving wreaths of lilies and ivy, as if she'd been someone important. A fund-raising committee had been organized which allowed a gravesite and a headstone to be purchased. Only last week, the University of Massachusetts, where she'd begun taking classes toward her graduate degree, had named a scholarship in her honor. All because that damned girl had noticed her in a restaurant. All because people thought once she was murdered, she had a story to tell, a worthless story as far as this man was concerned, a woman's story that had no beginning, only an end. She was nothing more than the bee that was humming nearby, which the man neatly swatted away from his ear as he jogged down Lockhart Avenue.

"Damn you," he said, to the bee and to Stella and to the woman he once thought he loved who had caused all this trouble in the first place when she turned him down. It was all their fault, especially the bee, for the damned thing wouldn't leave him alone. If he wasn't careful, he'd hear the sound inside his head and it would block out everything else, and then he'd be in trouble. He'd be running blind.

More fire trucks passed him, called in from North Arthur, but he kept on running, faster now, because there were more bees behind him. The bees smelled sweet, they had pollen from the laurels and the red clover coating their bodies, but they sounded terrifying. Before long, there were a hundred, and then two, and then it was a cloud that hummed behind him, keeping pace without effort. There was no way to run from them, but he thought there was, just as he'd thought the woman he'd gotten rid of in Brighton wasn't anyone worth remembering. He had no idea that bees like dead trees best of all; they always return to the comfort of heartwood gone dry if given a choice, for the wood in those old branches was so soft it was like marrow.

The man who was running was an out-of-towner; he couldn't know what was up in front of him. Unlike Will Avery, who always avoided the corner where the oak tree stood, since a single sting could kill him on the spot. Unlike Matt Avery, who knew enough about bees to feel comfortable when they swarmed. Matt understood that bees liked order and that unexpected or rowdy behavior would cause them to be agitated. That was one thing nobody wanted, an enraged swarm at his heels, but that's what the man who couldn't run fast enough had now.

Jimmy Elliot had helped pull the rowboat ashore. He had begun to chase after the figure he'd seen, but had to stop after a half-length.

He stood panting at the edge of Dead Horse Lane, trying his best to catch his breath. He vowed then and there to give up cigarettes. Actually, he made several promises to himself as he stood there on the shore, dripping water, sick with worry and love. Coming onto the shore, he was the only one to have seen someone take off. Just a shadow, just a glimpse, but Jimmy knew how easily it was to slip into the dark; he had robbed several houses in the neighborhood, and even though he'd given that up since he'd been caught and forced into community service, he hadn't forgotten what it was like. Just because people didn't bother looking at shadows, that didn't mean they weren't there.

It was a shadow who had the bees trailing after him, who jumped into a patch of stinging nettle when Dr. Stewart's old heap of a car rattled by. This shadowman, itching like crazy and running as fast as he could, had no particular escape route in mind; he'd follow the train tracks back to Boston, where he'd rethink and replan. And then he stopped unexpectedly, despite the bees. He thought he spied an elephant on the corner, gray and brown, bellowing as it loomed up before him. The man who thought nothing of murder, who would have willingly done it twice, stood there immobilized. His breath was hot in his cold, muddy body. He couldn't possibly be seeing straight. The trunk of the elephant was swinging out toward him. When the last dead section of the oak tree fell, it was dripping with honey; the bees were circling, one cloud, one being, as every bone in the body of the man who'd stopped running was broken, as everything he'd once been unwound in the soft, dark night.

They took Hap Stewart to the hospital in Hamilton, and from there he was flown to Boston for emergency surgery. Stella drove to the city with Dr. Stewart. They didn't speak on the ride in, but they didn't have to. Brock Stewart was going eighty miles an hour on I-95 and Stella wished he would go faster. They didn't bother to find a motel; there was no need for one. Stella was still wearing her wet clothes with Jimmy Elliot's shirt buttoned all wrong on top. She had water and frogs and weeds in her boots, and her hair stuck up, like feathers. She didn't care about any of that, nor the fact that she squeaked when she walked, nor the dark water she dripped all over the hospital lobby. They decided to camp out in the waiting room, where Dr. Stewart fell asleep some time near dawn. Stella, on the other hand, must have inherited something from Sarah Sparrow, for like Sarah she could stay awake all night long. No one would ever guess she hadn't had any sleep. No one would guess how hard she could wish for something.

The surgery lasted eleven hours, and for all that time Stella pictured Hap's face, his shining eyes, the way he'd been laughing in the moments before the oar had struck him. When Stella saw the surgeon approach, she shook Dr. Stewart awake and he blinked in the fluorescent light of the waiting room while the surgeon told them the good news. Someone else might not consider six months to a year of rehab good news, but Stella and the doctor most certainly did. One of Hap's legs would be shorter than the other, and he would most certainly walk with a limp, but even that was good news to them.

All along Dr. Stewart had been preparing for the worst, and when the surgeon left them, Brock seemed weakened. He sat back down in one of the plastic waiting room chairs, and he cried, the way he'd been known to when making rounds. The doctor's son, David, had been away on business and he arrived straight from the airport, shaken, having protected himself from the realm of sorrow ever since his wife's death. Now he collapsed in his father's arms.

"He's still our Hap. Six months of rehab at Hamilton Hospital. And be prepared when you see him—he's got a metal halo screwed into his head."

"Jesus. I was in Baltimore." The girl with the dark hair who was sitting with them looked vaguely familiar. "Is that Jenny Sparrow?"

Hap's father asked, confused, for he'd gone to school with Jenny and he knew she should be as old as he was. Ancient, at the moment. Worn out and useless and about a hundred years older than the girl on the bench.

"Her daughter," the doctor said. "Elinor's granddaughter."

"Was it a broken neck?"

"Thankfully, no. But almost as bad. A spinal injury." The doctor did not say that if the oar had hit him half a centimeter to the right or left Hap would have been paralyzed. "The halo's going to drive him crazy."

Stella had decided it didn't matter if Hap wasn't quite as tall; it didn't matter if his posture was sloped or if he limped, he still had his other best feature. She excused herself and phoned Juliet Aronson from a pay phone. Juliet hadn't been to a hospital since her father died, she was phobic about such places, but when Stella explained what had happened, she took a taxi and was there in under twenty minutes. When Juliet came flying down the hallway, Stella didn't recognize her friend. Juliet hadn't bothered with makeup; she was wearing a nightgown underneath her raincoat and had on plastic flip-flops. This was the way love walked in, barely dressed, confused, panic-stricken, overcome, not caring what anyone thought or what they believed.

"God, you look terrible," Stella said, as she led her Juliet down the hallway.

"You look worse." Juliet laughed out a noise that sounded broken.

Stella threw her arms around her friend; they hugged each other, then Juliet backed away.

"You're soaking wet."

"He has a halo. One of those metal braces that screw right into your skull. It's his spine that was hurt."

Juliet's face was tight, but she was pretty without all her makeup; without her bravado, she didn't seem any older then Stella. "I don't care what he has if he still has his integrity," she said. "That's his best feature."

In the postop room Hap Stewart was breathing slowly, deeply adrift inside the half-sleep of anesthesia which was only beginning to wear off. He thought he was in a boat floating on the black water. He thought there were mosquitoes in the air, and all around there was the steady droning of bees. He thought a beautiful girl leaned down close and whispered, *I'll always be here*. It was the voice from the telephone, the person who knew him inside out, Juliet Aronson. He smiled just to know she was there. A day starts out in one direction and ends in ways no one could imagine, with halos, with true love, with bees, with a swirling mass of stars below the fluorescent light, with good fortune where it was least expected to be found. Hap Stewart knew exactly who he was for one lucid moment, and that was more than could be said for most people. Before he sank back into morphine and sleep, he said *Lucky* out loud, as if that single word was his prayer and his protection, well worth repeating every day of his life.

II.

"SHE'S NOT DREAMING about snow anymore."

Matt was working out in the marsh, and Jenny had come to bring him lunch. She no longer had to buy tube after tube of titanium white now that her mother had moved on with her dreams.

"What is it now?" Matt asked.

"I think she's dreaming her life. I'm not going to have any choice but to know her."

They were only a few yards away from the spot where Constance Sparrow waited for her husband when he was at sea. Constance could stay underwater for nearly twenty minutes, and was often called upon to search for drowned sailors, each time hoping the man she searched for wasn't her own husband. She set out a lantern as a beacon to sailors; later, it became the Unity lighthouse, out on a line of black rocks. It was not far from here that the *Good Duck* had run aground, many year earlier, when the marsh was a deep harbor, perhaps the reason there were hundreds of peach trees growing up through the reeds. Or perhaps this abundance had been caused by women in love, who'd come to the marsh to make one final plea, with their peach stones tied on strings around their necks.

Either way, Matt had been hired by the town to cut down the seedlings that cropped up around the boathouse each spring, making it difficult for people to get their canoes into the water. He'd defended his thesis and accepted the job at the college. In the fall, someone else would have to be hired to clear away the fallen branches on the Elliots' property and bag the leaves on the common. Someone else would have to plow snow this coming winter, and then in April to power-wash the pine pollen off the sidewalks around Town Hall and the library. But at this time of year there would always be enough work for two men; next May, when classes let out, Matt would be back here at the boathouse, cutting down peach saplings, working so hard the only thing he'd hear was the echo of his own breathing, a steady rhythm.

Jenny took her latest paintings out of the picnic basket and arranged them in the grass. There was a girl with black hair. There was a garden where everything was green, except for a single azure bloom, hydrangea blue, sky blue, blue as the water had been when the marsh was a deep inlet where peach saplings destined for Boston Harbor had floated. Just last night, Jenny had experienced a dream that was filled with a strange pattern of red and blue lines, not unlike a spider's web. It wasn't until she painted the dream that she realized it was a human heart. It was her mother's life in color, in scarlet and indigo. Now, in the marsh, Jenny lay down with Matt for a few minutes in the grass. Her own heart beat ridiculously fast when she was beside him. Love was like that, like a dream you didn't quite understand, one in which you didn't necessarily know what you were looking at until it was right in front of you.

Love ambushed you, it lay in wait, dormant for days or years. It was the red thread, the peach stone, the kiss, the forgiveness. It came after you, it escaped you, it was invisible, it was everything, even to someone at the very end of their life, such as Elinor Sparrow. The more Elinor slept, the more she dreamed, but that didn't mean she wasn't still attached to this world. It was too late for medicine, for intervention, for hope, but it was not too late to give some things away. To her daughter, she gave the dreams of her youth. To her granddaughter, she gave Rebecca's bell, so she would never be silenced.

Sometimes Stella sat by her grandmother's bed and held her hand, and it was the only attachment Elinor Sparrow had to this world: the thread that pulled her back. Sometimes Jenny brought her water or tea, and this was the only attachment: the needle that pulled the thread. Sometimes it was Brock Stewart, carrying her out to the garden so she could feel sunlight, and this was the attachment she had to this world, the cloth that covered her and held her in place, so that she stayed with them like a leaf caught between branches, rattling, paper-thin, so translucent you could see right through into the next world.

But even those who are barely attached have their worries. Elinor fretted about what would happen to Argus after she passed on. If no one stayed on in Cake House, where would he go?

"When I die, you'll have to take him," she told Brock one day in the garden. She'd been dreaming of Argus. He was a puppy who refused to be separated from her. She tied him to a desk and told him to stay, and he just pulled the furniture along as he trailed after.

"Another animal that refuses to die? Elly, you can't do that to me. I just got rid of Sooner."

"Sorry. It's done. I bequeath him to you."

"Ah, Argus." The doctor leaned to rub the faithful dog's head. "Live well, but don't live much longer."

Elinor laughed. "You mean, mean man."

"I'm cruel," the doctor agreed. "I'm sure my cooking would kill the poor boy in no time flat, since he's used to your chicken and rice."

For so long Elinor had felt nothing, it still was a surprise to feel so much now. Anyone would think that being empty inside would make a person feel light, but in fact it brought with it a terrible heaviness. It was as though her bones had been made of iron all these years, her shoes made of lead. Only now, sitting with Brock in the garden, with Argus dozing at their feet, did Elinor slip off those shoes. The grass felt warm on her toes. Almost summer. Was that a dream, or was it real? She blinked back the sunlight.

"Where do you think old Sooner is now?" Elinor asked of the doctor's horse.

"He's still in my field. He's in the earth. In the grass."

The doctor turned and wiped his eyes with the palms of his hands.

"Who would have guessed you'd be crying over that old hay bag."

But that wasn't it at all, Elinor saw that from the look on his face when he turned to her. That was the attachment, that was the way he held on to her.

From up on the porch, there was the sound of voices, then laughter and a door slamming. Stella and Jimmy Elliot arrived.

"He had meningitis when he was eight months old," the doctor said of Jimmy. "I didn't think he'd make it. I took Henry Elliot aside and I told him he'd better prepare for the worst, but here he is on your front porch."

"Creating havoc," Elinor said, for Jimmy seemed to spend all his time at Cake House. Why, he'd brought Elinor a dinner tray the other evening and he hadn't even bothered to knock on her door. He'd called her Granny and put a vase of flowers on her dresser.

"Living his life," the doctor said. "Good for Jimmy Elliot. Why should he walk when he can run? Maybe he remembers how close he came. He's surely not going to let anything pass him by while he's here."

The doctor had been wrong about Jimmy the way Stella had been wrong about Hap. She thought he'd be thrown from a horse and break his neck, and now he was safe at home, working with a physical therapist from Monroe and watching TV. He was on the phone all the time to that girlfriend of his in Boston, so Dr. Stewart assumed he was improving each day.

"That's the age for it." Elinor remembered Jenny talking to Will constantly, as if she couldn't be pried away from the sound of his voice. She remembered the way she and the doctor kept their phones on their pillows, so it seemed they were together, even when they were not. "They've got a lot to say. For a while, at least."

"Like us."

Brock Stewart thought of how, when Hap first came to live with him, he used to bring the boy to pick violets, up on the hill behind Cake House, because Hap's mother had done so. They trekked to the hillside every spring, until Hap had let him know it was unnecessary to do so. *Grandpa, it's okay. You don't have to keep bringing me here. I remember this. I remember her.*

"Your horse is in the field." She had dreamed of that horse, once or twice. She had seen it running, in this world or the next. "Or so you say. But where do we go?"

"I used to think there was a plan, a rough plan, but a plan all the same," the doctor admitted. "Now, I believe there are a thousand plans. Every breath, every decision, influences the plan, expands it, shortens it, twists it all around. It's always changing. Those of us lucky enough to make it through the multitude of possible diseases and accidents get old. We get tired. We close our eyes."

"And then? Where are we then?"

Silly to ask him as though he knew, but in fact the doctor didn't hesitate. He took Elinor's hand and placed it on his chest, in the place where he knew his heart to be.

"There."

Elinor smiled and thought *At last*. At last someone had told her the truth. She could see it and feel it as the days bled into each other, until they were dreams. That was the way time passed now, so that yesterday was the same thing as today, even though a week had passed. They were still in the garden, even though seven days had gone by. There were weeds in the beds and chinks missing from the stone wall. The dark was sifting down.

"It's beautiful," Brock Stewart said of the garden Rebecca had begun long ago. Once a man started crying, he could never get away from it; it became a habit he couldn't break. The doctor had started that morning when Liza lost her baby, and now he barely noticed anymore. He could stand in a hospital corridor looking at his notes, and not even realize what had happened until the letters were swimming, the ink dripping down the page. He could be in a garden and believe it was raining, until he noticed nothing was coming down from the sky.

"It will be in ruin soon enough," Elinor assured him. "Keep your eye on it."

"Still beautiful. Even then."

Elinor was resting on the bench the doctor had given her as a present, but now she could barely sit up. She shifted and leaned her head against the doctor. She could hear the steady rhythm of his heartbeat.

"You were right," she said. "I'm tired."

There were thirteen sparrows on the stone wall; thirteen beds where the roses grew. Time had passed so quickly here. Elinor had turned around twice and it had all passed her by. But at least those iron shoes had been kicked off, the lead was out of her bones. She was drifting, she knew it, and she didn't even try to stop it from happening. She felt extremely light, as though she had air in her veins rather than her cold, frozen blood. She was exhausted, but the air smelled so sweet. The fresh green air of May.

Stella had insisted that her grandmother would live until winter, she had envisioned snow, but Brock Stewart knew there were no guarantees. He'd seen it with his own eyes: people he thought would survive lasted only days. Those he believed hadn't a chance to see morning went on for years. He knew that Elinor was growing weaker, that was a fact, too weak to wait for winter. Some days she dozed in the garden until it was nearly dark, the pearly milk light of May falling down on them.

There were evenings when the doctor had to carry her back to the house; soon enough, he had to carry her both ways, to the garden and back, wrapped in a blanket, even though the weather was fine. The doctor thought of his old horse in the field whom he missed more than he ever would have thought possible. He thought of Liza Hull kissing her baby good-bye, and of his grandson in his hospital bed, and of all the people he'd seen enter this world and those he'd helped leave it behind. He was a lucky man to be sitting beside Elinor in the garden in the last green days of May. He had loved her for so many years, he would just go on doing it, with or without her.

He knew that attachments were for the living, and so he did the honorable thing. He let her go. He leaned close so she would hear him say it was all right for her to leave him. They knew it was now; they could feel something shift the way it always did. Even Argus, who'd been whimpering, grew quiet. It was not a dream, but something more. She breathed out, and inside that one breath was every word that had been spoken, every step she had taken, everyone she had ever loved.

Above the stone wall, there stood one of the wild peach trees, possibly descended from one that had been set adrift long ago in the shipwreck, so close to shore. Or perhaps this tree had grown from a love token, tossed aside when it was no longer needed. The air itself smelled of peaches, here and all over Unity; when the breeze came up, petals fell like snow. If a person didn't move, if she was completely still, the petals streamed over her, catching in the hem of her clothes, in the strands of her hair, white as snow, quiet as snow, silent and fleeting and drifting down from above to cover her and carry her home.

III.

THE SERVICE FOR ELINOR SPARROW took place at the old meetinghouse on Chestnut Street in the last week of May, the season when gardeners are told to plant their tomatoes and corn, when children beg to stay up late now that the evening was bright, when the lion appeared on the western horizon in the nighttime sky and the lamb was nowhere to be seen. The family meant to leave Argus home when they went to the service, but he followed as far as Lockhart Avenue, at a surprisingly rapid pace for a dog as old as he. There was little choice but to stop the Jeep at the corner; Matt and Will got out and hoisted the wolfhound inside. The faithful deserve something, on this everyone agreed: kindness, at least, consideration, naturally; most of all, the right to their grief.

It was a large crowd who awaited them at the meetinghouse, nearly two hundred people, many of whom came back to Cake House for lunch afterward, traversing the rutted driveway for the first time in their lives. Many of the folks who had always been spooked by the notion of snapping turtles and drownings came to hang their jackets into the hall closet and meander around the parlor where Liza Hull had set the long trestle table with the good silver and several huge platters of sandwiches and cakes.

People spoke in whispers at first, then grew braver. Sissy Elliot, helped in by her daughters, roosted on one of the couches in the parlor, calling for fruit salad and tea. A few local children balanced their glasses of punch on the arrowhead case, then chased each other around the occasional table until their mothers told them to mind their manners. Hap Elliot, who was progressing nicely with his physical therapy, still used a wheelchair when he was in a crowd; today, he was nearly overwhelmed by good wishes. Juliet Aronson had taken the train in and was staying with Liza; at the luncheon she barely left Hap's side. She'd been right about his best feature, after all. Hap told her that he wouldn't blame her if she'd rather be with someone else, someone taller, for instance, someone who walked without a limp. Integrity, exactly as Juliet had foretold. As it turned out, height meant nothing. Precisely as she had suspected: everything that mattered was within.

Cynthia Elliot had volunteered to pour tea and collect stray plates, and due to the unexpected crowd, she was needed in the kitchen as well, to fix extra cucumber and salmon sandwiches. A guest book was left out on the dining room table, and signed by one and all: Eddie Baldwin, the plumber, had brought his entire family. The Fosters had come, and the Quimbys, including Marian, who looked at Will with moon eyes, just as she always had, even though she was a grown woman and a practicing attorney with three children of her own. She tried her best to flirt with him, but he just talked about Liza, endlessly, it seemed. There were so many neighbors that people who hadn't seen each other in five or six years now sat down over tea and discussed the intricacies of their lives. When someone left, someone else took his or her place. Cynthia Elliot had the good sense to commandeer her brother, Jimmy, who'd never made a sandwich in his life, and before he could complain, she set him to work spreading cream cheese on toasted rounds of bread.

Jimmy Elliot had become a hero of sorts, heralded for ignoring his community service and failing to chop down the last branch of the oak on Lockhart Avenue. He'd been invited to come talk to the third-grade class, whose students had protested the felling of the oak, and had, for one entire afternoon, held hands and pranced around the trunk singing.

Sometimes, you're smarter not to take orders, Jimmy told the rapt students when he visited their classroom, much to the dismay of Mrs. Cole, who'd been Jimmy's third-grade teacher as well and remembered him climbing to the top shelf of the coat closet and refusing to come down.

Doesn't anyone in this town see what's right in front of them? They're all terrible judges of character, Jimmy had said to Stella afterward. *I guess they'll figure out who I am soon enough. I might as well enjoy it while I can.*

They know who you are, Stella had told him. *So do I.*

Will Avery had also been put to use on the afternoon of Elinor's memorial service. He had helped Liza transport the large coffee urns, and was later sent off with a platter of tiny brioche to offer to the most elderly of the visitors, the ones who, once they were situated in a love seat or couch, only got up again for one thing: to leave. Jenny was the one who didn't seem to know what to do with herself; she stood in the front hall, as though ready to leave. But where would she go? She couldn't bring herself to abandon the hall closet, where Elinor's ashes were stored in a metal canister. She tried to walk toward the kitchen to help Liza, and found she couldn't take a single step.

"How are you holding up?" Matt Avery had brought over a strong cup of black tea.

"Absolutely fine." But, in fact, Jenny felt as though she was glued to the floor. She, who had found it so very easy to run away, now found she couldn't move an inch. "Terribly," she amended.

"Him, too."

There was the doctor, looking through one of the windows beside the front door. He could see into the garden, but it was a vision that was cloudy and green. What was he seeing? Elinor's last breath, broken into a thousand molecules? Was that what he was breathing?

Her essence, her self, the person he would miss every day, his worst patient, his nastiest neighbor, his most treasured friend.

"Stella's out there," he said when Jenny came to stand alongside him. When she looked, Jenny thought she saw her mother in the garden. She thought she saw Elinor crouched down, the way she'd been when she was grieving for everything she'd lost all those years ago. But it was Stella who was out there now, in the sweet, humid air. Stella who had seen snow, when instead there were only petals drifting down from the peach trees, who had seen time, when in fact there was none.

It was then Jenny found she could walk out the door. One minute she was standing there paralyzed, unable to go forward, the next she was on the porch. The wisteria was blooming, a twisted vine that scented the air. Bees droned, lazy, hypnotized by the wine-purple sugar. Argus was on the step, looking out toward the road, as though he expected his mistress to arrive any time. Jenny patted the old dog's head, then went across the lawn. On her way, she could hear the dog padding after her. She could hear the chatter of their neighbors' voices rising from within the house and the call of a cardinal in the woods. The bees had moved on from the wisteria to the laurel.

People used to believe that a spot of sugar placed in a baby's mouth would bring about a sweet life, but some children couldn't be force-fed; they had to make their own luck. These were the children who were forced to eat acorns and lily roots rather than sweets, they were fed by wild birds and had to be satisfied with liberty tea, made from loosestrife, or hyperion tea made from raspberry leaves. They had to make due with what they had.

Stella came over directly when she saw the metal canister that her mother carried. The garden gate shut behind her and she could hear the lock click shut. She had combed her hair back and a line of her natural color showed through. Star light, star bright. She had cried all night, so much so that her eyes hurt. Jimmy Elliot had sat beside her out by the monument. *This is what loving someone does,* Stella had told him. *Run away,* she'd advised. But the milk moon was above them, the one that made everything grow, like it or not, and Jimmy Elliot had remained where he was.

Later, when he walked Stella home, she had found a peach stone, left behind by a blackbird, right there on the road. She snatched it up, and once the stone was in her pocket, she felt some comfort. It was not every day you found something worth keeping, a token that could remind a person of what she had and what she'd lost and what was yet to come. Stella slept with the peach stone under her pillow. She dreamed it had fallen from a tree that was washed ashore when the old ship the *Good Duck* went down in the harbor, the day when the whole town smelled of peaches. She dreamed a girl in love had thrown it on the road after all her wishes had come true and a hundred trees had grown from that single stone. She dreamed her grandmother looked up and saw falling peach snow, so quiet it was nothing like a storm, so fragrant it could make a grown man cry.

Elinor had left Stella everything she had, enough for college, and for medical school if that was her choice. But the house, she had left to her daughter. Jenny. Henry Elliot had handed Jenny the deed to Cake House on the evening of her mother's death, made out and witnessed the year that Jenny had run away. The house had been hers all along. It was a house she didn't want, one she despised, the model of which was now being used as a dollhouse by a little girl in Medford, Massachusetts, who thought it to be the most beautiful house she had ever seen. House of windows and of wedding cakes, of pain that was never felt and of sleepless nights, of bird's-nest puddings, of invisible ink, of arrowheads, of laurel that was taller than any other in the Commonwealth, of bees that would never sting.

Jenny had thought they would scatter Elinor's ashes in the rose garden, but at the last moment, that had seemed wrong. Instead, they went into the woods. Argus followed them through the hedges as they went toward the Table and Chairs, past the lilacs, past the washing shed where Rebecca's portrait was still hidden behind the bricks. It was the time of year when the yellow warblers returned, when Baltimore orioles appeared once more, when one creature after another returned to Massachusetts, no matter how dark the woods might be. The spring azure butterflies, the dragonflies and damselflies, the wood thrush, the hummingbirds, tiny, but so territorial they would fight to the death to keep their home safe from trespass. Matt had arranged to have Rebecca's memorial bell on the common sounded, for the first time, and on this afternoon the pealing rose above the village, the way wind rises and then fans out, over houses and steeples, farms and shopping centers. The ringing reached farther than anyone would have imagined, all the way to North Arthur and Monroe, to Essex and Peabody. There were people walking down Beacon Street in Boston who swore they heard the sound of a bell on that day. In the Public Garden, children on the swan boats reached out as if to catch fireflies, although there was nothing but an echo which flew about in the air.

Jenny and Stella stepped carefully over the lady's slipper orchids that grew up through the pine bark and mulch. They walked past pitcher plants and trout lilies until they came to the place of the woods where it was always dark, where people in this part of the Commonwealth vowed there were wild roses, the sort that disappeared if viewed by the human eye. They followed the dog, who seemed intent on a particular path. It was not an easy route, but it wasn't impossible. Here, where there were thorn apples and water hemlock, was the very spot where Rebecca Sparrow was said to have appeared, beyond the rock formation of the Table and Chairs. Years from now local people would tell anyone willing to listen that blue flowers bloomed in this area year-round. They would insist that bees could be heard droning even on days when there was snow and ice. Close your eyes and listen, such people advised, then walk twenty paces farther than you thought necessary. Just when you're certain you've lost your way completely, you'll be there. Open your eyes.